ALL THE BROKEN PEOPLE

AMY RIVERS

Trade paperback ISBN: 978-0-578-42531-3

Ebook ISBN: 978-0-578-42547-4

Cover by Carl Graves

Author Photograph by Shannon Kaple

This is a work of fiction. Names, characters, events and incidents are the products of the author's imagination or used in a fictitious manner, except in the case of Juanita Jones. The story of Juanita Jones was taken from newspaper articles and from surviving family in Pickens County. The town of Jasper is described based on my memories of visits there. It's one of my favorite places, but my memories may be slightly different than reality.

For Betty

1

Small bursts of fog appeared and disappeared on the window in time with Alice's breathing. She rested her head against the glass, taking in the landscape as the car wound its way further from the city and into the gentle green folds of the Georgia mountains. The cab driver hummed along faintly to a tune only he could hear. Alice was glad he wasn't chatty.

Over the years, Will and Alice's visits to his hometown had been infrequent, and each time she felt like she was entering an alien world. Having grown up in a city in the dusty Southwest, Alice was taken with the Southern landscape, the friendly people and especially the kudzu. The green ornamental vine, which had been introduced to the United States in the nineteenth century for erosion control, had found the climate so hospitable it had grown rampantly, swallowing trees, power lines, old cars and even abandoned houses. Alice gazed out at leafy fingers creeping along the roadside, filling her both with the usual wonder and a new sensation she quickly recognized as dread.

Her phone began to vibrate in her lap, snapping her back to attention.

"Hi, Will," she said as cheerfully as she could muster. "I'm about twenty minutes away from your mom's house." Will had been pinging her phone with texts since she left the house and the micromanagement was beginning to chafe.

"Great. Let me know when you get there," Will said. The clicking of his keyboard in the background stopped and he added, "Take care of yourself, Alice." The line went dead, leaving Alice without the opportunity to take part in the conversation. For a moment, she could almost convince herself Will's words had been heartfelt. She held on to that hope with an iron grip, refocusing on the present.

"Burnt Mountain Road?" The driver drummed his fingers restlessly against the steering wheel.

"Yes, and then turn left onto Cove." She sat up straighter, paying closer attention to her surroundings now that they were approaching Mae's house. When they'd visited Will's mother together, Will had insisted on driving and Alice hadn't argued. Now, she'd be navigating on her own and she was nervous about getting lost in an area sparsely populated with people and densely populated with flora and fauna. She'd pulled up the map on her phone and was using its GPS to double-check their route, but her mind kept wandering to the task ahead. Alice had volunteered to look after her injured mother-in-law, but she lacked the confidence of an experienced caregiver.

When they finally arrived at Mae Bennett's house, the old family dog, Rosy, met Alice at the car door, tail wagging. Alice paid the driver, collected her bags and rang the doorbell, running her fingers through Rosy's fur as they waited. Rosy's days of being a ferocious guard dog had faded with her youth.

"Alice. It's so good to see you!" Margaret Bennett exclaimed as she opened the door wide and wrapped her arms around her sister-in-law. "Thank you for coming. I'm so glad you have a job that allows you to travel."

Alice pulled back gently and smiled. "My editor never fails to find something for me to write about no matter where I am."

"Please tell her how grateful I am."

Margaret looked more disheveled than Alice had ever seen her. She'd worn her role as eldest child in the family like a badge of honor, and Alice was flummoxed by how Margaret managed to be both a high-powered attorney and a dutiful Southern daughter. Alice was glad to see that even Margaret could be flustered.

As they carried her bags into the house, Alice took in the flowery wallpaper and pristine wainscoting that had been cared for so meticulously only its style gave away its age. Lace doilies covered the side tables. The doorknobs and lampshades bore filigree that lent a certain elegance to the home, though it was not to Alice's tastes.

"Mama's surgery went well, and the doctor says her hip will heal nicely," Margaret said as she set one of Alice's bags inside the guest room. "She'll need a lot of physical therapy, and she'll be very sore for a while. Lots of cuts and bruises from hitting the stone steps on the porch. She still doesn't remember the fall, but the doctor says that's normal with a concussion. I just got back from the hospital a little while ago. Let's get you settled in and then we'll go to see her. Unless you want to stop for something to eat first."

"That's okay. I'm not quite hungry yet, and I'm anxious to see Mae. I just need a few minutes to get ready."

The guest room had an expansive view of the lake. Alice loved staying there. She was enchanted by the sound of birds enjoying the feeders on the balcony and made a note to fill them with seed in Mae's absence. Looking out at the mist that settled over the water each morning never failed to make her smile. The thick scent of Georgia pine permeated every inch of the property.

Taking a deep breath, Alice changed out of her jeans and into some slacks. She always felt underdressed when visiting Will's family. The first time they'd visited, Will had changed for dinner—trading his jeans for crisp black trousers and a sports coat Alice had never seen him wear at home—and since that time, she had packed an entire suitcase with dressier evening clothes.

Grabbing her purse, she headed out to the living room and met Margaret at the door.

"Watch your step," Margaret advised as they walked down the front steps. "They get a bit shadowy as the days get shorter."

"Is this where Mae fell?"

"Yes. I've been pestering Mama for months to have my cousin Andrew put in a railing. Now I think we'll have to put in a ramp instead."

Alice looked at the beautiful stonework on the front patio. The steps and landing had been set by Mae's grandfather using rocks he'd dug out near the lake. Alice had always found them charming, but now, noticing the uneven surfaces, she wondered how Mae would be able to traverse the steps as she grew older.

Margaret searched around in her purse, pulling out a small set of keys. "Here are the keys to my mother's car. It's all yours while you're here."

Alice took the keys. "Thank you." She returned to studying the front porch when she noticed something reflective peeking out from a crevice. "What's this?" Stooping low, she reached her fingers into the space between two of the stone steps and pulled out a pack of cigarettes. "Huh. There are still a few in here, though they're flat as pancakes now. Does your cousin smoke?"

Margaret frowned. "He'd better not. I'm going to give that boy a piece of my mind."

Alice laughed. "They might not even be his. Besides, didn't I meet Andrew last time we visited? And isn't he nearly twice your size?"

Margaret smiled, but a fire blazed in her eyes. "Bigger and older, but I'd still give him a talking to if he was smoking around Mama's house." Alice felt a twinge of guilt at setting Margaret on her unsuspecting relative.

Margaret had locked the front door and was heading toward her car. Quickly, Alice tucked the cigarette package in an outside pocket of her purse and followed.

Alice wasn't sure what she'd expected but when they walked into Mae's hospital room she gasped at the sight of her mother-in-law. Mae had always been slight of build but she'd never appeared in public in anything less than conservative attire, with coifed hair and full makeup. Seeing Mae's diminished form folded up in a blanket, her usually curled hair lying flat against her head, Alice felt chills race through her body.

"Mama," Margaret said gently, approaching her mother's bedside and laying a hand softly on her shoulder. Mae stirred and opened her eyes.

"Oh." Her voice was shaky and weak. "Hello, darling. I was just napping."

"Mama, Alice is here to see you."

Mae shifted her gaze to Alice, who realized she'd been hovering in the corner. Alice stepped forward and pulled a chair up to sit beside Mae.

"Hello, Mae. How are you feeling?"

Mae smiled. "Well, I've been better, but the folks here have been taking good care of me."

"Are you having a lot of pain?"

"It comes and goes. The doctor says they'll get me up tomorrow to start walking around. I expect it'll be a little bit worse then."

"What happened, Mae?" Alice couldn't help but ask, despite being told Mae had no memory of the fall.

"I really don't know," Mae said, her eyes reflecting her confusion. She paused, the strain showing in her face as she tried to remember. "I was out walking Rosy and then I was here. It was the strangest thing. I can't quite remember, but it seems like someone else was there with me."

Margaret moved quickly to Mae's side and fluffed her pillow. "Now, Mama. We talked about this. You hit your head, and now you're having nightmares. The doctor said this is normal. In a few days, you'll be feeling much better." An awkward silence permeated the room.

Unsure what more to say, Alice launched into logistics. "Well, I'm going to start getting the house ready for when you come home. Is there anything you need?"

Mae sighed. "Just don't fuss too much over me, Alice. I'm sure I'll be back on my feet in no time." Alice doubted there had ever been a time in Mae's life when she couldn't look after herself. Having helped raise her little brothers while working an active farm, Mae wasn't accustomed to having anyone wait on her. Alice knew her presence added insult to injury when it came to Mae's sense of independence, though Mae's good manners would never permit her to say so.

Alice smiled reassuringly. "I'm sure you will. In the meantime, I'll do my best not to be a pest."

Mae held out a wrinkled hand and Alice took it, noting how delicate Mae's fingers were. "Thank you, Alice. I'm glad you came."

Alice could feel the tears welling up in her eyes. She wasn't used to tenderness. She patted Mae's hand and then, after checking in with Mae's nurse, she and Margaret said goodnight.

Returning to Mae's house after stopping for fast food, Alice and Margaret put the kettle on. Hot tea and a couple of old blankets in hand, they went down to the dock to enjoy the rest of the evening. The sun had set and the last bits of hazy light were fading. Luckily, it was too late in the year for mosquitoes and the solar lights running along the dock made for a pleasant retreat. For a while, the women sat in silence, gazing out onto the lake, its waters rippling gently in the cool autumn breeze. Alice hoped the tea would settle her stomach—she wondered if it was the food or the stress of the situation making her queasy.

"It's funny. When I think of the country, I always imagine it being so quiet. I'd almost forgotten how loud all the crickets and frogs and birds could be," Alice said with a smile.

Margaret nodded, but her mind seemed to be miles away. Alice sat back, intending to wait her out, though she couldn't help drumming her fingers softly against one of her blanketed legs. Patience had never been her strong suit.

Finally, when the waiting was beginning to become a physical burn in Alice's stomach, she broke the silence. "Are you enjoying living in Atlanta?"

"I've hardly had time to notice, the firm keeps me so busy, but it'll be worth it if I can make senior partner in the next few years. Then I'll have more flexibility." Alice smiled at the enthusiasm in her sister-in-law's voice. She could relate to Margaret's passion for her work, and it hadn't escaped her notice that Margaret's words were a near-perfect reflection of Will's own ambitions.

"Your mother seems to being doing well, in spite of everything that's happened to her."

"I wish she'd stop being so stubborn about living out here alone. The accident was bad enough, but this talk about someone being there when she fell? Well, it makes me very uncomfortable." Margaret's voice was strained and tired.

"Do you think your mother would ever consider moving into the city with you?" As much as she hated to prolong the conversation when Margaret was so upset, Alice needed to understand all the variables in their current situation. She knew Will would want a full report.

Margaret frowned. "No. I've asked her." She sighed. "I wanted her to come recover with me. I found a private nurse to take care of her while I worked. I was hoping a few months in Atlanta might change her mind about moving in with me, but then Will called and said you were coming, so she decided to stay here in Jasper." Alice could hear a hint of bitterness in her voice.

"I'm sorry if my coming here upset you, Margaret."

Margaret's face drained of color. "Oh, Alice. I didn't mean to make you feel bad. My mother would much rather be here. She's lived in this house for so long, I think it would be hard for her to start over somewhere else." Her frown returned. "I feel like I can't take care of her properly from Atlanta. Obviously, this fall confirms it. And Will always makes me feel like I'm shirking my responsibilities."

"Why do you think he does that?" Alice asked. She chided herself for sounding like such a journalist, but she was also genuinely curious, knowing what Margaret was saying was true. Will had never talked about his relationship with his sister in any detail. When he referred to her, it was with casual coolness, or more recently with evident disdain. Alice knew there was more to the story, but she'd never pressed the issue with Will, and she had to be careful now not to turn this conversation into an interrogation.

"It's complicated," Margaret started. "When Will was younger, everyone expected him to have this big future somewhere else. I never wanted to leave Georgia, and I guess everyone expected that, too. I imagine he felt like an outsider in our family sometimes."

"He always talks about all of you in glowing terms," Alice said, politely.

"It's not like that. My father was always pushing Will to expand his horizons. I don't think Daddy meant to, but I suspect Will thought Daddy didn't need him or want him here. Which was not the case, of course. Daddy talked about Will like he was the Second Coming." Margaret snorted. "We weren't one of those families where there was a farm or business the children were expected to run. We were free to choose. Then, while he was in college, Will got into some trouble here in town—an altercation so to speak."

Alice stared wide-eyed at her sister-in-law, allowing her mind to run wild with all the implications this new information about her husband's past presented. She was afraid if she spoke, the flow would dry up, so she nodded, urging Margaret to continue.

"That last time he left, we all knew Will was never coming back, not for long anyway. I had just graduated from college, and I was staying with my parents for the summer." Margaret's eyes were moist as she spoke of her family. "He came home late one night. We got in a fight. I told him he was selfish. He told me I knew nothing about his life. And that was it. We've barely spoken since."

Alice wondered what Margaret was holding back. It seemed strange that Will would stop speaking to his sister over one argument, but then, she'd never had siblings to have arguments with, foolish or otherwise. The fights in Alice's life had been life-threatening and soul-wrenching. She'd never pictured her husband's family as a backdrop for any sort of drama, and yet, she was sure there was more to the story.

"So, you two were close before?"

A doleful look passed over Margaret's face. "I used to think so, but I guess it's been a long time since Will and I really knew each other." Margaret's distant gaze made Alice shiver. She pulled her blanket up around her shoulders, gathering her thoughts.

"Well, I'm glad I get to spend some time with you while I'm here," Alice said, smiling. "I feel like there's a whole side of Will's life I know nothing about. It'll be interesting to see where he grew up and get to know the people around here. Plus, I've never had a sister of my own." Alice's words sounded corny but she was sincere.

"I really am glad you came, Alice." Margaret leaned over and patted her shoulder. "Just keep in mind that small towns like Jasper are brimming with folks only too eager to gossip. You can't always believe what you hear."

From inside the house, Rosy barked, causing Alice to turn in time to see a shadowed shape slip around the side of the house and disappear into the dark Georgia night.

2

"You know, you're dumb as a rock."

Larry Lee Simms shot his cousin and best friend, James, a hateful look, but didn't respond to the jibe.

"I said," James raised his voice, "you're as dumb as a damned rock."

"Oh yeah? Why's that?" Larry Lee was distracted. He barely noticed the change in James's tone.

"There's no reason for you to be hiding out, Larry Lee. If they suspected you, they'd have come and hauled you away by now." James grinned.

Larry Lee was itching to smack the smug expression off his cousin's face. This self-imposed captivity had Larry Lee wound up tight and ready to release some steam.

"I'm telling you, James. Carver showed up not five minutes after I got out of the last house. Feels like he's watching me and I'm not going back to prison. Not for this." Larry cringed at the shakiness he couldn't quite keep out of his voice when he talked about prison.

Silence descended over the two men like a shroud. Larry Lee and James were distant cousins in that way families in small towns could usually trace their roots to common origins. They'd been friends since birth, or sometime thereabouts, and kept each other company their whole lives. For days, they'd been lying low at the Simms house where Larry Lee lived with his mother Agnes. They'd spent most of their time adding to the line of empty Jack bottles lining the kitchen table.

"By the way, I talked to my sister. She says they'll be discharging the old lady soon." James interjected. Word of Mae Bennett's accident had spread like wildfire, being embellished at each stopping point along the gossip train. Having taken place less than a mile up the road from the Simms house, it was impossible for Larry Lee to avoid the topic. The eager look on James's face was enough to push Larry Lee over the edge.

"Who cares?" Larry Lee shouted, watching as his cousin's face dropped like a puppy dog who'd been kicked by his master.

Ever since news had spread about Mae Bennett's accident, he'd been waiting for the cops to show up at his door, an immediate response anytime anything bad happened in Jasper. His recent close call with the sheriff's department had left him paranoid. And paranoia made him impulsive, reckless. He was better off hunkered down, but after three days of being cooped up, he was so agitated, even the alcohol wasn't calming him.

"I'm out of smokes," he muttered, pawing at his back pocket as if the act alone would make cigarettes appear.

"Didn't you buy some yesterday?"

"Yeah. Maybe they're in my truck."

"Dumbass. You're always losing your cigarettes, Larry Lee." James crossed his arms over his chest and cast his eyes downward in full pout over Larry Lee's distractedness, but doggedly returned to the topic he'd started. "Anyway, the whole town's talking about it. Carly says Mrs. Bennett doesn't remember much about falling. Overheard the doctors talking about it."

"I'm not interested," Larry Lee said. His words were losing

their bite as he tried to relax. "That's all this town ever talks about —the Bennetts. I couldn't care less."

James shifted restlessly. "So, what are we going to do, anyway? I'm tired of spending all day hanging around this shithole with you and your mama." James dropped his voice to a near whisper on the last word.

"Then get the hell out," Larry Lee growled, and the venom in his voice caused James to pay more attention.

"Oh come on, Larry Lee," James said, his voice pleading, "I'm just saying, I think you're being paranoid. There's no reason to hide out. Let's get back to what we were doing."

"And what was that," Larry Lee spat. "Shooting cans? Odd jobs? Thieving? Ever since I got laid off from the factory in Tate, I can't catch a break here in town. Stupid people keep wagging their tongues. I need a damned job!" Larry Lee was pacing now. "I swear. It's like a black cloud hangs over this whole family."

James rolled his eyes and sank back down in the couch, ready for the coming rant.

"Damned Bennetts. Took our land. Ruined our reputation, the whole lot of us. They're the damned reason we can't get a leg up in this town. Something happens to a Bennett, the whole town's talking. What about the rest of us!" Larry Lee took another swig from the bottle, draining it. Then, instead of lining it up on the table with the other bottles, he chucked it across the kitchen where it landed with a loud *clank* in the corner of the room.

"Larry Lee!" A woman's angry voice shot down the hallway, followed by heavy footfalls. Agnes Simms thundered into the kitchen. She was not a big woman but she walked like a herd of elephants and was just as dangerous when riled. "You and James need to get the hell out of this house. You've been laying around like a couple of logs for days." Her eyes swept across the row of empty bottles and settled on the one in the corner. "And pick this mess up!"

Usually, when Agnes spoke, even a mean cuss like Larry Lee

hopped, but with more alcohol than blood flowing in his veins, he turned a defiant glare in his mother's direction. "Mind your own business, Mama."

Agnes launched herself across the room, landing so many punches into Larry Lee's face that all he could do was throw his hands up and try to keep her from doing any real damage. He was the stronger of the two, but his mother's temper was legendary. And she was fast—faster than her age and stature let on. Each punch caused a surge of pain and adrenaline but Larry Lee knew better than to interfere with one of Agnes's beatings. Once, he'd grabbed her hands in an attempt to stop her. He'd woken every night that week to scalding water thrown at him where he lay in bed until he finally couldn't sleep at all.

Agnes was generally content to use her fists, and she wasn't big enough to hurt him much anymore, but she was still an expert at making his life miserable. It was better to let her wear herself out. After a few more wallops, Agnes backed off.

"Get out of here, you mouthy son-of-a-bitch." She opened the refrigerator with pudgy fingers, pulled out a Coca-Cola and stomped back to her bedroom, the floorboards creaking warily with each step.

James stood. "Come on, Larry Lee. Let's go into town and get you some smokes. Take the edge off."

Larry Lee stretched his leg across the booth seat like he owned the place. He and James sat at the local diner where they'd scarfed down burgers and milkshakes. They'd been holed up in their booth for almost two hours and the waitress was starting to give them dirty looks, which they ignored like always.

James had been swirling a cold French fry lazily through a blob of ketchup, when he sat straight up, an amused expression on his face.

"Hey, Larry Lee. There's Miss High-and-Mighty herself."

Before he could act like he didn't care, Larry Lee had turned in his seat and saw Margaret Bennett returning to a booth on the other side of the restaurant. Margaret was a striking woman, handsome more than pretty, all sharp angles and an air of confidence that radiated like an aura. She was sitting across from a smaller woman who was slightly slumped in her chair, as if the weight of the world was heavy on her shoulders. "Who's she with?"

"I don't know. She don't look familiar. Maybe one of her friends from the city."

Larry Lee's face burned. He'd been sitting right here in this diner when he saw the front-page article in the newspaper: "Bennett Takes Top Law Job." Anything having to do with the Bennetts seemed to be news in this town. Larry Lee had read with mounting indignation at how Margaret had landed herself a junior partnership in one of Atlanta's most prestigious legal firms. It wasn't enough that the story made the front page; the whole town had buzzed about it for weeks. And since Larry Lee had gone to school with Margaret, people often assumed he knew her, bringing her up in casual conversation, which annoyed him to no end. Truth was, Larry Lee had asked Margaret out once and she'd turned him down flat, adding to his laundry list of perceived slights by the Bennett family.

On learning Margaret would be moving out of Jasper, Larry Lee had struck upon a vengeful idea. He had started lurking around Mae Bennett's house, getting his kicks on petty acts of vandalism. He'd been meaning to scare her, maybe even to run her off the property and out of town. *Would've served her right.* As usual, things hadn't turned out the way he'd planned. Harassing the old woman when there was no one around made him feel cowardly. Now with her laid up, the town was buzzing again about the famous Bennetts. Larry Lee felt the pot being stirred.

"Damn Bennetts," he muttered, but James's attention was still on Margaret and her companion. Larry Lee glanced back over at the woman sitting with Margaret. She looked tired, her eyes puffy, her wavy brown hair tangled, but she was attractive, soft and voluptuous. Everything Larry Lee liked in a woman, except she was sitting with his least favorite person. Regardless, he felt his body stir at the sight of her.

"Probably some prissy bitch from Atlanta," James said dismissively, tucking back into his petrified fries.

"Yeah, I guess."

Larry Lee leaned back against the window. His mind raced, his feelings in turmoil. The Simms family grudge against the Bennetts had been burned into him from the time he was born. The story of how his great-grandfather had been swindled out of a prime piece of lake property had fueled three generations of ill will. The mere mention of the name Bennett was enough to make his stomach turn. A sighting of one of the Bennett family colored his thoughts with rage.

Without meaning to, Larry Lee had torn his napkin into a million tiny fragments. Since the day he'd read the article about Margaret and her new fancy job, his fixation with the Bennetts had reached epic proportions. It hadn't helped that it was the same day he'd lost his factory job in Tate and had gotten into a real boxing match with Agnes. She'd drowned her sorrows in a bottle of whiskey and then spent the better part of an evening screaming at Larry Lee about his worthlessness and raging about the Bennett family, igniting in Larry Lee a misplaced need for vengeance. Agnes was a lousy mother but she was still his family.

From her vantage point, Alice couldn't help but notice the young woman at the back of the restaurant. When they'd entered, she had been listening closely to the conversations of two men sitting in the booth in front of her, though they didn't seem to notice. Alice got the feeling the woman was used to being overlooked, maybe even liked it, the way she eavesdropped with no apparent concern at getting caught. After a few moments, though, Alice found the woman staring at her.

She looked to be about Alice's age, but she wore the evidence of a life hard lived, from the stringy strands of dingy-looking light brown hair falling over sunken eyes to the leathery look of her skin. Despite her own childhood, Alice had a hard time imagining what a person might go through to look so worn so soon.

Alice returned her attention to Margaret, but after a few minutes she locked eyes once again with the woman at the back of the diner. It was a little unnerving, the way the young woman continued to stare in her direction. At first, she thought the woman was looking at Margaret, but she'd made eye contact with Alice so many times it was clear she was studying her, leaving Alice feeling both claustrophobic and exposed. The expression on her face was neutral, but there was a fire in her eyes that made Alice feel even more uncomfortable.

"Do you know who that woman is?" Alice asked, gesturing with her chin toward the young woman's table.

Margaret glanced over her shoulder. As she did, the woman leaned toward the wall, obscuring Margaret's view.

"I can't really tell, but the two guys in front of her are a whole lot of trouble. Larry Lee Simms and James Harris."

"You know them?" Alice asked.

"It's a small town, Alice. I know everyone." She frowned. "Though there are some people who I'd rather not know. And those two are at the top of the list."

Alice couldn't help but smile a bit at her sister-in-law's dramatic tone. "What did they do?"

"They're the town bullies. I'm surprised Larry Lee graduated from high school given how often he was suspended for fighting. And Pickens County has had a rash of burglaries. I suspect they're involved. So does local law enforcement, luckily. I called to make sure they were keeping an eye on my mother's house." She sighed.

"Honestly, I don't want to have anything to do with this crowd anymore, so I try not to think about it. As long as it doesn't affect Mama, then I don't care." Margaret took a sip of her drink. She glanced again at the two men and frowned.

"If you're done, I was thinking we could run to the medical supply store and pick up the things for Mama's bathroom. I want to get as much done as we can before I have to head back tomorrow, and they're closed on Sundays." Her voice had become professional and distant.

Alice nodded, pushing her plate away and gathering her coat, unsettled by the abrupt change in her sister-in-law's demeanor. They'd had a fairly stress-free day, but now Margaret's desire to get back to Atlanta was palpable.

As they walked toward the exit, Alice glanced over her shoulder and found three sets of eyes following her.

3

As he studied the carnage in front of him, Deputy Carver was unconvinced he was seeing the work of a wild animal—an easy explanation that simply refused to settle right in his gut. He'd been working for the Pickens County Sheriff's Department for so many years that he'd left his idealistic know-it-all days behind him and was content to admit he knew nothing. Enough law-abiding citizens had lied to him that he was suspicious of everyone and the scene before him had raised dozens of red flags.

"I don't buy it," Carver said once again, making note of the twitching vein in his fellow deputy's neck. Carver enjoyed being the thorn in everyone's side.

"What's your problem, Carver?" Morrison, the young deputy, was squarely in the middle of his jump-to-conclusion days. He wasn't a rookie, but close enough that he still thought he could call a case with little or no investigation. Carver rode him hard, seeing potential buried beneath the carelessness of his youth. Carver had been there too, and he cringed sometimes at memories of cases he'd flubbed by being too eager, invariably taking shortcuts he shouldn't.

"Right now, my problem is you, Morrison," Carver said, unwilling to budge an inch, waiting to see if Morrison would rise to the challenge. Carver had spent the day working on a series of burglaries only to be called off to this mess, and he wasn't in the mood for lazy police work. "I hadn't walked two steps into this scene before I could see we had a problem. Question is, why can't you?"

"It's not pretty, I'll give you that, but I don't see a shred of evidence this wasn't some wild animal attack. Or maybe the pack got into it over some food. Wouldn't be the first time we've seen feral dogs go after each other."

"Like this?" Carver asked, nodding his head to the grisly scene before them. They'd received a call about a dead dog in an abandoned house near the outskirts of town. They'd arrived to find more than just a dead dog. They'd found three big pit bulls—all showing signs of mange—torn to pieces, blood everywhere. It was grisly, but Morrison was right: finding dead animals wasn't new. Located in the woods of North Georgia, Jasper was rural. There were bear sightings daily, and pets sometimes met an untimely end at the claws of hungry wildlife.

This was different.

"Look over there," Carver indicated a dark corner near the back of the room. A filthy sleeping bag lay surrounded by trash and debris. "Looks to me like someone's been living here."

Morrison wrinkled his nose in distaste. "Yeah, that's nothing new. We're always running junkies and bums out of the old buildings around here. What's your point?"

Carver was beginning to lose patience. "Notice anything odd about the dogs?"

"You mean, besides they're being dead?" Morrison asked, his voice dripping with sarcasm.

Carver walked over to one of the corpses and tugged a glove out of his back pocket, pulling it over his fingers as he squatted. He reached down and pulled one of the dog's legs into the air. "Notice anything strange here?"

Morrison shifted uncomfortably and seemed to have to force himself to look, causing Carver to sigh in disgust. Morrison was silent for a moment, then he took on a peculiar expression. "That's weird. It looks like the paw was cut off."

Carver nodded. "The cut is clean, like it was made with a knife. They're all like that," he said, gesturing to the other corpses. "Last I checked, bears don't use kitchen knives on their meals. And look here," he pointed at the dog's neck, which was the only part of the body clear of damage. "Whatever happened here, it wasn't an animal. There's not a scratch on these dog's throats. Someone took a knife or something sharp to nearly every inch of this dog's back and rump, but the neck is clean. The paws are gone. You see what I'm saying?"

"I see what you're saying," Morrison parroted. His face had gone ashen.

Carver stood, sliding the glove off his hand gingerly, holding it between two fingers away from his body. "We need to get a crime scene kit in here."

"Yeah, okay," Morrison said, turning quickly toward the exit. Carver watched him go, his thoughts torn between irritation at the shoddy police work he was seeing these days and unease over the scene before them. What was going on in this town?

"Not a damned thing," Morrison announced a few days later as he joined Carver in updating the sheriff. "We took pictures of the wounds, obviously, but we didn't find the weapon. No discernible fingerprints. We didn't find anything that would warrant continuing to investigate at this time. If someone has been sleeping there, they haven't been back. We've been doing drive-bys."

"Thank you, Dave," the sheriff began, "What about the Mason burglary?"

"No leads," Morrison said, and he shuffled some papers in his hand. He was ready to launch into his next report when Carver interrupted.

"Sheriff, I'm not comfortable with dropping the investigation on the dead dogs. Something very disturbing happened out there and I'm worried—"

The sheriff waved a hand to silence Carver. "I know what you're going to say, Leland, but it sounds to me like there's nothing more we can do." Carver started to protest but the sheriff added, "We'll keep the case open, okay? You can ask around, but we've got to stay on top of the burglaries. I'm starting to get a lot of calls. Mason's house was what, the sixth or seventh incident? One thing at a time, all right?"

Carver stiffened but nodded. He hated being placated, and he wasn't a huge fan of the direction the department had taken these days. It felt so formal. So much paperwork. So many briefings. Some days he felt he'd spent more time filling out forms than actually patrolling the county. And while he knew the sheriff's office was only part of the equation, he was starting to feel disconnected from the community. It was an uncomfortable feeling. He used to know what was going on without having to look.

Morrison finished up the briefing, but Carver was only half paying attention. They walked out of the sheriff's office and Carver headed for his patrol car. He was supposed to conduct interviews to try and unearth some new information on the burglaries that were becoming epidemic, but his mind was still stuck on the dead dogs. He decided to drive out to the crime scene again.

"Hey, Carver," Morrison called from two spaces away. "If you find anything, let me know." Carver felt his lips turn up a bit despite himself. Morrison could be annoying as hell but he knew Carver.

Ten minutes later, Carver eased his patrol car into the overgrown driveway adjacent to the abandoned house. Crime scene tape crisscrossed the front doorway, but the door itself had long since been removed or destroyed. The roof was falling in, and weeds were beginning to pop up inside the house. Carver could see kudzu creeping toward the foundation. In a year or two, this whole area would be covered in leafy green and these old houses would fade away into the landscape.

As he approached the front door, examining the tape to make sure it hadn't been tampered with, something brushed against his forehead making him jump. He could see a wispy strand of string or thread caught in the doorframe but swaying on the breeze. As first, he thought it was a spider's web and he swiped at it, but when he examined the strand in his hand, he realized it was a hair. A long, light brown strand of human hair.

4

Margaret returned to Atlanta, and Alice spent the next few days getting the house ready for Mae's homecoming. Will had said to spare no expense, so she'd taken it upon herself to hire a contractor to build a ramp into the house and a railing for the steps. Finding someone to do the work on short notice had been no small accomplishment, but a few encouraging words from Will, and Alice was a woman possessed. She'd left enthusiastic messages on his voicemail after each completed task, detailing her visits with Mae at the hospital, and trying to put a positive note on the whole experience.

"You're really doing a good job, Alice," Will told her one evening, and she could hear the smile on his face. Her heart swelled. He'd been busy with the case he was working on, but Alice thought she heard concern in his voice every time he called. It can't have been easy for him to be away when his mother needed him, she thought.

"It's been a piece of cake." A slight exaggeration, but she told herself it was all in the name of love. What difference did it make for Will to know how difficult things had been, how little sleep Alice had gotten since arriving? What he needed was reassurance

Alice could handle the task at hand, and she was damned well going to give him that.

Mae's mobility would be significantly impacted for a month or two, and though she was using a wheelchair, her therapists encouraged her to walk each day to build her strength. Alice would help with all Mae's basic needs and drive her into town for doctors' appointments and for a variety of therapies. She stocked up on groceries and spent one evening making freezer meals so she'd be prepared for busy days when she might not have time to cook from scratch. Having grown up in the Southwest, Alice was used to a whole different way of eating. She kept having to remind herself her mother-in-law couldn't tolerate much spice.

Finally, Mae was ready to be discharged. Margaret took the day off to help transport her mother home. Alice lined the passenger seat in the car with extra blankets and pillows, so they could make her trip up the bumpy mountain roads as comfortable as possible. Luckily, the doctor had given Mae an extra dose of pain medication so she mostly slept on the drive from the hospital to her home —a winding twenty-minute journey through the back roads of Pickens County.

When they arrived, Mae looked at the new ramp and railing. "You've been busy," she said, smiling, her eyelids drooping slightly from the pain medication she'd been given.

"Don't worry, Mae. The ramp is sturdy but we can take it down when you're back on your feet if you'd like." Alice couldn't help but note the nod of approval from her mother-in-law.

The work of getting Mae out of the car and into her wheelchair left all three women winded. Mae leaned back silently as Alice pushed her wheelchair up the ramp and into the house. Margaret followed behind with Mae's things and the extra blankets and pillows, which she balanced precariously in her arms.

After they'd gotten Mae settled in bed and napping, Margaret and Alice retired to the living room with coffee and cookies, one of the Bennett household traditions Alice had always loved. Alice set down the refreshments and turned to answer the ringing phone before it could disturb Mae.

"The house is ready?" Will asked, without saying hello.

"Yes, Will," Alice said, biting back annoyance. She'd given him a rundown on every preparation she'd made, but he wouldn't stop interrogating her. He liked being in control of things. Really, it was a minor miracle he'd been so laid-back up to this point, but Alice was still stung. "The ramp worked perfectly and she's sleeping peacefully now in her own bed. She seemed pretty happy."

"Happy? How could she be happy?" Will's tone was both accusing and distracted. Alice could hear the click of the keys on his computer keyboard. He was calling from work and only giving her half his attention while he lambasted her.

A part of Alice wanted to argue with Will, to yell at him, tell him how selfish it was for him to treat her this way when he couldn't even pause long enough to be present in the conversation. After all, she and Margaret were taking care of things just fine and Alice wanted Will to see they were both capable of Mae's care.

Unfortunately that wasn't the way her relationship with Will worked. It never had been. For all his virtues, Will held a grudge. She'd been drawn to his confidence and self-possession; so much so that she found herself bending to his will more than she'd meant to. Perhaps, she realized now, more than she wanted to. It wasn't worth the trouble to get on Will's bad side.

"Listen, I've got to go. I have a meeting," Will said, before she had a chance to respond. "Give Mother my love." He disconnected abruptly. Another one-sided conversation on the books.

When Alice returned to the living room, her face must have betrayed how tired and stressed she was. Margaret walked up to her and put her arm around Alice's shoulder, giving her a brief squeeze before letting go.

"Thank you for doing this, Alice." Margaret's face was pained. "I feel so guilty for not being here."

Alice smiled at her sister-in-law. "Don't let your Southern guilt get you down. I'm happy to do it."

Margaret looked unconvinced. "Will's never going to forgive me for bringing you out here."

"There's nothing to forgive, Margaret. Your mother needed help and I'm able to give it to her. It's simple and I'm really glad to be able to be here," Alice said reassuringly, though she knew there was some truth to Margaret's fears about Will.

Later in the afternoon, a home health care worker stopped by to do an assessment. She suggested Margaret and Alice take a walk, since they'd be stuck to Mae like glue over the next few weeks. At least, Alice would. Margaret would be heading back to Atlanta before long.

Margaret pointed toward the lake. "Will and I used to jump off the boat dock behind the Hatcher house. Right over there, behind that big pine."

Alice smiled. Though her husband and her sister-in-law couldn't see eye to eye as adults, it was clear from the dreamy expression on Margaret's face that her memories of their childhood were warm. "Why not your dock?"

"Oh, we did that too, but we spent a lot of time with the Hatcher kids when we were young. Will and Jeff were good friends up until high school." Margaret had stopped walking and was looking out over the lake with a somewhat haunted look in her eyes. "Will always dared me to jump off. I was too scared. It wasn't until I was almost ten that I finally took the plunge. The water was freezing cold. I think it was still too early in the year to swim, but Will had been teasing me and I guess I finally had enough."

Alice waited for more, but Margaret shook away the memory

and started walking again. Before following, Alice stole one last look at the lake, and tried to picture her husband the way Margaret did. It was impossible. The Will she knew was too serious, too grown-up to spend a day playing by the lake. Alice wondered what he'd be like if they ever got around to having children. Lately, she'd pushed dreams of a family aside, not wanting to get her hopes up when their future was so uncertain.

As the two women made their way down the hill, Margaret shared other childhood memories and pointed out family landmarks. When they reached the paved road, they crossed and Margaret led Alice down a dirt road across the way.

"All the property on this side of the road belongs to my mother's family. She owns about 180 acres, right up to that rise over there."

Alice strained to see where Margaret was pointing. The sun cast the trees in front of them as silhouettes on a brilliant green and blue background. As they walked further on, Alice gasped with delight.

"Kudzu!" she exclaimed, causing Margaret to chuckle.

"It's pretty, isn't it?" Margaret said, "But don't get too close," she cautioned. "Snakes love to hang out under there."

Alice shivered. She hated snakes. "This is your family's land, too?" she asked.

"Uh huh. It's our own little kudzu patch. My cousin has a house about a mile up. He's a bit of a recluse." Margaret pointed ahead, but Alice was still staring out into the field of green kudzu leaves that rolled over the ground in waves and climbed up nearby trees and bushes. It was a little disorienting, the way the kudzu gobbled up everything in its path, making it difficult to get your bearings.

"It's so beautiful, but it gives me the creeps."

Margaret laughed. "Welcome to the South. Folks around here have been telling scary stories about kudzu for generations. *The vine that ate the South* and all that. Really, it's just a weed. It's hard to kill, but you can see all the areas where it's been pushed back."

Alice looked out across the other side of the road where the land had been cleared to make room for a house and several outbuildings. She could see Margaret's point, but from the corner of her eye, she still thought she sensed movement out in the green field.

Checking the time, they decided to return to the house, in case Mae's appointment was nearing its end. They headed back across the paved road and up the hill toward Margaret's childhood home. Off to the side, Alice noticed a small cabin hidden behind a thick copse of pine trees and vanishing under a layer of creeping kudzu, like the images she'd seen on the Internet. From what little she could see, it appeared the building was in a state of complete disrepair. Alice would have assumed it was abandoned had there not been a car sitting in the driveway.

"Who lives there?" She pointed to the broken-down house.

"The Simms family. They own a small piece of land here on this side of the lake, but as you can see," —Alice could hear the distaste in Margaret's voice — "They don't spend much time keeping up appearances."

"Do you know them?"

Margaret grimaced and nodded. "Oh yes, we know the Simms. Our families aren't exactly friendly. We saw one of them the other night at the diner, do you remember? Larry Lee Simms."

Alice wracked her memory, but the most vivid image from that night was the woman who'd been studying her. She tried to scrounge up an image of the men sitting nearby, but all she could see were those eyes staring daggers at her.

They approached Mae's house and saw the nurse standing at the door, waving them in. They quickly made their way up the drive. A few words with the nurse, and Alice's stint as primary caregiver was officially underway. Margaret said goodbye to Mae with promises to return the following weekend, then she headed back to Atlanta. Alice watched her taillights fading through the trees. As she turned to walk back into the quiet house, loneliness and isolation enfolded her like a familiar blanket, a relic of the past she thought she left behind.

Alice sat at the window looking out on the lake, a cup of coffee in her hands. The house was comfortably silent. Mae had spent the rest of the week and most of the weekend resting. Margaret had come out but was called away to work almost immediately, leaving Alice and Mae to their own devices. Mae's physical therapist had assigned bed-exercises that left her exhausted, but she did the exercises without complaint. It was easy to see where Will got his determination.

Alice would be driving Mae to the hospital for physical therapy two or three times a week, so she'd made a list of errands to run while Mae was in therapy. All the worry she'd suffered in anticipation of taking care of Mae was gone. Mae was already able to sit up on the edge of her bed and take small walks with her walker. With a pang of longing for her own mother who had died when she was a child, Alice gazed fondly at her mother-in-law, who was snoring lightly in her armchair.

Placing her empty cup on a coaster, Alice was about to wake Mae when her cell phone rang. A quick glance at the screen revealed the caller: Nancy Houghton—her editor at *A Woman's Life* magazine. Alice had been a regular contributor for over three years and loved the freedom and diversity that came with each assignment. Alice picked up the phone, silenced the ringer, and walked toward the kitchen, hoping to let Mae sleep a few more minutes.

"Morning, Nance."

"How's Georgia?" Alice could hear Nancy crunching something and smiled. Nancy was forever eating on the run.

"Beautiful, as always." Alice looked back over the lake. "There's a mist over the lake most mornings and when I drink my coffee, I feel like I'm in some fantasy commercial for Taster's Choice." She giggled.

"I've been thinking about story assignments while you're there and I think I have just the thing. It's a domestic violence piece." *Crunch, crunch, crunch.* "I'm filling slots for the spring violence-prevention issue and I ran across an interesting case from that area. The deadline is far enough out you should have time to get your hubby's mom back on her feet."

"Oh?" Alice's voice was strained. She'd never spoken about her own childhood experiences with violence, but for some reason she kept landing these assignments. She supposed she offered a unique perspective, but it didn't make writing about violence any easier on her soul.

"I know, I know. Another one, right? But listen, Alice. Your last two pieces had the highest engagement in our website's history. It's clear to me you were born to write these articles."

You have no idea, Alice thought. "Okay, so tell me about the case."

"It's an old one. From 1940. A young woman murdered by her husband. I ran across it during a random Internet search and it intrigued me."

"So, what's the hook? Why is this a story?"

"Well," Nancy paused. "He didn't just kill her. He mutilated her body. Cut off her hands, one of her feet. I mean, what makes someone do something like that?" Alice winced. "He was convicted and sentenced to life in prison, but he was paroled eleven years later and—get this—he remarried."

"Not surprising really," Alice said. "Women didn't have much recourse if their husbands abused them. And, for some reason, those guys never seemed to have much trouble finding new women to treat badly. It's surprising he was convicted at all."

Ignoring her, Nancy continued. "After they paroled him, he was killed in an accident."

"Probably got what he deserved."

"Maybe. I thought the case might make a good case study for an article about the evolution of domestic violence laws in the South. Especially with that progressive woman gaining ground in the Alabama Senate race."

"Where did the murder happen?"

"Tate, Georgia."

Alice walked over to the embroidered map of Georgia on her mother-in-law's dining room wall and frowned. "That's really close to Jasper."

"I know. I found the article about the case in the *Pickens County Progress*."

"That's the local paper here in town."

"Exactly. So, what do you think?"

Alice hesitated. She'd been hoping for something a little more lighthearted, but she'd never turned down an assignment before and she wasn't about to choose this moment for that particular first.

"Yeah, okay. It sounds fine, Nancy. Let me know if there's any particular angle you want me to take."

"Are you sure? You don't sound very enthusiastic."

"I'm sure. I'm getting ready to take Mae to the hospital, so I need to run. I'll start some research and get back to you."

After disconnecting, Alice went to rouse Mae but found her awake, a concerned expression on her face.

"Did Will call?" Mae asked, groggily. Every day when she woke, Mae asked after Will. Alice dreaded having to tell her no. Since Mae had gotten home, Will's calls became more infrequent. Mae had been sleeping at the time of his last call, and despite Alice urging him to call back, he hadn't. At first, Alice had been relieved for a break in Will's constant oversight, but seeing Mae's disappointment was beginning to make Alice angry toward her husband.

"No. It was my editor. She has a new assignment. Something local."

"Really?" Mae looked up at Alice with interest. Mae was a history buff and a wealth of knowledge on local goings-on. Alice knew she'd be picking Mae's brain for information, but she didn't want to distract Mae from her upcoming therapy.

"A murder from almost a century ago. I'll tell you about it later. Maybe you'll have some ideas about where to start my research, but if we don't get going now, we'll be late for your appointment."

Alice helped Mae to the bathroom, a simple task that now left Mae short of breath. Then they made their way slowly to the car. At the front door, Mae paused and furrowed her brow.

"What is it, Mae? Are you okay?"

Mae frowned. "I just had a strange feeling." Her face relaxed. "I like the work they did on this ramp. I think we should keep it up even after I'm back on my feet, so to speak."

Alice eased Mae into the passenger seat, glancing uneasily at the stone steps as they headed down the driveway.

"You know," Mae said quietly from the passenger seat, bringing Alice's attention back to the task at hand, "It may not be a good idea to go digging into the past. Folks around here are very private."

Alice snickered. "You sound like Will."

Despite the subject matter, Alice was looking forward to having a work project to keep her busy in her downtime. Mae wasn't a fussy patient and Alice found herself with idle hours to fill—a distraction from her growing misgivings about Will's infrequent calls. She decided to make a quick trip to the library to get acquainted with the reference librarian and pick up a few regional history books to start her research.

The Jasper library was located on a hill overlooking Burnt

Mountain Road, a main thoroughfare through Jasper. Alice parked her car and spent a few minutes admiring the marble statue of a boy reading to animals that sat nearby. When Alice was a little girl, the local library had been a refuge for her and there was something inherently comforting about being among all those books. She loved the contrast of the white marble against the vivid leaves, which were beginning to change color. A few had fallen onto the statue and Alice wiped them away.

As she made her way inside, she stopped by the circulation desk to ask a few questions. The woman at the desk appeared to be about Alice's age. She was slender with a very friendly smile and pretty eyes behind her oversized, but stylish, glasses.

"Hi there," said the woman, a little too loudly in the quiet of the library. Alice's easy feeling began to fade.

"Hello—"

Before she could say another word, the other woman said, "You're definitely a new face. I'm Charlene. Did you just move here or are you visiting?"

Alice cringed under the woman's probing gaze. "I'm visiting. Can you point me in the direction of the reference section?"

"Sure, but our reference librarian is on break. She should be back in a few minutes. Is there anything I can help you with?" Charlene's exuberance pelted Alice like hailstones hitting a tin roof. Alice often went out of her way to avoid overly friendly workers—she never felt comfortable having so much attention focused on her and Charlene's encroachment on her personal space was making her feel queasy.

"I'm doing some research for a story I'm writing. Local interest, that sort of thing."

"Ooh, a reporter? What newspaper do you work for?" Charlene's expression had *town gossip* written all over it.

Alice was beginning to feel annoyed. "I don't work for a newspaper. I write for a women's magazine." She tried to turn but Charlene cut her off again.

"Oh, wow! What's the story? I'm sure I can point you in the right direction. I know everything that goes on around here." There was no malice in Charlene's questions, and Alice could see she was trying to be helpful, but it was aggravating to be held hostage by this women's overeager information seeking. Alice would just as soon have remained anonymous during her stay.

"I'm sorry, Charlene. I'm kind of in a rush actually. I have to go pick up my mother-in-law in a few minutes. Can you point me in the direction of your regional collection?"

Alice saw a flash of irritation cross Charlene's face, but the woman regained her composure quickly. "Sure. This way." She walked around the desk and led Alice toward the other end of the building.

"You'll need to sign in and out," she said, indicating a clipboard on a nearby table. "This is our Georgia room. There are a lot of books about local history. Anything specific you want to read?" Charlene was still being polite but there was a hint of coldness in her tone.

"No, I'll just take a quick peek." Charlene turned to go but Alice jumped in, "Oh, my mother-in-law said I can check things out under her account. Is that okay? I have her card." She reached into her purse and held out Mae's library card for inspection.

"Well, you can't check out anything from this room. You can make copies, but you'll need to grab me for that. I guess it would be all right for you to check out books from the regular collection." Charlene looked at the card and raised her eyebrows. "You're Will Bennett's wife?"

"Yes," Alice answered as calmly as she could, though she felt like an ant under a magnifying glass. "Do you know Will?"

"You could say that," Charlene replied handing the card back to Alice. "Yes, you can use Mrs. Bennett's card." Charlene turned and walked away.

5

Larry Lee had slept off his bender and was out looking for work. He headed to the library to use the computers. He parked his pickup facing away from the library entrance and was about to climb out when a glance at the rearview mirror revealed someone exiting the building in a rush.

The woman from the diner—the one who'd been with Margaret Bennett—was walking out of the library, a small pile of white paper in her hands. The breeze caught her brown hair, flipping it over her face. She reached up to smooth it and nearly tripped. She gripped the pages tighter, wrinkling the edges, and slowed her pace a bit.

Larry Lee watched as she made her way to her car. She was an attractive woman. Her hair brushed against her shoulder blades and she was pleasingly curvy. He caught himself studying her, wondering where she'd come from, wondering if he might get to know her. Except, he reminded himself, she was consorting with the enemy. What was she doing with Margaret Bennett? And where was Miss High-And-Mighty anyway? Why was this woman in Jasper all alone? A ball of tension filled the pit of his stomach.

Larry Lee felt a sudden urge to start up the pickup and run her down, despite not even knowing her name.

Resisting the urge, he got out of his truck and walked briskly toward the library doors, shooting her a scowl as he did. She glanced back, and for a moment, their eyes met and a look of confusion crossed her pretty face. She wasn't wearing any makeup. He could see dark circles under her eyes. Larry Lee turned and walked into the library, feeling a twinge of discomfort as he thought about the strange woman's expression. He looked back over his shoulder, but she was out of sight.

"Good morning, Larry Lee."

Turning his attention forward, he found himself face to face with Charlene Walker, who had risen from her seat behind the circulation desk he'd nearly walked into. The sound of her voice—its high-pitched, flirty lilt—twisted the muscles in his shoulders tight.

"Morning, Leenie." He watched her cringe at the mention of this childhood nickname, which gave Larry Lee a jolt of satisfaction. *The best defense is a good offense*.

Charlene had graduated with Larry Lee's younger sister, Beth. The girls had been friends, or at least, Charlene was one of the few people Beth allowed to hang around her without tossing her away like a used tissue. Charlene had nursed a crush on Larry Lee for years. She was pretty enough. Too thin for Larry Lee's tastes, but her heart-shaped face and big green eyes were the sort of thing most men drooled over. Unfortunately for her, Larry Lee couldn't get past her boisterous personality and those ridiculous bug-eyed glasses she wore that aged her at least ten years. Mostly, he'd learned anything Beth touched was likely toxic: best to be avoided. "I'm going to use the computer. Still looking for a job."

"I hear they're hiring up at Big Canoe on the new housing complex."

Construction crews provided the most frequent work opportunities on the county job board. Larry Lee couldn't stand the jabbering of the men on the crews, so he tended to look for more solitary jobs. Not that Charlene needed to know any of this.

"Thanks," he said, and began moving away from the desk toward the fiction stacks, where a small bank of computers was tucked away from the regular library traffic.

"Good luck," she said, and then winked at him. Larry Lee nodded casually, careful to save his look of disgust until he was sure she wouldn't see his face. It didn't seem to matter what time or day Larry Lee appeared at the library, Charlene was always there, like a vulture waiting for her prey to drop dead. There wasn't a single part of his body that ached for Charlene Walker.

After taking a few brisk steps to put some distance between them, Larry Lee sauntered over to the computer kiosks and got started with his job search, his mind wandering to the woman from the diner. Who was she?

"More coffee?"

Larry Lee looked up from his eggs and shook his head. "No thanks, Patsy." The older woman clicked her tongue disapprovingly and turned to help other customers. He shifted uneasily in his seat.

"What a bitch," James said, stuffing a piece of toast in his mouth, oblivious as usual to the fact that they were seated in a public place where every word they said could be overheard. James didn't care what people thought about him, but then, he didn't have Larry Lee's sullied reputation. James rarely suffered from guilt by association.

Larry Lee had met James for lunch at the diner. His latest acquisition sat under a tarp in the back of his pickup truck waiting for a buyer. Having stolen goods in his possession always made Larry Lee jumpy, but until he found a job he didn't see much choice. He'd worn out his welcome with the few people left in town who'd shown any goodwill toward him or his family. Odd jobs were scarce and a little larceny was necessary to get by.

"Eh, she's all right. She's never much liked me."

James grinned. "No one much likes you, Larry Lee."

"You're telling me." Larry Lee took a few more bites, calming down as he ate. He'd found a few job opportunities, including one permanent job on a construction crew run by a man who he didn't know. That was always a plus. Most people who knew Larry Lee didn't want him around—he was a loose cannon with a history of violence. It wasn't his top choice for work, but beggars couldn't be choosers and steady work was steady work. "Sometimes I wonder if I should just pack up and leave town."

"And go where?"

Larry Lee shrugged. "I don't know. Maybe California. Somewhere to start fresh."

"What about your mama?"

"Well, that's the problem now, isn't it. She's stubborn as a mule. Won't go to the doctor, except when she needs a refill on one of her medications and they make her . . . Not that we can really afford it anyway." Larry Lee's head hung low as he continued. "She can't live on her own, that's for sure, and she'd kick my ass if I even suggested a home. Can't afford that either. As it is, I'm putting myself in a tight spot trying to get the money for her medications. *And* her booze. If I get caught again, they're going to throw the book at me. Everywhere I go, there's Carver. I've got to get down to unload the rest of that stuff on Tank. Makes me jumpy having it in the truck with Carver lurking around."

"You going down today?"

"Can't," Larry Lee sighed. "Told Mama I'd run some errands for her." Larry Lee felt a sudden rush of anger spread to his face. "When did it become my job to take care of Mama? Where the hell is Beth anyway?"

"Who knows?"

Larry Lee saw James's eye twitch at the mention of Beth's

name. Beth had been particularly harsh with James when they were younger. She knew he'd been in love with her, and so she took great pleasure in teasing and tormenting him endlessly. James was probably the only man in town Beth hadn't slept with.

As they got older, Beth's teasing lost its youthful carelessness, turning to straight up cruelty. She remained, to this day, the most likely reason James had never moved on, married, had kids—all the things you were supposed to have done by the time you'd reached his age. And for some reason, James was still in love with her. While Larry Lee was locked up, Beth ran off with some preppy football guy turned junkie, returning home only once to beg for cash. Not even his mother talked about her much these days.

Larry Lee shoveled another forkful of eggs into his mouth. "Yeah, well." He chewed and thought about how he'd ended up in this sorry state. Placing blame was like skipping stones for Larry Lee. He started with Beth and worked his way back to the Bennetts, keeping it as far away from himself as possible. It was ironic that both Will and Margaret Bennett, who everyone in town thought hung the moon, were the ones to leave while Larry Lee and his mother and James were stuck in this hellhole of a town.

Beth was the exception and who knew where she might be? Larry Lee was beginning to wonder if she was even alive. The last time he'd seen her, Beth was deep into methamphetamine use and it had already taken its toll on her scrawny body. She'd been so strung out, she hadn't recognized him. Of course, he'd just been released from prison and wasn't looking much like himself either but that was fine with Larry Lee. He didn't have an ounce of compassion for his wayward sister.

"Oh, hey. I was going to tell you. Carly says Mae Bennett's daughter-in-law is taking care of her," James piped up.

"So?" Larry Lee glared at his cousin, irritated at the interruption to his musings.

"So. *That* was the woman with Margaret at the diner the other night."

Now Larry Lee's interest was piqued. "Will's wife?"

"Yep. I guess, she's some kind of writer. Carly met her a few times while Mrs. Bennett was still in the hospital. Said she's real quiet."

"Will here too?"

During their school days, they'd come in contact only occasionally during some boys-will-be-boys backwoods shenanigans that ended up with one boy or another bloodied and bruised. Absentmindedly, Larry Lee rubbed a scar on his chin—a reminder of one of those rumbles. Nevertheless, he had no real gripe with Will Bennett except that he was, in fact, a Bennett and therefore evil.

Regardless, having Will Bennett around wasn't going to bode well for Larry Lee's plans. It was bad enough Will's wife would be keeping an eye on things, making it hard for Larry Lee to get around their property unnoticed. With Will back in town, he'd have to stay away completely. Will was the sort of person who noticed things.

"I don't know if he's here too. Carly didn't mention anything. Anyway, I thought you'd like to know."

Larry Lee didn't answer. His thoughts were drifting back to the incident at the library. He knew Will had gotten married, but there was something about his wife that didn't sit right with Larry Lee. Will was a few years younger than Larry Lee. He was the golden boy of his family and, really, the whole town. He'd graduated from some Ivy League school up north and become a big shot lawyer somewhere out west.

Larry Lee imagined Will would marry some supermodel, trophy-wife type of woman, all coifed and brainless. God knows that's the only type of girl he was ever seen around town with. The woman at the library, while attractive, didn't fit the mold at all. There was something damaged about her. If there was one thing Larry Lee could spot a mile away, it was damage. He'd noticed her puffy eyes while checking her out. She certainly didn't carry herself like the wife of a successful lawyer.

"Larry Lee?" The tone in James's voice suggested this wasn't the first time he'd tried to get Larry Lee's attention. The sour expression he was wearing confirmed it.

"What?"

"I said, the deputy just sat down and he keeps looking this way. Let's get out of here."

Larry Lee looked across the dining room and locked eyes with Deputy Carver. Balding and about fifty pounds overweight, Carver looked like a cartoonish version of a Southern lawman, but Larry Lee had had enough run-ins with Carver to know he wasn't a man to mess with. He pulled out cash to cover his breakfast and he and James ducked out the front door as quickly as they could. Larry Lee didn't look back. He didn't have to. He could feel Carver's eyes burning a hole in the back of his head.

On his way home, Larry Lee took the back road past the Salvation Army camp, which allowed him a slow drive by Mae Bennett's house on his way down the hill. His interest in the house and its inhabitant had become a bit obsessive of late. Now, knowing Will Bennett's wife was sleeping within those walls, Larry Lee felt an almost irresistible pull. As he neared the house, he noted there were no cars in the driveway. For a moment, he thought about approaching, but then he saw a familiar car coming up the road and thought better of it.

As he passed, Larry Lee saw Will's wife driving toward the house with her mother-in-law in the passenger seat. Her eyes were fixed on the road ahead, so intent on her task she didn't even spare a glance for Larry Lee as she drove by. *I wonder what her name is?* His heart beat a little bit faster.

Larry Lee pulled into a lake access road out of sight of the driveway and crept up to see what they were doing. He watched as the woman pulled a folded wheelchair out of the trunk, placing it carefully by the side of the car. She checked the locks so many times even Larry Lee was beginning to feel antsy.

Finally, she opened the door and helped Mae Bennett into the chair, wheeling her cautiously up a newly constructed ramp that partially covered the stone steps leading into her house. Neither woman said a word, and before long they were tucked away inside the house, leaving Larry Lee crouched in the bushes.

When he was sure the coast was clear, Larry Lee made his way back down to his truck and drove the rest of the way to his mother's house. Pulling into the driveway, he took a moment to survey the state of their property. It was a small parcel of land, but it might have been a beautiful one had Larry Lee or any of the Simms family ever felt the need to take care of it. Instead, they'd let the house and the surrounding land go. Any passersby might think the house uninhabited and that suited the Simms just fine.

Going in the front door, Larry Lee was surprised to find Agnes sitting at the kitchen table, a glass of water near her pudgy hand. He wasn't used to seeing her before dinnertime, if at all.

"Hey, Mama," Larry Lee said, sitting down in a chair beside her. He liked to gauge her mood before saying too much.

"Larry Lee, can you run back into town and get me some more antacid? My stomach's giving me fits and I used the last of it yesterday." Her face looked paler than usual.

Larry Lee sighed. Leave it to his mother to wait until he was finally back home to ask him for favors. Agnes wasn't yelling for a change. In fact, she seemed tired, lackluster. And with his mind on Will Bennett's wife, Larry Lee wasn't in the mood for a fight.

"Sure, Mama." He stood to leave.

"And Larry Lee." Agnes looked up at her son with drooping eyelids, her hot breath laced with the stink of vodka. "Get me another bottle?" She lifted the glass in a mock toast, a smirk gracing her sagging face.

6

Alice's heart raced as she fumbled in the dark for her robe. Mae's shrill shouts pierced the silence. It was the third night in a row Mae had woken with shrieks, and Alice was as rattled as she'd been the first night. Each time, Mae woke disoriented, but whatever images haunted her dreams disappeared as soon as she opened her eyes. For Alice, however, the anxiety wasn't so easily overcome.

Alice made her way down the hall, switching on lights along the way. When she entered Mae's room, Alice found her mother-in-law sitting up in bed, her delicate hands clutching her chest as if to restrain her heart from flying the coop. The hollering had stopped, but Mae's mouth was still wide open and she panted for breath.

"It's all right, Mae," Alice said, sitting beside the older woman and taking her hand. "Mae? It's all right," she repeated, trying to calm her own breathing.

"Alice," Mae said, clutching at Alice's hand, her breathing ragged. "This one was so real, so real. I can still smell cigarette smoke. He was right here." She gestured in no particular direction, still groggy.

Alice squeezed Mae's hand. "It's just you and me, Mae. Try and take some deep breaths." Something nagged at the back of Alice's mind. She looked around the room to be sure they were, indeed, alone, and then felt immediately foolish. "Do you remember your dream this time?"

Mae closed her eyes and was silent for a few moments. Alice wondered if she was starting to drift back to sleep. Then she spoke, her voice eerily calm. "I dreamed about the accident, Alice. About the night I was hurt. And I remember this time. *I remember.* I *was* attacked."

"What do you mean attacked?"

"I was walking Rosy, like I do when the evenings are nice. It was chilly outside. I remember pulling my sweater tighter. The woods were quiet. Quieter than usual, I think. And when I got to the house, I felt uneasy, like someone was watching me."

"Rosy was with you, Mae. She would have let you know if someone was there." Alice was trying to sound brave, but her heart was still racing.

"No, no. Rosy ran off." Mae paused to breathe. "She ran off to chase a squirrel, I think. And when I called her, she didn't come. I reached for my keys. And then someone was there, Alice." Mae told the story in her usual straightforward manner, but there was an edge to her voice. Alice stroked her arm gently but didn't interrupt. She realized she was hanging on Mae's every word.

"I felt someone grab my arm and push me, hard. It was darker than I thought. I lost my balance. I was trying to stop myself from falling. I didn't look back to see who was there. Then everything went black. I felt a pain in my arm and the next thing I know, I'm in the hospital."

"It could've been an accident," Alice said weakly, not putting much stock in her own words.

"Someone pushed me," Mae stated defiantly. Alice could see the worried creases on Mae's face as she struggled to remember more. "Someone was there, Alice. A man, I think. I could smell cigarette smoke. Someone pushed me down the steps." Mae's voice was becoming shrill again with each word.

For a moment, Alice was frozen, unable to react, to move, to speak. Fear gripped her heart, a fear she hadn't felt for many years. Shaking off the spell, Alice attempted to take control again, to steer her mother-in-law to a more palatable explanation. "You hit your head pretty hard, Mae. Your mind may be playing tricks on you. Remember, the doctor said that might happen."

Agitated, Mae shook her head, clasping Alice's hand tighter. "I know it sounds crazy, Alice. Margaret thinks I'm imagining things. The doctor too, but I'm quite positive. Someone was there. Someone pushed me down the steps, and I think . . . I think they meant for me to die there." The statement lingered in the air, sending a shiver down Alice's spine. Mae took a long breath, then turned to Alice. "Do you think we should call the police?"

Alice hesitated, torn between her desire to support Mae and her fear that Will would be angry if she gave in to Mae's hysteria. "It's the middle of the night, Mae. Why don't we wait until morning? I doubt they can do much in the dark."

Mae sighed. "Yes, I suppose you're right. We'll call first thing, all right?" She settled herself back into bed, pulling the covers up to her chin. "I guess we'd both best get some sleep."

Alice nodded, but as she rose to make her way back to her room, Mae said, "Alice, will you sit with me a while?"

"Of course." Alice walked back toward Mae's bed, sitting beside her. Even as Mae's breathing slowed, Alice's mind worked furiously. She couldn't imagine who would want to hurt her gentle, soft-spoken mother-in-law, but she knew Mae was not given to flights of fancy. And if someone had tried to kill Mae once, would they try again?

"Can you remember anything else, Mrs. Bennett? What the person was wearing maybe?"

Deputy David Morrison of the Pickens County Sheriff's Department was dutifully taking notes as Mae recounted her story. Alice could see disbelief etched all over his face, but she was thankful he was at least willing to pretend to take Mae seriously. In the light of the day, it seemed absurd to think that someone had deliberately tried to hurt Mae, but Mae was sticking to her story.

"As I told you earlier," Mae said, steadily, patiently, showing no sign of wear despite the repeated questions, "the attack came from the side. I didn't see anything at all. I just felt his hands on me."

"Are you sure it was a man?"

Mae hesitated. "No," she admitted. "But they left bruises. The hands were strong. It must have been." A twinge of uncertainty had entered her voice.

Deputy Morrison stood up. "Okay, Mrs. Bennett. I'll take a look around the property and then file my report." He turned to leave. Alice followed him to the door.

"Thank you, officer," Alice said. "I appreciate you coming out here to hear her story. I know it sounds strange."

He turned and smiled. "I'm sorry there's not more I can do." He took a few steps down the ramp, then turned again to face Alice. She noticed the sweep of his gaze as he took her measure. She blushed. "If you need anything at all, Mrs. Bennett, give me a call."

Alice hurried back into the house, away from those eyes. She was tired of being scrutinized wherever she went. Whether it was because she was Will Bennett's wife or some other reason, she felt like an animal being judged at the county fair. Only after she was safe inside the house did it occur to her that the deputy hadn't searched the property like he said he would. She could hear his tires on the gravel as he pulled away. Alice wasn't sure whether to feel irritated or relieved.

"Shall I make us some tea before we head into town?" Alice asked Mae as she walked past, heading toward the kitchen.

"Yes, that would be fine, dear," Mae said, distractedly. Alice wondered if Mae was suffering complications of her head injury and made a mental note to discuss it with Mae's doctor. She put the kettle on the stove to boil and nearly jumped out of her skin when she turned to find Mae standing silently behind her. Mae was becoming very proficient with her walker.

"Oh, Mae. You scared me half to death!"

Ignoring Alice's fright, Mae crinkled her forehead. "You know, I'm quite certain. I remember those hands on my arm, shoving me sideways. I reached for the rail, but of course, there wasn't one. It's possible, Alice." The desperation in Mae's voice made Alice's heart ache. She wanted to believe Mae's version of events, if only to placate her mother-in-law.

"Anything is possible, Mae," she replied, unconvincingly. The lack of serious attention from the sheriff's deputy had given weight to Alice's desire to discount Mae's theory and she wasn't doing a good job of keeping the disbelief out of her voice. Luckily, Mae was so distracted she didn't seem to notice. "Why don't you go sit down and I'll bring you the tea when it's ready."

Still lost in thought, Mae added, "I could swear I smelled cigarette smoke—" Her voice drifted off. Alice felt the skin on her neck prickle. She brushed gently past Mae and into the sitting room to her purse. Reaching into the front pocket, she retrieved the flattened pack of cigarettes. She couldn't believe she'd forgotten them until now.

"Mae, does your nephew Andrew smoke?"

Startled out of her reverie, Mae looked questioningly at Alice. "No. Why do you ask?"

Alice hesitated. There were lots of plausible reasons why the cigarette package had ended up wedged near Mae's front door. Maybe a visitor dropped it. Maybe the wind blew it over. It was probably a coincidence. She tucked the cigarettes back in her purse, making a mental note to call the deputy. "Margaret mentioned something the other day and I forgot to ask," she said dismissively, hoping Mae wouldn't notice her anxiety.

Mae chuckled as she moved into the sitting room. "Yes, Margaret would have his hide if she caught him smoking. She's always been like a mother hen to Andrew, even when they were children." The whistling of the kettle interrupted the conversation. Mae sat down in her armchair and Alice made her way back into the kitchen.

When they'd finished their tea, Alice got Mae into her coat and out the door for physical therapy. Alice nearly stumbled on the stone steps—awareness of the discarded pack of cigarettes weighing her down.

The frown lines in Will's forehead were deep and unyielding. Alice cringed. A few hours earlier, she'd picked Will up at the airport. He was all smiles. For a moment, she'd allowed herself to hope things might be better between them. They'd talked without the usual awkwardness, even laughing together as they made their way to Jasper, but when Mae told Will about filing a police report, Will's expression had turned dark.

"Alice, may I speak with you for a moment?"

Alice followed Will into the kitchen, feeling like a child banished to the principal's office. She braced herself for Will's temper, but he simply frowned quietly for several moments before talking.

"Did you talk to Mother's doctor about these fantasies she's having?" His voice was soft but there was danger there, an under-current of anger, resentment.

"I did. He said she shouldn't have any lasting effects from the fall. Her concussion was mild."

"But you let her call the police anyway?" His efforts to keep his voice calm weren't enough to disguise the accusation in his question.

Alice's apprehension gave way to irritation, but she tried to stay calm and to keep her voice steady. "Look, Will. I don't know your mother very well, but she's never struck me as the type of person who would make things up. Her nightmares those first few days were awful. And then, when she started talking about being attacked, the nightmares stopped. Like her mind was finally calm again. She's convinced it happened." Alice paused to let that sink in. "The deputy told me there wasn't much they could do about it. Filing the report made her feel better, so what harm did it do, really?"

For a moment, she thought about mentioning the cigarette pack, but Will was so convinced his mother was delusional, she figured it would only make him angrier.

"I suppose you're right. This is a small town, Alice. Maybe the sheriff's office will have some discretion," Will said, but his voice was tight. "When was Margaret up here last?"

"She comes up on the weekends, and she was here for Mae's doctor appointment a few days ago." Alice felt protective of her sister-in-law, but there was something else in Will's question that riled her: the insinuation that Alice couldn't evaluate the situation on her own. She'd been here for weeks, and still Will seemed hesitant to trust her.

"What did she think about Mother's claims?"

"She was concerned, of course, but she didn't dwell on it."

"Of course not," Will said, frowning again. "If it's not about Margaret's career, it's not important."

"That's not fair, Will. Margaret's job keeps her busy, just like yours, and she's been very helpful around here." Despite Alice's need to defend her sister-in-law, she regretted speaking as soon as Will turned on her. His eyes blazed.

"What are you implying, Alice? That I haven't done my part?"

The sudden fury in Will's voice gave Alice a start. She took a deep breath, hoping to defuse the situation. She would have to be the voice of reason. The thought made her feel agitated, resentful.

"Nobody said anything of the kind, Will. This is a very stressful time for your family. I think you all should take it easy on one another while we get Mae back on her feet."

Will looked as if he were about to say something, but Mae's voice interrupted his rant. Without another word, Will walked back into the sitting room. Alice stayed in the kitchen for a few moments, puttering around straightening things on the counter. She'd never pushed Will about his family before. As long as he stayed silent about his childhood, she felt safe doing the same. Now, it was like an unspoken rule. Still Alice couldn't help but wonder why her cool, calm husband seemed to fly off the handle so easily when it came to his sister. She had never paid much attention before to how petulant Will could be when he didn't get his way.

7

"Heard you were up at the Bennett house today?" Carver said as he took a seat next to Deputy Morrison in the department lunchroom. He'd been in town making his rounds and all anyone could talk about was Mae Bennett's daughter-in-law, Alice, like she was the newest attraction at the zoo.

Morrison nodded without looking up from his sandwich. *Here's the real animal,* Carver thought, as he watched a large plop of mustard splat on Morrison's plate. Another streak of yellow stretched from Morrison's mouth to the tip of his chin.

"Having some sandwich with your mustard?" Carver teased, grabbing a napkin from the counter and handing it to Morrison. Memories from raising his children surfaced frequently around the young deputy, who was not much older than Carver's youngest son.

"Thanks," Morrison said cleaning up the mess on his face. "Yeah, I got a call from Ms. Bennett—Alice—saying Mae Bennett thinks she was attacked."

"Attacked?" Carver scoffed. He'd been taking note of the eager expression on Morrison's face when he spoke about the young Mrs. Bennett and wasn't expecting the rest of the announcement.

"She says she remembers someone pushing her when she fell. Broke a hip, lots of bruises."

"I heard. Judging by your tone, you don't believe her?"

Morrison sighed. "Sorry, Leland. I know you see criminals around every corner, but I think Mae Bennett is old and she fell down her front steps."

"Did you find anything to suggest she's wrong?"

Morrison coughed. "No."

"But you looked? I mean, you went all the way up there to take her report, right? You did actually investigate, correct?" Carver scowled.

"I took down Mrs. Bennett's story. And Alice's."

Alice? Since when were they on a first name basis? Carver considered this a moment and then decided to poke his companion a bit further. "What about Alice Bennett? I haven't seen her. Is she pretty? I can't imagine Will Bennett having an ugly wife."

Morrison blushed. "She's, um, well, she's not what you would expect, I guess."

This response intrigued Carver. "What do you mean exactly?"

Morrison paused a moment. "Well, you know how Will always had some beauty queen girl on his arm in high school? Alice Bennett is different." He cleared his throat awkwardly. "I mean, she's beautiful, don't get me wrong, but she's substantial. You know?"

"Meaning what? She's not skinny?" Carver was enjoying the look of irritation on Morrison's reddening face.

"No! That's not what I meant. Never mind."

Carver laughed. "You sound pretty smitten, Dave. Best remember who you're dealing with."

The color in Morrison's face deepened. The Bennetts were an old family with roots that ran deep in this mountain town. Cavorting with Will Bennett's wife would be a disaster if you wanted to keep your standing in town. Morrison wasn't too young to understand the danger there, despite his obvious attraction.

"I'm not a fool," Morrison spat, "no matter what you think of me." His eyes were hard in stark contrast to the color in his face.

"Calm down, son." Carver couldn't resist the jab at Morrison's age, though he felt a little guilty at pressing the deputy so far. Morrison looked like he was going to implode. "I'm just joshing you."

Morrison threw away his half-eaten sandwich and stood. "Don't you have something better to do than yap at me?"

"Indeed I do," Carver said with a grin. He grabbed a can of soda out of the refrigerator and headed back to his car. He'd drive around town for a little while before continuing his interviews. Carver wasn't sure what he was looking for, but he figured he'd know it when he saw it.

With nothing to show from an hour of cruising Jasper's streets, Carver stopped at the Carriage House for some lunch.

"Hello, Patsy," he said, removing his hat as he took a seat at a table near the middle of the dining room. She made her way around the counter with a large glass of sweet tea.

"Here you go, Leland. What can I get you?" she asked, batting her lashes. Patsy was well into her sixties. She'd been flirting shamelessly with Carver for a few years now, ever since he and his wife had parted company. He wasn't about to let her know how much he enjoyed her advances. Maybe someday he'd ask her out, but not today.

"The usual, Patsy. Thanks," he said, scanning the room to inventory the faces, all of which he knew. The Carriage House was a daily stop for the Jasper Police Department, many of whom gathered for breakfast before or after their shifts. The sheriff's department was also represented today, including a few of the new recruits Carver had spent the last few weeks training. He rarely joined his colleagues, preferring to people watch, though he nodded anytime his eyes made contact.

"Hey there, Leland."

Carver looked up to see Jim Davis smiling down at him. Jim was wearing one of his funny t-shirts, his suspenders straining against his expanding belly. Carver had known Jim since they were kids—he was a frequent exception to Carver's solitary dining preference.

"Hey, Jim. Want to join me?"

"Don't mind if I do," Jim said, pulling out the chair opposite Carver. Jim Davis was another staple at the Carriage House. Patsy had a cup of coffee in Jim's hand before he saw her coming, his bushy white beard brushing the table and nearly dripping into his coffee. In a heartbeat, she was back with Carver's food.

"How's Judith?" Carver asked as he dug into the skillet Patsy had stealthily placed in front of him.

"Much better, thank you kindly," Jim replied with a smile. "She's getting her energy back. This last round of chemo was rough, but we're taking things one day at a time. You know the drill." Jim winked.

"That I do," Carver said, giving Jim a knowing grin. Both men had done a stint at the local AA. It wasn't uncommon. Pickens County had been a moonshine stronghold in North Georgia, and it wasn't a mark of shame to have gotten carried away. It was just a fact of life. Applying the AA phrase to Jim's wife lent levity to a situation that was otherwise tragic. Carver tried not to think of his own wife—his ex-wife now—driven away by the alcohol and the long, erratic hours of his job. She packed her bags the day their youngest left for college.

"So, have you seen Mae Bennett's daughter-in-law around town yet?"

"No, but young Morrison seems to think she's swell." Carver couldn't restrain the sarcasm in his voice.

Jim grinned. "She's a fascinating woman. I don't blame the

deputy for taking a liking to her. She's a looker, even if she doesn't seem to know it. And there's a lot to her."

Carver cocked an eyebrow. "That's what Morrison said. 'Substantial.' That's actually what he called her, can you believe it?" He smirked. "So, you've met her then?"

"Of course. She's been in here almost every afternoon. Doing some research for a story she's writing. I hear Morrison was up talking with Mae about her accident."

Carver groaned. "Yes, he was."

"Anything to her story?"

"You don't miss a thing do you, Jim?" Carver shook his head, though he couldn't suppress another grin. Living in a small town didn't lend itself to privacy. Word spread faster than a grass fire. "I don't know. Morrison doesn't seem to think so, but you can never tell. What with all the drug problems coming out of Atlanta, times are changing. Take all these burglaries. Never thought I'd see so much crime in Jasper."

Jim nodded. The two men sat in silence sipping their drinks. Finally, Carver put his napkin on the table and stood. "Well, back to work. Give Judith my love, won't you?"

"I will. And listen, Leland? Keep your eyes open."

"Something you want to tell me, Jim?" Carver's voice was strained.

"No," Jim said, his expression somber. "But something feels wrong to me."

Carver studied his friend another moment and then turned to leave. He muttered, "Me too, my friend," as he walked away.

8

"My goodness, Larry Lee Simms. I've never seen you around the library this often," Charlene Walker purred seductively from her seat behind the circulation desk. She winked at him. He tried to hide a shudder.

He'd been hanging around the library most days of the week, hoping to catch a glimpse of Alice Bennett. Larry Lee wasn't sure why he did it, but there was something about the woman that intrigued him. Of course, he'd find himself three beers into a tirade about the Bennett family by the end of every day as well. Having Alice in town—knowing she was Will Bennett's wife—Larry Lee's fixation on the Bennetts had taken on a new intensity.

It was Sunday afternoon and Alice hadn't been into the library for several days. Or, at least, Larry Lee hadn't seen her. He'd been careful to spend at least a half hour on the job boards so as not to arouse suspicion. Leave it to Charlene to notice his frequent trips.

"Searching for jobs," Larry Lee said, dismissively. "I get tired of driving all over the county to hear nothing but no. This is a lot easier."

"Mm hmm," Charlene was batting her eyelashes at Larry Lee, but the vacant look in her eyes betrayed the fact that her mind was elsewhere. "So, I was thinking, maybe you and me could go get some dinner this week?"

Charlene's smile was ferocious, causing the skin on his neck to tingle. She was good-looking, but her predatory gaze amplified by her long claw-like nails gave him the willies. She was like a wild animal you'd best avoid if you didn't want to get mauled. And she was tracking Larry Lee's scent.

"Let me think about it?" he hedged. "Mama's been feeling under the weather, so I may not have much free time."

Charlene's expression darkened at being rebuffed. "Yeah, okay," she said and went back to her work.

Relieved, Larry Lee walked through the interior doors then stopped when he spied Alice Bennett walking toward the entrance. Before she reached the doors, she turned. Someone was talking to her from her parked car. Larry Lee peeked around the corner in time to see Will Bennett get out of the car and walk toward his wife. He looked angry. She looked uncomfortable. They walked side by side, though about a foot apart, toward the door. Larry Lee barely had time to duck into the men's restroom before they would see him.

"Unbelievable," Larry Lee heard Will say in an exasperated tone. "You're supposed to be helping her, Alice."

"Can we talk about this later? I need to pick up a book and then we can head back," Alice pleaded in a low tone. Her voice faded as they walked farther into the library.

Looks like trouble in paradise, Larry Lee thought with a smirk. Inside his body he felt a jolt of something else—anger? Jealousy? Maybe even defensiveness? The more he saw of Alice Bennett, the more interested he became. Any other time, he might have been pleased to see the trouble in Will's marriage put on display, but the look of discomfort on Alice's face made him angry. In Larry Lee's mind, Will Bennett didn't have any right to be dissatisfied with his charmed life.

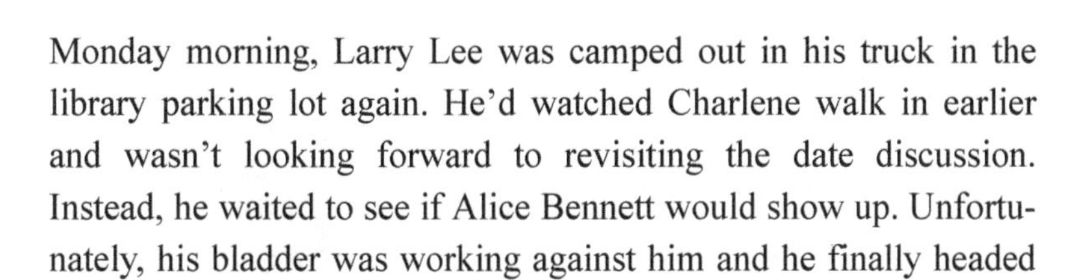

Monday morning, Larry Lee was camped out in his truck in the library parking lot again. He'd watched Charlene walk in earlier and wasn't looking forward to revisiting the date discussion. Instead, he waited to see if Alice Bennett would show up. Unfortunately, his bladder was working against him and he finally headed inside to use the restroom.

Returning to his truck, he was about to climb inside and give up his morning stakeout when he saw Alice's car pull off of Burnt Mountain Road. He ducked in front of his truck and stood near a bush, straining to see where Alice would park. The parking lot had filled up and she ended up driving around the far side of the building to find an open slot. Larry Lee inched up to the rear end of his truck, ducking down low to keep from being seen. He watched Alice walk through the library entrance, her arms laden with books and papers.

With single-minded focus, Larry Lee walked over to Alice's car and looked inside the window. He could see some papers lying on the passenger seat. He reached down and tried the handle, but the car was predictably locked.

"What're you doing, Larry Lee?"

Larry Lee nearly yelled as a hand touched his shoulder. He whirled around and found himself face-to-face with Deputy Morrison, one of his least favorite people in Pickens County. Despite having been responsible for only one out of six of Larry Lee's arrests, it was the one that had sent him to prison for almost a year. It figured Deputy Morrison would catch Larry Lee when he was actually up to something.

Attempting a dodge, Larry Lee said, "Jesus, Morrison. I'm heading in to look up some jobs. Been here nearly every day for the computers. You can ask Charlene," reflexively shoving his hands deep into his pants pockets. His voice conveyed annoyance, but his heart was beating rapidly.

"I'd be inclined to believe you, Larry Lee, but I've been sitting here watching you for the past ten minutes and I'm pretty sure you haven't been on the computers. And I'm quite positive this is not your car. What are you doing skulking around Alice Bennett's car?"

Panic. "I'm not skulking around no one. I don't even know who Alice Bennett is." Larry Lee hated the way his words got all ignorant-sounding and pathetic when he was nervous.

"So hiding behind your truck and then looking into locked car windows is your usual behavior, eh?" The deputy was enjoying Larry Lee's discomfort, which hacked Larry Lee off. He gestured at Alice's car. "What're you trying to get in there, Larry Lee?"

"I haven't done anything wrong. Looking at people's cars isn't a crime last time I checked. You've got no business bothering me, Morrison." Larry Lee's voice was becoming angry. He tried to keep his tone in check, but managing his anger had never been his strong point.

"I suggest you clear out of here, boy." Deputy Morrison had graduated a year ahead of Larry Lee and was fond of talking down to him. "I don't want to see you around Alice Bennett again."

Larry Lee thought Morrison was probably an okay guy, outside his uniform. As a cop, he saw the world in black and white like some overly earnest Barney Fife character and Larry Lee was firmly painted black in Morrison's book. Larry Lee wasn't stupid. He'd steer clear of Morrison, but the proprietary way the deputy spoke about Alice Bennett irked Larry Lee.

"It's a free country," Larry Lee replied.

"And it's a small town, Larry Lee. Unless you want to end up in the county lockup again, I suggest you keep your distance."

It wasn't right that Alice Bennett could walk around town like she owned it and he couldn't even use the library. Larry Lee wanted to argue, but the look on Deputy Morrison's face gave Larry Lee bad memories of his time in county lockup. He turned and walked to his truck without another word.

After leaving the library, Larry Lee headed to the drugstore to buy some cigarettes. His smoking had reached epic proportions, matched only by his drinking. Either way, he'd become a regular at the drugstore, the home of cheap liquor and cheaper smokes—and his mother's medications when he could afford to fill them. Walking into the store, though, he nearly changed his mind.

Standing behind the counter was another of Larry Lee's least favorite people in Pickens County: Jeffrey David Hatcher. Larry Lee and Jeff had been on opposite sides of the social spectrum for as long as he could remember. Jeff had been friendly with Will Bennett growing up, and *those boys were going places* or so the locals said. Larry Lee always found it a little ironic that Jeff was still working at his dad's drugstore almost twenty years after graduation. And yet, somehow, Jeff never failed to make Larry Lee feel small.

Luckily, there were a few people in the store—enough to keep Jeff on his best behavior. And Larry Lee needed a cigarette to calm his frazzled nerves.

"Pack of smokes," Larry Lee said quietly as he approached the counter. "And Agnes's pills if they're ready."

Jeff smirked at him. "Hey, Larry Lee. How's the job hunt going?" Larry Lee hated the way his problems seemed to be common knowledge around town.

"It's going," Larry Lee said, biting his tongue so as not to keep talking. Nothing good would come from letting himself be baited by Jeff Hatcher.

Jeff sniggered. "Must be a sign of something. Guess no one wants you around here, huh Larry Lee."

Larry Lee shoved his hands into his pockets, fighting the urge to pummel Jeff right then and there. "Can I get some cigarettes, please?" Larry Lee looked around nervously, noting he was now the only customer in the store.

Jeff disappeared for a moment. He returned with a white pharmacy bag, which he set on the counter. He reached around and pulled a pack of cigarettes out of the display behind him, sliding them across the counter to Larry Lee and making change for the dollar bills Larry Lee offered. Larry Lee was pocketing his change and turning to go when Jeff laughed out loud, getting Larry Lee's attention. He turned to face his tormentor.

"Funny you came in. I was just thinking about your sister, Larry Lee? I haven't had that particular piece of ass in my backseat for a long time. How is little Beth Ann? Thought I saw her in town the other day." Jeff scratched his crotch crudely, a malicious look on his face. "Guess she's ready for some more of this."

Larry Lee could feel the skin on his neck prickle. He drew in a long deep breath, trying to stay calm long enough to make his way out of the drugstore, but try as he might, he couldn't move his feet toward the door. It was like the mere mention of his sister's name had frozen him firmly in place.

"Of course," Jeff continued, a grin stretched wide across his face. "Everyone's had that particular piece of ass. And I mean everyone." It was clear he enjoyed making Larry Lee squirm. Larry Lee felt himself losing control. His heart raced and the urge to spring across the counter was becoming physically painful to resist. He curled his fingers tightly around the bag in his hand, taking comfort in the crackle as he squeezed tightly. He turned to face Jeff, but kept his feet planted.

"Shut your damned mouth," Larry Lee growled.

Jeff laughed cruelly. "Guess she ran out of return customers around here, eh Larry Lee? Maybe you should go find out where she's whoring around and find a job there. Such a happy family reunion. Slut sister. Loser brother. Together," Jeff feigned a romantic expression. "Forever."

Larry Lee's fists were clenched so tight they were starting to turn cold. His resolve was wearing thin.

"Can't think of a place dumb enough to give you a job—"

"That's enough," a voice from behind Larry Lee sounded, breaking the tension and freeing Larry Lee from his rigid stance.

He turned and found himself nearly nose to nose with Deputy Carver. Seemed like he couldn't escape his least favorite people today. Lucky for him, Jeff had been too caught up in his taunts to notice Carver walk in.

The sheriff's deputy leaned past Larry Lee and slapped a newspaper down on the counter. "You better be getting home, Larry Lee," he said, but his fiery eyes were trained on Jeff, who'd gone very pale. Thankful for the reprieve, Larry Lee didn't wait to see what happened next. Gripping his items like a lifeline, he hurried to his truck and drove straight home where the trouble wouldn't get him locked up.

9

After a disastrous weekend with Will, Alice was relieved to get back to work on her article. She'd been halfway to the reference room when she realized she'd forgotten the papers she needed in her car. As she stepped into the parking lot, she saw the same man she'd been seeing around the library talking angrily with the sheriff's deputy. They were standing next to her car, so she decided to go back inside without her papers. She'd caught the man looking at her and was relieved to see the deputy reading him the riot act.

Alice was settling in to do some research when Deputy Morrison walked up to her table.

"Hello, Alice," he said, pulling out a chair across from her without waiting for an invitation. "Mind if we chat for a moment?"

"No, of course not." She put down her pen and gave the deputy her full attention, curiosity overcoming her irritation at being interrupted. As he took a seat, she noticed once again how young he was. Morrison was only a bit taller than Alice and certainly no more than a few years older, with curly hair and a stubble-free face that seemed almost cherubic, though he was not nearly as handsome as Will. She'd begun to compare all men to Will even before they were dating seriously. Something about her husband made other men pale by comparison for Alice, even now with their relationship in turmoil.

Since taking Mae's report, Deputy Morrison had checked in twice to make sure Mae was okay. With no new information, Mae was feeling very discouraged and her dreams were turning ugly again. Each visit left Alice feeling frustrated, and she didn't like the way the deputy looked at her with desire in his eyes. She knew that look.

"How's Mae?" The deputy spoke with great fondness. Alice knew he'd grown up with the Bennetts in the local Baptist church. It seemed like everywhere she looked, there were connections in this town. For a moment, her mind wandered to her own childhood. Then she caught his eye again and blushed as he studied her.

"She's doing all right. Getting around much easier, though she still has pain. The doctor says she should be able to drive again in about six weeks."

"That's good." Deputy Morrison seemed distracted. "Has she remembered anything new about the night she fell?"

Alice felt the hairs on the back of her neck prickle. "No. Why? Has something happened?"

The deputy hesitated. "Well, it may be nothing. I was talking to the doctor yesterday and we were thinking about the bruise on Mae's right arm."

Alice frowned. It bothered her that the doctor was talking about Mae without her permission, but in such a small town, she figured privacy was sometimes a luxury. "And?"

"Well, it occurred to us that Mae landed on her left side."

"Yes, that's where most of her injuries are." Alice felt herself getting impatient.

"Given Mae's age, it's likely she bruises easily. The fall was very traumatic. But . . ." and finally Alice got what he was trying to say.

"You think someone may have pushed her hard enough to

bruise her right arm?" She pictured the ugly bruises on Mae's delicate skin. Fear spread across Alice's chest, a tightening wave threatening to take her breath away.

Once again, the deputy hesitated. "It's possible. That's why I wanted to talk to you alone. I don't want to scare Mae, but I'd like to come back out and search the grounds again, a little wider of an area this time." He fumbled with his words. Alice wondered why. "And I need Mae to make a list of everyone who'd been out to the house over the weeks leading up to the accident."

It was Alice's turn to pause. "Are we safe up there?" Having lived in a city all her life, Alice had loved the remoteness of Will's childhood home. Now being reminded of the isolation took on an ominous quality.

"Yes. I've already talked to the lake association president, and he still has a small community watch program. Mae's been living up there alone for months. We'll step up patrols, but that area has always been a very safe place to live."

Alice wasn't so sure. They chatted for a few more minutes before the deputy got up to leave. As he turned away, Alice said, "Wait a second." She reached into her purse and pulled out the pack of cigarettes. "I found these next to Mae's front steps the first night I got here. We thought they must have belonged to her nephew. He comes up to do odd jobs now and again." Alice handed the pack to Deputy Morrison.

"Okay, thanks. I'm sure it's just trash that blew up in the last big wind," he said, but Alice saw a flicker of recognition on the deputy's face.

Alice decided to take Rosy for an early walk, wanting to avoid the mountain roads in the dusk. Every shadow suddenly seemed menacing. They crossed the road and headed toward the kudzu patch, when Rosy caught scent of something and took off at a dead run. Alice jogged a few paces up the road calling the dog's name, but gave up, knowing Rosy would come back shortly. She always did. Alice ambled up the road.

Rain over the weekend had left the kudzu patch a gorgeous lush green. Alice stepped to the side of the road and pulled out her phone to take a picture.

"Be careful. There's a lot of mud over there."

The woman's voice pierced the silence of the landscape, startling Alice. She turned to see a short, stout figure in khaki pants and a floral shirt, well-worn gardening gloves on and a pair of shears in one hand. The woman stood in front of a small house, trimming her rosebushes, which erupted with a rainbow of colors. She looked at Alice curiously, removing her gloves. "You must be Mae Bennett's daughter-in-law?"

"Yes, I am. I'm Alice." Alice walked across the road and took the woman's outstretched hand. It was warm and moist from work in the hot sun. "How did you know?"

"Joylyn Clement." The older woman's handshake was strong and sure. She looked to be in her seventies, but her hands were callused from manual labor and she appeared much sturdier than Mae. "I've seen you and Rosy out for your evening walks. Mae used to stop and chat when she was out with Rosy. Would you like to come in and have some tea?" Joylyn gestured to her house.

"Thank you. I probably shouldn't though. Mae will wonder where we've gotten off to."

"The kettle's already on. Rosy took off after the squirrels she likes to chase. She'll have cornered the critter up a tree. I'm sure she'll be a little while." Joylyn had already started walking back toward her front door. Alice sighed and followed.

Once both women were seated, Joylyn asked, "How's Mae doing?"

"Much better, thank you. She's still using a walker, but her hip is getting much stronger."

"It was sweet of you to come up and take care of her." Joylyn sipped her tea, but she studied Alice all the while. "I heard someone pushed her."

Alice sputtered, nearly choking on her tea. "Where did you hear that?"

Joylyn giggled. "It's a small town, dear. Secrets don't stay secret for long around here. Everyone in town is talking about it. And about you."

Choosing to ignore the last comment, Alice said, "Well, we're not exactly sure what happened, but Mae remembers feeling someone push her and there seems to be some evidence she's right."

"I've known Mae my whole life. If she says she remembers being pushed, I reckon she was."

Alice pondered this statement. "I simply can't imagine someone attacking Mae right at her front door."

Joylyn smiled, but it wasn't a comforting smile. "Bad blood runs deep in this part of the country. You'd be surprised what the quiet country folk around here are capable of." She took another sip of her tea. "I wouldn't be one bit surprised if Larry Lee Simms were to blame."

"Larry Lee Simms?" The name sounded familiar. A vague image popped into Alice's mind of the two men at the diner on one of her first nights in town. "I think Margaret mentioned him," she said, idly, trying to remember which one was Larry Lee. No matter what she did, her memories landed back on the woman at the back of the diner.

"The Simms and the Bennetts have been at each other's throats for generations. I guess we all thought the feud had died down when Mae's husband passed, but maybe that's not the case."

"Feud? You mean like the Hatfields and the McCoys?" Alice couldn't keep the amusement out of her voice. She was reminded of a cartoon she'd loved when she was a child, an episode of which featured the famous feuding families.

"I know how it sounds, but this is Georgia, the land of moonshine and property disputes. Both of which play into the trouble between the Simms and the Bennetts." The look on Alice's face must have given away her feelings of disbelief, because Joylyn continued, "It's a different world than you're used to."

"I'm beginning to see that," Alice replied. The unassuming town of Jasper she'd visited with Will was revealing itself to be a complicated, sometimes frightening place. She was pondering this when, looking out across the kudzu patch, Alice saw Rosy loping through the green vines.

"Here comes Rosy. She must have given up her quarry. I'd better go." She rose to put her teacup in the sink, but Joylyn waved her away.

"I'll take care of it. Give Mae my love. Tell her I'm bringing up a pie tomorrow."

"I will. It was nice to meet you, Mrs. Clement. Thank you for the tea." Alice offered the older woman her warmest smile. She got the feeling Joylyn was someone she would be glad to know.

Alice turned and walked out the front door, calling Rosy as she went. Rosy came panting up and nuzzled her nose into Alice's pant leg. They walked back toward Mae's house past the shambles of the Simms place. She couldn't help but look over her shoulder constantly, unable to shake the feeling she was being watched.

"The soup was delicious, Alice." Mae patted daintily at her mouth with an embroidered cloth napkin that looked as though it had been in her family for generations. It was the first meal they'd had at the dining table. Mae had preferred the comfort of her armchair up to this point, and Alice felt like making it special.

"Thank you. My grandmother used to make it for us when we were little. She had a huge vegetable garden and the soup was always full of all the fresh veggies we'd gather."

"Is your grandmother still living?"

"Oh, no. She passed away when I was still very young." Alice felt a familiar tug of sadness in her chest. "Our family was never really the same." Embarrassed at her emotional reaction, Alice changed the subject so as not to have to elaborate. "That reminds me. I met Joylyn Clement on my walk today."

Mae smiled. "Joylyn's a character. She's been living in that house all by herself for nearly a decade. Her husband died young and her only son moved up north a few years ago."

"She invited me in for tea and asked me to tell you she'd be bringing up a pie tomorrow."

"Joylyn is famous for her peach pies. You're going to love it. Peaches plucked right from her orchard, I imagine."

Alice wasn't interested in pies. Joylyn's words about family feuds had been nagging at her since she'd left. She hesitated, having spent so much of her life learning to avoid talking about her own family that she felt strange prying into Mae's, but a need for answers firmed her resolve. "Joylyn mentioned some problems with another local family. The Simms? I think Margaret pointed out their house when I first got here."

Mae frowned. "Another thing Joylyn is famous for besides her pies. That woman loves gossip, bless her. She should know better than to worry you, though. Especially with things so far in the past."

"She said your families have been fighting for generations. Apparently, the whole town is talking about you being pushed. Joylyn suggested Larry Lee Simms might have had something to do with it."

Alice watched Mae closely to gauge her reaction, but Mae's face stayed frozen in a frown, her eyes gazing steadily ahead of her. "Larry Lee was in Margaret's class in school, I think. Has had quite a few run-ins with the law. I see him every now and again when I walk Rosy. They live right down the hill."

Alice mulled over this information, then decided to continue. "What happened, Mae? With the Simms?"

Mae sighed. "Remember when I said it might not be a good idea to pry into local affairs? Well, in the South, people hold on to their grudges. They get passed down from generation to generation. The Simms were a moonshining family. They may still be. That sort of thing still goes on in this part of the country."

Alice listened intently, intrigued. She'd experienced firsthand Will's inability to forgive and forget but had always attributed it to his personality. The cultural aspect piqued her curiosity.

Mae seemed to lose her train of thought. Alice, worried, leaned in closer, but Mae snapped to and smiled. "Don't worry, Alice. I'm just thinking back. Anyway, my father-in-law owned a lot of land around Jasper. It was part of the original homesteads and the property boundaries weren't very clear in those days. He sold a parcel of land to the Simms family when they moved into the area. The Bennetts were God-fearing Baptists and Will's grandfather did not stand for alcohol of any sort, especially moonshine. That put him at odds with the Simms almost immediately."

"A few years before he died, old man Bennett hired a surveyor to clarify some of the property lines. To put in the estate papers. They found a discrepancy in the boundaries for the parcel he'd sold to Simms. When Bennett brought it up with Simms, they nearly came to blows." Seeing the disbelief on Alice's face, Mae explained. "In those days, property disputes were pretty common. Boundaries were often marked by piles of rocks or ruined foundations. Cases still go to court today, as hard as that may be to imagine."

"What happened?"

"Old man Simms took a shot at Bennett one day. He didn't injure him, mind you. Both men were getting so old, neither one could see past their noses. But the sheriff was called in and Simms was thrown in jail. The Bennetts held a lot of sway in town. Simms was released, but not before the judge found in favor of Bennett regarding the land boundaries. Unfortunately for Simms, one of his biggest distilleries sat on the land they lost, hidden up behind some trees. Bennett tore it down immediately, claiming a moral victory as well as a personal one.

"The feud has been going on ever since. Agnes Simms used to run her grocery cart into mine when we saw each other at the Piggly Wiggly. When my husband died though, things seemed to settle down. Or maybe neither Agnes nor I get into town much these days." The last comment was intended to lighten the mood, but it didn't quite hit its mark. And Mae added, "Either way, there aren't enough Simms or Bennetts left in town to keep up the fight." Mae smiled, but Alice's imagination had been ignited.

"For heaven's sake," Alice said, unable to conceal her shock. "Do you really think Larry Lee Simms might have been the one who pushed you?"

Mae considered for a moment, but then shook her head. "No. It's hard to believe Larry Lee would bother hurting an old lady like me. After all, I've barely seen any of the Simms since Bill died. Losing our husbands seemed to create an informal truce between Agnes and me. Larry Lee's younger sister Beth left town years ago, and Agnes doesn't leave the house much anymore. Larry Lee only came back to town a few years ago, and he's been keeping to himself." Though Mae offered this explanation calmly, her face stayed scrunched in a frown.

Alice decided she would talk to Deputy Morrison the next day, just to be sure.

10

"Larry Lee! If you don't cut that out, I'm going to string you up."

Agnes Simms's face was red with rage. Larry Lee was sitting at the kitchen table, his feet propped on the tabletop, throwing an old tennis ball against the wall. He'd been at it for hours. Seeing the murderous look on his mother's face, Larry Lee couldn't help but grin. He was feeling mean and pent up like a caged animal. Provoking Agnes gave him a sense of accomplishment, even though he knew she'd be beating on him any minute.

Larry Lee put the tennis ball on the table. It was filthy from having been chewed by their old dog Ace. Ace was long gone but the tennis ball still held enough bounce to keep Larry Lee entertained. He was bored. James had picked up a position on a pulpwood crew and had been out of touch for days. Avoiding the library and the possibility of running into Alice Bennett or Deputy Morrison or Carver or Jeffrey Hatcher or any of the other growing list of people he wanted to stay away from, Larry Lee was at loose ends. So he drank and pissed off his mother to pass the time.

"Go back to bed, Mama."

Agnes filled up the doorway, her housedress bedraggled from

days of sweat and sleep without a wash. Larry Lee could smell her body odor from his seat across the room. Agnes looked weak, but Larry Lee didn't doubt for a minute she'd hit him if she got close enough. Her balled fists confirmed his suspicions.

"What are you doing home anyway?" she asked. Larry Lee could hear a wheeze in her lungs as she spoke, but he was in too foul a mood to feel concern for his mother.

"I live here, Mama. Where else would I be?"

"I'm warning you, Larry Lee. Don't you run your mouth off at me. This is my house and don't think for a minute I won't send you packing." The force of her words made Agnes cough.

Larry Lee waited silently for her to quiet down before saying, "Over your dead body." His voice was measured and cold as steel. Alcohol coursed through his veins—liquid courage. He often mouthed off to his mother, but this time, as the words came out of his mouth, he realized he meant them. Larry Lee was reaching his limit. He'd had enough.

Agnes must have sensed the change, too. The blood drained from her face, but she forced her lips up in a sneer. "Go get a job, you drunk." She snatched a pill bottle from the table, then turned and waddled back to her bedroom.

Larry Lee laughed out loud. Sure he was drunk, but his mother hadn't gone a day without hitting the bottle since Larry Lee had returned home. He could see the yellow in her eyes, same as his father before he died. And the pills she was taking, the ones you weren't supposed to mix with alcohol, were disappearing fast. Larry Lee may have been a lot of things, but naïve was not one of them. He knew she wasn't long for this world.

Doubting very much she'd make another appearance this evening, he picked up the tennis ball and was about to target the wall again when there was a knock at the door. Dropping the tennis ball, Larry Lee bolted upright. No one ever knocked on the Simms door. He should've gotten up to answer it, but something had him spooked.

Another knock, louder this time, and then a voice Larry Lee hadn't heard in years. "Mama? Mama, it's me."

"Beth?" Larry Lee opened the door slowly. The woman on the other side was a stranger, an apparition, yet her voice still made his stomach turn. Small and mousy, Beth Simms looked like something the cat dragged in. He realized he'd seen her lurking around town but hadn't recognized her. Larry Lee could see her hip bones and ribs poking out beneath a too-tight, threadbare shirt. Her cheeks looked sunken. He was sure if he looked closely, he'd see track marks on her arms.

"Larry Lee?" Beth appeared startled. Looking past him, she asked, "Where's Mama?"

"She's in bed. What're you doing here, Beth?" Larry Lee stood in the doorway and made no move to let his younger sister in. His sister was the last person on earth he wanted to see. *Ever.*

"I came home to see Mama, that's all." Beth moved forward, but Larry Lee held fast.

"You aren't welcome here, Beth."

"Who died and made you God?" Beth snarled. "You can't keep me out of my own home, Larry Lee."

"Your home? Who do you think has been here taking care of things while you've been off running wild? Who's been taking care of Mama? Paying the bills. Putting food on the table." Larry Lee didn't care if what he was saying was true or not; he was on a roll. "Who always cleaned up your damned messes, Beth? It's bad enough I have to take Mama's crap. I don't feel like taking any of yours. Why don't you go back where you came from?"

Rage flared up in Beth's eyes and she took on the crazy look that always signaled trouble. Beth was trouble, for herself and for everyone else she came in contact with. It had been a while since Larry Lee had seen her like this—wild with rage. Without thinking, he shifted away from her, but still blocked the door.

"Who are you to tell me to leave, Larry Lee? Aren't you a little old to be living with your mama anyway? I heard you can't get a job to save your life." Beth sneered. She never failed to hit him where it hurt. As much as he hated to let her get to him, her words were like a sledgehammer to his pride. What little there was left.

Wounded, he said, "It hasn't exactly been easy trying to make a life for myself here, you know."

"Whose fault is that?" she spat.

"Yours, Beth. It's always your fault!" Larry Lee tried not to yell, but the volume of his voice climbed. "And what do you care anyway? You didn't even have the decency to see me. I was locked up for your damned disaster and you didn't even visit. You left Mama stranded here while you ran off with what's-his-name." The words flew out of Larry Lee's mouth. "She's sick, you know? Mama. She's old and weak and here I am taking care of her. Where've you been, Beth? If you're looking for a handout, she ain't got nothing to give you."

Beth leaned in, but Larry Lee stood his ground.

"You always did think you knew better than any of us, but you don't know anything, Larry Lee." Her voice was small and for a moment, Larry Lee could see the ghost of the little girl he used to play in the woods with. Then he remembered the mangled remains of Oscar Clement's face and his time behind bars and the anger surged again.

"Leave us alone, Beth." The words hissed through his teeth like steam escaping a break in a pipe. He wasn't surprised to feel his heart beating hard and fast in his chest.

"Get out of my way. I want to see Mama." She shoved past him and stalked back toward the bedrooms.

Larry Lee heard his mother's voice, "Beth?" and then the bedroom door slammed shut. A flicker of worry passed through Larry Lee's heart, but then, deflated and utterly drained, he decided his mother deserved whatever she got from Beth. He walked out the front door without looking back.

~

With Beth at his house, Larry Lee decided the best thing to do was to stay away for a while. The list of places he could go and still avoid people in Jasper was growing smaller every day. He decided to drive into Atlanta and try to sell a few things. His funds were dwindling and his mother would need her medications soon, a fact he usually confronted with mild frustration, but with Beth in town his frustration had turned to rage. How dare she tell him to get out of the way in his own house? How dare Agnes call him a drunk when everything he did was to support her?

Larry Lee was grateful for the fast flow of traffic and the anonymity of the freeway. He needed time to think. What was Beth doing back home? Time had been hard on Beth, and Larry Lee had felt a momentary pang of sympathy when he cast eyes on the bedraggled stranger at his door, but Beth's famous attitude was still intact and it didn't take long to rub Larry Lee the wrong way. He didn't know why she'd come back, but he was sure it would mean more trouble for him.

He drove south through Atlanta toward the Bluff, an area where he'd had to come claim Beth more than once when she'd gone on a heroin bender or gotten herself in trouble for failure to pay one of her dealers. He'd made a connection in the neighborhood and began making his own trips down to fence stolen merchandise far enough from home to know it wouldn't be traced back to him. No one cared about the Bluff. It was perfect, though immensely dangerous.

Driving past broken-down buildings and dilapidated houses, Larry Lee was reminded of the injustice of it all—the haves and the have-nots. The Simms and the Bennetts. He felt both a sense of belonging and repulsion at this part of the city, along with a healthy dose of fear. The Bluff was known for its high crime and Larry Lee wasn't stupid. He knew better than to think he was immune to the violence. He'd left the Bluff on more than one occasion with black eyes and other bruises, not to mention the time that gangbanger had broken his ribs for bumping his car. Hadn't left a scratch on the car but his ribs still hurt when the weather got cold.

Pulling into the cracked driveway of a run-down blue-shingled house, Larry Lee scanned the area before stepping out and walking briskly toward the front door, his duffle bag slung over his shoulder. As he approached the door, it swung open. A behemoth of a man held the door open, looking Larry Lee up and down with suspicion.

"I need to see Tank." Larry Lee said from the bottom step, his muscles tense and ready to spring back toward his truck if things got out of hand. Most of these guys were so strung out, it didn't take much to push their buttons. Sometimes nothing at all.

The other man paused. Larry Lee wasn't a slight man by any means, but the sight of this giant gatekeeper had Larry Lee's stomach clenched. Without a word, he gestured over his shoulder toward the interior of the house, leaving Larry Lee to follow.

Larry Lee stepped inside the door and winced as the screen door clicked back into place. He did not step forward. The gatekeeper disappeared down the hall and Larry Lee waited. After a few moments, a smaller, mangy-looking man with long hair and a ratty beard sauntered down the hall. He was bare-chested, and his sweatpants were frayed at the waist.

"Whatcha got, Larry Lee?" The man's voice was raspy from drug use and a hard life.

"A few watches." Larry Lee reached into his bag and handed over several items, which Tank examined for some time before saying, "I can give you four hundred. Can't take this one though," he handed back one of the watches. "It's engraved. Too easy to track."

Larry Lee nodded, threw the watch back into his bag with the intention of dumping it in the first garbage bin he saw, and the exchange was done. As Tank closed the screen door behind Larry Lee he said, "Your sister came through here yesterday. She's not looking very good."

Larry Lee shrugged, though he felt his pulse quicken. "I haven't seen her in years. I don't know what to tell you." He picked at a loose baseboard with the tip of his boot, his eyes glued to the floor, waiting for more. There was always more when it came to Beth.

Tank looked at Larry Lee thoughtfully. "Listen, man. I don't think you'd better come around here for a while. And if you see Beth, tell her if she comes around here, they're going to kill her. You don't mess with the boys that way."

Larry Lee made to ask a question, but Tank closed the door hard in his face, lending finality to his words.

Larry Lee wondered what Beth had gotten herself into this time. Even she had better sense than to piss off these guys. *She's out of her goddamned mind!* He got back behind the wheel of his truck, slamming his fists into the sun-heated vinyl and yelled. As if things weren't already bad enough.

11

Carver felt frustrated. So, when he saw Larry Lee Simms speed by on his way back into Jasper, his ticket writing hand started itching. He turned on his lights and stepped on the gas in pursuit. As he rounded a bend, he saw something small and metallic fly out of the driver side window and land somewhere in the kudzu that engulfed the side of the highway. Larry Lee slowed down and pulled over.

Carver parked, got out of his car, and walked up to Larry Lee's truck.

"Deputy Carver," Larry Lee said, his face stony, his back pressed into the seat. He glared, but Carver could see a line of sweat on his brow.

"Hey there, Larry Lee. Where's the fire?"

"Huh?"

"You were speeding, son."

"Bullshit. I was going five miles over the speed limit."

"What d'you think speeding is, you smartass. Christ, Larry Lee. You get a little stupider every time I see you."

This was the nature of their relationship. Carver had busted Larry Lee a number of times, but he also felt a responsibility to keep Larry Lee from further trouble—insofar as that was possible. Carver rode Larry Lee hard, and Larry Lee pushed back equally hard. He was a pain in the ass, but Carver also felt some sympathy. He knew what Larry Lee's home life was like.

Carver sniffed. "You been drinking?"

"No, sir," Larry Lee replied, now visibly nervous.

"That's good, since I believe drinking is a parole violation. Am I right?"

"Yes, sir." Now Carver had Larry Lee on the run. Larry Lee only got polite and compliant when he was scared shitless.

"Why don't you step out of the truck?"

Larry Lee opened the door and stepped out onto the dirt. His clothes looked like they hadn't been washed maybe ever. He reeked of cigarette smoke and the dark circles under his eyes told the story of sleepless nights.

Carver took a quick peek inside the cab, knowing he wouldn't find anything. Despite Carver's jab, Larry Lee was not stupid. Anything incriminating was now lying in the kudzu and Carver wasn't about to go find it, a fact Larry Lee undoubtedly relied on.

"What'd you throw out the window back there?"

Larry Lee had clearly been expecting this question. "I don't know what you're talking about, deputy." He simpered.

"Goddammit, Larry Lee. Why is it you can't keep your nose clean? I have a feeling you're the one who's been busting into people's houses, and I'm of the mind that throwing you back in the can would go a long way to keeping the residents of Jasper—and their possessions—safe."

Now Larry Lee was sweating and shaking. Carver was torn. He didn't have any evidence to support arresting Larry Lee, but he'd gambled with his words and was pissed Larry Lee looked so guilty. He really didn't want to throw Larry Lee back in jail. He knew it hadn't been a pleasant time the first go-round.

"Here's what we're going to do, Larry Lee. I'm going to let you go. No tickets. No problem, right? But I tell you what. If I wasn't sure it was you thieving before, I am now and I'm going to be watching you like a hawk. You step one toe out of line and I'll have you back in the county lockup faster than you can say dumbass."

Before Larry Lee had a chance to reply, Carver turned and walked back to his squad car in a huff. He realized he'd been holding out hope Larry Lee wasn't involved this time—that maybe, just this once, Carver had the wrong guy. When he drove by, Larry Lee was still standing by his truck, looking for all the world like he was frozen in place.

Larry Lee's head felt like it was going to explode. He kept his body still and rigid as he watched the back end of Carver's car round the bend, but as soon as the deputy was out of sight, he let loose. A guttural scream from deep down in his abdomen—one that had been brewing and stewing for months, maybe years—pushed its way out and he kicked up dust clouds as he threw a full-on tantrum right there on the side of the road. He felt the rush of the cars going by and wondered what he must look like, but the release felt so good he couldn't stop.

The proverbial noose was thick and tight around his neck. He knew he'd been operating on borrowed time—that it was only a matter of days or weeks maybe before Carver or Morrison or some other twerp caught him with stolen goods and back to the clink he'd go. He'd been bullheaded enough to believe he could stay one step ahead, even if it was a small step, but now Larry Lee knew that Carver knew. And as much of a nuisance as Carver had been, following Larry Lee around like a stalker, he'd let him go. The thought made Larry Lee howl with frustration. He realized that as much as he didn't want to return to prison, what lay ahead of him now was completely unknown. He had no idea how he would make ends meet. He would have to go on welfare and the shame was too much for Larry Lee.

As he raged, his mind cycled furiously over the events of his life and, particularly, those of the last few weeks. He wanted to turn his truck around and leave town now, without a backward glance, but how could he? Larry Lee hated his mother and his sister, but they were his family. And you did for family. Didn't matter if they beat you down. His mother could mistreat him, his sister could whore it up all over town, but who would he be if he didn't try to fill his father's shoes? To be the man of the house, such as it was.

Larry Lee's voice began to crack with strain and he realized his face was wet with tears. He wondered when they'd started. Dropping to his knees, Larry Lee gave himself one last moment of weakness, pounding his fists into the ground and letting out the last ounce of frustration before picking himself up and heading for home. What else could he do?

"You didn't see anything else, Ms. Clement?" Morrison asked, taking notes on a small pad he'd pulled out of his breast pocket. Carver wondered what the deputy was writing. They'd been sitting in Joylyn's living room for nearly twenty minutes and had uncovered exactly zero pieces of useful information.

"Joylyn," Carver said, placing the tea she'd handed him on a side table, careful not to miss the doily. "Are you sure you haven't seen any kids messing around out here? Because kids these days are pretty stupid and I wouldn't put it past them to think this was funny."

Joylyn frowned. "Leland, I spend about five or six hours every day in my garden. The rest of the day I'm on my porch. I see everyone who goes by here. My fence was intact this morning, everything pristine. Now it looks like a tornado hit. My roses are ruined. I was outside all day with the exception of one hour—one hour I spent in town getting my hair done, as I told you nearly half an hour ago. In that time, someone set about to destroy my property. Do I think it was a bunch of kids getting their jollies? No, I do not."

Her matter-of-fact monologue made Carver grin. Joylyn Clement was tough as nails. She'd lived in this town, in this house, her entire life. She'd spent the last seven of those years on her own, and this was the first time Carver could remember her ever making a call to the Sheriff. Joylyn didn't ask for help. She owned a shotgun and knew how to use it. She wasn't about to let the deputies get away with anything less than a full-scale investigation.

"Ms. Clement, we—" Morrison started, but Carver interrupted.

"Joylyn. Stay calm. We'll figure out who did this, but we want to make sure we have all the facts. You say there's nothing missing. Are you sure? Because we still have a burglar on the loose and this may be related."

Joylyn's expression softened. "I've looked, Leland. No one was in the house, only the garden. And I didn't see a thing when I got back from town. Just the mess." Her face darkened, and Carver thought she suddenly looked every bit her seventy-two years. "Do you think the person who attacked Mae Bennett—?"

"We don't know for sure anyone attacked Mae Bennett," Morrison said, trying to calm her. Carver could have told the deputy this tactic wouldn't work.

Joylyn turned her laser gaze on Morrison. "*I* know, Deputy Morrison. Mae says she was pushed." She moved toward the front door, ushering Morrison as she did so. "She was pushed."

Carver laughed at the startled look on the deputy's face as he was herded toward the door. "Okay, Dave. Let's go look around and see what we can find. I'll check in with you later, Joylyn." He tipped his hat and followed Morrison out the door. Joylyn closed it behind them, though she remained at the window as they walked around the wrecked boards and plants that used to be Joylyn's lovely garden.

"There's nothing here," Morrison grunted a few minutes later, kicking at one of the loose boards. Carver sympathized with Morrison's frustration. It seemed like every time they were called out these days, they were met with a disaster but no clues. And unlike some of their other cases, Carver knew for certain this one had nothing to do with Larry Lee Simms.

As he was about to call an end to their search, Carver spied something strange on the board Morrison had kicked. The board had settled, resting awkwardly on a mound of broken rose branches, and Carver could see something orange underneath. Turning over the board revealed some orange spray paint. Hurriedly, he and Morrison turned over the rest of the fence pieces and found themselves with a puzzle. After a few minutes of work in the hot sun, Carver stood, wiped his brow, and pondered what he was seeing. Someone had scrawled the word YOU in bright orange letters across Joylyn's fence and then hacked it apart.

12

A few days passed without incident and, with Mae feeling better every day, Alice decided it was time to get serious about the article she was working on. She'd done the preliminary research into recent domestic violence laws and court cases in Georgia, but she'd been avoiding delving into the murder her editor had found so fascinating, well aware of her propensity to dive head first into hopeless cases. Now that she'd gotten to know some of the details of the case, she felt that familiar pull.

In 1940, a young woman—a mere girl really—was brutally murdered by her husband. The victim was young, popular, and pregnant. That the case hadn't been swept under the rug was in itself a miracle given the time period, but it also stood out because political careers had been made by it. The case helped the career of assistant prosecutor Herman Talmadge, who eventually became Governor of Georgia, following in his father's footsteps, and then a longtime United States Senator.

Despite the press and notoriety, Alice was finding little information on the story. Incredibly, it seemed to have been mostly forgotten in Pickens County. Alice was determined to find people who remembered the victim, Juanita Jones, if she had to talk to each and every person living in Pickens County. She made it a mission, but it was also a welcome distraction from the stresses in her life, despite the grisly nature of the crime.

Her first stop was the *Pickens County Progress* office. When she arrived to find it closed, she decided to walk down to the Carriage House and have lunch. Alice loved that restaurant, with its collection of rolling pins and freshly baked pies. She'd discovered their homemade granola on a visit with Will a few years earlier and she couldn't pass it by. It was a hot spot for local law enforcement, with the courthouse located next door, and she loved to sit and sip coffee while people-watching.

Alice had nearly finished her dish when an older man with a long white beard approached her table. "How's the granola?" he said with a smile. He wore a funny graphic shirt under suspenders and Alice couldn't suppress a grin.

"Delicious. We met a few weeks ago, right? You're Jim Davis."

"Hey," he chuckled, "that was my line. I'm Jim Davis." He reached out a hand, leathery and tanned from outdoor work. "And you're Alice Bennett."

She shook his hand and gestured to the chair opposite her. "Would you like to join me, Jim? I'm waiting for the *Progress* office to open up."

He took a seat and the waitress brought him a cup of coffee as if on cue. "I'd be delighted, but I can't stay long. My wife isn't well, and I try not to leave her alone too long." He took a sip and smiled. "Can't resist my daily stop at the Carriage House though. How are you enjoying your time in Jasper? How is Mae doing?"

"She's doing much better, thank you. Now, if I could only convince her son," Alice added with a sigh, immediately regretting airing her frustration. She'd had another awkward discussion with Will. It started out pleasant enough, but Will wouldn't allow himself to accept Alice had everything under control.

A broad grin stretched across Jim's face. "Will Bennett. I

haven't seen him in years. I remember when he went off to Emory. Full scholarship. That boy was going places." Jim chortled. "Obviously not back home."

Alice blushed. "Will's job keeps him pretty busy." She wondered why she still felt the need to paint a positive picture of Will for others.

Jim nodded. "How're you holding up?"

The question made Alice feel strange. She was getting used to having random strangers ask her about Mae. Hardly anyone asked how she herself was doing. In Alice's hometown, people had made it a point not to know you. Especially Alice. She was used to being snubbed. "I'm doing well, thank you for asking. Just trying to get some work done in between Mae's appointments."

"That's good news," Jim said, but then his brow crinkled in a frown. "I hope you don't mind me asking, but is it true what everyone is saying about Mae's fall?"

"What exactly do they say?" Alice was curious about the direction the local gossip had taken. She'd heard Joylyn Clement's theory, but she wondered if the rest of the town shared her opinion.

"Mae was knocked down and nearly killed by someone trying to break into her house?"

Alice hadn't considered burglary as a possible motive, but apparently the folks in Jasper had. "Well, if they were trying to rob her, they failed miserably. It looks like whoever was responsible took off right away."

"Poor Mae," Jim replied, his eyes downcast as he considered Alice's words. After a moment of silence, he perked up again. "So, what are you looking for at the *Progress*?"

"I'm a writer and I'm working on a story about some laws in Georgia. I've been researching a murder case that happened back in the 1940's. Juanita Jones. Do you know it?"

"Girl murdered in Tate?" Jim asked, and when Alice nodded he said, "I remember hearing the story. As you can see, I'm too young to remember directly." He grinned at her. Alice smiled back, but she noticed a woman at the next table leaning in to hear their conversation. She had a sour scowl on her face.

"The *Progress* printed a story a few years ago and I'm hoping to speak with the reporter to get a feel for the case. My article is actually about evolving domestic violence laws in Georgia, but my editor mentioned the girl's murder so I'm trying to follow up."

"That's pretty heavy stuff. And a word of warning . . . the folks around here may not like being reminded. The girl's murder was particularly gruesome, a definite black mark on local history." Jim's expression was friendly, but his words felt heavy on Alice's heart.

He finished up his cup of coffee and then stood. "Well, Miss Alice, thank you for inviting me to join you. It's been a real pleasure seeing you. I'm sure we'll run into each other again. Give Mae my love."

"I will. Nice to see you too, Jim." As he walked out the door, the woman sitting behind him stood as well, throwing her napkin on the table and stalking out of the restaurant in a huff.

After meeting with the editor at the *Progress*, Alice walked toward her car with a renewed sense of purpose. The Juanita Jones story was still shrouded in mystery, but she had gotten some good sources for her case study, including the contact information for the reporter who'd written the news article. As she walked past the courthouse, she admired the marble. The town of Tate where Juanita Jones lived and died had been a company town, the headquarters of the Georgia Marble Company. Juanita Jones's husband was an employee at the marble company and Juanita had died in a company house. Downtown Jasper was full of Georgia Marble.

Alice was so lost in thought she didn't notice the man walking toward her until he'd literally knocked into her shoulder, sending her papers scattering, nearly throwing her down.

"What the . . .?" she exclaimed as she regained her balance and stooped to grab her notes before they flew into the street. When she looked up, she recognized the man from the library. He was the one who'd been talking with Deputy Morrison.

"Why don't you watch where you're going?" he said, but he bent down to pick up a folder and handed it to her.

"I could say the same to you," Alice said, gruffly. She couldn't believe the audacity of this man. He'd nearly knocked her over and wasn't the least bit sorry. She could smell alcohol on his breath. It made her stomach turn.

Alice was about to say something, when she heard a familiar voice from across the street. "Larry Lee Simms, what the hell are you doing?" It was Jim Davis, making his way toward the scene of the collision.

The surly look on Simms face disappeared. "It wasn't my fault."

"I was standing right across the street, Larry Lee. I saw you walk directly into Alice." Jim had made it across the street at this point and planted himself in front of Larry Lee, who seemed to cower under his glare. Instead of arguing, Larry Lee tucked his head down and walked away in a huff, muttering to himself.

"Are you all right, Alice?" Jim asked, helping her arrange the rest of her fallen items.

"Yes, I'm fine. That was Larry Lee Simms?"

"You've heard of him?" Jim asked, though he didn't seem surprised.

"Joylyn Clement brought him up the other day." Alice didn't mention her previous run-ins with Larry Lee, though she could now easily picture his face as one of those in the diner upon whom the strange woman had been eavesdropping.

Jim laughed. "Yes, I guess she would have. There's no love lost between Joylyn and Larry Lee Simms."

"Why is that?"

"Larry Lee beat up her son Oscar pretty badly. He was in the hospital for a month. Larry Lee ended up in prison, and Oscar left town for good as soon as he was recovered. He rarely comes to visit." Jim's expression turned sad. "The whole Simms family is nothing but bad seeds, and Larry Lee's mama Agnes is the meanest woman to ever walk this earth."

"Joylyn told me about the issues between the Simms and the Bennetts."

"Joylyn sure is gossipy. And I guess she told you about her theory? About Larry Lee?"

Alice nodded.

"Larry Lee is a reckless fool. He's mean and stupid, especially when he's drunk, which is all the time lately . . . but I don't see Larry Lee attacking Mae Bennett. I could imagine him getting into a brawl with Will, but . . .?"

"What does Larry Lee have against Will?"

Jim looked decidedly uncomfortable. "There's a lot of bad blood there." Jim scratched his head. "I'd better get going. I need to get groceries or the wife will have my hide." He smiled. "Take care of yourself, Alice."

When Jim reached his truck, Alice waved. She was disconcerted by Jim's vagueness about the relationship between Will and Larry Lee Simms. Despite Jim's reassurance, Alice wasn't so sure Larry Lee hadn't hurt Mae.

Rattled by her encounter with Larry Lee and still mulling over Jim's words, Alice turned around and walked toward the Woodbridge Inn, hoping to calm down a bit before driving back to Mae's house. She and Will had stayed at the Inn now and again when they visited. She crossed the bridge over the railroad tracks and gazed down the overgrown line of tracks, deep in thought.

The first time she and Will had visited Georgia, it had been like entering another world. Of course, Alice had been terrified. With her own rocky family background, her desire to impress Will's parents was almost suffocating. It had taken days to pick out her wardrobe for their three-day trip. Will had teased her the whole time, realizing nothing he said would convince her everything would be fine.

"They'll love you," he'd said, wrapping his arms around her as she stared in the mirror.

"You think so?"

"Of course."

Alice was a hard sell. There were bits about her past she would never reveal, not even to Will, and meeting new people was always a little intimidating. They'd ask her questions and she'd have to answer as honestly as she could without giving herself away. Looking down at the ring Will had placed on her finger the previous week, Alice had felt a surge of fear.

"Tell me about them again." And he had. He'd talked about his parents and his sister with zeal, and yet, Alice always felt like he wasn't breaking the surface. That was the way it had always been with Will. He was reserved. He explained his private nature away through his Southern upbringing, but Alice suspected there was more to the story. Nonetheless, she never pried, lest she be forced to give up her own secrets. Instead, she and Will had created a picture-perfect life together, at least on the surface.

She should have known the past would catch up with her. Little by little, Will began to notice her reluctance to socialize with others, especially when alcohol was involved. Alice threw herself into her work, and with Will's busy schedule, the distance that grew between them seemed a natural progression, justifiable. The time when he held her, the moments when they smiled and laughed together, became fewer and far between. And then Will started to show his frustration.

It started with a party at Will's law firm. Most of the time, Will was understanding when she found an excuse not to attend those sort of functions, citing a work conflict or a headache, but she was careful not to say "no" so often he would see a pattern. That night, the firm was celebrating a big victory and Will had made it clear all the spouses would be expected to attend. The affair was black tie, which made Alice feel horribly conspicuous. She was an attractive woman, but it seemed every female lawyer and lawyer's wife were waifs with perfectly manicured nails, unnaturally coifed updos and dresses that looked like designer one-of-a-kind originals, with a different dress for every event.

Will was the object of relentless attention from his female colleagues, whether Alice was present or not. And he liked the attention; she could see it written plainly on his face and in the way he responded. Will blamed his flirtatious nature on his Southern roots, chiding Alice when jealousy got the best of her.

The night had been rainy and cold. It was one of those nights that had Alice shivering in her boots, haunted by the ghosts in her past: fists, screams, crying, darkness. After her grandmother's death, Alice had ended up living with her alcoholic father, a man so vicious Alice spent most of her time at home behind a locked door, as quiet as she could be so as not to catch his attention. She waited anxiously for Will to get home, feeling sick to her stomach.

Her relief when he arrived was soon replaced with agitation. With barely a word, he stalked toward the bedroom, changed into his tuxedo and was headed back to the door when he seemed to notice Alice for the first time.

"That's what you're wearing? Tonight?"

Alice ran her hands self-consciously down the sides of her black dress. True, it was simple, but she'd paired it with the pearls Will had given her for her birthday. Up to that point, she'd been feeling very sophisticated. "What's wrong with this?" she asked, trying to hide her disappointment.

Will seemed on the verge of an answer, but instead he glanced at his watch, sighed and said, "We'll be late. Let's go."

They rode in silence to the waterfront restaurant, and Will walked ahead of her as they entered the dining room. He was greeted boisterously, and they mingled their way further into the crowd, Alice trailing behind her husband who seemed content to let her remain a shadow.

Alice could smell the alcohol floating around the room. It seemed everyone had gotten an early start at the bar. She approached the bartender, ordered a soda water with lime, which she would nurse all night with effort. Will appeared beside her, ordered a martini, and leaned against the bar, surveying the party-goers. Alice watched her husband, wondering who he was looking for.

She was about to start a conversation with Will when one of the senior partners walked up to them, gripped Will roughly by the shoulder, and leaned in, rubbing against Alice with his shoulder.

"Nice work, Will. Really. Excellent job." Each word was slurred and pungent with drink. The man's face was inches from Alice's, though he was nearly shouting as he spoke. His hand was still on Will, but his eyes were molesting Alice from head to toe. She inched back into the bar, trying to escape.

"You remember my wife, Alice?" Will said, but when Alice looked up at him in silent thanks, this having been his first introduction of the evening, she realized he was still looking into the crowd. "Excuse me a moment, please" and to Alice's utter dismay, he walked away, leaving her with his drunken partner.

"You're looking very ravishing tonight, Anne." The partner leaned in further. "I had forgotten Will's wife was so beautiful."

"It's Alice," she corrected, but not wanting to offend anyone Will worked with, she added, "thank you." She inched to the side, hoping to gain some space without seeming rude.

"Bartender! I'd like to buy this lovely woman a glass of champagne."

"Oh, no thank you," Alice stuttered, holding up her glass. "I already have a drink."

"This?" The man plucked the glass of club soda from her hand, setting it down hard on the bar just out of her reach, sloshing its contents onto the shining surface. A glass of sparkling wine appeared in front of her. The bartender gave her a wink, clearly oblivious to her distress.

Alice peered past her pursuer, looking desperately for Will. When she finally found him, he was leaning in closely to a woman in a blue dress, slit nearly to her thigh. She laughed at something Will said, and he gave her a smile Alice hadn't seen since they'd been dating. It was the same smile that had won her over, put aside her insecurities and ultimately landed her in his bed. Alice felt raw fury building inside her, warming her cheeks and twisting her stomach.

"Come on, darling," the partner said, bringing Alice back into the moment. "You're not going to turn me down, are you?" He handed her the glass of champagne.

For a moment, Alice considered putting the glass back on the bar, making her excuses, and hiding in the ladies room until she could get Will to take her home, but she glanced at Will, and saw the woman in blue with her hand on his arm, whispering into his ear, turning years of "I should know better" into "this'll show him" in a matter of seconds. She tossed back the bubbly liquid, feeling a trickle down the side of her mouth. Her suitor laughed raucously.

"That's right, darling. Let's have another."

A few hours later, Alice and Will were back at home. The car ride had been heavy with stony silence, but Alice had been too drunk to notice much. It wasn't until he closed the front door behind them that Alice became aware of Will's mood.

"You're drunk," he said, his tone full of disgust.

"Oh, come on, sweetheart. Everyone at the party was drunk." She slid down onto the couch, kicking off her shoes.

"Not everyone at the party was being fondled by my boss." Alice could hear the anger in each word but couldn't make herself feel sorry.

"I guess that woman in the blue dress with her hands all over you wasn't your boss then?" Alice heard the words leave her mouth and an alarm went off in her brain, sobering her. She was drunk, something that had never happened before in front of Will, and she was goading her husband, picking a fight, as she often did when she drank. One look at his face told her she had crossed a line, but the thought of that woman touching Will—*her* Will—and the smile on his face as it was happening was enough to fuel her alcohol-laced boldness. "If you want to fuck the women you work with, you don't have to make me watch."

"How dare you," Will snarled, looking meaner than she'd ever seen him. If she had expected remorse or guilt, she was disappointed. For the first time in their relationship, she felt afraid of her husband, threatened. It was a feeling she understood well, and her fight response surged within her.

"How dare I?" she practically screamed. "I didn't even want to go to that ridiculous party, Will. You told me I had to. And then you left me alone with that letch of a man. Do you know what he did to me, Will? He put his hands on my breasts, at a party, surrounded by your fucking colleagues, and now here you are yelling at me. As if I meant for it to happen. As if I wanted it." She realized she was the only one yelling. Will's tone had been calm, dangerous. She ignored all the red flags and screamed, "Fuck you, Will!"

Alice had been fidgeting with a water glass she'd left on the coffee table as she spoke but she was surprised to find she'd picked it up. Driven by rage, she threw the glass hard in Will's direction. It met its mark. Will grasped at his face, and Alice could see blood seeping between his fingers. The coppery smell hit her nostrils, bringing her to her senses. She saw the look of horror on her husband's face and realized she'd become her father.

Without another word, not even to ask Will if he was okay, Alice ran into the bathroom and locked the door, barely making it to the toilet before the vomiting began. For what felt like hours, Alice lay against the cold tile floor, swimming in a sea of shame and regret.

In the morning, she woke up with her face pressed against the bathroom tile, the smell of vomit rank in the air. She stumbled out into the hallway, her head throbbing, making the walls look as though they were swaying. It was before dawn and the house was still shrouded in darkness. Afraid to face Will, she went to the kitchen for some water. The broken glass and a trail of blood drops made her hang her head in shame. Working up the nerve, she'd walked down to their bedroom, only to find it empty. Will's travel case was gone.

She lay down in their bed and cried.

Three days passed before she heard Will's key in the door again. Alice was sitting on the couch, typing an article, having unwillingly dragged herself out of bed only when her phone began ringing every few minutes, her editor frantic at not being able to reach her.

Alice's hair was unkempt and she hadn't showered since the incident. The sound of the key startled her. She'd honestly begun to believe Will was never coming back. The reality that they would be face-to-face filled her with dread. She'd never liked to deal with confrontation sober.

Will walked in the door and froze, staring at Alice with angry eyes. Alice shrank under the ferocity of his gaze. The house they shared was Will's and she knew that when the shit hit the fan, she'd be the one to leave, but the relative calm of the past few days had created a false sense of security. She imagined the fight to come. The accusations. The explanations. Assuming Will would let her explain, which didn't seem likely the way he was glaring at her now. No matter which way you looked at it, Alice couldn't see a way out of this disaster. Resigned, she stood. "I'll pack."

The silence that enveloped her as she walked down the hallway was earsplitting. Alice had expected yelling, screaming, crying—maybe even violence. Those were things Alice could handle. She understood violence. Will's glare and his stony silence cut her heart like a knife, but what did she expect?

She'd been packing in their bedroom for almost two hours when Will finally approached her. "I want to know why? How could you do that to me?" His tone was cold, but his eyes brimmed with hurt. The cut on his cheek was beginning to heal, but the bruise surrounding it was an ugly greenish hue. Alice wondered how he'd explained it to his colleagues.

She searched for the right words to justify her actions. The scene from that night still stung—Will flirting with the woman in the blue dress, leaving her in the roaming hands of his disgusting partner. In the end, she realized it was a time for some truth. She looked him straight in the eye and, in a quiet voice said, "My father was an alcoholic." Then, ashamed at having shifted the blame, she added, "I'm an alcoholic."

Will's eyebrows had arched in surprise. "An alcoholic?" Then his face darkened. "Your father? You told me he died when you were a baby."

"I lied."

Will sat down at the foot of the bed, facing away from her, his shoulders slumped, weighed down by a heaviness Alice knew all too well. She'd always hated the lying.

"My mother and I went to live with my grandmother when I was six. My father was an abusive alcoholic." Alice could hear how wooden her words sounded, but talking about her father seemed to flip the switch, shutting down her emotions. "My mother died when I was ten, and my grandmother's health wasn't good. When she passed away, I had to go back and live with my father." Alice took a breath and steadied herself.

"I didn't have anyone else. I told myself that if I could survive him, I would get out of there and make something out of my life. Something good."

Will turned slowly. "So, your father is still alive?"

"No. He died when I was nineteen." She knew he'd want to hear more, but the words were choking her. She looked away from Will and continued, "Growing up, I missed a lot of school. Broken bones. Trips to the emergency room where I had to convince adults I was okay, knowing they either wouldn't or couldn't help me."

Alice walked to the window and looked out into the city. "By the time I was a teenager, I'd started sneaking swigs out of his bottles. The alcohol numbed the pain and before long I was as out of control as he was. Drinking gave me the courage to defend myself. To fight back. To start the fights before he could. After he died, I couldn't stop. It took years to get sober." She fell silent, trying to slow her breathing, to keep the tears at bay.

One of the things that had drawn her to Will was his self-control. When she mentioned she didn't drink much on their first date, Will hadn't asked why. He'd simply ordered an iced tea and continued on with the conversation. Over the years, they'd each have a glass of wine with dinner on occasion. Alice didn't feel the same pull she had when she was at the mercy of the bottle, though there were times when keeping up appearances for her husband was exhausting. On the other hand, she avoided parties and situations where she knew the booze would be flowing, avoiding temptation.

After coming clean, more excruciating time passed with Will sitting still as the dead on their bed and Alice held in a state of suspended animation, unable to move forward or back. Her suitcase lay open between them. The sleeve of a shirt she'd folded and unfolded at least a dozen times while she waited hung loosely over the edge like it was trying to escape.

Eventually, Will got up and walked to the living room. When Alice finally worked up her courage, she followed him, taking a seat beside him on the couch.

"I feel like I don't know you, Alice," Will started. Alice felt her heart squeezed within her chest. "But I want to try and make this work. I love you. You have to promise me this will never happen again."

A wave of relief flooded Alice's system and her eyes welled with tears. "Of course. Oh, Will. I'm so sorry. Can we start over?"

"I think I'd like that."

Alice was too busy being grateful for his forgiveness to wonder what the implications were. And even then she hadn't given him all the details of her childhood. She'd never told Will the ugly truth that would surely drive him away forever, the story of her father's death. Disoriented by the memory, Alice stumbled over a railroad tie as she headed back to her car.

Afternoon tea with Joylyn had become a regular part of Alice's day, so she wasn't surprised to find refreshments already set out when she approached Joylyn's house one afternoon. She'd left Rosy at home to keep Mae company, opting for a bit of time on her own for some introspection. Some of the local boys had hauled away the ruined fence and put up new picket. The bright white paint prodded at Alice's senses, a stark reminder of violence that had been done there. After clearing away the wreckage, Joylyn found that some of her prized roses were salvageable. The garden looked sparser, but neat and well-loved again.

When they finished their tea, Joylyn suggested they take a walk. Since Alice had restricted her walking route to the road between Mae's and Joylyn's houses, Joylyn started off in a different direction.

"Where are we going?" Alice asked as Joylyn led her along the paved road toward town.

"You'll see," Joylyn smiled. The road began to incline and Alice was surprised to have to struggle to match Joylyn's pace. The older woman was sturdy and strong despite her age. The air was cool, but the humidity made Alice sweat. They crested the hill and Joylyn led Alice toward a small white chapel with a little cemetery nestled beside it.

"What's this?" Alice asked, a bit apprehensive.

"I thought you might like another history lesson, seeing as how you're writing about this area. This is Sharptop Baptist Church."

"Sharptop?"

Joylyn pointed to the mountain peak behind the church.

"Sharptop is a major landmark around here." As she looked, Alice remembered Will pointing out Sharptop Mountain on a trip to meet his mother. "My husband and I were married here. So were Mae and Bill."

They made their way toward the cemetery. It was a lovely place, quaint and picturesque, the type of landscape Alice often associated with north Georgia. They stopped in front of a simple marble tombstone.

"This is my husband, John." Joylyn said his name tenderly.

"Mae told me he died very young."

"Yes. He was a few months shy of his thirty-fifth birthday. Oscar was a toddler. It was a terrible time." Joylyn pointed at the next few headstones. "His mother, father and both brothers are buried here too."

Alice looked at the dates on John's siblings' graves and gasped. "They were just babies."

Joylyn nodded. "Something about that family. All the boys had a weak constitution. John always had a cough or a cold. Finally, one day, his heart gave out. His mother died a few years later. She'd been in ill health for years. I think John's death finally convinced her it was her time to let go."

"And Oscar?"

Joylyn smiled. "Oscar takes after his mother. He'll probably live to be 102, especially in the city with all the newfangled medical inventions they have available."

Alice's heart ached at the tragic display in front of her. For a moment they stood in silence, then Joylyn moved past her husband's grave and headed a few rows over.

"Here's Mae's husband, Bill." The dates of Bill Bennett's life and death were etched into the left side of the tombstone. A space on the right awaited Mae's demise. Alice always thought it morbid that a living person's name would already appear on their headstone, but she supposed being buried next to your loved ones was a comfort for some people. She couldn't help but wonder why Will had never brought her here.

The women walked quietly around the cemetery, with Joylyn stopping every few feet to relate some story.

Looking at her watch, Alice said, "I need to head back. Mae's going to start wondering where I am."

"I'll come with you. I want to check on the old girl." Joylyn smiled. The women turned to walk back toward the lake when out of the corner of her eye, Alice thought she spotted a familiar name on a small marker situated apart from the rest, as though it were forgotten.

"Does it say Simms?" she asked, craning her neck to read the headstone. The name was nearly illegible, as if someone had taken a tool and tried to scrape it away.

They approached the grave. "Is this Larry Lee Simms's father?"

Joylyn shook her head. "No, his is over here." She pointed past the vandalized headstone to another nearby.

"Whose is this?" Alice asked. "I don't see any others that say Simms."

Joylyn frowned. "I'm not entirely sure. Honestly, I don't pay much attention to the Simms folk buried here."

Alice kneeled down and placed her fingers against the stone. "The last two numbers could be zero and two. The stone itself is new though. Could it be from 2002? Doesn't Larry Lee have a sister?"

"Yes, but that isn't her. She was still living around here back then."

"What was his sister's name again?" Alice rubbed away at the stone with her fingers, but no matter how hard she tried, she couldn't make out the letters in the name.

"Her name was Beth Ann. And believe me, we'd all know if Beth Simms was dead. We might have all been spared a lot of misery."

13

It had been almost two weeks since Larry Lee had picked up a paying job, and he was restless to the point where even a trip to his favorite local watering hole couldn't stop him from fidgeting on his barstool.

"You want another one, Larry Lee?" Larry Lee loved this bartender. He was one of the old-timers who never cut Larry Lee off, no matter how belligerent he got. Then again, he'd never cut Larry Lee's father off either.

"Nah, I need to get back home and check on Mama." Larry Lee thumped his glass on the counter harder than he meant to.

"How's your mama doing?"

"Same as ever." Larry Lee could see the old man had no real interest, so he didn't belabor the point. Not many people in town gave a rat's ass about how Agnes Simms was doing. She was all vinegar. Larry Lee got up and stretched. He was feeling a little buzzed, but he could make the drive home half-asleep.

"Thought I saw Beth and some guy the other day."

Larry Lee bristled. "Yep. Beth dropped by the house the other day. I don't know about the guy though. He wasn't with her."

"She staying?"

"I don't know. I don't keep up with Beth much."

The bartender snorted. "I reckon not." It wasn't a secret that Larry Lee had done time for one of Beth's "situations." Where Larry Lee was trouble, Beth was a natural disaster sweeping through town. No one had much sympathy for Larry Lee. He'd been a screwup his whole life, but the incident with the Clement boy—well, it seemed that everyone knew something wasn't right about it.

Slapping some cash on the bar, Larry Lee headed out into the sunlight.

"Son of a bitch!" he exclaimed. One look at his truck and bile rose up in his throat. Someone had taken a key to the paint, leaving deep scratches and gouges along the driver's side. Larry Lee walked slowly around the truck and saw the vandal had been thorough. Running his fingers along the gouges, he felt as if the scars had been scraped painfully into his own skin.

Larry Lee's truck wasn't much to look at, but it was still probably his most valued possession. He wasn't in there that long, was he? How could someone do this in broad daylight?

Larry Lee turned in manic circles, searching the parking lot for any signs of the culprit, muscles tight and ready to pounce. He could feel blood pulsing through the veins in his neck, creating so much pressure in his head he felt it would explode.

"Dammit! Dammit! Dammit! Dammit!" he shrieked, pounding his fists into the hood of the truck. Larry Lee was used to his life being full of garbage, but it seemed things were taking a turn for the worse.

~

When Larry Lee arrived home, his mood was so dark it cast a gloom around him. He was relieved to find the house quiet. He walked straight to the fridge, grabbed a beer, and was kicking off his shoes when he heard the creak of Agnes's bedroom door.

"Larry Lee? Is that you?" His mother's voice sounded strained.

Reluctantly, Larry Lee answered back, "Yes, ma'am," hoping to avoid any more drama. He heard the door squeak and then the thump as it hit the wall. Agnes's footfalls were soft on the hallway, causing the hairs on Larry Lee's neck to prickle. There was nothing soft about Agnes. Despite being short in stature, you got the impression she was made of solid rock and her demeanor was more a steamroller than a kitten.

"You okay, Mama?" Larry Lee asked as Agnes appeared at the end of the hall.

Agnes's skin was pale and the rings under her eyes were dark. Concern flooded through Larry Lee, crumbling his resolve to be surly.

"Do you need the doctor?"

Agnes shook her head and sank down into the armchair across from Larry Lee. "Of course not. I'm fine. Just didn't sleep very well. Ran out of those pills that help me sleep." She fidgeted in the chair, shifting her weight as if she couldn't get comfortable. Her eyes darted to the front door. Larry Lee felt a knot in his stomach.

"The ones I picked up a few days ago? You're already out?" Larry Lee looked around. "What's going on, Mama? Is Beth still here?" Larry Lee hadn't seen his sister in a few days, but he knew she was still lurking around town.

Agnes hesitated, then said slowly, "I was thinking. Your cousin David up in Tennessee? Last time I talked to Bertha, she said he was building a cabin on the land he bought. I was wondering if maybe you might go up and help him with the building." The words should have sounded like a suggestion, but out of Agnes's mouth they sounded more like a death sentence.

Larry Lee tried to process this new information but her nervous behavior had him on edge. As Agnes's gaze wandered again to the door, Larry Lee spoke up. "You expecting someone?"

A flash of fear crossed Agnes's face, but it was quickly replaced by anger. "Did you hear what I said to you?" Agnes roared, her voice growing in volume with each word until she'd reached a shrill scream.

Larry Lee was unnerved. He was used to his mother's anger, but her behavior now was erratic and the fear in her eyes was enough to send Larry Lee's stomach flip-flopping like a fish out of water.

"Why are you trying to get rid of me?" He eyed his mother suspiciously, muscles tensed, ready to spring out of reach if necessary.

Agnes sighed. "You've been hanging around here too long, Larry Lee. Jobs are scarce. You need to get out of here and get a life of your own."

"This have something to do with Beth showing up? Why is she here anyway?"

"She's your sister, Larry Lee. No need to treat her like she's garbage."

"Why not? I spent more than a year in prison because of Beth and what did she do? Ran off, that's what. The way I hear it, she's been burning bridges with some really dangerous people, probably all strung out on drugs as usual. And who's been taking care of things around here? Me, Mama. Now, suddenly Beth's back and you're trying to send me away from my own house? Tell me why."

Larry Lee's voice was angry, but there was something else there too. A sense of betrayal. He'd been taking care of Agnes for years, without a hint of Beth's whereabouts. He'd always suspected Agnes felt more for Beth than for him. Sure, Agnes had laid into Beth more often than Larry Lee, but that was because Beth had a sharp mouth and a nasty temper. Larry Lee suspected Agnes hated him for loving his father more than her. This seemed to confirm it.

Agnes looked over at the front door and then spoke angrily again, avoiding the question altogether. "Larry Lee, you're a grown man. You have no business living with your mama anymore."

Larry Lee shot back, "And what am I supposed to do, Mama?"

Almost as an afterthought, he added, "Who's going to be here to look after you? Beth? She's a junked up whore. Always has been."

Agnes glared at him, her eyes black with anger. "You got an hour to pack up your shit and get out of my house, Larry Lee, or I'll call the cops and let them into your room." Larry Lee flinched, knowing what they would find. He'd gotten rid of most of the contraband from his illicit activities, but there were a few trophy items that could easily land him back in the clink.

"And you can tell James not to come around here no more either." Agnes stood shakily and stomped back down the hallway, slamming the door to her bedroom hard enough to rattle the dust off the floorboards.

Larry Lee sat back, chugging the remnants of his beer. *What the hell is going on around here*, he thought gloomily. He lobbed the can at the kitchen wall and stalked off to his room to pack.

Stuffing random pairs of pants and shirts into his duffle, Larry Lee stormed around his room, knocking into walls unnecessarily and hoping to rile Agnes as much as possible before making his departure.

He kicked through piles of his father's old clothes, feeling a pang of guilt that was nowhere near as potent as the rage and betrayal coursing through his veins. Since coming home from prison, Larry Lee had been living like an unwelcome guest in his own house. At first, he'd tried to stay positive, to get back to real life, but you didn't walk away from your transgressions in a town like Jasper. Everywhere he looked there were closed doors.

He opened up the closet and shoved his father's work coat aside to reveal a cardboard box full of other people's treasures, some for sale. Agnes's failing health was expensive business. She'd been too proud and stubborn to seek financial help, and with Larry Lee interminably unemployed, he'd had to resort to stealing to pay for the things his mother needed.

Larry Lee felt his stomach clench as he sifted through the box. He wasn't a thief, not really. Mean, yes. Angry, yes. Certainly not someone you'd want to get on the wrong side of, but even Larry Lee had his pride. Until necessity intervened and he had to bury his pride like a dog burying a bone in the backyard to be forgotten. He'd started out opening car doors and taking anything he could get his hands on, but the bills mounted and soon he was staking out lake houses and breaking in. Many of the older families on the lake still left their doors unlocked, so at first it was easy.

He remembered being in Mae Bennett's house once, not long ago. He'd taken to walking along the lake road, feigning a casual stroll whenever anyone passed him. One day, he saw Mae leave the house with Joylyn Clement and he took the opportunity to snoop. Of course there were valuables to be taken, but being inside the Bennett house stirred something deep inside him. Curiosity seized hold and he found himself going carefully through the living room, picking up picture frames and books. He kept looking over his shoulder expecting to get caught, until finally his anxiety overcame him and he crept out, but not without a few small prizes.

For a few weeks, he'd expected to have a sheriff knocking at his door, but when it became clear he wasn't going to get caught, the urge to break in again started gnawing at him until he finally began staking out Mae's house, looking for any opportunity to get inside.

Nothing in the cardboard box had come from the Bennett house and luckily there were only a few things left he hadn't been able to sell, mostly jewelry he'd been afraid to unload in town. He threw the remaining items in his duffle bag and then reached up inside his closet to pull down his secret stash. He checked the contents and stuffed them back in its hiding place, out of sight.

Bang. Bang. Bang.

"Larry Lee! You'd better get your ass out of here!" Agnes's shrill voice rang in his ears and she pounded on his bedroom door.

"Get off my damned back, Mama!" Larry Lee yelled back, but he quickened his pace. As he finished packing, his mind wandered back to the Bennetts again.

A storm brewed inside Larry Lee Simms. A mix of fury and betrayal twisted his stomach into knots. Never one to focus inward, Larry Lee felt a burning desire to lash out. To hurt everyone who'd ever hurt him. To seek vengeance for being born into a horrible family in a small-minded and unforgiving town. He wanted to yell, to pummel the nearest person, to cause pain and destruction.

Slinging his duffle over his shoulder, he stomped toward the kitchen, pawed through the cupboard until he found Agnes's emergency wad of cash and pocketed it. Then, Larry Lee walked out of his childhood home, slamming the screen door so hard it sagged on its hinges.

14

As reluctant as she'd been to dig into the life of Juanita Jones for her article, Alice was now hooked. It started out slowly. Alice found a few articles in the local paper about the murder and the resulting trial before the trail went cold. Then she found a few more articles in an Atlanta paper. Small inconsistencies between the articles started keeping her up at night. Soon, she was at the Courthouse waiting to speak to the clerk about finding the trial records.

"May I help you?" An attractive older woman with a lovely Southern lilt in her voice looked up over the counter. Alice stepped forward, resting her folder on the countertop.

"I'm looking for some information about a trial that happened in 1941."

The woman sighed. "Do you have the case number?"

"Well, no. I've been researching from newspaper articles, but I can give you the name of the defendant and the trial dates."

The woman sifted through her desk, looking for a pad of paper. Her movements were slow and casual, either from lack of interest or irritation at being put to work on a historical case. Maybe both, Alice thought as she watched the woman's sloth-like speed. Alice's stomach twisted a bit. She didn't blame the woman for her disinterest, but she felt a twinge of indignation on behalf of Juanita Jones.

Finally, having retrieved a stack of brightly colored sticky notes and a pen, the woman said, "Give me as much information as you have."

Alice rattled off what she knew. J.M. Carney was arrested in late October for the murder of his young, pregnant wife, Juanita Jones. A coroner's inquest ruled that her death was due to strangulation. Carney was tried, convicted, and sentenced to life in prison in April of 1941.

Looking up at Alice with barely concealed frustration, the woman said, "Well, the records will be down in the vault, if they even still exist. I'll have to go down and look."

"Is there anything I can do to help?" Alice asked hopefully, worried that if she wasn't materially involved in finding the file, her request would be relegated to the bottom of the stack.

"No. It will take some time." She passed Alice the paper. "Put your name and number here and I'll give you a call if I find something."

Alice obliged and the woman set the note aside, confirming Alice's suspicions. She then returned to her computer, effectively dismissing Alice without another word.

Reaching the marble patio outside the courthouse, Alice plodded along to her car more loudly than necessary, taking her aggression out on the white marble in the walkway. She thought about the Georgia Marble Company in Tate and the fact that Juanita Jones was killed in company housing. *Why didn't anyone help Juanita Jones?* Alice exhaled, puffing out her cheeks and letting the air flow slowly over her lips.

Alice spent every morning for the rest of the week in the Georgia history room at the library, researching Georgia laws and investigation procedures, but always with an image of Juanita Jones in her mind.

Afterward, she'd head to the Carriage House for lunch. Jim

would often join her and spend half-an-hour regaling her with local gossip. Each conversation shed light on Will's disconnect with his hometown. Alice tried in vain to picture her well-mannered, impeccably dressed husband as a player in the stories she was hearing. It seemed both she and Will had put as much distance as possible between themselves and their pasts.

"And the thing was, Billy didn't even want the job," Jim hooted. He'd been telling a story about a friend of Will's from high school who'd been beaten out for a job by a local rival. "Tom and the boys went up to Billy's house one night and drug him out in his pajamas. Gave him one good walloping."

With a look of disgust, Alice asked, "Did that include Will?"

Seeing her expression, Jim's face fell and he adopted a more somber tone. "Well, I'm sure it did. He and Tom were pretty inseparable in school."

Alice frowned. As far as she knew, Will wasn't in contact with any of his high school friends. The way Jim talked about Tom and Will, she couldn't imagine having such a close friend and losing touch so completely.

"Does Billy still live around here?"

Jim sighed. "No. He got into an accident after they graduated and his family moved away."

"What kind of accident?"

"I don't really remember," Jim said, but he shifted nervously. "I know he injured his spine. Ended up in a wheelchair and his folks took him somewhere where he could get better treatment. Though I suspect they'd had quite enough of this town."

"And what about Tom?" As unsettling as Jim's stories were, Alice felt a tug of temptation to investigate her husband's past further.

"No, Tom moved away after graduation. I haven't seen him here since then."

Seeing Alice's disappointment, Jim changed topics, keeping things lighthearted for the rest of their visit, but Alice couldn't stop picturing the young man in the wheelchair. Something about the story struck her as odd, and she couldn't stop thinking that she understood why Will buried memories of his hometown so deep. She also wondered how little she knew about her husband.

On Friday, Alice was finishing up a cup of coffee and packing up her things when she felt someone watching her. She looked up, expecting to see Jim, but instead found herself locking eyes with a familiar woman sitting across the dining room. The woman was petite, much shorter than Alice's five-foot-eight-inch frame, and painfully thin. Her light brown hair was pulled back in a messy ponytail, but instead of looking stylish, on this woman it looked lazy.

Alice studied her papers, but the other woman stared hard at her across the room when she looked back up. Alice's curiosity got the better of her. She had resolved to get up and introduce herself when the woman rose swiftly and left the restaurant, letting the door bang shut behind her. Her exit caused an uncomfortable silence to fall over the dining room, with most patrons looking toward the door, momentarily wrenched out of their conversations. Then, one by one, their eyes turned to Alice. It lasted only a moment, but the effect was immediate. Alice felt entirely out of place, scrutinized like a bug under a magnifying glass

Conversations resumed. The buzz of human noise returned the restaurant to its previously cozy atmosphere. Alice gathered her things and made her way to her car, deciding to stick closer to Mae's house until after Will's visit. Whatever was going on in town, she wasn't a part of it and she was pretty sure she didn't want to be. For the first time since she'd arrived, Alice yearned to go home.

Approaching her car, Alice could see a piece of paper, partially trapped under the windshield wiper, the corners flapping in the breeze. She grabbed it expecting to find a flyer for a local store or upcoming event. Instead, angry handwriting filled her vision. The pen had been pressed forcibly into the paper, leaving it on the verge of tearing in some places and blotted with ink in others. The capital letters screamed at her.

WILL'S WHORE
GO HOME
YOU DON'T BELONG

~

Alice was beginning to see Mae's house as her only refuge. Each new rattling event in town sent her flying back home to Mae. She took comfort in their daily routine and in Mae's presence. Despite all the drama, and in spite of her continued pain, Mae was generally upbeat and calm, a feeling which Alice craved and absorbed.

Parking her car near the front door, Alice grabbed her books and bags and headed into the house.

"I'm back," she called softly, in case Mae was sleeping, but when she entered the sitting room, she found Mae in her armchair, a worried look on her face. Alice tossed her things on the couch and rushed to Mae's side, adrenaline coursing through her veins. "What's wrong, Mae? Are you in pain?"

Mae looked at Alice as if she hadn't seen her coming. "Alice? Oh, Alice. I'm glad you're back."

Alice started to relax, figuring Mae would have told her right away if she were sick. The older woman's nightmares had been coming and going, so it wasn't unusual for Mae to slip into a contemplative space from time to time.

"What's the matter, Mae?" Alice pulled over a chair and took a seat next to her mother-in-law, leaning in to give Mae comfort, marveling at the intimacy that had developed between them. Physical closeness had never come easily to Alice.

"The strangest thing happened a little while ago," Mae looked toward the door. "A woman—she looked so familiar—stopped by this afternoon. I'd just gotten up from my nap and I wouldn't have ordinarily opened the door, but Joylyn said she'd be stopping by again so I went to see if it was her."

Mae paused for breath, and Alice wondered what could have possibly happened that would make her so agitated.

"She didn't give her name, but she asked me to pass a message to you." Mae looked at Alice curiously. "She said, 'tell your girl to keep her nose out of our business.' That was it. She turned around and left without another word. I called after her, but she ignored me and drove away quickly. She looked so familiar, but I can't seem to place her."

Thinking about the note she'd received and the strange incident in the restaurant, Alice asked, "Was she small? Light brown hair? Maybe a little younger than me?"

Mae looked puzzled. "No, not at all. She was an older woman. I'm sure I've seen her before but I can't for the life of me recall where. Maybe Margaret would know." Mae's words drifted off and she stared back out the window at the lake.

"I'm sorry that happened, Mae. I can understand why you're upset." Alice patted Mae's arm softly as she spoke, though her own thoughts were racing.

Mae smiled, putting her hand over Alice's. "I'm not upset, exactly. It was a very strange visit though. I worry about you."

Alice frowned. Besides taking care of Mae, her only activity in town was researching a murder that occurred over seventy years ago. It couldn't possibly be the "business" she was to keep her nose out of, could it? Alice went to work on dinner, but she couldn't keep her mind off of Mae's visitor and the note on her windshield, wondering if they were connected.

Later that evening, Alice took Rosy for a walk. They'd taken their usual path by the kudzu patch and, as was becoming a habit, Alice had stopped in to Joylyn's house for some tea and conversation. She liked the older woman very much, though like Jim, Joylyn was full of colorful stories about the area, some of which made Alice feel very uneasy. Having been born and raised in the mountains outside of Jasper, Joylyn wasn't always the best source of information on things that happened in town, but she knew the hills like the back of her hand and she could tell you most anything about every family that had lived in the area for generations.

In fact, she was the only person besides Jim thus far who'd even heard of the Juanita Jones murder case. Despite the grisly details, the murder of Juanita Jones had slipped eerily out of the public consciousness—not even a local legend remained. As she researched the story, Alice felt compelled to bring Juanita's case to light. She hoped her article would remind people of the young woman whose life was cut so very short.

"How's the story coming?" Joylyn asked as they settled in for tea.

Unlike other people in town, Joylyn seemed unfazed by the research Alice was doing. When Alice had mentioned the uninvited visitor to Mae's house, Joylyn brushed it off with a "ignore those busy-bodies." Alice still wondered if she knew more than she let on.

Alice sighed. "Slowly but surely. It's been difficult to find information about the case, but I finally got my hands on the court transcripts and that helps. You and Jim are still the only ones in town who've even heard of the case."

"Have you been getting much help?"

Alice shrugged. "Not really. It's not that people are lying to me, but it seems they're not inclined to open up. Some days I wish I could drop this project, but this magazine accounts for most of my income and I'm not in any position to lose my job right now."

"Have you been down to Tate? I'm pretty sure there's still some family in the area. They have a pretty active historical society too."

"No, not yet. I thought I'd take a trip down there next week, after Will visits. Mae's been doing really well and I'm hoping he'll be relieved to see her improvement."

Joylyn frowned. "I'm sure he's worried about his mother." Something in her tone didn't support her words. "I'm surprised he's come to visit as often as he has, but I guess that'll be because of you. He hasn't shown much interest in Mae's health over the years."

It wasn't the first time Joylyn had seemed less than complimentary toward Will. Each time, it startled Alice a bit. Until Joylyn, she'd never met anyone who spoke about Will in anything less than glowing terms. When it came to Mae and Margaret, Joylyn had nothing but nice things to say, but each time Will's name was mentioned, she darkened.

Before Alice could press Joylyn, they heard the shrill cry of a dog in pain. Alice bolted upright, nearly overturning her chair in the process, and both women raced into the garden.

"Rosy!" Alice called, worried.

"She probably tangled with a skunk again. They hang out in the kudzu at times. She's gotten herself sprayed a few times. You'd think she'd learn her lesson."

Alice scanned the field but there was no sign of the dog. "Rosy!" she yelled louder this time. After a few minutes, there was some rustling in the kudzu. Alice's anxiety grew by the minute. Finally, Rosy's pale brown hide could be seen slowly making its way toward the edge of the kudzu patch. The dog emerged from the foliage and limped across the road toward Alice. Alice could see the dog's ragged breathing and the smear of red across her fur.

Alice and Joylyn went out into the road to meet her, Joylyn muttering, "What did you get yourself into today, girl?"

Alice knelt and examined the dog. Just above her right hind leg, there was a large gash. Blood was caked on her fur, and there was a slow but steady stream of blood flowing down her leg. "What in the world?" Alice said, patting Rosy's head to calm her. Rosy whimpered softly and kept her leg off the ground. "Joylyn, can you watch Rosy for a few minutes while I go get the car? I think she needs to see the vet."

"Of course," Joylyn said, but her voice was uncharacteristically shaky. Alice looked up at the older woman and saw that her face was as white as a ghost.

"Are you okay?" Alice asked, concerned.

Evading the question, Joylyn knelt next to Rosy, pulled a handkerchief out of her pocket and tied it tightly around the wound on the dog's leg. "Come on girl. Let's go sit in the grass." She led a hobbling Rosy toward a patch of soft grass near the gate and slid a garden chair up next to her.

Looking back over her shoulder, Alice saw that Joylyn had gone inside. A moment later she reappeared. Joylyn gazed out into the kudzu field, stroking Rosy's head soothingly with one hand, a shotgun in the other. Alice took off for Mae's house at a jog.

15

Carver was heading toward the lake to confront Larry Lee Simms. He should have been happy but something nagged at him. Despite his warning, another break-in had occurred. There wasn't a shred of evidence at the scene, but Carver was pretty certain he'd find something on Larry Lee this time, especially if he caught him unawares. There simply hadn't been enough time to hide the evidence, if things had indeed played out the way he thought they had. The call had come into the station less than twenty minutes prior.

Pulling into the Simms driveway, Carver was both relieved and on edge at seeing Larry Lee's truck parked haphazardly in the drive, a long jagged scratch etched deep into the paint. A quick peek in the truck window revealed a large box sitting in the passenger side, which Carver eyed cagily, feeling thrilled with the idea of catching Larry Lee red-handed, and also wary. He made his way to the door and knocked, loud.

"Sheriff's department. Open up," he shouted, his voice gruff. The wind whistled through the trees. Carver waited. After a few minutes, he tried again, this time pounding hard on the door, which creaked under the force. "Larry Lee!" he bellowed.

He was about to walk back to his car when Larry Lee opened the door. Carver was appalled to see Larry Lee's disheveled appearance. He looked like he was coated in about an inch of dust.

"What?" Larry Lee shouted, then, seeing Carver standing there, he leaned back, adopted a defiant expression, and crossed his arms. "What can I do for you, Deputy Carver?"

"There's been another break-in, Larry Lee. I want to know what's inside the box in your truck."

Larry Lee snarled. "This is private property. You got a warrant?"

"No," Carver admitted. "But if you don't show me what's in the box, I'll be back here in an hour and search your whole house. How would that be, Larry Lee?"

Carver expected more fight, so he was surprised when Larry Lee sighed and stepped out onto the porch. He made his way to the truck, pulled out the box, and opened it wide. The mess inside certainly wasn't what Carver had expected.

"You going somewhere?" he asked, genuinely intrigued.

"Mama threw me out," Larry Lee said without emotion, though Carver heard him mumble "ungrateful bitch" under his breath.

"No kidding. Where are you headed?"

"Fuck if I know," Larry Lee replied and Carver felt a pang of sympathy for the pathetic lump of man in front of him. "Satisfied?"

"Where've you been the last few days, Larry Lee?"

"Not that it's any of your business, but I've been looking for work. You can ask Charlene. I've been up at the library 'bout every day now." Larry Lee's tone was still petulant, but he looked deflated.

"What happened to your truck?" Carver asked.

"Someone took a key to it." Larry Lee looked dolefully at his truck.

Suddenly, there was a loud crash inside the Simms house. Carver moved toward the front entrance, but Larry Lee beat him there. His defiant expression had been replaced by a worried one.

"Is your mama all right?" Carver asked, attempting to edge past Larry Lee who was blocking the door but making no attempt to enter.

"She's fine. If you're done, I've got to finish packing up my shit. I forgot a few things, and it took me the last half an hour to get her to let me back in."

Carver could see Larry Lee wasn't going to budge until he left, and given that he had no grounds to press the issue further, he relented. As he was backing out of the driveway, he looked back at the broken-down house, wondering what was going on inside. A figure peered out the window, darting back behind the curtain as soon as they saw him looking. Carver was sure he'd seen long, light brown rather scraggly looking hair.

After leaving the Simms house, Carver headed up the hill toward the Salvation Army campground above, passing by Mae Bennett's house on his way. When he reached the campground, he pulled into a parking lot and turned his car around. He sat for a few minutes looking down the hill. The thick pine trees made the area look isolated, even though there were houses dotted all along the lakefront. This seclusion that most of the residents sought also made them targets for burglary and a haven for other criminal activity. Only a few weeks ago, Carver had busted a drug ring using the land below the Salvation Army site as their headquarters, and not a single neighbor had noticed a thing, or so they told the investigating officers.

As his eyes crept further down the road, Carver made a mental map. Mae Bennett's house sat on the lake less than half a mile down on the right. Then the Simms house on the left. And about a mile down, on the other side of the paved road, sat Joylyn Clement's property. His mind drew a line from house to house and he wondered how the things that had been going on in Jasper might be related. It couldn't be a coincidence that all three families had been seeing their share of trouble lately.

On a whim, Carver drove slowly back down toward the highway. As he crested the hill, he saw the tail of Larry Lee's truck heading toward the intersection and then turn left toward Jasper. He was nearing the Simms driveway when another car, a silver coupe, nondescript, pulled into the drive. A few minutes later, it pulled out again. Carver could see that a man drove the car. The passenger seat, which had been empty before, was now occupied by the same shaggy head of mousy brown hair Carver had seen in the window. It certainly wasn't Agnes Simms—the form was too slight.

Carver stopped and watched as the silver car moved slowly toward the intersection and then turned left, heading into Jasper only seconds behind Larry Lee. He was pretty sure the car belonged to Agnes Simms, though he hadn't seen her drive it in years, and she definitely wasn't in the car now.

And then, Carver knew. Beth Ann Simms had come home.

"Beth Simms?" Morrison asked incredulously. "She's been gone, what, five, six years?"

"Not quite that long. It was awfully peaceful after she left. Didn't you go to school with her?"

Morrison scowled. "She was a few years behind me, so no. I never really interacted with any of the Simms until I started working here. First time I talked to her, I was giving her a warning for smoking dope. Not that it helped."

Carver laughed. "Yeah, that's not a surprise. Back in the day, I think Beth made her rounds with most of the men in town—old, young, didn't seem to matter to her."

"You?" Morrison baited Carver, grinning.

"Of course not," Carver said. The very thought of Beth Simms left a bad taste in his mouth. "Anyway, I'm pretty sure it was her in the car. Can't imagine who else would be skulking around Agnes's house. And honestly, I can't think of a single reason why Agnes would kick Larry Lee out if it wasn't for something to do with Beth. Larry Lee's been pretty much keeping her alive for years."

"True," Morrison replied, though Carver could see his attention was somewhere else. He'd been on the phone when Carver reached the office.

"Am I boring you, Deputy?"

"Sorry, Leland. I just got off the phone with Alice Bennett."

"Oh, for Chrissake—"

"No, listen. She was calling from the vet's office. She was out walking the dog yesterday and she got hurt."

"Alice got hurt?" Carver asked impatiently, his mind still on the Simms family.

"No, the dog. The vet says he thinks someone attacked Mrs. Bennett's dog. Cut her with a knife or a piece of sharp metal."

Now Morrison had Carver's full attention. "When was this?"

"Yesterday afternoon. Alice says she was visiting with Joylyn Clement and the dog ran after a squirrel. When she came back to Joylyn's house, she was hurt."

Carver was already on his feet, though his thoughts were all jumbled. Petty theft was definitely Larry Lee's MO, but mutilating animals, that was something new and it didn't fit. Carver couldn't help but wonder if darker forces were at work. He chided himself on letting the disturbing nature of these crimes get to him. Whatever the answer, Larry Lee Simms was in the middle of it, whether he knew it or not.

16

Larry Lee backed his truck into a shady spot across the street from James's house, a broken down duplex on the outskirts of town. Exhausted and still covered in sweat from exertion, he folded his arms over his chest and laid his head back on the seat. He must've fallen asleep, because he woke up to a persistent rapping on the window and a stiff neck.

"Larry Lee?" James banged on the driver's side door now, a worried look in his eyes. "What're you doing here?"

Larry Lee shook off his grogginess and opened the door. James stepped back as his cousin exited the vehicle. "Can I crash with you for a few days?" Larry Lee asked, stretching his arms high over his head and yawning.

"Sure, man. What's going on? You and Agnes get into a fight?"

Larry Lee shook his head. "She kicked me out."

"Really?" James asked, though he didn't seem altogether surprised. Rather, he seemed distracted, looking back over Larry Lee's shoulder toward the intersection of the main drag. Not that Larry Lee paid him much mind. He was too busy being irritated at his sudden homeless state.

"Ungrateful bitch," Larry Lee muttered.

James took one of Larry Lee's bags and the men made their way into his house. The interior was shabby, but James had put in some comfortable old couches and Larry Lee was happy for the refuge. He and James had grown up together like brothers and, from the beginning, James had followed Larry Lee around like a puppy. Larry Lee liked the attention and was grateful for a place to go when things heated up around his house. Larry Lee loved James a whole lot more than anyone else in his family, including his actual sibling.

James popped open a beer and handed it to Larry Lee, then grabbed one for himself and took a seat on the other couch. "So, what happened?"

Larry Lee frowned. "I honestly don't know. I walked in today and Mama suggested I go up to Tennessee to help David build his house. I doubt David would want me up there, you know, since I busted his nose that time." Larry Lee and his cousin David had hated each other their whole lives. "I think she's trying to get me out of town and I think it has to do with Beth."

James arched an eyebrow. "Beth? What about Beth?"

"She showed up at Mama's door a few nights ago." Larry Lee caught James up on everything that had been going on in town. When he got to the keying of his truck, his lip quivered.

James pushed his shaggy hair out of his eyes and exhaled. "Whoa, man. What stupid bastard would even think about keying your truck? Everyone around here knows it's yours. I can't think of anyone who'd want to mess with you and face the consequences."

"I don't know, but when I find out, I'm going to take a key to his face." The words hissed through Larry Lee's gritted teeth. He pondered James's comment. It was true. He couldn't think of anyone in town who'd be dumb enough to wreck his truck.

As he drank his beer, Larry Lee thought about what little there was left for him in Jasper. He thought bitterly of all the people who'd treated him badly, and his mind wandered until it found its way to Alice Bennett. Since the moment she walked into town, his already dismal life had gotten nothing but worse. Finishing his drink, he crunched the can in his hand, feeling the jagged edges of tin tug at the flesh of his palm.

With the weekend approaching and no jobs on the horizon, Larry Lee and James were of the mind to load up on booze and lie low. Though Agnes never left the house these days, Larry Lee figured it was better to at least pretend he'd gotten out of town for a few days, so his mother would calm down. Then maybe he could talk some sense into her.

Heading down Main Street toward the package store, Larry Lee contemplated the sweet call of whiskey when he spotted his sister coming out of the drugstore. He hadn't seen her since they'd run into each other at his mother's house, and he still had no idea what she was doing back in town. When he'd reappeared at Agnes's door to get a box he'd forgotten, Beth had been there, raging. He hadn't even seen Agnes that day. When Deputy Carver showed up at the door, he'd been trying to get past Beth to check on Agnes, but she'd torn the place apart trying to keep him out. The deputy's visit had quieted Beth down long enough for him to leave.

Today, Beth carried a small package she tucked up under her jacket with one hand while pulling her hood over her head with the other. Larry Lee watched her duck around the corner and slink into a waiting car like a cat evading capture.

Years earlier, Beth had been the notorious town floozy, leaving a steady string of broken hearts and empty beds in her path. Beth used people like they were nothing, completely inconsequential, and she used her body to get what she wanted. No one in the Simms family would ever be mistaken for levelheaded, but Beth was a piece of work, even for a Simms. Her temper was volatile, and she'd been on the verge of being expelled for fighting, among other transgressions, when she dropped out of high school. She'd spend her day working at the drugstore and all night carousing.

At the time, Larry Lee had been attempting to make something of his life. Coming from a dysfunctional family with no money, he signed up for the Navy after scraping by with a high school diploma. Getting away from Pickens County had been a revelation for Larry Lee, and for a while, he thrived within the structure and discipline the military provided.

Then the novelty wore off, and Larry Lee's general distaste for authority and rules, combined with a nasty temper and deceiving nature, became his undoing. At first, Larry Lee received only minor sanctions over bouts of public drunkenness and suspected theft. His aptitude for critical observation, a skill he honed early on to avoid the brunt of Agnes's temper or the ever-watchful eyes of local law enforcement, was an asset his superiors were reluctant to part with, but Larry Lee's ongoing bad behavior soon proved he wasn't a salvageable soldier.

One night, in a drunken brawl, he beat a fellow sailor to the point of unconsciousness—not that the fight had been one-sided. Larry Lee hadn't even been the instigator. He never could say no to a fight. He narrowly avoided a court-martial, owing in large part to his buddy-buddy relationship with his superior officer and a lack of witnesses willing to come forward. Nevertheless, he was dishonorably discharged and sent home to Jasper.

Upon returning home, Larry Lee had tried to be an adult—if not responsible, then at least independent—and to live a life of his own. He'd found steady work on a construction crew and was renting a small house on the outskirts of Jasper. Beth was still living at home with Agnes. Larry Lee made the obligatory visit once a week to his childhood home, but he didn't linger.

He and Beth had never gotten along well. Since returning to town, Larry Lee realized Beth had moved beyond trouble. She was a disaster waiting to happen, for herself and for everyone around her. Beth being his little sister, Larry Lee had often stood up for her, defending her against venomous tongues and clenched fists. Now Beth was so strung out on drugs that even the slightest thing would provoke her and, despite her petite frame, when she fought, she went for blood.

A year had passed with Larry Lee keeping his nose clean and avoiding his family as much as possible when Beth started dating the Clement boy. The Clements were a mountain family, hearty and hardworking. The relationship between Beth Simms and Oscar Clement was the topic of speculation almost from the get-go, and Beth relished the attention.

One night, Larry Lee got a call from Agnes screaming about something happening to Beth. When Larry Lee arrived home, he found his mother so agitated she was shaking and his sister sprawled on the couch, her skirt ripped, dirt on her knees and a fat lip caked with blood. Larry Lee thought he noticed a swell around her midsection, but she shifted and pulled an afghan over her legs before he could be sure.

"What happened?" Larry Lee asked, cautiously. Beth was small, but she was mean like Agnes and there weren't a lot of people in town who would take her on, least of all Oscar Clement. Oscar was a strong young man from years of mountain living, but he had a reputation for being gentle. When Larry Lee found out the two were dating, he'd been baffled at what Oscar saw in Beth, and shocked Oscar's mother hadn't put a stop to it directly.

"That boy attacked your sister!" his mother screeched. "He raped her!"

Larry Lee scrutinized his sister. She definitely looked like she'd been in a scuffle, but it was hard to imagine anyone, especially a pansy-ass boy like Oscar Clement, getting the upper hand on Beth. "That what happened?" he asked Beth, unable to hide his disbelief.

Beth sniffled dramatically, but Larry Lee saw her lips turn up slightly at the sides. "You calling me a liar, Larry Lee? Some brother you are."

Larry Lee was still looking at Beth with a skeptical eye when Agnes smacked him upside the head. Ducking away, he said, "For fuck's sake, Mama. What did you do that for?"

"That boy had his way with your sister." Somehow Larry Lee doubted it, given Beth's reputation, but Agnes was on a roll. "What kind of a man are you, Larry Lee? You're weak, like your father. Always with a bottle in your hand." Agnes's words hit the mark. Larry Lee's father had died a hopeless alcoholic, but Larry Lee had loved his daddy more than anyone. Anger churned in his gut as Agnes continued, "You don't go and take care of that asshole, you're the sorriest son a woman ever had and I wash my hands of you."

Perhaps he should have fought back, or maybe just left—avoided the whole situation until things blew over—but Beth was his sister, no matter what a whore she might be, and family honor was about all Larry Lee had to sustain him. Despite his misgivings, Larry Lee nodded and walked out the door, heading for the park where Beth had last seen Oscar. A few hours later, Oscar Clement was in the hospital, black and blue, with broken ribs and a face swollen beyond recognition, and Larry Lee Simms was headed to jail.

17

Will sighed, running his fingers through his hair. Alice sat across from him, her anger burning bright. With Mae napping a few feet away, Will and Alice tried to keep their voices low, but the argument was escalating.

"You're starting to sound crazy," Will said, exasperated.

Alice fumed. "Don't call me crazy. I'm telling you what the vet said." After hurrying back to the house, Alice had given Mae a half-hearted excuse about Rosy and drove back down the road to pick up the dog and take her to the vet. When she arrived, she found Joylyn still holding her gun tightly and staring out into the kudzu. The field of green took on an even more sinister feel than usual. Alice felt uneasy, but she decided not to question Joylyn about the gun. She put Rosy in the backseat on some towels she had hastily laid out.

By the time they got to the vet's office, Alice had convinced herself Rosy had tangled with an animal and had come out the worse for wear. She wondered if they should change their walking route.

After a few minutes of examination, the vet looked up and asked, "You say she got into a fight?"

The look in his eyes made Alice doubt her own story. "Well," she said slowly, "She took off after a squirrel, like she always does, and the next thing I knew she was limping across the road bleeding. So I assumed . . ."

The doctor quietly looked at the gash in Rosy's leg again and said, "Could she have been near some farm equipment? Maybe in someone's barn?"

"I don't think so," Alice replied. "She wasn't gone very long and I don't think there are a lot of houses around there. A few small cabins here and there, but mostly just forest."

"Well, this wound wasn't made by an animal. See the edge here," he pointed to the torn skin. "The cut is clean. This might have been done by a sharp edge on a piece of equipment. Or a knife."

"A knife?" Alice heard her voice catch. "You think someone might have done this on purpose?"

The doctor hesitated, but the look on his face made Alice shiver. "I didn't mean to scare you. It's an odd injury." Alice was left to her own thoughts while the vet called in a tech to help sanitize and stitch up the wound. When Rosy was all cleaned up, the vet handed Alice a bottle of canine painkillers and gave instructions to keep Rosy in the house and resting as much as possible. The tech fitted Rosy with a cone to keep the dog from licking at her wound. Rosy looked up sadly as Alice carried her to the car.

Thinking back on the experience now, Alice was struck by how easily she accepted someone may have intentionally hurt Rosy, but her husband's unwillingness to even consider that possibility put her on edge. From the minute he stepped in the house, Will had been treating Alice like she was certifiably insane, and for once, she wasn't buying it.

"Look, Will," Alice began, taking a deep breath and trying to keep her voice steady. "Something's going on around here, and I'm worried about leaving Mae alone, even when she's all healed up. Maybe we could look into a retirement home nearby."

Will rounded on her angrily. “The whole point of you coming here, Alice, was to keep Mother from having to go to one of those places.”

Alice couldn’t understand why Will was so angry. Hadn’t putting Mae in a nursing home been his idea in the beginning? She thought furiously of ways to defuse the situation, but her frustration was growing. “Maybe she could come and stay with us?” Alice suggested.

Will sighed, his shoulders finally relaxing. “I doubt she would. And, anyway, given our schedules, I’m not sure she’d be happy with us.”

“I think we need to speak with the police again. If the attack—” Alice paused, seeing Will’s shoulders tense again at the word. “If Rosy’s injuries are somehow related to Mae’s accident, we really need to think seriously about her safety here.”

“You think someone is trying to get to my mother?” Will asked, mockingly, his features ugly and unkind.

“I think,” she started, looking away from Will so she could keep from getting any more riled up, “that something odd is going on and until we understand what it is precisely, it’s not safe to leave your mother on her own.”

Will stalked across the room, grabbed his jacket and keys and headed toward the door. The last rays of sunlight streaked in through the lakeside windows.

“Where are you going?” Alice asked, unable to hide the accusation in her voice. It wasn’t unusual for Will to walk away from an argument and come home with beer on his breath, something that never failed to put Alice in an even fouler mood.

“Out,” he said, closing the door rather harshly behind him.

In the early hours of the morning, Alice heard the creak of the door to her room. A faint light spilled in as Will crept across the room. A quick glance at the alarm clock revealed it was only a few hours until dawn. Still smarting from their argument, Alice lay still and watched her husband. He removed his shirt and laid it across the bench at the foot of the bed. Then, he walked quietly out into the hallway, closing the door behind him. Alice could hear the shower water running, pounding on the tile like a hammer on her heart.

Alice and Mae sat at the dining room table, finishing up breakfast and sipping cups of hot tea, when Will emerged from the bedroom. Alice had never seen Will look so unkempt, especially around his mother. He was usually fastidious in his grooming, unwilling to greet anyone if even a hair was out of place.

Mae, however, smiled up at her son. "You look like you did when you were a little boy, like you just rolled out of bed."

Will looked up at his mother sleepily. "I had a late night." He poured himself a cup of coffee and sat down at the table opposite his wife.

"Yes, I heard you creeping home in the wee hours of the night," Mae continued, her words making Will blush. Alice wondered how much of their argument Mae had heard the previous evening. "I'm going to go check on Rosy." Mae eased herself up and used her walker to make her way back to her room, where Rosy was curled up on the floor snoring away. Mae's hip was getting stronger and she was able to navigate without the walker much of the day.

After Mae was out of earshot, Alice whispered. "Where were you last night?"

Will looked uncharacteristically unsure of himself. "I went down to one of the local bars and ran into a few people I knew."

"I didn't realize there were still people you associated with here in town." Will had been very clear with Alice that, other than family, there was nothing tying him to Georgia. Alice might have felt some relief if not for the look of shame on Will's face.

"This person hasn't lived here for a while."

Alice felt her chest tighten. "Person? Why are you playing the pronoun game, Will?"

Will had the decency to look down when he said, "An old girlfriend."

"You hung out with an old girlfriend until three in the morning?" Alice asked, her voice dripping with venom, as she remembered the early morning shower Will had taken. Emotion surged through her body, a confusing combination of rage, jealousy, and betrayal.

"Listen, I was thinking. Maybe it's time you came home." Will's awkward attempt to change the subject sent Alice's pulse racing. His voice was soft, nearly pleading—so unlike every exchange they'd had in recent months. The change was extremely unsettling. "Mother is getting around pretty well on her own. Maybe we could hire someone to help her with errands and doctors' appointments."

Alice looked at her husband like she was looking at an alien. "What about your mother's safety, Will? What're you thinking?"

Just as Will was going to answer, Mae walked back into the room, an odd expression on her face. "Alice?"

"What's wrong, Mae?"

"Did you move my medicine?"

Alice furrowed her brow. "No. They're right next to your bed. Why? Are you in pain? Do you need me to get them?"

"No," Mae paused. "I think someone's been in my room." Mae held out a pill bottle and opened it, spilling the contents into her hand. Amid the small group of white oval pills were a few yellower, thinner pills.

Alice picked one up. "What are those?"

"I don't know. And I know they weren't there yesterday when I took my medicine. I counted them, so I could decide if I needed a refill from the doctor this week."

Alice looked across the table at Will and was surprised to find his face had gone pale. His hands trembled slightly on his coffee mug.

Turning back to Mae, Alice said, “Are these the pain meds?”

“Yes.”

“Why don’t we put them away for today and take them in to the pharmacy tomorrow. We can get a new refill and have them take a look at what these other ones are. The pharmacist probably made a mistake,” Alice said soothingly. For now, she altogether ignored Mae’s story about having counted the pills, hoping to assuage Mae’s worry.

Mae nodded distractedly and walked back to her room, leaving Alice with the bottle of pills.

She turned to Will. “Do you still think I’m crazy?”

Will stared at her, his face frozen. “Alice, there’s something I need to tell you.”

Having been through a lot in her own life, Alice had learned to be prepared for bad news. It came in waves and it came on the heels of death, violence, and betrayal, but Alice had been lulled into a false sense of security with her honorable, always so put-together husband. Now here she was putting up emotional defenses she’d worked hard to keep at bay with Will.

“When I was in college, I used to come home to visit every summer.” Will’s speech had the cadence of a man making his way down death row to the electric chair—slow and heavy. “The summer of my senior year, I was pretty stressed. I’d barely passed one of my major courses, and I was heading out to the bar a lot.”

A jolt of shock hit Alice’s heart. Will rarely admitted weakness and she’d always assumed he’d been the perfect student—top of his class. She waited for him to continue, wondering where this was going, dreading whatever might have incited this sudden need to confess in her husband.

“I went out every night and came home so tossed I’m surprised I made it home alive. My father finally put his foot down, but not before I'd gotten myself into some trouble." Will shifted anxiously in his seat. "I had a fling with a girl in town. She slept with everyone and I was drinking too much. It only happened a few times, but before I knew it, she was showing up everywhere talking about marriage. I was disgusted and broke it off with her. I wasn't kind." Shame filled his eyes and something else—*could it be fear?*

"That was the old girlfriend you ran into last night?" Alice asked, morbidly curious to see where this story would lead. The possibility that Will might have hooked up with this old flame again, especially given how poorly he spoke of her, made Alice sick to her stomach.

"Yes." Will took another shaky sip of his coffee and winced. "Cold," he said, setting the mug away from him. "Anyway, Beth started some nasty rumors about me after I broke it off. She told everyone I'd gotten her pregnant. I was terrified word would get back to my mother and father. My father was already disappointed with me, and dating a person like Beth—well, I didn't want to admit to it. I couldn't bear to see the look on his face. So one night, I waited for her outside the bar."

A cold chill ran up Alice's spine as she pictured her husband, lying in wait like a predator. She wasn't sure she wanted to hear the rest, but if there was one thing Alice had learned in her life, it was that silence didn't make things disappear.

"When she came out, I yelled at her and pushed her against the wall. I thought she'd be scared and leave me alone, but she smiled. Then she started to laugh. It made me so angry I hauled back and punched her hard in the stomach. The smile disappeared and she slid down the wall, moaning and grabbing at her stomach. I left her there."

"Was she all right?" Alice was horrified. The vision she'd nurtured of her loving, gentle husband collapsed around her like a house of cards.

"I don't know." Will's eyes bore holes into the dining room table.

"You didn't check to see if she was all right?" Alice couldn't hide the disgust in her voice.

"I left a few days later for senior year and I never saw her again."

Alice could feel the bile rising up in her throat. "Until last night?"

Will nodded. "I'd already had a few drinks when she walked in. I thought about getting up and leaving, but I was still angry about our argument and felt bullheaded. She walked right up to me and sat down beside me at the bar." Will stopped to take a breath. "We talked a little bit and it was like old times."

"Old times?" Alice wanted to throw up. "What did you do, Will?" Her voice was barely more than a whisper.

"It's just . . . No, you wouldn't understand. My father's probably rolling in his grave." Suddenly, as if struck by a lightning bolt, he looked at Alice, his eyes wide as he took in the look of horror on her face. "Nothing happened, Alice. I'd never do that to you, especially with someone like Beth Simms."

"Simms?" Alice asked. "As in Larry Lee Simms?"

Will's face flushed. "How do you know Larry Lee Simms?"

18

Larry Lee's paranoia was beginning to take over. He had been staying on James's couch for several days when it occurred to him that James hadn't been all that surprised to hear Beth was back in town. He wondered what that meant? The events of the past few days tore through his mind like a tornado. Beth showed up. His mother kicked him out. His truck was vandalized. It couldn't be a coincidence, could it?

He'd been sitting around contemplating things until his brain hurt. He decided he needed to get out of the house for some fresh air. He made his way slowly toward downtown Jasper, forgoing a stop at the library, intent on wandering. He'd just passed the clock tower on Main Street when he spied Beth.

She stood on the sidewalk behind the drugstore with Jeff Hatcher. Though he towered over her, he leaned slightly away from her as they talked. His posture suggested he might need to make a run for it. The two were arguing. Larry Lee pulled over behind a parked car and rolled down his window a bit, though it wasn't necessary. With the engine off, he could clearly hear the shrill sound of Beth's screaming.

"Back off, Jeff! I don't care what you think about it. I never have. And I don't answer to you. If you're not man enough for this, go back to your mama."

Jeff's voice was low and hoarse making it impossible for Larry Lee to make out what he said, but his tone was tense.

"Of course not!" Beth let her hands fall to her side, but her fists were clenched tightly. "I'm not stopping because you're scared shitless. Man, I thought you had more balls than this."

It made Larry Lee crazy that he couldn't seem to catch the gist of the argument. His insides were at war. On the one hand, he was stricken by some deeply ingrained instinct to jump to Beth's aid, as much as it wrenched at his gut. On the other hand, he hated Beth intensely and had already done more than his fair share of sticking up for her—enough for two lifetimes. He should have driven away, but with everything happening lately, with all the questions rolling around his head, he needed to hear what they were saying.

Larry Lee watched his sister's reaction as Jeff spoke in hushed tones, his shoulders sagging in defeat. Her face, which had been an ugly red, began to lighten. Her fists unclenched and her fingers relaxed. Finally, she smiled. It wasn't a pretty smile, but maybe it was the best she could do.

"That's my man." Beth reached up and kissed him on the mouth, leaving her hands at her side. Tail between his legs, he turned and walked toward a car parked across the street. Beth watched him go with a look of pure malice that made Larry Lee's skin crawl.

For a moment, Larry Lee sat in his truck feeling utterly confused. Seeing Beth was stirring up all kinds of memories for him. Knowing she was up to something fueled his paranoia. Why had she come back to Jasper? And what was she doing with Jeffrey Hatcher?

Larry Lee was so caught up in his thoughts he didn't notice Beth approaching his truck until she was only a few feet away, closing the distance fast.

"Open up, big brother," she yelled. Her eyes were fierce and she was scowling.

Larry Lee rolled the window back up and then opened the door wide, forcing Beth to take a step back, giving him some much-needed distance and buying him a few seconds to collect his thoughts. He got out of the truck and shut the door behind him, then stood awkwardly against it.

"What're you doing here?" she asked, eyeing him suspiciously.

"What, in Jasper? I live here, or had you forgotten. The real question is, what're you doing here, Beth?" Larry Lee examined Beth. She had big dark bags under her eyes and her hair looked like it hadn't been washed in weeks. He noticed a gash on the side of her arm that had gone to scab. "What happened to you?" he asked, gesturing toward her arm, trying not to sound too interested.

Beth crossed her arms so the wound was pressed against her chest. "You spying on me, Larry Lee?" Her voice was a ferocious growl. Larry Lee felt the hairs on his arms stand on end, like an animal under attack. He didn't remember ever feeling real fear around Beth before.

"Hell no." Larry Lee kicked at a small rock near his foot, suddenly wishing he'd gotten out of town when he had the chance. His temper flared. He stared daggers at his sister. "I'm not the one who has to explain myself, Beth. Here you are, again, and my life is going to shit. Got me kicked out of my own damned house. What are you up to?"

Beth smirked. "Mama should have kicked you out a long time ago. You're a grown man, Larry Lee. Go get a life." She paused and lowered her voice to a whisper. "Your truck looks like shit."

Larry Lee clenched his jaw tight. "You know what, Beth? You're a fucking bitch." He climbed back into his truck and revved the engine to make a point, but as he pulled away from the curb, Beth was still smiling.

~

Heading back toward James's house, Larry Lee pulled into the drive-in and ordered a Coke with change he'd scrounged from James's dresser. He put his feet up on the dash and sipped at the cold soda, using the straw to crunch the crushed ice around—a nervous habit that drove James crazy.

Something was not right. Jasper was a small town and there was one thing Larry Lee could always count on: nothing ever changed. This one fact had been the bane of his existence lately. He couldn't do anything in town without the taint of his past thwarting his efforts to move on, but the slow pace and lack of progress was also a source of comfort. Larry Lee knew when he walked into the drugstore, he'd get yelled at or thrown out, depending on who was behind the counter. He knew when he went to the library, Charlene would hit on him. There was something very reassuring about predictability.

With Beth back in town that comfortable feeling was gone from Pickens County. Something was definitely wrong. As Beth skulked around town, a black cloud opened up and dumped down shit on Larry Lee's head.

A sheriff's cruiser rolled by the drive-in. Larry Lee sunk down in his seat, though no one in town could mistake his truck at this point. The ruined exterior was an eyesore even in the run-down neighborhood James lived in. He'd seen Deputy Carver on James's street more than once now, obviously bent on catching Larry Lee in the act of something. After the last close call, he'd been extra careful about keeping his nose clean and his tracks covered.

Wanting nothing more than to get back to his couch, crack open a beer, and zone out, Larry Lee was getting ready to pull out of the drive-in when he remembered he really needed to stop by the library to check his email. He wasn't optimistic about a job offer having come in, but if he checked, he'd feel better about doing nothing the rest of the day.

When he entered the library, Charlene was in her usual position behind the circulation desk, but Larry Lee could see she was ticked off about something. The way she sighed and banged the keys on her keyboard was unnecessarily rough. She hadn't noticed him walk in at first.

He made his way quietly by her, thinking he might get off without her seeing him, when she looked up, her eyes ablaze.

"Have you ever once thought about how much trouble you bring on yourself, Larry Lee?" Her voice was raised, and Larry Lee looked around in embarrassment.

"What're you going on about, Charlene?" Normally, he'd use her nickname to goad her, but it didn't seem like she needed any more goading and Larry Lee wasn't sure he wanted to be on the receiving end of her bad mood.

"I mean, in the years I've known you, I've heard you rant about everyone in town. How people don't give you a chance. How someone treated you badly. Did you ever stop to think about how you might be causing that reaction in people?"

Larry Lee was genuinely surprised by Charlene's behavior. He was used to fending her off, but he never once thought she'd been paying any attention to what he'd been saying all these years. It was strange. Charlene might be one of the only people in town who actually listened to Larry Lee. He almost felt guilty for being so mean to her. Almost.

"I don't know what's got you so worked up, but I'm going to go use the computers."

He had started to walk away when Charlene muttered, "You're a user. You and your sister both."

Larry Lee whipped around, ready for a fight, but Charlene had gotten up and gone into the office, shutting the door behind her. He wanted to follow her, to demand she explain what she had meant by that. He was still riled from his run-in with Beth, and he wasn't taking kindly to being put into the same category with her.

Heading back to the computer bank, Larry Lee chose a station in the far corner. He logged in to his email, verified the lack of correspondence from any potential jobs, and sat back in his chair to think. Larry Lee rarely spent much time thinking about his own role in his life. When he robbed someone's house, he knew it was wrong, but he didn't feel guilty. He needed the money. He usually felt his actions were justified, that the odds were against him, and he had to make his own way in the world. Now he wondered if Charlene had a point. Was he responsible for the things that happened to him? The way people looked at him, talked about him, always saw the worst in him?

Maybe it was the truth, but Larry Lee wasn't ready to accept it. He still thought people like Will and Margaret Bennett got all the breaks, while people like he and James were left with the dregs, the shitty jobs, the busted-up cars. He pictured his mother and Beth holed up in the shabbiest house on the lake, a house he was no longer welcome.

Though he'd started out thinking about responsibility, his thoughts had quickly become a tirade about inequity and unfairness. All of it seemed determined to pull him under, to beat him down until there was nothing left. Some people might feel depressed or hopeless, but Larry Lee wasn't made that way. He felt white-hot fury brimming under the surface. He switched off the computer, pushing in his chair so hard it hit the table with a loud thudding, garnering dirty looks from nearby library patrons.

"Mind your own business," he snarled at no one in particular. He hightailed it to his truck, slamming the door and flooring the engine as he raced down the road toward James's house, where the promise of his cousin's ratty old couch and the bottle of whiskey he'd stowed in his bag for such an occasion awaited.

19

"I understand, Mrs. Pruitt. We're doing everything we can—"

"Not nearly enough, as far as I can see." Mrs. Pruitt was a small, round woman whose family had lived near the lake for generations. Her house was the most recent to be burgled. Carver was itching to finish taking her statement and start looking around, but the diminutive Mrs. Pruitt wasn't ready to let go of her audience.

Unlike the previous burglaries, Mrs. Pruitt's window had been smashed in plain sight of the road, and her house was a disaster. Mrs. Pruitt was angry, but Carver suspected she was also suffering some shock. Luckily, Pruitt's daughter and son-in-law lived with her, and both were on their way home from work to help.

"I need to take a look around. It would be very helpful if you could make a list of anything missing," Carver said kindly, handing the older woman a notepad and pen. He hoped giving her a job would give him a few peaceful moments to take stock. Mrs. Pruitt took the notepad but gave Carver a glare that said she understood what he was up to.

The scene around the window was textbook. The burglar had sent a large rock through it. Glass shards were strewn about the floor and the rock lay where it had come to rest against the leg of a chair. The window had then been unlocked and pushed open. Carver had looked for footprints outside when he'd arrived at the house, but the spot was lush with ground cover. The suspect's shoes had crushed the plants but avoided leaving imprints in the dirt beneath.

He stood and let his eyes travel the path of destruction. It looked as though the intruder had walked toward the back of the house, opening drawers and scattering contents as they went. Oddly, only the top drawers had been disturbed, and as Mrs. Pruitt followed him through the house, she noticed nothing missing. Mrs. Pruitt's bedroom had been rifled through, but the intruder had failed to look through the majority of the drawers and cabinets, with most of the damage focused around the bedside table.

The house had two bathrooms on the main floor, and both had been turned inside out, the medicine cabinets swept clean with pill bottles strewn about the floor. Several bottles had been opened and upturned, leaving a rainbow of tablets and capsules lying around. Carver bent down and picked up one of the bottles that had been opened.

"What's this?" Reading the label, he added, "Loratadine?"

"Allergy pills," Mrs. Pruitt replied. "I believe those are Chester's. He's been sniffling since the trees started blooming." She gave a disapproving snort. "My daughter marries a Northern man, and the poor child can't breathe our fine Southern air."

Carver smiled. "Well, I guess nobody's perfect." Mrs. Pruitt wasn't alone in her general disdain for "foreigners," which included anyone from north of the Mason-Dixon line.

"Do you keep any narcotics or controlled substances in the house?"

Mrs. Pruitt looked baffled. "You mean—drugs?" She'd spoken the last word in a near whisper despite it being just the two of them.

"I mean medications, Mrs. Pruitt. For pain. For anxiety. Anything that would require an ID to get at the pharmacy."

"No, nothing like that. I had an old bottle of pain medicine they gave to Walter before he died, but I threw it out years ago." She looked him square in the eyes, challenging him to question her. He only smiled again.

"Okay, I'm going to take a look around the rest of the house, but please have your daughter look through these medications and let me know if anything important is missing."

With drug activity increasing throughout the county, this break-in looked like a clear-cut drug seeking mission. The homes along the lake, mostly occupied by older residents, were a boon for junkies looking for prescription narcotics. Whoever had been in the Pruitt house hadn't been so lucky. Still, there was something odd about this incident, something that didn't sit right. Whoever had broken in had been looking for something specific. The rest of the mess felt staged—enough wreckage to make it harder to know what was missing. Larry Lee was Carver's prime suspect for burglaries in the area, but while Larry Lee was careful, he wasn't calculated. Anyway, drugs weren't Larry Lee's thing and Carver's suspicions turned quickly to Beth Simms.

He took another careful look around the house, hoping something might stand out to him, but when he left an hour later, he had come up empty.

~

The police cruiser was stifling and there wasn't much of a breeze outside to help cool things down. Carver was irritable as sweat trickled down his neck.

It was his own fault. He'd been tailing Larry Lee Simms for nearly a week, as often as his schedule would allow, and he'd started to think Larry Lee was the most boring person in Georgia history. If Larry Lee had decided to lie low, he was excelling in his efforts. Other than trips to the convenience story for cigarettes, Larry Lee rarely left the house. He was staying with his cousin James, and James worked from early morning to late afternoon. The house was quiet. And yet, Carver had made it his mission to keep tabs on Larry Lee.

Why? Wiping a trickle of sweat away from his eyes, Carver asked himself this question once more. The minute Larry Lee had hit town after being released from prison, Carver knew it was a matter of time before he was sent back. Carver also knew Larry Lee was a victim of circumstance. It did not excuse his behavior, but Carver had known the Simms family since before Larry Lee and his sister Beth were born—back in the days when Larry Lee's father was a regular at the bar where Carver wasted away his youth, ruining his marriage and alienating his children in the process.

Carver had gotten sober. Larry Lee's father had gotten dead, leaving his kids at the mercy of his wife, Agnes. And mercy wasn't a word Agnes Simms was familiar with.

The guilt had begun then as a whisper that kept him awake at night. Every time Carver picked up Larry Lee for petty theft or fighting. Every time Beth Simms was seen climbing out of the backseat of some yahoo's car. Every time Carver was called out to the Simms place on some domestic disturbance, he felt the weight of every drink he'd shared at that bar with Harold Simms.

When Larry Lee ended up in prison, Carver had been both relieved and crushed.

It hadn't been the same with Beth. When she'd left town, Carver had felt the relief with none of the remorse. There was simply something about Beth that made him believe she was a lost cause. Larry Lee was different. He reminded Carver of himself. Carver's dad had also been a drunk, but Carver had been fortunate enough to have a mother who loved him in her way. She hadn't been an affectionate woman, by any means, but she'd worked hard to support her family, to get her boys through school, to help them make something of themselves. Carver was pretty sure he'd broken her heart twice over every time he picked up the bottle.

Distracted by his thoughts, Carver was frustrated to look up and see Larry Lee's truck rolling toward his parking spot. Larry Lee pulled up alongside Carver and rolled down his window.

"Nothing better to do than keep an eye on me, eh Carver?" A wave of cigarette smoke spilled out of the truck and rolled into Carver's cruiser. He waved it away, disgusted.

"Just trying to keep you on the straight and narrow," Carver said with a wink.

"Ah, I'm touched," Larry Lee replied. He wore a smug expression but beyond that, Carver swore he saw something softer, something surprising. Carver could see Larry Lee's eyes were clear and bright, like he hadn't yet started into the drink. Maybe Larry Lee had turned a corner. Carver wondered whether the outcome would be good.

20

Alice slept fitfully Sunday night and woke Monday morning feeling tired down deep in her bones. Will had flown home Sunday evening, but the entire day following his confession over breakfast had been emotional and exhausting, with Will practically begging Alice to come home. His fervor only served to fuel her feelings of suspicion and betrayal.

"Would you really have me leave your mother alone? After everything that's happened?" Alice had finally asked, seeing Will was determined to have his way. In the past, she'd have bent to his desires easily, seeing him as the more solid and rational of the two of them. Now she had her doubts.

"Of course not," Will responded, though she could see he was taken aback by her question, as if he wasn't thinking of Mae at all. She suspected Will's pleading came from his guilt over seeing Beth Simms rather than any real desire to have Alice come rushing home. His lack of concern about his mother was shocking. Alice simply could not abide the selfishness.

"She's not ready to leave her home, Will. Every day since her fall, she's worked hard to recover. Every setback—the nightmares and now this problem with her medications—she's determined,

Will. If none of that has convinced her to leave, I'm not sure anything will. She wants to be in her own home."

Alice could see the color rising in Will's cheeks. "Don't you think I know that, Alice? But it's not safe here. With Larry Lee and Beth Simms both lurking around . . ."

"Oh please. You think your ex-girlfriend is going to come attack us? Or does this all boil down to the famous feud?" Alice couldn't keep a hint of sarcasm out of her voice. She still couldn't quite wrap her mind around the idea of a real feud, and her patience with Will had run its course.

"No. Not exactly." Will ran his fingers through his hair, his face twisted in a scowl. "The trouble between the Simms and the Bennetts was never like this. Not since the beginning. I mean, we sort of hated each other from a distance. Any altercations were minor, more a matter of chest-thumping, not a real threat."

Exasperated, Alice said, "Well, then whatever is going on around here is no different than anywhere else. We'll take better precautions, but there's no way I'm leaving Mae."

Will still insisted on a long talk with Mae about moving into a rehabilitation facility, both in terms of continued care and security, but after the initial shock of finding her medications had been tampered with, Mae had stubbornly resolved to stay at home. A thorough search of the house revealed no other signs of a break-in, and Mae became convinced the pharmacy had made a mistake and she simply hadn't noticed. Again, Alice had her doubts. She was anxious to get to the pharmacy to get the whole incident sorted out, hoping without faith that Mae was right.

She was determined to see Mae through the recovery process. The thought of leaving early wasn't even an option for Alice. She wasn't going anywhere. Will's refusal to understand that was a source of heartbreak and frustration. He'd left town like a petulant child who hadn't gotten his way and Alice had to admit she wasn't terribly sad to see him go.

Alice took a long, hot shower then put the kettle on before

making her way to Mae's room. She found her mother-in-law awake and already dressed.

"Good morning, Mae," Alice said, after knocking softly on the door.

"Good morning, Alice. Did you sleep well?"

Alice hesitated. "No, not very, but maybe I'll lie down for a nap after we get back from the doctor."

Mae nodded. "The last few days have been very stressful. My son can be annoyingly stubborn."

Not wanting to air her own feelings about Will's behavior, Alice simply said, "I'm sure he's doing what he thinks is best."

"It's been a long time since Will called this place his home." Mae sighed. "Ever since his father died, Will's been drifting further and further away. I think Jasper is too small for him."

Alice knew there was more to the story. Despite Will's vague descriptions of high school animosity and the family feud, the look on his face when she mentioned Larry Lee Simms was enough to convince her Will was holding something back. She remembered Jim Davis's story about Will's friend Tom and the boy who ended up in a wheelchair, wondering if Larry Lee had been there. It seemed that Will's history with Larry Lee Simms predated his relationship with Beth by miles, though he'd never mentioned it.

"We have about an hour before we head into town. Are you ready for some breakfast?"

Mae nodded and slowly made her way down to the dining room without her walker. Easing herself into her chair, she said, "Hardly any pain this morning. Just stiffness."

Alice smiled. "I bet the physical therapist will like to hear that."

Mae chortled. "She'll be happy to put the pain back into the mix."

Alice nodded sympathetically. She'd gone through physical therapy after a bad break had left her with weakness and chronic pain in her arm and shoulder. Physical therapy helped her regain normal function, but not without a lot of pain. She rolled her shoulder absentmindedly, thinking if physical pain could alleviate the emotional damage, she'd take it.

When they'd finished eating, Alice cleaned up the breakfast dishes, then they went out to the car, the prescription bottle rattling in Alice's purse and grating on her nerves. As she got into the driver's seat, she took one last look around the property and was irritated to see the flowers, the trees, the peaceful mountain landscape, all without a hint of the menace that had become a regular part of their lives.

Since the pharmacy wouldn't open until after the doctor's appointment, Mae and Alice headed straight for the physicians' offices located in the north wing of the hospital. When Dr. Slater asked about Mae's pain, Alice decided to bring up the issue with the meds in case a new prescription needed to be written. Dr. Slater shook the pills out into her hand and frowned.

"You got these filled here at the hospital?"

Alice nodded. "Yes, not too long ago. Mae had only taken one of the new pills. She was counting them when she noticed the mistake. We were going to take it straight to the pharmacy, but I wondered if we'd need a new prescription."

Still looking concerned, Dr. Slater asked, "Mae, is your pain manageable?"

"Yes," Mae said, though worry now began to show on her face as well.

"I'd like you to start taking ibuprofen then, as needed, instead of the prescription medications."

Mae nodded. "That would be good. I don't like how sleepy those pills make me anyway. It's the reason I haven't taken them more often."

"Now, I don't want to alarm you, but I'd like to call in the pharmacist."

Alice gasped. "Why?"

Dr. Slater hesitated. "I've known Bill Manning for ten years and I trust him. If this was a mistake from his department, he needs to know about it right away."

Alice frowned. "Do you recognize those other pills?"

"I do. And the interaction between them could be fatal." Dr. Slater turned to Mae. "I am very thankful you examined these before taking them, Mae."

Mae nodded, but the shock on her face was startling. Alice took her hand.

Dr. Slater excused herself and returned a few minutes later with an older man in a white coat.

"Mae, this is Bill Manning, the pharmacist here at the hospital." Mae shook the man's hand. "Bill, I want you to take a look at this."

Bill poured the pills out onto a sterile tray he'd retrieved from the cupboard and without delay he said, "Oh, no. Good gracious." He frowned, and Alice watched as the color drained from his face. He turned the bottle in his hand to read the label.

After a few more moments, he said, "I don't understand, Michelle." He looked at Dr. Slater with a very serious expression. "I filled this prescription myself. These pills aren't even from the same area of the pharmacy, and since they're both controlled substances, we triple-check these prescriptions. I'm one hundred percent positive this bottle contained only the Oxycodone when I filled it."

Dr. Slater nodded. "I thought you would say that." Then, turning to Alice and Mae she said, "I think we need to involve law enforcement."

~

Mae and Alice had spent most of Monday in town, first at the doctor's office and then at the police station. The hospital pharmacy had been put on lockdown while an inventory was conducted. Bill Manning was put on paid leave pending an investigation, which he accepted without complaint, obviously distressed by the incident. Alice sympathized, but the whole situation left her brain reeling. Somewhere between the pharmacy and Mae's house, someone had put Klonopin, a benzodiazepine used to treat seizures and panic attacks, in with Mae's Oxycodone. The combination could have been fatal, especially for a person whose body had been weakened by trauma. Would someone want to kill Mae? Who would have had the opportunity? And was this a second attempt?

Other than Alice and Will, Mae had not been in contact with anyone since the prescription had been filled, but Alice *had* been out of the house for several hours on Friday while taking Rosy to the vet. Deputy Morrison and an officer from the Jasper Police Department had searched Mae's house and property.

Margaret took Tuesday off and came up to Jasper to spend the day with Mae. Alice had a meeting scheduled in Tate for her story, and though she wanted to cancel, Margaret urged her to go, assuring her they'd be quite safe. Alice only relented because Margaret planned on staying all day. Alice had no intention of leaving Mae alone again, even for a few minutes, until this whole medication debacle had been resolved.

Driving down the highway from Jasper toward Tate, Alice tried to bask in the gorgeous Georgia scenery, but she was distracted. She'd agreed to meet Sally Jenkins, a local historian, at Millie's Diner on the outskirts of Tate. As she neared the town, she remembered a Christmas a few years back when she and Will had visited and he'd brought her down to Tate for the holiday house tours of the Historic Tate House. As the home of the Georgia Marble Company, Tate was known for its marble and the Tate House was constructed out of a rare pink marble quarried right in its own backyard. It was a gorgeous house with elegant gardens used for summer weddings. The Christmas decor had transported Alice back in time. She'd fallen in love with everything Georgian on that trip.

She spied the red roof on Millie's Diner and found a spot in the parking lot. Having arrived a few minutes early, she took the time to check her email and make some preliminary notes. She'd been vague on the phone about what she was hoping to research in Tate. Since receiving the message to get out of town, Alice had been more reserved when talking with people about her work. She hoped to develop some rapport with Mrs. Jenkins before springing such a grisly line of inquiry on her.

Alice entered the restaurant and asked for a table for two, telling the hostess she was meeting someone. She ordered coffee and let her mind wander as she gazed out the window at the Georgia countryside.

"Alice Bennett?" A woman's voice woke her from her reverie.

"Yes," she said, standing to take the other woman's outstretched hand. "You must be Sally. Thank you for meeting with me."

Sally Jenkins was a good half a foot shorter than Alice and quite stout, but she had a cheerful face and her smile reached all the way to her eyes, putting Alice at ease. "Not a problem. I love nothing as much as talking about Tate."

As Sally took a seat, Alice asked, "You were born here?"

"Yes. Well, in Atlanta, but back in those days that was the closest hospital. My family has been here in Tate since I was a girl. My father worked for Georgia Marble and we lived in company housing for many years."

"What was that like?" Alice asked.

"Oh, it was pretty ordinary when I was a girl, but the history of the company was riddled with interesting gems. Back in the days of Sam Tate, all employees were provided with housing, but they weren't allowed to own their own houses or build on company land. On the other hand, Tate was very interested in the education of children. Georgia Marble Company built and maintained schools for both the white and black children." Sally spoke energetically, jumping from topic to topic with the skill of a pro.

Alice began taking copious notes as Sally regaled her with tales of growing up in Tate and the history of the area. In between topics, they ordered and ate lunch. As the conversation began to taper off, Alice decided it was time to get to the point.

"This sounds like such a nice place to live," Alice said, then added, "I'm working on a piece about the evolution of some of Georgia's laws, and I ran across a murder case that happened here in the 1940s. It involved a Georgia Marble Company employee, J.M. Carney?" Alice paused and silently groaned as she watched Sally Jenkins's face become a mask.

"Is that what you're here to research? The murder of Juanita Jones?" Sally's tone was guarded.

"I'm surprised you've heard of her. Most of the people I spoke to up in Jasper had never heard about the case." Alice was trying to keep her tone light, but the wall of resentment emanating off of her companion was palpable.

"I wasn't born yet, of course, but my parents were already living here in Tate when Ms. Jones was murdered. My parents were good friends with the Jones family."

Alice sensed danger, but she felt like she was finally getting somewhere and so she plodded ahead. "They were? Do you know, does the family still live around here?"

"Look, Mrs. Bennett," the shift in formality was an unnecessary indication of the turn the conversation had taken. The irritation in Sally Jenkins's eyes was enough. "Tate is a beautiful, historic Georgia town. We've had our share of trouble, but we choose to focus on the great things about living here. I've certainly got nothing to say regarding the murder of Juanita Jones. And speaking on behalf of her family, I suggest you use your time here in our beautiful state to a more productive end. Excuse me." Laying her napkin on the table, Sally Jenkins rose, gathered her bag, and walked out the door without so much as a passing glance. Alice, however, was aware that several pairs of eyes were on her.

Alice finished her coffee, paid the bill and walked toward her car with feigned calmness, fighting back the urge to run. Disappointed by the direction her meeting had taken, Alice headed back to Jasper and decided to hit the library before returning to Mae's. She was thinking about Juanita Jones, who'd been so savagely murdered and then almost entirely forgotten. Alice felt frustrated at coming up empty-handed when she was so close to learning more about the poor woman.

Researching Jones's story was making Alice a little bit crazy. She found herself thinking about her father more and more, and the result wasn't pleasant. As she pulled into the parking lot and got out of her car, she thought about what it might have been like if her father had lived and answered for his crimes.

She was so lost in her thoughts she didn't notice the truck with the ugly gouge down its side heading slowly toward her until she'd nearly walked into its front end.

"Hey! Watch out!" a man's voice yelled from the driver's side. Alice looked up, startled, and found herself gazing at the red face of Larry Lee Simms. What surprised her most was the look of fear when their eyes met.

Alice hopped onto the sidewalk and said, "I'm so sorry. I didn't see you coming." She expected a harsh retort like their previous run-in. Instead, Larry Lee pulled into an open spot, got out of the truck and walked toward her. She shifted the books in her hand to the middle of her torso, a subconscious move to defend her body from an oncoming attack.

"Look, I'm sorry. I thought you saw me coming," Larry Lee said nervously. For a moment, Alice stood there dumbly, the shock making it impossible to think of anything to say.

She studied Larry Lee Simms, the subject of so much speculation and family history. He was a tall man who'd obviously spent some time drinking lately—his beer gut, though small, was visible through his gray t-shirt. He looked like he hadn't slept in a few days, or shaved. The hair growth on his face was ragged and unkempt, but it was clear from his build that he could handle himself physically. She'd already experienced his infamous temper. Alice wondered if this man could have hurt Mae. She searched his eyes for signs of guilt.

"I'm fine." Alice turned as if to leave, but Larry Lee reached out and grabbed her arm. His grasp had been light, but she jumped and he let go as if he'd received an electric shock. "Don't touch me," she said, her voice higher and more unsteady than she would have liked.

Larry Lee shifted his weight from one foot to another, glancing over his shoulder nervously. "I wanted to apologize for knocking you down the other day. In front of the courthouse. I wasn't thinking."

Alice studied Larry Lee, not knowing exactly what to say. Finally, she settled on, "It's all right. You didn't hurt me." She was relieved to hear the confidence restored to her voice.

"I'm Larry Lee," he said, though he kept his hands shoved down deep into pants pockets. "I guess you probably know that already," he added, looking down at his shoes.

"Yes, and I'm sure you know I'm Alice Bennett. Will Bennett's wife." She added the last comment for no other reason than to see Larry Lee's reaction. He had none.

Larry Lee shifted his weight and let his eyes wander everywhere but Alice, unusual in a town where everyone seemed to stare. He looked like he was going to say something, but the words wouldn't come. The silence between them was thick and awkward.

Alice checked her watch. Normally, she'd have made excuses and been on her way, so as not to keep Mae waiting, but something in Larry Lee's posture, his obvious discomfort, tugged at Alice's heartstrings. She was tempted to reach out and take his hand, though she cringed at the thought. What would Will say if he knew she was sympathetic to Mae's probable attacker? Thinking about it made her sweat.

As if on cue, a Pickens County sheriff's cruiser rolled up the drive to the library. Alice saw Larry Lee stiffen, and for a moment, she understood what it must be like to be the scapegoat in a small town. She'd never considered how much anonymity she'd had in her own hometown, one small miracle in an otherwise disastrous life. She also wondered why the sheriff's office seemed to show up anytime she was at the library. She fought back a wave of paranoia. As the car rolled to a stop in front of them, Deputy Morrison rolled down the window. "Everything all right here, Alice?" His gaze at Larry Lee was hard as steel.

"Yes, everything's fine." Alice watched Larry Lee, who seemed to be shrinking into himself, trying to become invisible. She'd heard all the stories about Larry Lee's run-ins with law enforcement. Seeing him shrivel, she felt bolder. "Mr. Simms was just apologizing for bumping into me the other day." She saw Larry Lee raise his eyebrows slightly in disbelief.

"That so?" The deputy's expression could have made water freeze. Alice felt sorry for Larry Lee. It was obvious from the deputy's expression he didn't need much of an excuse to find fault with Larry Lee.

"Yes, sir." Larry Lee looked back at Alice. "Have a good day, ma'am." He turned and shuffled off to his truck and slowly exited the parking lot, not making eye contact with either Alice or Deputy Morrison as he left. The deputy pulled into the now free spot and got out to talk to Alice.

"I don't think I've ever seen such a tough guy turn into such a pussycat. How do you do that, Deputy?" The corners of her lips turned up as she watched Larry Lee drive away, surprising her.

"Larry Lee and I go way back," Deputy Morrison said with a sigh, then added, "But he never goes all tame like that for me. Guess it must be you." His gaze lingered over her body a moment too long before he looked back out again at the now empty drive-way. "Looks like I need to have another talk with him."

"Not on my account I hope," Alice replied, running her fingers clumsily through her hair, self-conscious but determined to get Larry Lee off the hook, "This was my fault. I was distracted and almost walked right into his truck."

The deputy looked at Alice with concern, though she couldn't help but notice his eyes leave her face again. "Is everything okay? Anything happen with Mae?"

Alice shrugged off the discomfort she felt under Morrison's gaze and tried adding some levity to the situation. "What? Since yesterday? No, Margaret is up at the house today, so I'm working on the story I'm writing. I had a less-than-satisfactory meeting with a woman in Tate."

The deputy nodded, but Alice could see his mind was elsewhere. She glanced down the driveway again, but when she turned her attention to the officer, he was still looking at her. Seeing her notice, he finally shifted his gaze. "Well, listen. I was hoping I'd run into you. We've finished with the pharmacy inventory and the pills in Mae's bottle definitely didn't come from the hospital. I need you to go through the timeline on Friday with me again."

He escorted Alice into the library where they spent what felt like hours going over everything that had happened the past few days. By the time Alice headed home, she was almost tired enough, almost frazzled enough, to want a drink.

21

Alice chewed at her cuticle nervously. She sat on Joylyn's porch, waiting while Joylyn fetched some tea. With Rosy at home recuperating, Alice had driven to Joylyn's cabin, too spooked to take even the shortest walk without her furry companion.

"Here you are," Joylyn said, propping the screen door open and handing Alice a mug of tea before securing the door and taking a seat beside her. They were seated on two wooden armchairs Joylyn's father had made nearly half a century earlier. Alice ran her free hand along the wood, taking comfort in the smooth timeworn surface.

"How's Rosy?" Joylyn asked.

"She's pretty annoyed she has to wear a cone and we won't let her outside much, but she seems to be healing up pretty well." Alice chuckled. "She mostly lays down beside Mae and pouts."

Joylyn smiled. "Sounds like Rosy. She's an outdoor dog for sure. What did the vet say about her injury?"

Reluctantly, Alice replied, "He said it looked like someone cut her." Studying Joylyn's reaction, she added, "But you suspected that, I think."

Joylyn nodded, though she kept her eyes locked on the kudzu patch across the road.

"When you got out your gun the other day, what were you thinking, Joylyn? Who were you expecting to have to shoot?"

For a long time, Joylyn didn't answer. Alice could see a story simmering in her friend's posture, so she waited, albeit impatiently. She sipped her tea loudly to break the silence. When she couldn't take it anymore, she finally said, "Will told me something when he was here. Something about Beth Simms."

Joylyn's reaction was immediate. Her body stiffened and her breathing grew heavy. "Beth Simms," she muttered.

"He saw her this weekend."

For a moment, the older woman's eyes were wide with shock, but then she sighed. "He would." The disapproval in her voice wasn't subtle. For a moment, Alice could see why Will was so hell-bent on keeping his relationship with Beth a secret.

"Listen, Joylyn. I wanted to ask Mae about this, but I didn't want to upset her so I'm asking you. What do you know about Beth Simms?"

"More than I ever wanted to know." Joylyn shifted in her seat and took a few purposeful breaths, looking out into the kudzu field. "My son Oscar dated Beth Simms for a while. It was a year or so after Larry Lee came back from the Navy. He was still living on his own in town, so it was just Agnes and Beth up here at the lake. Beth had been sleeping her way around the county, and when Oscar told me he was seeing her, I nearly lost my mind. I reckon it was the biggest fight we ever had." She finally looked at Alice. "You know how I feel about the Simms family?"

Alice nodded, but stayed silent to allow Joylyn room to talk.

"My issues with the Simms family have nothing to do with your in-laws. Lots of families hold grudges around here, that's nothing new. I don't get involved in the feuding unless it concerns me. And there have been a lot of troubled kids around here in my lifetime. In that way, the Simms are hardly any reason to get all worked up, but I grew up with Agnes Simms and knew that family was trouble long before Agnes brought Larry Lee and Beth into the world."

Joylyn rubbed a wrinkled hand to her brow. "I can start talking myself in circles about the Simms family. Anyway, Oscar and I went rounds about Beth Simms. He told me he was in love. I told him she was bad news. It wasn't just the other men, mind you, although that was bad enough. No, Beth was a known drug user and Oscar—well—Oscar was naive. Despite it being the two of us, he'd led a fairly sheltered life up here in the mountains. I can see now I shouldn't have pushed so hard, but Oscar was my only child. Hindsight and all that."

"What happened with Oscar?"

"One night, Oscar went to see Beth. He was getting ready to head back to graduate school. When he wasn't home by midnight, I started to worry and called the sheriff's office. An hour later, I was at the hospital, wondering whether my son would ever wake up. He had broken bones and was in pretty rough shape, but the damage to his face was horrific. It took several surgeries to put him back together again and he almost lost an eye."

"Oh, Joylyn."

"The sheriff's office picked up Larry Lee Simms and charged him with the assault. No one ever said a word about Beth, but I knew if Oscar was hurt, it wasn't Larry Lee's fault. Not really."

"I'm so sorry all that happened, Joylyn, but I'm not sure I see what this has to do with Will?"

A fire burned in Joylyn's eyes, but she took a deep breath before continuing. "What happened to Oscar has nothing to do with Will. He was away at college at the time. He and Oscar had never been friends despite my friendship with Mae, but everyone knew what had happened to Oscar.

"Will came home to spend a few months with his mother and father the summer after Oscar left town for good. There was something wild and desperate about Will that summer. Mae sent him down once a week to help me out around the house. I've never seen him so out of sorts. That was back when I still made regular trips into town, and one day I saw them."

"Who?"

"Will and Beth. I was coming out of the drugstore and they were walking down the street. They weren't touching, but it was pretty clear they were together. Will saw me and he ducked into the nearest store. When I saw him the following week, I was livid. We got into an argument. He begged me not to tell his parents he was seeing Beth. He knew what had happened to Oscar but he still fought with me like I was trying to take away his new toy. He swore it was not serious and that, since he was heading back to school soon, it would end. "

Alice raised an eyebrow. "Only it didn't end, did it?"

Joylyn frowned. "No. It didn't." She sighed. "Listen, Alice. I don't really know what happened. Maybe no one but Will and Beth do, but Will left for college not too long after and Beth had definitely been roughed up. There were a lot of rumors, but then, there always were when it came to Beth Simms. Will never really came back home after that, not for any length of time. Beth left town shortly after. I doubt anyone was sad to see her go—certainly not me. Hearing she's back in town—well, that's not good news. Not for any of us." The bitterness in Joylyn's voice was so strong it made Alice's mouth feel chalky, but it was the worried look in her eye that chilled Alice to her core.

Fear gripped her heart as Alice let the story sink in, but a nagging question surfaced. "Joylyn. You said Oscar's injuries weren't Larry Lee's fault. What did you mean?"

"When I called the sheriff's office that night, they were already on their way to the park where Oscar mentioned he was meeting Beth. When they got there, they found Larry Lee dragging Oscar's body toward the woods. He told them he and Oscar had gotten into a fight and they arrested him." She paused.

"Funny thing though. Oscar was a strong boy, but the sheriff's deputies didn't find a single defensive wound on Larry Lee. It was like Oscar didn't even try to fight back. Unfortunately, Oscar still doesn't remember what happened very well. His head was badly injured. There was a lot of swelling on his brain—traumatic brain injury, they call it now." Seeing the look of concern on Alice's face, she added, "He's okay now. He has some scarring on his face and chest, but he recovered, thank God. He's got some really amazing doctors up where he's living."

"Wait." Alice frowned. "Are you saying you don't think Larry Lee was the one who beat up your son?"

Joylyn set her tea mug on the wooden table between them with a loud thump. "I know my son, Alice. He was a gentle boy, but he wasn't a wimp. I can't see Oscar standing there letting Larry Lee beat him to a pulp. The two boys weren't in the same class and they didn't know each well—our families didn't socialize. Why would Larry Lee beat up Oscar?"

"Because Beth told him to?" Alice responded, though a much different image was forming in her mind.

"I don't think so. I think he went up to the park and found Oscar already down."

"You think Beth attacked your son?" Alice couldn't get the incredulity out of her voice. "From everything I've heard about Beth, a strong breeze could knock her off her feet." Her attempt at levity was met with a stern stare. "I've seen her a few times around town. I'll grant you, she was probably in better shape back then. Now she looks like she's been used and abused pretty thoroughly. Still, I can't see her holding her own against a grown man."

"Don't underestimate Beth Simms. What she lacks in size, she makes up for in pure meanness."

Alice looked at her friend skeptically. "You make it sound like she's evil."

Joylyn's face was sobering. "Someone beat my son so badly he was almost unrecognizable and then left him to die. The first thought I had when I saw him was that I was looking at the work of pure hatred. Maybe I'm wrong, Alice, but I don't think it was Larry Lee who hated my son that way."

They each settled into their chairs, and this time, the silence stretched for miles, putting some much-needed distance between them and the taint of the story Joylyn had told. But the silence ended when Joylyn said, rather abruptly, "Alice, I'm quite certain Bill Bennett owned a gun. Might be a good idea for you and Mae to find it."

It felt nearly impossible to refocus on work, but once Alice made her way into town later that afternoon, she was glad she'd let Mae convince her to go. "You're only the third person I've found who's even heard of Juanita Jones," Alice said with a big smile. All the stress in her personal life had been pulling Alice away from her work. As much as she hated to admit it, she needed to make some progress on her article or tell her editor she couldn't do the job. Joylyn had referred her to Owen Thompson, a man whose family had owned the local garage in town for as long as automobiles had been on the road.

Owen grinned. "Well, to be fair, Mrs. Jones was murdered a long time ago. The reason I know about her is actually because of her husband. My grandfather did maintenance work for the prison crew Juanita's husband was working with after his release from prison. Grandpa Thompson worked on the truck that ran over Carney, so the story became a piece of our family history."

"I don't know much about the accident. It was mentioned briefly in a newspaper article."

Chuckling, Owen replied. "Accident may not be the right word. I expect the ole boy got what was coming to him. The man driving the truck was never charged. More like lauded as a hero."

Alice grimaced. She'd experienced too much vigilante justice in her life to take casual talk of retribution lightly. And with everything happening with Mae, she simply couldn't find the humor in Owen's story.

"Was there anything else you remember?" she asked, finishing up her notes.

"No ma'am. I think I've told you everything I was ever told. Sorry if it's not much help."

"Oh no, you've been a great help," Alice said. "I feel like I've been on a wild goose chase for weeks now."

"I can imagine. The people around here are pretty protective of their own. They can be a little stubborn."

Alice smiled. "I'd say so. Although I've heard quite a lot of venom about a few other characters."

"That would be the Simms family, I imagine."

"How'd you guess?"

"It's a small town, Mrs. Bennett. People have been talking about you since you got here. I feel like we're already old friends. The story of Mae's accident has been making the rounds as well."

"Joylyn Clement has been filling my head with stories of feuds and unimaginable violence. It seems like such a quiet place. It's hard to picture."

Owen nodded. "That's the funny thing about small towns. Take Juanita Jones, for example. I don't think anyone ever imagined something like that could happen in Pickens County, but it did."

Alice thought for a moment and then took a chance. "What about Beth Simms? I've heard all sorts of things about Larry Lee, but when I ask about Beth, people don't have much to say, except she was bad news and she got around."

Owen hesitated, and then said, "Well, that may be because it's you doing the asking."

"Me? Why does it matter?" Alice scrunched her nose in consternation.

Again, Owen paused, as if considering his words carefully. "Because you're Will Bennett's wife."

"What does that have to do with anything?" Alice began to feel agitated at the direction the conversation had taken. The idea that people were holding back because she was married to Will was frustrating.

"Listen, Mrs. Bennett . . . Alice. I think there are times when history is better left in the past, but with Beth roaming around here again, I think it's best to level with you. Your husband and Beth Simms ran around together one summer. It didn't last long, but the whole town was talking about it. You'd rarely see them together. Mostly up at the bar. Will seemed pretty nervous anytime anyone said two words to him when they were together. I can imagine he didn't want his folks finding out, though I can't imagine they didn't, eventually. When Will's father was alive, the animosity between those two families was legendary. Things settled down recently, but back then, I wouldn't have wanted to tell my parents I was seeing any Simms—much less Beth, who had a reputation that would make a sailor blush." Owen laughed, but then his expression became serious.

"Beth was never a good girl. Larry Lee at least gave it a try. He joined up with the military and, even after he was kicked out, he tried real hard to make it on his own. He should have tried it in some other town, because his family always dragged him back into the thick of things."

"What do you mean?"

"Anytime Beth got in trouble, Larry Lee was there to bail her out, clean up her messes. He got in more fights and spent more nights cooling off in jail because of Beth than any brother deserves. Then there was the business with Oscar Clement." Owen got a distant look in his eyes and was silent a moment.

"Oscar left town. Will went back to college. Things settled down for a while. Until the summer when Will came back." He wiped his brow, though Alice didn't see any signs of sweat. She wondered if it was a nervous habit.

"Will told me about dating Beth, Mr. Thompson. I don't understand what this has to do with anything, though. He's sure Mae doesn't know about their relationship."

"That may be. Even back then, Mae spent most of her time up in the mountains and she was never one for gossip." He grinned sheepishly.

"After Will left, Beth was changed. She wasn't just trouble anymore. She was a certifiable disaster. Vandalism. Violence. Drugs. If it was illegal or immoral, Beth was waist deep in it. I never understood how Beth managed to stay out of jail, or really how she even survived her lifestyle, but you didn't stay around her long enough to find out. I swear, the town heaved a collective sigh of relief when she left."

"So you think people aren't talking to me about Beth because of Will's relationship with her? That was so many years ago. Why would it matter?"

"Well, with Beth back in town—"

Alice sighed. "As interesting as all this may be, Mr. Thompson, here's what I really want to know, since you seem to know a lot about the Simms family. Do you think Larry Lee Simms would hurt Mae?"

"Maybe," Owen hedged. "Anything is possible, of course. But Alice," he took her hand across the table. "I don't think Larry Lee is the one you have to worry about."

22

"Jesus Christ, Larry Lee!" James walked in the front door after work and was taking in the carnage, his face twisted in anger. At least a dozen smashed beer cans littered the floor of the living room, and Larry Lee was lying half passed out on the far couch, barely hanging on to the can in his hand.

Larry Lee tilted his head up wearily, saw the expression on James's face, and laid his head back down again, closing his eyes. If he could make this day go away, he would.

"Fuck sakes, James. Keep your damn voice down." Larry Lee had intended to put some fight in his words, but the alcohol had done its job too well. He didn't even turn his head as he spoke.

"Look," James said, stepping around the garbage on the floor and taking a seat on the opposite couch. "You're my best friend and I love you, but you can't lay around here drinking all day. I'm tired of spending time after a long shift cleaning up after you. And you've really outdone yourself this time."

Larry Lee scowled, his words slurred. "What're you saying? Are you going to kick me out too, James?"

"No," James replied, but he was studying the floor like it could save his life. "But this is where I live, Larry Lee. My landlady's going to have a shit fit when she sees."

Larry Lee grunted. "I'll clean up the trash, man. Sheesh, relax. No reason why your landlady would even come in here anyway."

James looked at Larry Lee with eyes as wide as an owl's. "You've got to be kidding me, right? I'm not talking about the beer cans. I'm talking about the fence and your goddamned truck."

Now Larry Lee was alert. "What're you talking about?" He sat up quickly and then thought better of it as the room spun. He braced his hands against the couch to steady himself.

"The goddamned fence, Larry Lee. You took out the whole left side. Hell, your truck is only a foot away from that wall," he said, pointing toward the front door.

Larry Lee was on his feet and out the door in seconds. Sure enough, his truck sat on the lawn, having taken out half the fence. Larry Lee was so shocked, he stood there, gaping. Splintered pieces of wood stuck out from the mangled front fender and a new layer of damage had been done to the already tortured paint. Finally, in a strangled voice, Larry Lee shouted, "What the fuck!"

The sunlight caused Larry Lee's head to throb, but raw fury kept him moving. He walked over to the driver's side. The window had been broken in, leaving jagged shards of glass all over the front seat and floorboard. It even looked like someone had taken one of the glass shards and ripped up the upholstery. In a fit of rage, Larry Lee started pounding his fists into the door until bloody spots appeared in the dents.

James rushed over to Larry Lee. "Cut it out!" he said through gritted teeth. "You want the police out here before we can get the truck moved?"

After a moment, Larry Lee seemed to come to his senses. "Who did this?" he whispered, his eyes wide and bright with confusion, emotion turning his face an ugly purplish-red.

James seemed puzzled. "You telling me you didn't do this?"

"Of course, I didn't do this." Larry Lee was so exasperated he was beginning to feel faint. He looked up and down the street, but not a soul moved. "Where are the damned neighbors? Somebody had to have seen this happen?"

"A lot of things happen in this neighborhood nobody sees. It's one of the reasons I live here. The neighbors don't get involved. Now, go get your keys and let's get the truck back out on the street." James kicked at the ground. "Dammit, I'm going to have to pay to replace the fence."

Larry Lee gazed at the ground. James was his boy. He was still in shock over the latest attack on his personal property, but his mind wandered back to his run-in with his sister and his encounter with Alice Bennett. The scorn in Deputy Morrison's eyes when he gave Larry Lee the boot. Carver pulling him over and nearly catching him with the last of the things he'd stolen. His mother kicking him out. Larry Lee had often said how it seemed like the whole world was against him, but it wasn't until that moment that he really believed it. His heartbeat sped up as he glanced around nervously, the feeling of being watched making his skin prickle.

Fueled on anger and adrenaline, Larry Lee drove slowly up the mountain, on a mission of sorts, though not entirely sure what he hoped to gain. After taping up the window of his truck, Larry Lee and James had just sat down when the landlady nearly banged the door down. Apparently the neighbors did notice some things because someone had called Mrs. Johnson and boy was she was fit to be tied when she showed up at James's door.

It took nearly half an hour to calm her down, complete with promises to repair the fence and an understanding that Larry Lee was not to be staying on the premise for more than two more weeks. Both men had grudgingly agreed and hadn't spoken a word about it after she left. Instead, Larry Lee's mind was focused on Alice Bennett.

"That's got to be it," Larry Lee said, almost the second Mrs. Johnson had left. "I had a run-in with Alice Bennett this morning."

"I thought Morrison told you to stay away from her," James replied with a yawn.

"He did, and I've been doing my best, but I had to go to the library today. I made sure she wasn't there when I arrived, but when I was pulling out of the parking lot, she walked out in front of me. Nearly ran her over. Thought I was going to have a heart attack." Larry Lee snorted. "I was worried she'd report me so I got out and tried to make nice, but Morrison pulled up right then and got involved."

"So, what? You think Alice Bennett came over and drove your truck through the fence?" James said, incredulously. Even Larry Lee couldn't deny how ridiculous the idea sounded.

"Nah, man. But Morrison? He shows up every time I see her. Like he's tailing her. And the way he looks at her, it isn't brotherly love he's got for Alice Bennett. You should have seen the way he looked at me when he saw me talking to her."

"You think Morrison jacked up your truck?"

This possibility had more merit. Morrison had been the thorn in Larry Lee's side ever since the incident with the Clement boy. He'd never be one of Larry Lee's favorite people, but siding with the Bennetts put Morrison squarely on the side of the enemy. Paranoia fully fueled, Larry Lee stood up and said with confidence, "That's exactly what I think."

An hour later, he was in his truck, driving the back way up to the lake. He parked his truck up the hill at the Salvation Army camp and walked down toward the Bennett house. As he approached, he could smell smoke. People were beginning to use their fireplaces, but it had been a warm day and it didn't smell like wood smoke. As Larry Lee rounded the corner, he saw a small but steady stream of smoke coming from below Mae Bennett's house. Curious, Larry Lee approached with caution.

A small pile of grass and leaves had been set alight on the side of the house, too close to be safe. No one was tending the fire. For a moment, Larry Lee hesitated. He looked around, convinced Alice Bennett or even a workman would come around to check on the fire they'd started, but the house was quiet. He began to sweat. He didn't want to be seen at Mae Bennett's house, but the flames were starting to lick the siding of the house and before he knew it, Larry Lee was sprinting toward the errant fire.

He looked around for a source of water, but when he didn't see one, he started stomping at the grass fire, hoping to smother it without getting burned. The tinder was dry as a bone and despite his best efforts, the flames continued to spread. He was jumping up and down frantically when he heard a car pull into the driveway with footsteps racing in his direction. When he looked up, he stared into the eyes of Deputy Morrison.

"What the hell, Larry Lee!" Morrison yelled, then ran for the front porch.

"Water!" Larry Lee yelped as he leapt aside, feeling the heat of the fire through his jeans. He watched as Deputy Morrison finished dousing the grass fire with a hose coiled neatly on Mae Bennett's front porch, in plain sight of the road. Alice Bennett stood on the front porch staring icily at Larry Lee, despite his repeated protestations of innocence.

When the fire was put out, Deputy Morrison spoke quietly with Alice before turning his attention to Larry Lee. Alice walked into the house, shutting the door behind her. Larry Lee could hear the clicking of the lock sliding into place.

"So, tell me again, Larry Lee," Morrison said, and Larry Lee could tell there wasn't a thing he could say that the deputy would believe. Hell, he wasn't sure he'd believe it himself.

"Like I told you, I was taking a walk. Someone broke into my truck this afternoon and I needed to blow off some steam. I parked up at the camp and was walking down when I saw the fire. I would've put it out myself if you hadn't come along."

"Mm hmm," Deputy Morrison said, nodding. "A Good Samaritan, right? And you didn't see anything suspicious."

"No, sir," Larry Lee said, though he could hear the agitation in his voice. He'd come up here half-cocked, ready to teach the Bennetts a lesson, and it figured that it all went so wrong. Everything always went wrong for Larry Lee, especially where the Bennetts were concerned. Larry Lee sighed.

"I need you to come down to the office with me, Larry Lee. I'll get your statement and then have someone drive you to get your truck."

"Am I under arrest?"

Deputy Morrison gave Larry Lee a hard look. "No, but I'd think about laying low if I were you."

"That's all I've been doing lately. A lot of good it's done me," Larry Lee muttered.

"Listen." Larry Lee was surprised to see worry in Deputy Morrison's eyes. "Someone is trying to scare the Bennetts. Maybe worse. I don't think you set this fire, but you damned sure have the worst luck in the world. Or maybe I'm wrong."

"No," Larry Lee shook his head. "I think you're right." He could see that Morrison's concern was not for him, but for Alice Bennett. Either way, he was relieved to hear that even Morrison wasn't fingering him for whatever was going on with the Bennetts.

"Anyway, if you didn't set the fire, it's lucky for Mae Bennett you came along when you did. Either way, I'm going to get a statement from you and I'm going to be keeping an eye on you."

Larry Lee chortled. "So, more of the same. You and Carver."

Agitated, Morrison added, "I know you think I'm your enemy, Larry Lee, but I'm not, and really, I don't have to be. You're your own worst enemy." The deputy opened the back door of his cruiser and gestured for Larry Lee to get inside.

~

The three men sat around the table, silent but tense. Larry Lee had been taken to a small conference room at the sheriff's office, and as Morrison took his statement, Deputy Carver walked in, insisting he merely wanted to listen.

For the first time in his life, Larry Lee spilled his guts. No smirks. No sass. He simply told the two deputies everything that had happened lately, making special note of all the damage done to his truck. He figured he deserved at least a little sympathy given that he'd maybe saved Mae Bennett's house from burning down.

"So, who have you pissed off lately, Larry Lee?" Carver asked when Larry Lee had finished his tale and was guzzling the Coca Cola he'd been handed.

"You mean besides you," he gestured to the two deputies, "my mother, James, the Bennetts and pretty much everyone else in Pickens County?" His body felt heavy as he spoke. "The question is who haven't I pissed off lately. I'm not even trying right now."

The look Carver gave Larry Lee was just this side of compassionate and it made Larry Lee squirm.

"Noticed Beth is back in town. Is she planning on staying?" Morrison asked.

"I really don't know. She showed up at my house a couple of weeks ago and it wasn't two days later Mama kicked me out." Larry Lee thought about Beth and how badly things had been going for him since her arrival. He'd been so caught up in all the intrigue with Alice Bennett and then the vandalism of this truck that he hadn't spent much time thinking about how Beth factored in to the equation. The look on Morrison's face told a different story. "You think Beth had something to do with the fire?"

Morrison wrinkled his forehead but didn't answer.

"Truth is, Larry Lee, we don't know what's going on around here, but we can't help but notice how you keep popping up in the middle of things. Beth's reappearance doesn't exactly make us feel any better," Carver said, looking at Larry Lee with a meaningful expression, though he didn't quite understand it.

Larry Lee matched Carver's stare. "So, what're you going to do about it? Because keeping to myself isn't getting me anywhere. My truck is a fucking eyesore. Whoever took it and smashed it through the fence this morning is costing me money I don't have."

"I don't know, Larry Lee," Carver replied, honestly. "Maybe it's time to get out of Dodge for a while. If things keep happening while you're not around, at least we'll know for sure it's not you."

23

"I'm serious, Alice. This is getting out of hand." Will's angry voice was so loud over the phone that Alice had to hold the device a few inches from her ear. She was already getting a headache and dealing with Will wasn't helping.

"I hear what you're saying, Will, but your mother doesn't want to stay in a hotel." Alice had repeated this statement at least half a dozen times. It was clear Will was beyond caring what either his mother or his wife thought. And honestly, Alice wasn't entirely in disagreement. Seeing Larry Lee Simms standing across the street when the deputy had knocked on her door alerting her to the fire, Alice was furious. The events of the past few weeks had taken their toll and she'd had enough.

Deputy Morrison had assured her Larry Lee couldn't have started the fire. His showing up was either one of the unluckiest coincidences in the history of the world, or there was something else going on. Maybe both. Either way, Alice wasn't happy. She'd asked Mae if they could go into Atlanta for a few days, but with Rosy still healing and Mae's mobility still on the mend, Mae wasn't interested in being anywhere but home. Alice could see where Will got his stubborn streak.

Alice heard Will building up to another verbal assault and she cut him off. "Look, Will. Unless you want to come out and force the issue, I can't make Mae leave the house. She's comfortable here. The sheriff's office has decided to have an officer drive by the house several times a day. In the meantime, the fire may have been an accident. We were lucky it didn't reach the house, but we're fine." She couldn't help but pack a little *as if you cared* into that statement. Alice wasn't used to being forceful with Will, but the longer she stayed in Georgia, the more independent and capable she felt, despite all the craziness going on around her.

She focused on her breathing, waiting for the next onslaught. Instead, she was caught off guard by the change in Will's tone. "It's just that, if anything happened to you . . ." His voice cracked, and he broke off. She could hear his rapid breathing and wondered, momentarily, if Will was crying, though she immediately dismissed the thought as ridiculous. In all the years she'd known Will, she'd never seen him cry.

Not knowing what to say, Alice waited for him to continue. "I'd feel a lot more comfortable if you two were staying somewhere else. There aren't enough people at the sheriff's office to offer you the amount of protection you need." Will's words and tone were ominous, making Alice shiver. She struggled to remain calm.

"It's pretty clear to me someone is trying to get under Mae's skin. Deputy Morrison is taking this very seriously, and we'll try to be more vigilant until he has this figured out."

The silence between them stretched for miles.

Finally, Will sighed. "Okay. I don't think I can come out this weekend, but I'm going to try and take a few days off next week so I can stay a little longer."

Alice felt both thrilled at the prospect of having Will around for longer and worried. Will was an ambitious junior partner at his law firm, but keeping his position meant long hours and a willingness to prioritize business over personal life. Alice understood, mostly, why Will hadn't taken more time off to be with Mae. Intellectually it made sense, even if it didn't feel right. "Can you do that? Will the partners let you have the time?"

"I don't really care what they think, Alice." Her breath caught in her throat. "I need to be there. With you." They said goodbye and disconnected. Hope erased the irritation and fear Alice had been feeling, as visions of a happy reunion—a fresh start—with her husband consumed her. *This is why I'm here*, she thought.

By Thursday afternoon, Alice was reconsidering Larry Lee Simms as a likely suspect for the bad things that had happened to her and Mae. He was an easy target, and despite the sympathy she'd felt for him at the library, it was eerie how he managed to be in the wrong spot at the wrong time, every time. Her paranoia was fed by a near constant snubbing from the people she interacted with in the course of her research and the lack of progress in the investigation about the fall and the fire. Larry Lee's name kept coming up in the conversation, fueling the bitterness she felt. The only bright spot for Alice was Will's imminent arrival.

As she drove into Jasper, Alice looked out at the kudzu covering the trees on the side of the road. It reminded her of the town itself: a layer of growth over all things, beautiful and sinister. The town, which had seemed so open and welcoming when Alice arrived, now felt cold and closed to her. Even the librarian, Charlene—who'd been so helpful in Alice's first few weeks, if not a little bit annoying and overly familiar—had been distracted and unable to fulfill Alice's requests, citing computer glitches or lost materials. Work on her article had come to an almost complete standstill, and Alice was thinking about throwing in the towel for the first time in her professional career.

The only thing stopping her was the image of her father, his drunken eyes looking on her cruelly as he said, "You're nothing,

Alice. You're never going to amount to anything more than your whore mother." Alice had fought hard to escape the abuse, and then she'd struggled against the grip of alcoholism, which seemed almost like her father reaching out from the grave, trying to pull her in with him. Nothing had ever come easily to Alice, but despite all the tragedy in her life, Alice had made something of herself through hard work, determination and grit. She was a professional journalist with a successful husband. Maybe a chance at a real family, children of her own someday. She wasn't about to squander this chance at happiness, not to mention her sobriety.

It had been several days since the fire, and Alice found herself looking over her shoulder wherever she went, expecting to see Larry Lee Simms watching her. She had made the decision not to tell Will about Larry Lee's involvement, or lack thereof, knowing it would set Will off again. Instead, she'd glossed over the details of the incident and spent her time fending off Will's demands that she and Mae head for safer ground.

At Mae's insistence, Alice had gone back to her regular routine, spending a few hours each morning in town doing research. The one thing she'd finally gotten Mae to agree to was the purchase of a cell phone for times when Alice was away from the house. Alice had the locks re-keyed and was thinking about having a security system installed in the house. She'd hoped Will would help her sort it out, but he'd been too focused on trying to get them to leave. Alice had added it to the list of things she'd have to do herself, something she minded less and less as the days wore on.

Parking her car near the courthouse, Alice made her way to the Carriage House for lunch. She took a small table in the back of the restaurant and tried to be invisible. She'd almost made it through when she heard her friend Jim enter the restaurant, saying boisterous hellos to everyone he met as he made his way back to Alice's table.

"Good morning, Mrs. Bennett. Thanks for saving me a seat,"

he said, sitting down across from her as if it was the most normal thing in the world. Alice could feel eyes on her but she tried to ignore them as she offered Jim a small smile. Jim was oblivious to the tension—or at least he chose to ignore it—which made her feel a little bit more relaxed.

"Hello, Jim."

Looking concerned, Jim said, "Why the long face, Alice?"

She hadn't realized how close her emotions were to the surface until she felt warm tears welling up in her eyes. Embarrassed, she patted her eyes with her napkin. "Oh, it's been a rough couple of days," she said, trying to sound as casual as possible. Alice was unnerved by the knowing expression on Jim's face.

"I hear Mrs. Jenkins down in Tate wasn't too friendly."

"She's not the only one. How did you know about that?"

"Like I said before, it's a small community, Alice. People talk."

Alice sighed. "It's so frustrating. The more I learn about Juanita Jones, the more I feel for her. She was so young. The brutality she suffered was unspeakable. I wish I could tell her story but everyone clams up when I ask, or doesn't have a clue what I'm talking about. I can't just reprint the few newspaper articles I came across, and I haven't been able to reach the journalist who wrote the original article I read. He's retired and out of town."

It occurred to Alice that her interest in the story really was more about Juanita Jones and less about where it fit in the evolution of Georgia state laws, if at all. She was curious about Juanita herself—what kind of woman she'd been, her dreams and aspirations. She kept asking herself how this story had been forgotten so completely. Alice knew what it felt like to be overlooked, to be trapped in your own personal hell with no one around to care. She realized part of her motivation in choosing a writing career was to create something that would continue living even when she was gone. Her legacy. And unearthing the story of Juanita Jones was helping her come to terms with her own lost youth.

"Sally will come around. Folks around here are very protective."

"I keep hearing that." Alice sighed wearily. "I don't know, Jim. Ever since our meeting, I can't get anyone to talk to me. You're about the only person around here who is even willing to be in the same room with me." Alice smiled at him. "Are you breaking some code or something?"

Jim laughed. "I can't imagine anyone thinking they could shut me up." He winked. "I'll talk to Sally, if it'll help."

"Would you?" Alice beamed. "Oh, Jim, if you could get her to talk to me, even for a little while, that would be such a huge help. If I can't get any further with my research, I'm going to have to give up on this article and I don't want to do that to Juanita."

"I'll see what I can do." He patted her hand, then his face darkened. "I heard you ladies had some trouble up at Mae's house."

Alice sighed. "Good news travels fast around here, eh?"

"That it does. I heard Larry Lee Simms was lurking around."

Alice couldn't stifle a laugh. "It's funny. All I've ever heard about Larry Lee Simms is he's trouble. And yet, they can't seem to pin anything on him. How's that possible?"

"Larry Lee has gotten himself in a lot of trouble over the years, no denying it. It's hard, in a small place like this, to move past it. Forgiving and forgetting is not in our nature." His eyes drifted around the restaurant, stopping on a small figure near the front window. "Besides, Larry Lee isn't the only cause of trouble around here."

Alice followed his gaze and locked eyes with the woman from the diner her first night in Jasper, the one who'd left her feeling so scrutinized. "Is that—?"

"Yes, it is, my dear. Beth Ann Simms, Larry Lee's younger sister. And let me tell you, if Larry Lee is trouble, that young woman is the devil herself."

~

Alice sat in her car across the street from the restaurant sorting through her notes when she looked up and spied Beth Simms exiting the restaurant and walking swiftly toward the drugstore. When she didn't enter, but instead ducked around the far corner, curiosity got the better of Alice. She slipped out of her car and followed.

Approaching the corner, she could hear shouting.

"How dare you tell me what to do!" Beth paced back and forth between two parked cars on the street behind the drugstore, shrieking in her cell phone.

"Look who's talking about right and wrong! Well, you can go fuck yourself. I said it before and I meant it. I'm not doing you any favors. You know what I want and I'm not settling. You owe me."

Alice stood with her back against the building, listening to Beth talk, wondering who was on the other end of the line. When Beth stopped talking, Alice waited a minute before peeking around the corner. Beth sat on the hood of the one of the parked cars, facing away from Alice's hiding spot. Alice could see she hugged her chest tightly, her fingertips visible on her sides. She rocked back and forth. For several moments, Alice was mesmerized by the movement. Then Beth let out a guttural howl that sent the hairs on Alice's neck standing on end.

Shaken, Alice was about to leave when Beth's phone rang again. She put it to her ear and listened, her chest rising and falling heavily with emotion. The conversation lasted a long while, and it seemed to calm Beth down. Finally, she spoke.

"All right. I'll pick you up."

Alice had just enough time to duck back around the corner before Beth got into her car and started driving away, thankfully in the opposite direction from where Alice was hiding.

As Alice walked back to her own car, she pondered what she'd heard. She could still feel Beth's agitation deep down in her bones. Watching the other woman rocking reminded Alice of times when she'd wrapped her arms tightly around herself, an act of physically holding things together when life seemed about to fall apart. Alice's heart went out to Beth. Whatever was going on with her, it was clear to Alice that it was breaking her down.

On the other hand, Alice thought as she settled into the driver's seat, whoever Beth was talking to seemed to have bitten off more than they could chew.

24

As Larry Lee drove back toward his mama's house, he noticed a lone mourner at Sharptop Baptist Church. When he was younger, he'd spent a lot of time at the small cemetery near the chapel. His father was buried there, and for years after he died, Larry Lee made regular visits to his grave. Now, a figure was hunched over a grave near where Larry Lee's father rested. Curious, Larry Lee pulled into the church parking lot, wincing at the loud crunch of the gravel. After parking, he eased out of the truck, closing the door as quietly as possible and walking toward the cemetery. He hadn't made it far when he recognized the mourner. It was Beth.

Larry Lee froze. Beth was on her knees, her hood pulled up over her head. A few stray strands of hair peeked out around her face. Larry Lee expected her to turn and see him at any moment, but she seemed not to have noticed his approach. He watched her for more than ten minutes, prepared for the inevitable confrontation, but she never moved a muscle.

Then, he noticed her shoulder shaking. Much to his horror, Larry Lee realized his sister was crying. Her body spasmed with grief. From where he stood, it was hard to tell which grave she was kneeling in front of. It wasn't their father's. This grave stood apart from the area where his father rested. Larry Lee couldn't imagine anyone whose death would have such a profound effect on Beth.

Her sobbing, which had begun silently, picked up volume as the moments passed. She gulped in huge breaths of air, sniffled, and wailed like an animal in pain. Finally, she reached forward and touched the headstone. He heard a scraping sound like metal on stone. He could make out a shiny object in Beth's hand, sawing away at the headstone. Mesmerized by the scene in front of him, all Larry Lee could do was stand and watch.

Then, a new sound escaped Beth's lips. It started as a chuckle, low and hard to hear. Then it became a menacing roar: maniacal laughter that made Larry Lee shiver. She stood and began kicking at the headstone, guffaws becoming louder and more shrill as she exerted herself. Then, in a flash, she turned to the road and ran back toward the lake and Agnes's house. Not once did she look in Larry Lee's direction, consumed as she was in some kind of mania, leaving Larry Lee rattled.

When he was sure she was gone, Larry Lee walked slowly toward the grave, passing many familiar names on the way. He knelt down, settling into the indentions his sister had left on the grass. White powder and flakes dusted the surface of the grass nearest the headstone, the carnage from Beth's wild attack. He could see his father's grave marker in the next row.

Larry Lee put his hand up to the headstone. The name was completely illegible, marred by Beth's rampage. Running his fingers over the deep gouges, he realized the marker was made of concrete, not marble or granite—a burial for the poor. He noticed some of the scratches were older, smoothed over by the passage of time and exposure to the elements. He wondered again who was buried here.

~

Despite his mother throwing him out of the house, Larry Lee had stopped by nearly every day to drop off medicine or groceries. He crept in the door, leaving things on the kitchen table, not yet ready to exchange words with Agnes. He was still reeling from his stop by the cemetery when he pulled into the driveway.

"Larry Lee? That you?" his mother's voice came down the hall.

"Yeah, Mama." He laid the bag he'd brought on the table and was about to leave when Agnes entered the room. He'd seen Agnes looking bad, but the apparition approaching him made his blood run cold. Agnes's skin was gray, and he could see where her hair was falling out in clumps. She sat down heavily at the table and looked up at Larry Lee, her eyes bloodshot, one lid drooping. Or was it swollen?

"You don't look so good," Larry Lee said quietly, his voice hoarse.

"Don't feel so good either," Agnes replied. There was no fight left in her, and despite how badly she'd treated him, Larry Lee felt pity for the wretched woman sitting there. He took a seat across from her, still wary.

"What's going on, Mama?" he asked.

"I wanted to tell you . . ." she started, then her eyes grew wide.

From behind Larry Lee, the door creaked open. Beth stood there, smiling, a cold sinister smile. "I'm here, Mama. No need to trouble Larry Lee with your problems." Beth's eyes were red-rimmed and puffy, but she still looked insane, dangerous. Larry Lee looked back to his mother, but she'd shut her mouth tight and cast her eyes to the table.

"Mama?" Larry Lee said. He could see the old woman's hands begin to shake.

"Go on and get back to bed now," Beth cooed. Agnes stood unsteadily and walked back down to her bedroom, closing the door gently. Larry Lee thought he heard the click of a lock. He stood and faced his sister.

"What are you doing here, Larry Lee?" Beth growled, her eyes fierce with hatred.

"I don't see how that's any of your business," he replied, but he kept his distance. Beth's shoes were thick with mud, her face streaked with dirt. She followed his eyes down to her shoes.

"Better be careful out there, big brother. The ground is so thick with mud, you could be swallowed right up. No one would ever find you." She kicked off her shoes, smearing mud across the entryway. Larry Lee shuddered.

Padding across the room, Beth reached for a glass. "I'd ask you to stay, but I'm just not up to entertaining guests right now." The word *guests* rolled off her tongue like poison, a reminder that Larry Lee was no longer welcome in his own family.

Larry Lee walked slowly toward the door, angling his body to keep his sister is his sights. Normally, he'd be all too happy to fight it out with Beth, but this new version of his sister was unsettling. He knew what she was capable of, and he suddenly couldn't wait to get away from her. He walked out the door and got in his truck.

When he turned back toward the house, he saw Beth staring at him through the screen door. If looks could kill, he'd have been six feet under.

Larry Lee was sitting in the dark on the floor of James's apartment when James got home from work that evening. Flipping on the light switch, James jumped at the sight of his cousin. A second later, he started yelling, his voice still shrill from fright.

"What the fuck, Larry Lee!" He threw his car keys onto the kitchen table and grabbed a beer out of the fridge. "Every day it's some goddamned new thing with you."

James sat at the table and chugged his beer. Larry Lee made no move to stand. He studied James. They'd been friends since they were kids. He couldn't remember them ever having so much as argued, but James seemed more and more agitated with Larry Lee these days. It was one of many things in his life that had been turned on its head these past few weeks.

Larry Lee felt nearly unhinged after his run-in with his mother and sister and simply didn't have the energy for another confrontation. He was hoping to find a nice, neutral topic—turn the focus of the conversation away from himself.

"How's the job?" he asked.

To Larry Lee's surprise, James's face flushed.

"It's fine," James said, noncommittally, but Larry Lee could see the vein bulging in his neck, a sure sign of tension. The only time he'd ever seen James look so nervous was when he was lying, usually to the cops, but he'd never lied to Larry Lee. And they weren't even talking about anything serious.

"What's going on, James?" Larry Lee asked, his hackles raised.

James's expression hardened. "What do you mean, what's going on? It was a long fucking day. I'm tired. I come home and you're sitting in the dark like some weird zombie. I'm sick of all the bullshit, Larry Lee."

Larry Lee kept his gaze locked on James, which seemed to unnerve his friend. Finally, James scooted back in his chair, rose, and headed toward the door, grabbing his keys in the process.

"Fuck it. I'm going to go get something to eat." He was halfway out the door when he turned to face Larry Lee and asked in a conciliatory tone that sounded forced, "Want me to pick something up for you?"

Larry Lee paused. He was looking into the face of his oldest friend, feeling overwhelmed by suspicion. Over what? He couldn't say. Probably nothing. He tried to shake it off but the feeling stayed.

"Nah, I'm fine," Larry Lee said. James walked out the door into the night. Larry Lee switched off the light and sat back down on the floor, alone with his thoughts.

25

Jim was as good as his word and Alice was surprised to get a call from Sally Jenkins the following day.

"I'm sorry for storming out the other day, Mrs. Bennett," Sally said, her voice distorted with discomfort. "As you can imagine, that wasn't a very happy time in Tate."

Alice hesitated, wanting to watch her step and keep Sally talking. "I understand, Ms. Jenkins. I want you to know—I really want to tell Juanita's story, to honor her memory."

"I'm still not entirely comfortable talking with you about it," Sally managed, "but Jim Davis vouched for you and I trust Jim." She faltered, then continued. "People around here don't take kindly to dragging out dirty laundry, even when it's been forgotten by most. There was a lot of bad blood after the murder, as I understand it."

"I can understand why," Alice said. The line fell silent, leaving Alice to wonder whether she'd been hung up on. "Ms. Jenkins? Are you still there?"

"Yes. Listen, I'd like to think a little bit more about what I might be able to share with you."

Alice's heart deflated a bit.

"All right. Can I give you a call in a day or two?"

"I'll call you," Sally said, then disconnected abruptly, giving the whole conversation a clandestine feel. Alice sighed, disappointed, but rather than spend more time worrying about it, she decided to feel hopeful that Sally Jenkins might come around.

Alice put her research on hold for the rest of the afternoon in favor of some long-overdue yard work. The bushes around Mae's house needed tending, and Alice, after a fairly heated debate with Mae, was determined to cut back the plants near the front door, making it easier to see around the house and harder for anyone to hide.

She spent several hours hacking away at the bushes and bagging leaves and brush for removal when the sun came out strong and bright from behind the clouds. She went inside the house looking for a straw hat and found Mae sitting at the window, gazing out at the lake.

"It's getting hot out there," Alice said, walking past Mae to get a glass of water from the kitchen.

"I always loved living here," Mae said absentmindedly when Alice returned to the living room. "When the kids were younger, they'd spend hours every day swimming and canoeing on the lake. We're close to town but far enough away we always felt safe letting the kids play on their own. I always imagined grandchildren fishing off the dock like Will and Margaret used to."

The pain in Mae's voice was palpable. Alice and Will had been talking seriously about having children when Alice had gotten herself drunk and ruined everything. She had been hesitant. Given her allusions to an unhappy childhood, she felt Will should be more sympathetic about her fear of bringing children into the world. Of course, she'd never told him all the details, so maybe it was unreasonable to expect him to understand. She made a mental note to come clean with Will as soon as possible. If their marriage was going to work, they both needed to lay it all out on the table.

Alice took a seat across from her mother-in-law. "Are you feeling okay, Mae?"

Mae smiled. "Yes. I've been thinking about this place. Maybe it's wrong for me to cling so stubbornly to it. When Bill and I bought this house, this top section wasn't built. Bill's aunt was living out in the boathouse. We added this floor when we had Margaret." Mae's focus drifted again, as if scenes from the past were playing out before her eyes. "Margaret taught Will to swim. They were inseparable when they were little. Will toddled after Margaret, and she always looked out for him. I wish I knew why they've grown apart."

"Sometimes it's hard for siblings to stay close, especially when they live so far apart."

"Alice?" Mae looked searchingly into Alice's eyes. "Do you think Will would ever consider moving back here?"

Alice felt a little pang in her heart. Once upon a time, she'd harbored a wish that Will might want to move with her here to the Georgia mountains. She'd craved the stability of his family, not having had much of her own, but even Alice wasn't sure she'd want that now. Not wanting to create a false sense of hope, but also wanting to avoid hurting Mae, she hedged. "I guess time will tell." From the look in Mae's eyes, Alice could tell the older woman sensed she was being placated.

As she looked out the window, Alice noticed the bird feeders. "I'm going to mix up some sugar water for the hummingbirds," she said. With a small glass of the nectar, she walked carefully out onto the deck, filling each feeder, enjoying the cool breeze coming off the lake. Moving her gaze to the dock, she noticed something blue sticking out from behind one of the legs of the pier.

Walking back inside, she went to the far window and looked out again, but she couldn't make out what it was.

"Do you see that?" She pointed toward the dock.

"I'm not sure," Mae said as she moved closer to Alice. She

frowned. "Maybe something floated over from one of the other houses."

"I'm going to go check it out."

Alice grabbed a sun hat and headed out the front door. She walked down the stone steps that lined the side of the house, leading down the hill toward the lake. The lake level was down. Alice walked past the side of the dock toward the water's edge, watching her feet to avoid slipping on the steep hillside. When she neared the water, she screamed, and everything went black.

"She's alive." Deputy Morrison held Alice by the arms, speaking gently but firmly. "Alice, did you hear me?"

Alice could feel the deputy's hands on her arms, but his voice was distant. Her ears were ringing loudly and it was all she could do to focus on her breathing. As soon as she'd seen the body in the lake, Alice had been gripped by darkness. Luckily, she'd screamed so loud that Mae had heard and called the police. The EMTs had pulled Joylyn Clement out of the water, strapped her onto a gurney and were carrying her up the hill, slowly since the incline was steep.

"What did you say?" Alice managed, her voice weak.

"Mrs. Clement is alive, Alice." Morrison led her up the hill and onto the dock to take a seat on one of the benches and wrapped a heavy wool blanket around her. An EMT kneeled in front of her and began wiping at her cheek, her gauze coming away bloodied. The sight of the blood brought Alice back to her senses.

"Oh my God! What happened?" she nearly shrieked. Feeling hysteria creeping in again, she focused on the details of Deputy Morrison's face. She could see another group of officers searching the shoreline, taking photographs and asking questions of neighbors who'd come to see what all the commotion was about.

"We don't know." Deputy Morrison scratched his cheek,

bringing Alice's attention to the stinging sensation coming from her own face. "Ouch." She flinched as the paramedic cleaned the cuts on her face.

"Sorry, ma'am. It looks like your cheek hit some rocks near the water. I'll have this bandaged up in a second." The young EMT looked kindly at her and worked quickly.

Morrison continued, "Mae called us and we found you out here near Joylyn. You must have fainted. Thankfully, Mrs. Clement's body was only partially submerged. She was lucky—she could have drowned or succumbed to the elements if you hadn't found her."

"Is she going to be okay?"

"She's in pretty bad shape. It looks like she took a severe beating. Cuts and bruising all over her face and neck. She hasn't regained consciousness so it'll be some time before we know what happened. I can't imagine why she was here. Mrs. Bennett mentioned that Mrs. Clement was a frequent visitor, but she didn't stop by today."

Alice shook her head. "No, I've been home all afternoon with Mae."

"You didn't notice anything unusual?" Morrison asked, pulling out a notebook and pen.

"Not at all. I spent most of my time right here on the side of the house pulling weeds and trimming back the brush. I'm sure I would have heard something."

"It looks like Mrs. Clement had been laying out there for a while. When she wakes up, hopefully she'll be able to tell us what happened."

"When she wakes up? Do you know when that will be?"

Deputy Morrison frowned. "No. She's unresponsive. We're not sure when she'll wake up or how much damage there might be." He placed a reassuring hand on Alice's arm, but his touch was entirely unwelcome, causing Alice to shiver.

The paramedic finished cleaning Alice's wounds and began

gathering her things. Alice caught sight of her own blood on some white gauze and began to shake. Up to that point, she had managed to fend off memories of the past, keeping them at a dull roar in the back of her mind. Now, no matter how she tried, she couldn't keep her mind off that night so many years ago. Images of her father came flooding back in full force, unbidden and unwelcome. For once, Alice let them come.

After returning to the house, Alice lay down on the sofa to rest. Too tired to resist, she closed her eyes and soon she was sleeping, dreaming.

It had been deceptively quiet that day. Alice had come home from her miserable job at the lumberyard near her house and poured herself an illicit glass of her father's cheap whiskey as she did every night. She wasn't old enough to drink, not legally anyway, but being caught by the police didn't worry her.

On days like these, by dinnertime she'd be slurring her words—an alcoholic's daughter doing what came naturally. Most nights, Alice would be making dinner when her father walked into the kitchen, ranting about the noise. If she had a good day at work, she'd pacify him and the two would step into a slippery world of booze that would allow them to slide past each other without friction. If she had a bad day, she'd look for a fight, and she never failed to find one.

That night, however, the house was quiet. Alice began making dinner, awaiting the sound of his footsteps on the floor behind her, but they never came. By the time she'd put dinner on the table, she was overcome with nervousness. Quiet in her father's house was always a sign of impending danger. The last quiet moment they'd spent was the day her mother had died. Her father had been on a perpetual rage bender since then and Alice had learned to fear the quiet.

"Daddy?" she called tentatively, keeping the table between her body and the hallway where, at any moment, a furious monster would no doubt come hurtling down, fist clenched, eyes glazed. She realized she was holding her breath, but silence hung heavily in the air.

Slowly, Alice crept down the hallway toward her father's room. The door was closed and Alice knew better than to open it. Instead, she leaned her face close to the door, listening and hearing only the drumming of her heart in her ears.

"Daddy?" Her voice was barely more than a whisper. She waited minutes that seemed like hours before reaching down and turning the doorknob. Pushing the door painfully slowly, Alice felt fear coursing through her. She expected, or maybe hoped, she'd find her father, facedown on the floor in a pool of his own vomit. It had happened before. When she'd opened the door just enough to peek around the corner, she was overwhelmed by the acrid smell of blood that hit her like a wave, taking her breath away.

She threw open the door and there he was, his body sprawled halfway out of bed with his head lying on the floor. The blinds were down and the room was cast in a ghoulish half-light. Something dripped from the area near her father's neck and a puddle formed below his unmoving hand.

Alice's feet felt like they were glued to the floor and it seemed like time stood still. She tried to convince herself to move forward. *Maybe he's okay*, she thought, but even as the words formed in her mind, she knew there was no truth to them. Finally, she was able to inch forward. She reached out a hand to touch her father's back and could feel the heat coming off his body before she made contact. That gave her pause. Whatever had happened here had just happened. She surveyed the room and looked back at the door, expecting someone to appear.

"Daddy?" she said again, this time to confirm that her father could not answer her. She reached down to feel for a pulse and gagged when her hand came back covered in sticky blood. Backing away from her father's lifeless body, she stumbled into the hallway and slid down the wall, wiping furiously at the carpet to get the blood off her hand. She heard a shrill, frantic scream piercing the thick air in her house and looked around wildly, searching for the source, before she realized it was coming from her own mouth.

Whatever happened next had always been a blur. Before long, the police were pounding on her door and coming down the hallway, though she did not remember calling them. She remembered seeing blood smeared along the walls and what finally brought her to her senses was an officer asking her what she'd done. Finally, her brain snapped to attention and she screamed, "I didn't do it!" It had taken time to clear her name—time when everyone around her thought she was capable of murder. It was her rock bottom and though it had taken years, she had climbed out of that hole, but the memories could swallow her whole if she let them.

26

Carver had just decided to give up his self-appointed task of following Larry Lee when things finally got interesting. In fact, he'd been on his way home when he saw Larry Lee's truck heading up toward the lake. It was late, and Carver was tired. Agnes Simms lived that direction, so there was no real reason to follow, but something in his gut told him to make the effort. Larry Lee wasn't living with Agnes at the moment, so why visit at this time of night?

Of course, following anyone up this particular stretch of road at night was a challenge. There were no other cars, so Carver decided to take the back road up to the top of the hill and then double-back to catch Larry Lee on his way up. When he reached the Salvation Army camp, he was surprised to see the truck approaching in the distance. Hoping he hadn't been noticed, Carver pulled in beside one of the buildings and waited for Larry Lee to pass. Instead, Carver heard the truck approach and then the engine stopped.

"Dammit," he muttered under his breath, easing his car door open and hoping he could peek around the corner quietly enough. From his hiding spot, he wasn't sure where Larry Lee had parked. With each step near the edge of the building, his boots crunched and he cringed. When he finally got closer to the parked truck, he could hear an argument taking place in the cab. It was loud and had masked the sound of his approach.

He might have turned around. He certainly wasn't going to catch Larry Lee in the act of robbing a house out here, but two things bothered him. First, Larry Lee wasn't alone. The passenger appeared much shorter and he might have suspected it to be a date, except for the second thing. The passenger was shouting. Carver could hear a near constant stream of yelling from a distinctly female voice. The driver held his head down low, and as far as Carver could tell, he never did respond. If this was a date, it wasn't going well.

Finally, the passenger got out of the truck, slamming the door behind her. Carver stayed still, waiting to see what would happen next, but while the woman began walking down the hill toward the lake, the driver stayed put.

Lovers' quarrel? Carver couldn't imagine Larry Lee finding the time to get a date under the current circumstances. The whole town knew Charlene the librarian had a thing for this bad boy, but Larry Lee had never returned her advances. Besides, the woman who'd exited the car was rail thin and much too short to be Charlene Walker.

Carver couldn't see well enough in the darkness to make out either the passenger or the driver for that matter. For a moment, he was stumped. If he got back in his car and drove away, Larry Lee would see him and whatever might be up would be interrupted. On the other hand, Carver wasn't in the mood to watch whatever kissing and making up might be in store once the woman cooled off.

He decided to wait it out. He walked slowly back to his car, sat in the front seat with the door still open and waited. He'd been sitting for nearly an hour and was ready to swing back into the car and go home when the truck's engine started up again. Tires spun, kicking up gravel, as the truck sped off down the lake road.

Carver hesitated only a moment before getting behind the wheel, slamming the door and taking off down the road after Larry Lee, but that moment's hesitation, and the particular position he'd chosen to park in, delayed his start long enough that when Carver made it down toward the Simms house, Larry Lee's truck was nowhere to be seen.

The Simms house was dark. Agnes's car was parked outside. There was no movement. No reason to interrupt the quiet.

Carver headed back into town, still thinking he'd catch up to Larry Lee. He drove all the way to James's house. Larry Lee's truck was nowhere to be seen, but the lights were on inside the house, the curtain parted. As Carver drove by, he could see Larry Lee Simms slumped on the couch, his head tilted back in sleep. As he drove home, Carver realized someone had made Larry Lee the perfect scapegoat and they'd all been dragged along the wrong trail.

It wasn't until their morning debriefing that Carver heard about what had happened to Joylyn.

"They have her in ICU." Morrison had taken them through the facts of the case, his voice flat, his posture deflated. Carver was in shock.

"The Bennetts didn't see anything at all?" Carver asked thinly. "It happened right outside their house."

"You can't really see that part of the dock from the house, I looked," Morrison piped up, suddenly defensive. "Alice was lucky to have noticed Joylyn's jacket—"

"Alice? Jesus, James! Your crush on Will Bennett's wife is getting ridiculous. Since she got here, the whole town's going insane over that woman and you're right at the front of the pack, licking her boots."

"Now, wait a sec—" the sheriff interjected on Morrison's behalf.

"Unbelievable," Morrison huffed over the sheriff's protestation, but his cheeks were bright red.

Carver's face was hot with fury, and though he felt guilty for unloading on Morrison, it felt good to let out some steam. Carver had known Joylyn Clement his whole life, even harbored a crush on her before she got married to John. The idea of someone attacking Joylyn was overloading his system. If Carver had a breaking point, he was pretty sure they'd reached it.

A stalemate ensued. Morrison glared. The sheriff looked exasperatedly from one deputy to the other. Finally, Carver broke the silence.

"I'm sorry," Carver said to the sheriff. He wasn't about to apologize to Morrison. "I'm very disturbed by the direction things are taking here. We're still having break-ins but they're different than before, more erratic. I've been keeping an eye on Larry Lee Simms; he's not responsible for the latest ones for sure." He babbled, thinking out loud in hopes that something would begin to make sense.

"Joylyn was targeted," Morrison offered.

Carver shot him an incredulous glare. "Brilliant. How long did it take you to figure that out?"

"Carver," the sheriff warned.

Carver adopted a face he hoped conveyed remorse even if he didn't feel it, but he was done apologizing. His mind was racing.

"Sheriff. I followed Larry Lee up the hill last night—I thought it was Larry Lee anyway. He was parked at the Salvation Army camp and there was a girl with him. It was late. I think they had a fight because she got out of the car and walked off. He took off a while later, bit of a rush. Left the girl there—not sure where she went—but on my way home, I saw Larry Lee at James's house, asleep."

"Your point?" the sheriff asked, his impatience coming through.

Carver was about to respond when Morrison interrupted. "I think his point is that someone was up near the lake late last night in Larry Lee's truck. Everything seems to be centered on the lake community and Larry Lee is the common factor. Maybe he's guilty. Maybe not, but someone sure knows we'd suspect him."

"It was strange," Carver added distractedly. He was thankful Morrison had followed him along his current train of thought, but something wasn't quite right. "I heard whoever was in that truck raising a commotion. It's hard to believe anyone could get yelled at like that and not yell back."

Morrison stood. "Once again, we have more questions than answers. Looks like I'll be paying yet another visit to our friend, Mr. Simms. Seems like he's at the middle of this whether he likes it or not."

27

A pounding at the door startled Larry Lee awake. He put his arm over his eyes, thinking the pounding was coming from his brain, a symptom of another night spent drowning his misery in cheap booze. Before long, the banging was accompanied by a voice he recognized all too well. He groaned.

"Larry Lee! Open up. I need to talk to you."

"Just a goddamned second!" Larry Lee shouted, searching for his jeans, which he finally found bunched up near the foot of the couch. Having been cooped up in James's place, not wanting to risk another run-in with the police, Larry Lee felt prickly and irritated. He pulled on his jeans and hobbled to the door. As he flung it open, he yelled, "What do you want?" He regretted it almost immediately as he found himself face-to-face with Deputy Morrison.

"You smell like hell, Larry Lee," the deputy said, waving away the odor dramatically.

"Yeah, well, there's not much to do when you're being held prisoner." He gestured to the wreck that was once James's living room.

"They'd certainly make you shower in prison," Morrison said sarcastically. "I need to know where you've been the past few days, Larry Lee."

"You hard of hearing? What did I just say?"

"You're telling me you haven't left this house in the past two days?" Deputy Morrison eyed him skeptically.

"Not even to get some smokes," Larry Lee confirmed haughtily, leaving out his visit to his mother's house, a visit he'd been trying hard to forget. "James has been stocking up so I can 'lay low' as you so eloquently ordered me to do."

The deputy frowned. "Has James been driving your truck?"

"Shit no." Larry Lee's back ached from spending too much time on the couch. He stretched. "James wouldn't be caught dead in my truck, especially now that someone fucked it up so badly."

"Where is it now then?" Deputy Morrison looked behind him toward the street.

"You woke me up to ask me about where my truck is? It's right across the street, you stupid—" but his voice trailed off when he saw that his truck was not where he'd left it. "What the hell? Someone stole my goddamned truck!"

Larry Lee made his way toward the street, his feet still bare, his jeans still unbuttoned. He reached into his pockets, first one and then the other and muttered, "Keys."

Turning around, he went past Morrison and back into the house, where he proceeded to turn the room upside down looking for his keys. Rage surged through Larry Lee's veins, making him feel absolutely out of control. He wanted to scream.

"Where *is* James?" Deputy Morrison asked from the doorway, snapping Larry Lee back into reality.

"At work, I guess. He's been working on a construction site over in Big Canoe for a few weeks."

The deputy raised his eyebrows, but said nothing. "Maybe he took your truck to work?"

Larry Lee looked at the deputy dumbfounded. "I don't see why he would. He has his own car and it's definitely not where he usually parks it."

"You're sure you haven't been up by the lake in the last few days?"

"I said I hadn't. I'm not stupid, Deputy. You told me to stay away so I'm staying away."

Deputy Morrison nodded in acknowledgement and turned to leave, but before closing the door he said, "Funny though. Since several people saw your truck parked up at the camp again this morning." He closed the door, leaving Larry Lee sitting in a heap, agitated and confused.

It didn't occur to Larry Lee until much later that the deputy didn't even care his truck had been stolen. He didn't offer to take a report. Didn't offer even a word of sympathy. It would probably be this way forever if he stayed in Pickens County, being everyone's scapegoat and no one's concern. The thought was depressing and Larry Lee was feeling pretty sorry for himself when James walked in.

He took one look at the living room and started in on Larry Lee. "For God's sake, Larry Lee. This house is not your personal pissing ground." He stomped over to the refrigerator to pull out a beer, but came away empty-handed. "You drank the whole case?"

"Nice to see you too," Larry Lee spat. "What happened, you ask? Well, let me tell you since you obviously don't give a shit. Someone stole my truck and I was searching for my keys, which are gone too."

"These keys?" James reached into his pocket and pulled out a key ring with a few keys on it. He tossed it to Larry Lee, who eyed him suspiciously.

"You had them?"

James shrugged. "I accidentally picked them up on my way out this morning. Didn't figure you'd miss them since you aren't going anywhere."

"You should have brought them back," Larry Lee said. "What if I'd had an emergency? Needed to go somewhere?"

"Where you gonna go, Larry Lee? You don't have a job. You don't have a place to live, and you're not supposed to be traipsing around town. The law's got you in hiding, right? Where are you gonna go?" James's tone was indifferent. Just one more person who didn't really give a damn about Larry Lee. Larry Lee could feel his control slipping, his stomach churning with fury.

"Did you take my truck?" Larry Lee lashed out at his friend, seeking a target for the cold rage storming inside him.

"That piece-of-shit truck?" James sniggered and in the blink of an eye, Larry Lee was on him. He landed a few punches before James managed to shove him off, wiping at a split lip, his cheek already beginning to swell.

"Dammit," James muttered, spitting out bloody saliva on the living room floor.

"You deserved it, you son of a bitch," Larry said, his body still tense, waiting for James to take a swing at him. Every ounce of pent-up energy and aggression was coursing like blood into his fists, waiting to be released. Instead of fighting, James stood upright, his expression resolute, angry but cold.

"Get the hell out of here!" he yelled at Larry Lee.

Any other day, Larry Lee might have tried to sweet-talk James into changing his mind, but the weeks had worn Larry Lee down and their fight had taken the last of his energy. Hearing James tell him to go drained the last bit of adrenaline, and with it, his pride. He grabbed his bag, stuffed a few random articles of clothing inside, and left, slamming the door behind him. His keys were back in their spot in his pocket, but his truck was still nowhere to be seen.

Larry Lee trudged into town, mopping at the sweat on his forehead and neck until his sleeve was soaked. He stopped in at the drugstore to get some water and a pack of cigarettes, which he knew would have to last him awhile—money was running out.

Then he shuffled down Main Street toward the courthouse. It was too early for lunch, but he decided to stop in at the Carriage House for a cup of coffee, knowing it would be quiet at this time of day.

He walked straight back to a table in the corner, barely visible from the front door, flagged down a waitress and ordered a cup of joe. He was busy nursing his coffee when he heard the door open. He looked up in time to spy Beth's mousy head as she took a seat at a table near the window. Her seat was angled so Larry Lee couldn't quite see her face.

Seeing Beth gave Larry Lee a gnawing pain in the pit of his stomach. Their whole lives, anytime something bad had happened to Larry Lee, Beth was somewhere nearby. One thing was painfully obvious—if Beth was back to stay, Larry Lee would have to go—it was a simple matter of self-preservation. He pressed himself into the wall to make sure he couldn't be seen.

More tables began to fill as the lunch hour approached and Larry Lee was relieved at the distraction. The crowd provided a useful buffer between himself and his sister. Unfortunately, in order to avoid her, he was stuck at his table until she left; so he decided to order some lunch. A quick look in his wallet gave him an idea of what he could afford. Not much. The last of the money he'd stolen from his mother, plus a little he'd pilfered from James, was nearly gone. He needed to get a job. Maybe he'd look further out of town for a change.

When the waitress came to deliver his meal, Larry Lee looked up and saw James walk in the door. Instinctively, he began to raise his hand to wave him over when James took the seat across from Beth without hesitation. They were both turned away from him facing the window, and Larry Lee leaned out as far as he thought was safe. He watched as they talked, both faces twisted in anger. Finally, Beth smiled and Larry Lee watched in horror as she leaned across the table and kissed James full on the mouth, then got up and walked out of the restaurant without another glance. James, looking guilty, paid the bill and left shortly thereafter.

"Not hungry?" The waitress's appearance at Larry Lee's table startled him. He looked down at his untouched plate.

"Not much. Can you box this up for me?"

"Sure thing." She returned with his food and a meager amount of change, which he stuffed into his pocket rather than leaving a tip. Larry Lee walked cautiously toward the door, making sure the coast was clear before he exited the restaurant and made his way toward the library.

28

Alice drove Mae to the hospital for her physical therapy. While she waited, she stopped in to check on Joylyn. There had been no change. It made Alice's stomach turn to see the yellowing bruises on Joylyn's swollen face. It looked as though someone had clawed at Joylyn's skin, leaving trails of angry red lines down her cheeks and on her neck. Mae had been asking to visit, but Alice had been reluctant, not wanting to upset Mae further. Seeing Joylyn's face, Alice was sure she'd made the right decision and yet, she wondered if a visit to Joylyn would convince Mae that getting away from Jasper for a while was the right thing to do. When Alice picked her mother-in-law up from therapy, Mae's first words were, "Let's go see Joylyn."

Grudgingly, Alice agreed. They made their way slowly toward Joylyn's room. When they walked in, Mae gasped and squeezed Alice's arm. "Oh my Lord," she whispered.

"I spoke with her doctor earlier. They say her vitals are good, but she still hasn't woken up, which is actually a good thing because it's giving her body more time to heal."

Alice helped Mae over to the armchair next to Joylyn's bed. Mae took her friend's hand, stroked it gently and murmured words of comfort. Still looking at Joylyn, she said softly, "Joylyn was the first one there when Bill died." Alice could see tears welling up in her mother-in-law's eyes. "She was there before the ambulance arrived. She did CPR even though we both knew he was gone. I don't know what I would have done without her."

She paused and then asked, her voice shaking, "Who could have done this?" Mae's eyes turned to Alice and for the first time, Alice saw fear.

"I don't know, Mae." Alice walked over and stood beside Mae, resting a hand on her shoulder, unable to find any words to comfort her.

The previous evening, Alice had another heated discussion with Will. He was frantic when she told him about Joylyn Clement, begging her to take his mother to Atlanta, but in spite of everything, Mae was adamant about staying in her home in the Georgia hills. Alice wondered if the sight of one of her dearest friends, beaten to within an inch of her life, would weaken Mae's resolve.

There was a knock at the door, and Alice shifted in time to see Deputy Morrison enter the room.

"Oh, hello Alice. Mae. I didn't know you were in here."

For a moment, Alice felt a rush of indignation at the intrusion and Morrison's uncanny way of finding her wherever she went. He may have been well-meaning, but his constant presence made Alice feel ill at ease. With Mae in the room, however, she pushed her feelings aside and stood to shake the deputy's outstretched hand. "We stopped by after Mae's therapy appointment to check on her. The doctor says there's not much change."

"I spoke with her doctor a few minutes ago. They're optimistic she might wake up today, maybe tomorrow. She's been stirring. Her son Oscar should be here within the hour."

Mae perked up. "Oscar is coming?"

Deputy Morrison nodded. "No one is sure how much care Joylyn will need when she comes to. I think Oscar is planning on taking her home with him as soon as she's able to travel."

Mae looked rattled. Alice sat down again and put a hand on her mother-in-law's shoulder. "It makes sense, Mae. You told me Oscar's been trying to get her to move up with him for years. I know she didn't want to leave her home, but things have changed." Alice looked over at the fragile woman lying there, unnaturally motionless.

"I suppose so," Mae replied, but Alice could see the sadness in her eyes.

The Bennett house had been quiet all afternoon, with Alice and Mae moving gingerly around one another, neither wanting to broach the subject of Joylyn Clement or the horrible things happening in Mae's previously sheltered life. Tension in the house was thick. Over dinner, the clank of spoons hitting soup bowls began to grate on Alice's nerves. Finally, she said, "Mae, we should talk about going to Atlanta. Or maybe even you coming back home with me and Will."

Mae sighed. "I know I've been stubborn, Alice. I've lived in this house nearly forty years and it's hard to imagine living away from it."

"I understand. But it's not safe right now. I don't know what is going on around here, but I don't mind telling you I'm scared. Seeing Joylyn today brought home how real this is, how vulnerable we are, especially up here in the mountains. Whether it's Larry Lee Simms trying to terrorize us or not, we're sitting ducks up here. Will is right. The sheriff's office doesn't have enough manpower to keep us safe all the time."

Mae nodded, and Alice could see how much effort it took. She could empathize. After her father's death and the investigation that followed, no one seemed to understand why Alice would stick around in a town where she'd been abused, shunned and even accused of murder. Alice could never properly explain how the thought of leaving was much scarier than the thought of staying.

"Why don't we start off small?" Alice suggested. "We'll go stay at a nice resort in Atlanta, like we're on vacation. I'll make arrangements for physical therapy in one of the hospitals there."

Mae's eyes brightened. "A vacation sounds nice."

"I'll find someone to keep an eye on the house. We'll stay in touch with Deputy Morrison while we're gone. Hopefully by the time we're ready to come home, they'll have sorted this whole mess out."

Alice pumped as much enthusiasm as she could into her words, though she doubted the police would manage to uncover much more with them gone than they had with them here.

"Okay. I think that will work."

Alice saw the uncertainty in Mae's eyes, so she pushed ahead hoping to keep up the momentum. "I'll start making arrangements tomorrow. Why don't you call Margaret and fill her in on our plan?"

Both women stood and headed toward the living room, leaving their dinner dishes on the table for Alice to clean up later. They'd made it as far as the couch when the doorbell rang. Mae took a seat near the phone and Alice went to open the door.

Mae never received unannounced visitors, and the last one—the unknown woman with the warning—wasn't pleasant. Alice jumped when she opened the door to Larry Lee Simms.

"Alice? Who is it?" Mae's voice was coming nearer, but Alice was too shocked to speak. Then she heard a gasp. Mae stood in the hallway and stared at Larry Lee with an expression of horror. Her face had gone pale.

"You!" Mae's voice traveled down the hallway with more force than Alice had ever heard. Alice looked back and saw her mother-in-law begin to shake. Leaving Larry Lee standing at the door, she rushed to help Mae to her seat. She heard the door click behind her and realized Larry Lee had followed them in, shutting the door behind him.

Alice turned. “Get out of here!” she shouted, but despite her anger, she couldn’t hide the quiver in her voice. Larry Lee froze in place. Alice was surprised to see fear on his face.

Larry Lee looked disheveled, like he had neither slept nor washed up in days. His eyes were pleading, and there was nothing menacing about him now. “Please, Mrs. Bennett, I need to speak with you.”

A determined expression had taken hold of Mae’s face. “It was you.” Mae couldn’t get any more words out.

Alice looked at her mother-in-law, confused, but seeing the look in Mae’s eyes, Alice suddenly knew, without a doubt. Once again, she turned to Larry Lee, but this time she placed herself between Mae and the man in front of her, ready to fight if it came to that.

“You pushed her, didn’t you?” As she spoke, Alice searched for her phone, spotting it a few feet away on a side table. Larry Lee followed her eyes and saw it too. He reached down, picked it up and handed it to her.

“Go ahead. Call the police. Hell, I’m surprised they’re not already knocking the door down.”

Alice had been thinking the same thing. Maybe this thought made her hesitate. Maybe it was the desperation emanating off of Larry Lee in waves. Keeping a firm grip on the phone, she asked, “Why are you here, Larry Lee?”

Shifting his weight from foot to foot, Larry Lee looked like a captive animal ready to bolt. He didn’t seem threatening. He seemed lost and terrified.

“Something’s going on around here.” He rubbed his hands together nervously. “Something . . . I don’t know . . . I think someone is trying to set me up. I’m starting to think it may be my sister, Beth.”

Cautiously, Alice said, “Did your sister attack Mae?”

Larry Lee looked at Alice, the truth revealed in his eyes before he even spoke a word. "No. I did."

Alice's finger hovered over the call button on her phone, but Larry Lee had made no move and she hesitated.

"I pushed Mrs. Bennett. I was drunk and angry. I was walking down the hill and when I saw her walking her dog home, I flipped out. I wasn't trying to kill her. I wasn't thinking."

"Who cares what you were trying to do. The truth is, you almost *did* kill her," Alice spat, disgusted with what she was hearing.

"Look, I'm a screwup. I always have been. I'm not making excuses for what I did, and I will stand right here while you call the cops, but please hear me out."

"Why?" Alice asked, stunned by the coldness in her own voice.

Larry Lee looked down to the floor. "Because something bad is happening around here. Something else. Something that doesn't have anything to do with me, regardless of how it looks. And you may be the only person in town who'll believe me."

29

Alice let her hand fall to her side, but she kept a firm grip on the phone like a lifeline. "Have a seat," she said, gesturing to the armchair nearest the door. She led Mae back toward the sofa, positioning herself again between Mae and Larry Lee.

Mae seemed to be recovering from her initial shock. Her eyes shone brightly when she asked, "What do you need to tell us, Larry Lee?"

Larry Lee shifted uncomfortably in his seat. Now that he'd been given permission to speak, he seemed tongue-tied. "Ever since the night I pushed Mrs. Bennett—" His voice shook. He didn't make eye contact with either woman as he spoke, his face downturned as if examining every fiber in the carpet. "Everything has been going wrong. Not like things have been all that great anyway, but it seems like I'm always in the wrong place at the wrong time, you know?"

He shot a quick glance in Alice's direction and their gazes locked. There was so much resignation in his eyes, it made her heart ache, despite her best efforts to stay angry.

"I don't know when Beth got back to town, exactly. She's been gone a long time. Everyone seems scared of her. Even Mama. And I don't know why, but I feel the same. She's wild and . . . deranged. I've never seen her like this before."

He became more agitated as he rambled. Alice let him speak without interrupting, sure anything might set him off.

"It's like the other day with the fire. I was on the way to my mother's house when I saw the smoke."

"Did you see Beth that day?" Alice asked, apprehensively.

"No. Then Morrison showed up and he assumes it's me. That's the way it always is around here. They assume it's me. And I admit, sometimes it is. Maybe *most* of the time, but not this time."

"Why would Beth set the fire?"

After a few moments of silence, Larry Lee shrugged. "I don't know. I've never understood Beth's reasons for doing the things she does. I'm not even sure it was her, but I know it wasn't me. And she keeps popping up around town and I know enough to know she's up to something. I just don't know what it is."

Alice looked to Mae for a cue, but her mother-in-law sat silently, her hands folded in her lap, a thoughtful expression on her face. Alice wondered what she must be thinking. Here she was, confronted by the man who had, admittedly, attacked her and left her for dead, and she seemed eerily calm. That, more than Larry Lee's presence in the room, sent Alice's heart racing.

Mae noticed Alice looking at her and smiled. "I'm all right, Alice." To Larry Lee, she said, sternly, "Did you hurt Joylyn Clement, Larry Lee?"

"No," he replied steadily, but he didn't elaborate. Alice saw no traces of guilt on his face, but he didn't offer any further information. Instead, he looked crestfallen, like he couldn't believe anyone would suggest such a thing.

Alice suspected she'd worn that look a time or two. She thought back on days when she was the one everyone looked at when anything went wrong. Her growing compassion for Larry Lee was at war with her loyalty to Mae.

"What is it that you want us to do?" Alice asked, more snappishly than she'd intended, unable to quell the tumult within her.

"I want you to be safe," he said simply, and Alice was astonished to find him looking directly at her when he said it. She felt herself blush. "I want you to know, whatever I've done in the past, this time, it's not me."

Not knowing what to say or how to react, Alice strained to keep her voice steady as she said, "Okay. You've had your say, Larry Lee. I think you need to go."

Larry Lee nodded and stood. Alice rose and stepped toward him, looking back at Mae to say, "I'll see Larry Lee to the door, Mae—Mae?" But her mother-in-law was lost in thought.

Alice's mind was ablaze as she followed Larry Lee to the door. She felt like the very fabric of her life was unraveling. Coming to Georgia had forced her to face parts of her past she'd been trying to forget, bringing to light the fact that in doing so, she'd taken some serious missteps. Most alarming was how little she seemed to know about the man she'd married and his life before her. There was a distinct possibility that her perfect, stable life was a lie.

She was so wrapped up in her own thoughts she almost ran into Larry Lee, who'd stepped over the threshold and then stopped abruptly.

Flustered, she said, "Good night, Larry Lee." They were standing on the same spot where Larry Lee had struck out at Mae Bennett in drunken wrath, nearly killing her, whatever his intentions. The thought made Alice shiver.

Larry Lee had turned and was facing Alice now, his eyes deep in a shadow cast by the porch light. His expression was a mask of tight, barely controlled emotion. For a moment, she was afraid. All the sympathy she'd felt inside, the control she'd felt she had, erased by the darkness.

"Alice," he said, his voice husky and vulnerable. "Alice, I don't think it's safe for you here." It looked like there was more he wanted to say, but he held his lips tight together, barring the words from escaping his mouth.

"Is there something you're not telling me?" she asked, anger welling inside her. She had had enough of the stalling, the lying, the subterfuge. She was tired, and Larry Lee was a convenient outlet for all the tension she'd been holding in. She was on the verge of exploding, or imploding, and she knew how self-destructive she could be.

Larry Lee stepped back, instinctively, as if scorched by the venom in her voice. Alice wondered how many people had taken their rage out on Larry Lee Simms.

"No. I've told you everything I know. I've seen you in town, Alice. You're out there riling people up. This is a small town. Even *I* hear the talk. I don't know what my sister is up to, but I've seen what's been happening around here and I'm worried."

"About Mae?"

"No," and for a moment, his expression turned almost tender. "About you?"

Alice was unnerved, and as she stood there, she felt weak, terrified. Larry Lee, of all people, was poking holes in her carefully constructed armor. That made her mad. Enraged. Steeling her nerve, she laughed, cold and hard. "About me? Why are you concerned about me, Larry Lee? You haven't exactly been friendly since I got here. So, you'll have to excuse me if I don't swoon over your concern for my welfare."

The words shot out of her mouth like bullets, full of venom and fire. Even as she said them, she knew that Larry Lee was not really the target of her fury. As she looked into his eyes, she saw she had wounded him with her words.

He sighed. "You're not the first or the last person who's ever accused me of lying. I'm not asking you to forgive me for what I did to Mrs. Bennett. I'm not even asking you to understand why I came here. I want you to be careful. Take Mrs. Bennett away somewhere, until whatever is going on stops."

There was no threat in what Larry Lee said. He looked at her with such depth of emotion that she felt awkward and uncomfortable. She couldn't take another moment of his gaze.

"Good night, Larry Lee," she said again, and this time she went inside, locking the door behind her.

Alice sank back into the couch across from Mae pondering what Larry Lee had said. Her thoughts were interrupted by Mae clearing her throat.

"Are you all right?" Alice asked, suddenly concerned. If she was feeling overwhelmed, she couldn't imagine how Mae must be taking the news. But the look on Mae's face was still calm, which puzzled Alice.

"I'm fine, dear. I was thinking we could have some tea."

"Are you sure? It's almost bed time."

"I am. There are a few things I think we need to talk about."

Alice cringed. She was aware that Larry Lee's full attention had been on her the last few minutes of his visit. Even Alice could see Larry Lee had some kind of feelings for her, not that she could even begin to understand why or what those feelings might be. What could Mae be thinking?

Like a student dreading punishment, Alice made her way to the kitchen to make tea, her shoulders slightly hunched in submission. Or maybe exhaustion. It was hard to sort out all of her own feelings.

When she returned to the living room, placing a cup and saucer on the table near Mae, Alice was nervous. She wasn't sure she could take whatever Mae was about to say.

Mae sipped her tea thoughtfully, then said, "Will is my only son and he was my baby. As a parent, you're blissfully ignorant of how the world will shape your child. The world is full of possibilities, but it's also full of dangers and you tend to overprotect, to shelter."

Alice wondered where Mae was going. She wondered if Will

had told Mae about their recent troubles, that her mother-in-law might see her as one of those dangers.

"Will's father and I, well, we tried to give our children every opportunity in life. Jasper is a small town, but we had money and we used it for a better education, private lessons, extracurricular activities—hoping Margaret and Will would become productive and responsible adults." She smiled. "You would probably say we spoiled them." Then her expression darkened.

"It's hard to be objective, to see how your children have turned out, until it's too late to change anything."

"Will and Margaret are both smart and accomplished professionals. You did a wonderful job raising them," Alice said, trying to reassure Mae though unsure why she would need to.

Mae gave Alice a small smile, but her expression remained somber. "I won't deny it. Will and Margaret have achieved all the things we hoped for them. Except, I notice Margaret's sense of duty weighs her down. And Will . . ." she paused. "Will is so sure of himself, so proud and arrogant. Sometimes I think we sheltered our children too much."

Mae sat so still that Alice began to wonder if she was dozing off, but soon she spoke again. "You know, my family were mountain folk. Quiet. Self-sustaining. I worked from the time I was small and if I did something wrong, I got paddled."

Alice winced, imagining gentle Mae as a child being struck by her parents.

Mae snickered. "Don't worry. It didn't happen very often. In the early years of our marriage, before we had children, Will's father and I struggled to make ends meet. Not because our families couldn't help us, but because we wanted to make our own way. Then, when we had children, we shielded them from toil. It's a shame really. We should have made them work harder. Will especially."

The serious tone in Mae's voice dragged Alice's mood lower. A revelation was on its way, and she wasn't sure she wanted to hear it.

"Mae, we're both tired. Why don't we get you to bed and then we'll talk some more tomorrow over breakfast."

"No," Mae's voice was soft but stern. "I've sat by quietly for years, protecting my children, sometimes from themselves. It's time that stopped, I think."

"Protecting them from what? Mae, you're scaring me."

Mae hesitated, but she continued, "When Will was in college, he was wild. He came home every summer, but we saw him less and less. He'd sneak in at all hours. I knew he'd been drinking. His father preferred to deal with him, but I always knew. I'm his mother, after all.

"The last summer he came home, Will started seeing Beth Simms. I heard the ladies talking about it one day at the salon. I never told Will's father. He would have been furious, but I knew Will was just passing through, so I never brought it up with him. You see, my feelings towards the Simms family were never as strong as Bill's. I knew Will would go back to college, and I didn't expect he'd come back. Then, after Will left town, I heard a rumor."

Alice sighed. "I think I know what you're going to say. Will told me he dated Beth briefly one summer. I know things got ugly when they broke up. He told me he hit her." Mae did not look surprised. The thought still stung, but Alice had had some time to adjust to this new vision of her husband. At least Mae's story wouldn't blindside her.

"Yes, I heard that as well but not only that. Beth may have been pregnant."

Alice felt the blood rush from her face, and for a moment she felt faint. "Pregnant?" she asked, her voice weak. "Are you saying Beth and Will may have a child?"

"I don't know," Mae said.

"I don't understand. What do you mean?"

"I truly don't know. I never asked. I never investigated. I didn't want to know. I never said a word about it to anyone, not even Will. I wanted it to disappear, and before long it did. Beth left town and no one really mentioned her after. For a long time, I even convinced myself I'd imagined the whole situation, but if Larry Lee is right, if Beth is back in town . . . Well, I think she might be trying to get to Will. The only way I can see for her to do that is through me. And you. It's probably best for us to go stay with Margaret in Atlanta for a little while."

30

Larry Lee's truck hadn't been parked outside of James's house in days and Carver wondered if Larry Lee had actually taken his advice. A small part of him hoped so. A bigger part knew Larry Lee was usually looking for trouble. Running wasn't in his nature. Carver wondered how Morrison's visit with Larry Lee had gone, how it had ended. Maybe Morrison had been able to get through to Larry Lee? Whatever the outcome, Carver was running out of steam—investigating the break-ins, the animal mutilations and trying to tail Larry Lee was simply too much for him.

Carver was mulling over the events of the previous weeks when he noticed someone familiar walking quickly away from the hardware store on the edge of town. Her hair was dingy, her already petite figure looking gaunt. Carver wasn't in a good position to follow her as she walked around the corner, but he had finally caught his first good glimpse of Beth Simms. He pulled into a parking spot across the street and waited, hoping to see what car Beth was driving, whether she was with someone, but she never reappeared.

Making his way across the street to the hardware store, Carver thought about Beth. He'd never felt empathy for her, the way he'd done for Larry Lee. There was something about Beth that was cold, always had been. Larry Lee was wounded and angry, but his actions were somewhat predictable. His sister was aloof, erratic—dangerous. She didn't want help, and those who tried to give it often found themselves worse for the wear, particularly her brother.

As Carver entered the store, the bell above the door dinged the way it had for fifty years. It was a comforting sound. Approaching the counter, Carver grinned at the stringy teenage boy working the cash register.

"Hey there, Daniel. Is your dad here?"

The runty youth smiled awkwardly. "No, sir. He went out for some kind of meeting. Left me in charge." The kid's face beamed with pride. Carver remembered a time when the boy's father had been standing behind the counter for the first time, same wiry frame, same goofy grin.

"Listen. Did you help a young woman a few minutes ago? Small? Light brown hair?"

Daniel's face turned pink, and he looked guilty, like he'd been caught with his hand in the cookie jar. "Yes, sir." He gulped.

Carver guffawed. "Did you give her all the cash in the till?"

"No!" Daniel's expression had turned defiant and terrified. Carver was afraid the kid was going to have a heart attack right then and there.

"I'm teasing you, Daniel," Carver said, and was glad to see the boy's features relax. "She flirted with you, eh?"

Daniel hesitated. "Yes, sir." His face reached fire truck red in the spectrum.

"Nothing wrong with a pretty girl flirting with you, Daniel," Carver said softly. "I'd be careful with this particular girl. She has a bad habit of hurting the boys she flirts with."

Daniel nodded with a hint of regret. Carver suspected the kid didn't get flirted with too often.

"Was this the first time she's been in?"

"No, sir. She came in a few weeks ago and bought a bunch of things. Some camping supplies—a tent, a tarp, some rope. She said she was working on her mama's house too so she bought some tools."

"Did she buy a knife or something like that?"

"Yes, sir. A hunting knife. Actually two. One was a big serrated one. I told her it wouldn't work for cutting down trees. Told her she needed an axe, but she said the knife would work for what she was cutting through."

The teen's words were so casual. He sold hunting and camping supplies all day. It clearly hadn't crossed his mind the supplies might serve some nefarious purpose. Carver was glad. That little bit of innocence gave him some hope.

It took the rest of the morning for Carver to track Morrison down. He finally found the deputy at the Carriage House. Carver sat down across from Morrison without being invited and got a glare for his troubles. Carver waited until Patsy had set a glass of iced tea in front of him before he launched into talking.

"Have you gotten results back from the crime scene?"

Morrison held up a hand. "Before I tell you, I've got something to say. Yes, I like Alice Bennett. She's a kind and interesting person. I have no romantic feelings for her."

Carver grinned. "Mm hmm. Been planning that speech for days, have you?"

Morrison sighed. "Yes, crime scene got back with some preliminary results. No prints. The blood appears to be Joylyn's. The only thing they can say for sure is Joylyn suffered blunt force trauma. There are ligature marks around her wrists, but most of the damage appears to have been made by fists."

"Any cuts? Like with a knife?"

Morrison looked hard at Carver. "Not really. Some bruises and abrasions from being dragged around, some broken skin that bled a little bit, but nothing about any cuts. Why?"

Carver was silent for a while, deep in thought, his mind working furiously through various scenarios, each worse than the last. Trouble was, he had no proof of any of it.

"Did you talk to Larry Lee?" he asked.

Morrison looked taken aback by the sudden change in topic. "Yeah, he was hanging out at his cousin's house."

"I realize that," Carver said impatiently. "And?"

"He says he's been hiding out, never left the house. I told him we saw his truck up at the camp. It wasn't parked outside of the house when I got there, and I tell you what Carver, he was pretty upset to see it gone."

"How so?" Carver sat up a little straighter, giving Morrison his full attention.

"He ran out of the house yelling. He couldn't find his keys. They weren't where he was expecting them to be. I asked him if James might have taken his truck, but he said no. James's car wasn't parked nearby, so I tend to believe him. As I was driving down here, I saw Larry Lee in the park. He's got his duffle bag with him, looked like he'd been sleeping there. No truck."

"Did he say anything?" As soon as the question was out of his mouth, Carver's thoughts were elsewhere. He wondered again who the man in Larry Lee's truck had been that night at the Salvation Army camp.

"I didn't stop to talk to him." Morrison finished off his iced tea, threw his napkin on his half-eaten plate of eggs and stood. "I've got to get back to the office, get some reports finished. See ya."

As Morrison walked away, Carver murmured a goodbye, but kept his thoughts focused on the mounting pile of information that seemed to shine a spotlight on Larry Lee Simms, but this time as the victim.

31

Alice started packing almost immediately after helping Mae to bed. She was surprised to find that she wasn't angry at Mae or at Will. She would never again look at them as a model for the perfect family, but she was beginning to understand them better. What she saw scared her. The next morning, she dropped Rosy off at one of the neighbors' houses, grateful for the offer of dog-sitting while they were away. She ran errands all over town, picking up prescriptions, setting up alternate therapy appointments for Mae, and stocking up on supplies they'd need to keep themselves away for some indefinite amount of time.

By midday, they were checking in to an Atlanta area resort. They settled in, and Alice felt herself really relax for the first time in weeks. Mae slept peacefully the first night, lending the overall impression that they were finally safe. It was only a few days before Alice realized she was going to go stir-crazy in their new setup. They'd reserved a two-bedroom suite that was roomy and full of natural light. Still, both women felt the burden of their captivity.

Mae sat by the window, gazing out onto green manicured lawns and watching the children play in the pool near their building. She sighed. "Maybe you can stop by the library while you're in Jasper and check out a few books for me?" There was desperation in her tone.

Alice laughed. "Of course I will. I'm feeling cooped up too, but I won't be gone more than a few hours."

Mae smiled, returning her attention to the window.

Alice was glad Mae was a woman who seldom complained because Alice was nearing her breaking point. Despite having finally gotten Mae to a safer place, Will was dissatisfied. He was flying in on Saturday, leaving Alice two days to finish up her business in Pickens County before she'd have to contend with Will.

Neither Alice nor Mae had mentioned Larry Lee or his sister since arriving in Atlanta. Both women seemed to need some space to contemplate, and Alice was glad of the silence. Getting Mae out of Jasper diminished much of the fear she'd been feeling, but she knew she would have to confront Will. If Will's relationship with Beth was at the root of their troubles, Will needed to deal with it. Otherwise, Mae might never be safe again in her own home.

About halfway to Jasper, Alice got a call.

"Alice?" a familiar female voice asked when she answered. "This is Sally Jenkins."

Alice was nearly overcome by shock. She hadn't heard from Sally after their last conversation, and with all the recent drama, Alice had given up on whatever information Sally might be able to give her.

"I was wondering if you'd have a few minutes to meet with me today? Maybe over coffee?" The woman's tone wasn't exactly friendly, but neither did she sound irate the way she had when Alice had been with her a few weeks earlier. Alice owed Jim Davis a big slice of pie next time she saw him.

"I'm sorry Mrs. Jenkins. My mother-in-law and I are staying in Atlanta for a few days, and I need to get back. Would you be able to meet tomorrow?"

"How about lunch at the barbecue stop on 515? North of Talking Rock. Do you know it?"

"I'm sure I'll be able to find it," Alice said, uneasy at the out-of-the-way location, but desperate to get some information she could use to finish her article.

"I'll see you at noon," Sally said, and then hung up again, as abruptly as she had before.

Alice had pulled onto the shoulder of the road. Given that she'd be spending another day in Jasper, she decided to turn around and head back to the resort. Her errands would wait another day.

She spent much of the drive back to Atlanta brooding about Will. She thought back on the conversation she'd overheard Beth having the day Alice followed her behind the drugstore. Who had Beth been talking too? Her son? Or daughter? Would Alice soon find herself face-to-face with a child with Will's eyes? *Teenager now*, Alice mused. Then she remembered the uncontrolled rage in Beth's voice that day. What would happen to a child raised by a mother like Beth?

The next morning, Alice packed up her things early, made sure Mae was settled, and headed back to Jasper. Driving up the freeway, she went over all the things that had happened since she arrived in Georgia. She was surprised to realize that she'd been distracted from the troubles in her marriage. Being apart from Will gave her a chance to breathe. She wondered if she'd been so stuck on saving their relationship she'd lost perspective. After all, she was learning things about Will she never would have imagined. Could she have been so seduced by the promise of a "normal" life that she was willing to turn a blind eye to serious flaws in his character?

I wonder if the same thing happened to Juanita Jones, Alice mused. *Was she so caught up in her need for love that she'd failed to see what a monster she was married to?* Alice knew these situations were never that simple. Looking at her own history, she could see how people might have suspected her of murdering her own father. Everyone in their neighborhood knew he was a drunk. They knew he beat her, that he'd been beating her and her mother forever, but no one had done a thing to help. Of course, they knew she was a drunk too. She'd imagined killing him a thousand times at least, but in the end, someone else had done the deed.

Alice had been traumatized by the horror of her father's death, and also the sweet sense of relief she felt when she was sure he was gone. She was at loose ends, but she was free. The feeling was short-lived, however. She was taken into custody immediately and held for days before the district attorney finally decided he didn't have enough evidence to prosecute her. They never did figure out who'd killed her old man.

Moving slowly into the heart of town, Alice was lost in thought and nearly drove right through without stopping when something caught her attention as she neared the corner on Main Street. A woman, small and mousy, was pulling playfully, yet forcefully, on the sleeve of a taller man, still standing in the doorway of a restaurant. Alice knew immediately the woman was Beth Simms. The woman's slight stature and her aggressive manner were a dead giveaway. Alice shrieked when the man finally stepped out onto the sidewalk and she saw who it was. She watched helplessly as Beth Simms curled her scrawny arm possessively around Will Bennett's waist.

Alice hardly remembered a thing that happened next. She found herself in the library parking lot without quite knowing how she got there, pressure building in her chest as she tried to hold herself together long enough to turn off the engine. Will wasn't due in Atlanta until tomorrow. He'd sent her a copy of his itinerary; she was sure of it. After seemingly endless moments of inaction, rage coursing through her system like poison, Alice pulled out her cell phone to send a text.

Hi honey. What time does your flight get in tomorrow?

Her back felt hot and sticky against the car upholstery. She needed air, but she was afraid to roll down a window, afraid the scream she was holding in would rear its ugly head again. She certainly didn't need or want the added attention. After a few minutes, her phone buzzed.

I caught a morning flight out today to surprise you! Mother told me you're in Jasper. Can we meet up after your meeting? The Carriage House?

This time, Alice didn't hold back, screaming loud and long as she beat her fists against the steering wheel. The image of Beth Simms's hands on her husband sent icy stabs of pain through her chest. What was he doing with her? And why had he lied? *Well,* she thought, *that's a stupid question. He lied so he could see her.*

Tears began spilling down Alice's face. She rarely cried, and it was more often out of anger than sadness. Today, it was both. She could feel the fragile life of her marriage slipping through her fingers. It took nearly thirty minutes to compose herself, and really, what finally got her out of the car were the strange looks of the patrons coming out of the library.

On autopilot, she walked into the library, made a pit stop at the bathroom to wipe her eyes, gathered the books Mae had requested, and checked out. As Charlene handed her the books, she asked, "Are you all right?"

Alice clenched her teeth, remembering her first interaction with Charlene, realizing everyone in town knew her husband better than she did. "I'm fine."

The librarian looked at her with sympathetic eyes, none of the usual swagger she usually donned while Alice was around, which only made Alice's anger fiercer. But she held it in and made her way to the restaurant where she was meeting Sally Jenkins, opting to forgo her trip to the courthouse out of self-preservation. Besides, she'd need time to figure out how to deal with Will. She remembered she hadn't texted him back.

Yes, the Carriage House around 1:30.

A moment later.

See you then. Love you sweet pea. Alice's fingers turned white as she gripped the steering wheel, feeling Will's pet name for her sink into her flesh like a knife.

32

It wasn't often Larry Lee was genuinely surprised. Things often went the way he expected them to, usually awful. Every now and again Larry Lee wondered how much of his bad luck was his own fault, but being angry at the world was a lot easier than taking stock of his own culpability. A shot of Jack Daniels never hurt either.

When Larry Lee had shown up on Mae Bennett's doorstep, he expected them to call in the cavalry. He was almost looking forward to it. Morrison or Carver would show up, or one of those new rookie deputies itching to prove themselves. They'd have slapped some cuffs on him, and he would've been enjoying three squares a day in county lockup. Not a pleasant thought, but in many ways preferable to the way things were going.

Instead, Alice Bennett had shocked him by listening. She hadn't exactly been friendly, but given the fact that Larry Lee had nearly killed her mother-in-law, Alice was surprisingly patient. Even Mae listened, though he suspected she was the more likely of the two to turn him in. He still wasn't entirely sure why they didn't, but their talk lit a fire under him. Larry Lee was going to find out what was happening. He was going to be the hero for once.

After leaving the Bennetts, Larry Lee had made the long hike into town, finding a park bench to curl up on near the outskirts. He didn't have anywhere else to go, and he was out of ideas. He'd spent the better part of the next two days hanging around the woods near town, returning to the park at night. The weather was getting colder, and he knew he wouldn't be able to continue staying out of doors. He thought of Mae Bennett lying on her porch step and felt an unfamiliar pang of guilt.

By the third day, he was hungry. He'd run out of provisions—two candy bars and a soda he'd been carrying around in his jacket pocket—and needed to make a trip to the drugstore. The walk gave Larry Lee time to think. The first thing that came to mind was seeing James and Beth at the diner. He was puzzling over the memory when he heard a car coming up behind him. He could hear it slowing, and a quick glance over his shoulder revealed a sheriff's vehicle. *She called the cops anyway*, Larry Lee thought. He really couldn't blame Alice, but he was disappointed all the same. He stopped and waited as Deputy Carver hoisted his heavy frame out of the car.

"Hey, Larry Lee. Get in. I'll give you a ride into town."

Larry Lee eyed the deputy suspiciously. "Er, no thanks. I need the exercise."

Exasperated, Carver motioned impatiently at Larry Lee. "Get in the damned car, Larry Lee. We found your truck. I need you to come in and answer a few questions."

"What kind of questions?" Larry Lee was happy to hear about his truck, but he wasn't about to get into a police car without knowing what was going on. "Am I under arrest?"

Carver grinned. "Should I arrest you?" His belly fat bulged out over his belt and Larry Lee could see sweat stains under both arms, despite the chill in the air.

"I ain't done nothing," Larry Lee said, ashamed to hear the quaking in his voice. "So, no. You don't need to arrest me."

"Let's go. I don't have all day to argue with you."

Warily, Larry Lee nodded and made his way to the deputy's car. Carver shut him in the backseat and they drove into town. By the time Carver let him out of the car, Larry Lee felt like a caged cat ready to scratch his way out. He realized how stupid he'd been, admitting to pushing Mae Bennett. He should have argued, denied, or at least feigned ignorance, not that anyone would have believed him. When he looked into Alice's eyes, he knew she already knew. They were going to lock him up and throw away the key. Larry Lee wished he'd left town when he had a chance. No, actually, he wished he'd never come back in the first place.

Carver had pulled into the county impound lot, and Larry Lee could see the bed of his truck sticking out around a corner. After a few formalities, Carver led him into the yard and over to the truck. As they approached, Larry Lee saw a huge dent in the front end. His heart sank. His truck looked like it belonged in a junkyard.

"Found it down near Tate. Looks like it tangled with a nearby tree. The tree didn't look all that great either," he added, seeing Larry Lee's anguished face. "You really didn't do this, did you?"

"Fuck no," Larry Lee spat. "Of course, I didn't."

Carver looked at Larry Lee curiously, with something like compassion on his face. The look made Larry Lee feel agitated. "Who had access to your truck?" Carver asked.

Larry Lee thought for a moment. "No one. I have the only set of keys." Then he remembered James having taken them with him by accident the other day.

Carver must have seen a change in Larry Lee's expression, because he asked, "What? What are you thinking?"

Trying hard to put his face in neutral, Larry Lee replied, "Nothing. Just pissed off about my truck. Can I take it?"

"Well, there's an impound fee." Carver paused. "I know you haven't been working, so I'm guessing you can't pay it."

Larry Lee turned and walked toward the exit when Carver said, "I guess I could spot you the fee." Larry Lee blinked at the unexpected kindness in Carver's voice and then looked away as emotion swelled within him. Carver had never been kind to him. No, that wasn't true. Carver had stood up for Larry Lee in the drugstore when that asshole Jeff was trying to start something, but he couldn't afford to let his guard down. Larry Lee turned again, facing the deputy.

"Why? What do you want?"

"Why can't you ask for help, Larry Lee? Why does everything have to be so hard?" Carver sounded exasperated. He studied Larry Lee for a moment longer before saying, "I was thinking maybe you could drive your truck right on out of town."

"That an order?"

"More like a suggestion. I don't know what's going on around here, but your name keeps coming up in the conversation. Seems to me you're begging to be back in prison."

Carver hesitated, then added. "You know I'd bust you in a minute if I caught you doing something wrong, but I don't see you as the type of man who'd beat up an old lady and leave her to die." Carver paused. Larry Lee's head swam. He'd never beat up Mae Bennett? What the hell was going on here?

"In fact," Carver continued, "I don't think you have it in you to kill anyone." The look he gave Larry Lee sent shivers down his spine.

Larry Lee's heart began to race. If Mae Bennett had called the sheriff, why wasn't he under arrest? This whole situation was like a puzzle and Larry Lee hated puzzles.

"Besides. Whenever there was trouble for you, your sister was somewhere close by. Seeing as she's back in town . . ."

"What's this got to do with Beth?"

Carver sighed. "Honestly, I don't know, but I've seen her skulking around town for a few weeks now and I don't much care for coincidences." He turned and walked away from Larry Lee, putting an end to the conversation.

Carver spoke with the impound lot supervisor and a minute later, he handed Larry Lee a paper releasing his truck.

"Think about what I said, Larry Lee," Carver said. He walked to his car and drove away, leaving Larry Lee completely flummoxed.

Driving back through town, Larry Lee was unsure what to do next. He didn't have a place to stay. He knew he'd have to go confront his mother at some point. After all, she couldn't stay in that house on her own for long, and all the evidence said Beth damned well wasn't going to take care of her, but he wasn't ready for that scene yet. Instead, he drove around town, aimlessly.

He was heading back to the main street when he saw his sister's scrawny frame ducking into a room at a run-down local motel. *So, that's where she's staying,* he thought. He pulled around the block and walked cautiously back toward the motel. As he approached the room she'd gone into, he could hear voices raised in argument.

"Beth, please," a man pleaded, sounding desperate.

"Not until you give me what I want," Beth cooed, sending a shiver down Larry Lee's spine. The window to the room was cracked allowing their voices to carry, but the curtains were drawn. Larry Lee wished he could see who she was talking to.

"I can't, Beth. I'm married. I love my wife."

Beth laughed. "You didn't say no last time I saw you."

Larry Lee began to feel uneasy, but he couldn't pull himself away. He glanced over his shoulder to see if anyone was around. The street was quiet, save for the voices coming from his sister's hotel room.

"That was a mistake, Beth. You knew I'd had too much to

drink." Larry Lee heard the sound of bedsprings, followed by the sharp buzz of a zipper being pulled hastily. "Get off of me!" the man shouted. Larry Lee could hear his teeth were clenched.

"No!" Beth shrieked. "You will do exactly as I say, or I will drive straight up the hill and talk to your wife about the last time we were together. I doubt you'll stay married for long."

"I never touched you, Beth. You know it. Anyway, she's not there. She and my mother left yesterday."

Larry Lee gasped. Will Bennett. What was Will doing with Beth? Why was he in Jasper?

"I'm resourceful, Will. Don't you think I can find her?"

"You stay away from her," Will said forcefully, all hint of pleading gone in a flash.

"All I'm asking is for one last time together, Will." Beth's voice was sweet and seductive but laced with menace. Larry Lee actually felt sorry for Will Bennett, who was clearly in over his head.

"Hold me, Will," Beth pled. The desperation in her voice sounded genuine. "Just for a while." Will groaned.

A thud behind Larry Lee made him jump. He turned as a janitor walked around the corner, emptying the trash. He locked eyes with Larry Lee, but Larry Lee was already backing away. He jogged to his truck and sped away, thoughts of Alice Bennett heavy on his mind. Why would Will Bennett be in Jasper with Beth? Did Alice know? Larry Lee headed toward his mother's house to clear out of town. He was finally convinced, whatever was going on, he didn't want to be around for the fallout.

33

Alice silenced her phone, barely able to keep herself from hurling it across the parking lot. She pulled out her notes and prepared for her meeting. Turning to work had always saved her in the past.

As she scanned her notes, she was reminded that Juanita Jones tried to run away, to leave her abuser. Like so many victims of domestic violence, her attempt at escape had put her in greater danger—she'd been killed mere days after her return. *Brave girl,* Alice thought sadly. It was so hard to know the right thing to do when your world was turned upside down. *If only she'd made it out.*

Thinking about Juanita Jones in light of all the turmoil in her own life was heartbreaking. She pictured an idealistic girl—popular, lots of friends, full of life—cut down before she'd even had a chance to begin. Unlike Juanita, Alice had never had friends. Her home life had been such a disaster that she mostly kept to herself rather than let anyone in. She wondered what Juanita Jones would have been like if she'd been spared—if someone had seen the collision course she was on and had saved her. Alice had had to save herself in the end. *Juanita Jones tried to save herself,* Alice thought sadly, her heart aching for the young woman.

Alice hadn't realized how long she'd been lost in thought until she saw Sally Jenkins emerging from an old station wagon and approaching her car, a look of concern mingled with reservation.

Alice opened up the door and stepped out. "Hello, Mrs. Jenkins."

Sally gave her a sympathetic look. "I'd hate to see what the other guy looked like." Alice realized her face must be blotchy and puffy from crying.

Putting on her best smile, she replied, "Sorry. It's been a rough couple of weeks."

Sally nodded. "I heard about Joylyn Clement. Poor old thing."

"Yes," Alice said, averting her eyes as tears began to flow. When she looked up again, Sally's expression was soft, kind. She reached out a hand and gave Alice's arm a gentle pat.

"Let's go have some lunch," she said.

The two women walked into the restaurant and were seated in a quiet booth near the back. Alice was thankful for the tall seat backs, which gave them a modicum of privacy. They ordered and while they waited, silence descended, thick as molasses. Finally, Sally Jenkins said, "I'd like to apologize for being so rude the other day. Not many folks around here remember Juanita Jones and sometimes we like to keep it that way. Especially in Tate. It was a horrible thing. The *Pickens County Progress* wrote an article about it a few years back and it stirred up a lot of bad memories."

"I'm not interested in sensationalizing the murder, Mrs. Jenkins, and I understand you want to protect the community. I'd like to tell Juanita's story, at least as much as I can piece together, but I can't do it on my own—not properly. I need your help."

Sally was quiet for a few moments before saying, "Okay. I'll see what I can do about connecting you with her relations." She slid a thin folder out of her purse and handed it to Alice. "I spoke with Juanita's great niece. She became the keeper of old newspaper clippings and things related to the murder when her father passed away."

Alice took the folder and flipped through the papers inside.

"This is amazing," she beamed. "Thank you, Mrs. Jenkins. I've never seen some of these articles. I didn't realize how many of the newspapers around here covered the murder. I didn't see any of these in my searches."

"As I said, it was a horrible time. When Herman Talmadge got involved in the murder trial, the powers-that-be in Atlanta took notice. Otherwise, I'm not sure it would have gotten the attention." Sally Jenkins paused. "Well, that and the nature of the crime. Honestly, I've never heard of anything so ghastly."

Alice nodded, but her own experience had clearly been very different from Sally Jenkins's. She could imagine this level of horror and much worse.

Alice brimmed with newfound confidence in her ability to pay tribute to the short life of Juanita Jones. She basked in the satisfied feeling of accomplishment for as long as she could. When lunch was over and Alice was saying goodbye to Sally Jenkins with a promise to touch base the following week, Sally's face darkened. "Listen, Mrs. Bennett. Talking about Juanita Jones makes people uneasy, me included. What J.M. Carney did to Juanita was evil, to say the least. But . . ." She hesitated, causing Alice's anxiety to rise. "Well, there are other monsters out there. Be careful."

Sally turned and walked purposefully to her car leaving Alice standing alone in the parking lot, unsettled. Alice wondered if there would come a point in her stay here when someone wasn't warning her about dangers and secrets. She'd always seen her husband's hometown as a peaceful haven—now that illusion was gone forever.

Making her way back toward Jasper, taking the road through Talking Rock, Alice tried to focus on the task ahead. She wasn't sure what she would say to Will, and she was dreading it. He'd lied to her, despite the fact that she'd been taking care of his mother for weeks under his constant scrutiny and disappointment. It took every ounce of willpower she had to not drive right through town and back to Atlanta. Instead, she parked across the street from the Carriage House where Will was standing outside, his hands in his coat pockets.

As she approached, he held out his hands to her. She let herself be swept up into a hug, but Will must have felt her stiffness because he let go of her rather quickly. He looked back at the door of the restaurant, avoiding her eyes. "Are you hungry?"

Alice shook her head. "Not really. My meeting was over lunch so I've already eaten, but we can go in if you'd like to. I'll have some tea."

Will crinkled his nose. "No, that's okay. I ate a late breakfast. Let's head back to Atlanta. Are you done here?"

"Yes, I'm finished with my business today. How about you?" Alice couldn't help baiting him.

"I came up to see you." There it was—the lie. Alice wanted to punch him in the face. She wanted to throw herself at him and take out every bit of fear, grief and anger she'd felt in the last few weeks. The urge was so strong but she fought it back. The weak woman she'd been when she arrived in Georgia was gone. She was in control.

"Where's your car?" she asked, her voice flat.

"Oh," Will said, nervously, "I decided to take the shuttle up since you already have a car. Didn't see the need to spend extra money." More lies. She knew how it went. The lies multiplied because once you told one, you had to tell others to cover up the first—a never-ending cycle that she realized she'd never outgrown. She had labored under the false assumption that her precious husband was better than her. He studied her reaction the way he did when he wanted to gauge whether she was in agreement. She fought hard to keep her expression neutral.

"Do you want me to drive?" he asked.

"No," she said, gripping the keys tightly. They walked to the car, Alice keeping some distance between them. She slid into the driver's seat and moved her things into the back to make room for Will. A stony silence settled between them. It was as if nothing had changed and everything had changed all at once.

They headed south on the road to Tate. As they wound through the country roads, Will finally sighed loudly and said, "Alice, we need to talk." He sounded defeated.

"I don't want to talk right now, Will. Please, let me drive." Her own voice mirrored his, lackluster and without hope. Each breath she took in his presence felt heavy and sedating. When they got back to the resort, she would excuse herself to the bedroom and sleep for as long as she could to avoid what came next.

As they headed back out to the highway, Alice glanced in the rearview mirror anxiously. The atmosphere in the car had shifted to something more ominous.

"What is it?" Will asked.

"The guy behind us is right up on my tail." Alice said, her teeth gritted. She accelerated to give herself some room, but Alice could hear the car behind them revving its engine in response. Before she could say anything more, she was jolted forward as the car rammed into them.

Will's face beaded with sweat. He looked around as though searching for someone to save them. The car rammed them again, this time harder, forcing Will's body forward with a jolt. Alice had to hold on tight to the steering wheel to keep them on the road. The crunch of metal on metal made her ears throb painfully.

"Will!" Alice shrieked, but the car hit them again, this time at an angle. Alice lost control of the wheel, jerking it roughly to the side. She slammed on the brakes, but the car skidded off the road and through the barbed wire fence into the nearby field. They hit a ditch, hard, throwing them both into the dashboard. The last thing Alice remembered was a white puff of smoke as the airbags deployed, followed by darkness.

34

When Larry Lee pulled in front of his mother's house, he realized it would be the last time he'd see it. Relief washed through him. He remembered returning after being discharged from the Navy, his head hung down in shame. Then, he'd looked forward to the comforts of home, but Agnes, who'd never been an easy woman, seemed to have hardened over the years. With Beth out of the house, all of her pent-up wrath was now aimed directly at Larry Lee. Needless to say, his welcome was not warm, but, despite a solid try at living on his own and making something of his life, once he'd gotten back to town, it was like he could never escape.

Larry Lee wasn't sure what kind of reception to expect when he walked up to the door and knocked. He really didn't want to see his mother, but he needed a few things from the house if he was going to make a clean break. And he wanted to tell her to her face he was done with her for good.

He felt a twinge of guilt about leaving town. Partly because of his mother's failing health, which seemed to have taken a turn for the worse now that Beth was back, but mostly it was because of Alice Bennett. After the scene at the motel, he knew she was headed for trouble. Beth had made it clear that if Will wouldn't do what she wanted, she was going to make his life a living hell, and Larry Lee knew she could. He didn't really care what happened to Will—Will had made his bed, now he had to sleep in it—but Alice never asked for any of this.

After three attempts at knocking on Agnes's front door, each louder than the one before with no response, Larry Lee reached down and turned the doorknob. The door squeaked open, as he knew it would. He had never bothered fixing the lock.

As soon as Larry Lee crossed the threshold, he knew something was wrong. Agnes was no housekeeper by any stretch of the imagination, but the house looked like it had been hit by a tornado—chairs overturned, old plates with food still on them scattered over the floor. A putrid stench permeated the house, nearly sending Larry Lee back outside for fresh air. As he made his way toward his room, the wreckage and smell continued to get worse.

Larry Lee's room was the first one on the right. He went straight in and saw it was in the same state of disarray. Luckily, most of the things in the room had belonged to Larry Lee's father and not him. Agnes had moved in all the old man's junk while Larry Lee was gone and, having nothing much of his own, Larry Lee hadn't bothered to get rid of it. It appeared whoever had torn the place apart was bent on destruction. Nothing had gone without a rip or tear, a slash or hole. Walking to his closet, Larry Lee reached up into the corner shelf and felt around until he found what he was looking for.

He pulled out a wooden box. A relic from his year in high school shop class, the box was Larry Lee's final project. It was about the size of a shoebox, and his initials had been burnt clumsily into the wood. The lid lay askew over the top. When Larry Lee opened it, he was relieved to see it had not been ransacked. Inside were some photos and papers, as well as the hunting knife his father had given him for his fifteenth birthday. Larry Lee put the lid back on and carried the box toward the door. A quick glance confirmed none of his clothes or any other personal effects could be salvaged.

He was about to leave the house—to walk straight out the front door and never return—but something held him back. His mother hadn't made a sound since he entered the house. Now the silence beckoned him. He turned and looked at Agnes's bedroom door. It was closed, as usual, and he inched toward it. He knocked twice, lightly, not wanting to incur his mother's wrath, not when he was this close to being free. To his surprise, the door swung open. The curtains were drawn and the room was bathed in darkness.

"Mama?" Larry Lee called, his voice barely more than a whisper. When there was no answer, he opened the door the rest of the way and was met by a scene taken straight out of one of the gory horror flicks he'd watched as a kid.

Agnes's body was splayed across the rug, her eyes were open and there was a look of terror frozen on her face. The pool of blood around her torso had congealed—she'd obviously been lying there for a while—and Larry Lee could see stab wounds all over her body, too many to count. Most disturbing were her hands, or the lack thereof. Someone had hacked off Agnes's hands at the wrist.

Vomit rose in Larry Lee's throat. His hands shook. His breathing was ragged. The room began to spin, the smell of death and decomposition assaulting his senses with force now that he knew the source of the stench. The state of his mother's body—the brutality of it all—made him feel fear like he'd never known before. It took hold of his heart and clenched at his chest until he felt like he might explode.

He backed out of the room, closing the door behind him as if he could shut his mind to what he'd seen. He scrambled out of the house frantically, retching violently when he reached the porch. His stomach spasmed as he vomited, first the contents of his stomach and then nothing at all—the image of his mother's broken body on the floor pushing at his skull with each heave.

He staggered to his truck, throwing his box on the passenger side, his wheels kicking up dust as he sped out of the driveway. Only later did it occur to him that his mother's car was not parked in front of her house.

It had taken hours for Larry Lee to pull himself together. He wasn't entirely sure how he made it down the mountain, but he pulled into the first parking lot he reached, parked his truck haphazardly near the back of the lot, closed his eyes and wailed. His eyes were dry, but the sound coming out of his mouth was unearthly, building deep in his gut and surging forward without conscious effort. He sat like that until his voice grew hoarse. Only then did he begin to feel anger, bubbling up like a pot left unattended.

He pictured his mother's broken body and felt emptiness inside him, a black hole growing more massive by the second. Who could do such a thing? He realized there was now nothing tying him to Jasper, no one that needed him in this town or in the whole wide world, but first, he had unfinished business to address. Larry Lee drove north for an hour, pulling into a small gas station where he used the pay phone to contact the Jasper Police Department and report his mother's murder. He spent the night in his truck at a rest stop nearby, tucking his truck between two big rigs and letting utter exhaustion take hold.

He'd woken up with the sun, feeling motivated like he'd never felt before. In the early afternoon, he finally made his way back to town. His first stop was the library, where he put in applications at jobs in three different states, letting fate decide where he would go. Whatever happened next, he knew that he was done with Jasper for good. He walked past Charlene without a glance, both coming and going.

For a while after, Larry Lee cruised around town, determined to find his sister. He drove by the motel where he'd overheard the clandestine meeting between Beth and Will, but the curtains were closed and no one was around. On a hunch, he stopped by the drugstore. Beth had worked there briefly as a teenager, and since he kept seeing her there, he suspected she was hanging around a lot now.

"Have you seen my sister, Beth?"

The woman at the register looked up. Recognizing Larry Lee, she scowled. "No, I haven't. And you can tell her that the next time we see either one in here, we're calling the police. She got Jeff stealing other people's prescriptions for her. We had to let him go. Lucky he's not in jail. Idiot."

Larry Lee walked out without responding, feeling more confused than ever. He couldn't care less that Jeff had lost his job, but he couldn't imagine how Beth could have made that happen—Jeff's dad owned the drugstore. Larry Lee wondered if Jeff had given Beth access to the pharmacy's coffers.

With nothing left to do and a few hours to kill, Larry Lee drove up to James's house to wait. James had been working out at Big Canoe for most of the month, so Larry Lee was surprised to see movement in James's house. He felt a rush of adrenaline as he thought through his confrontation with James. He needed to know what James was up to, what he was doing with Beth. A small part of him hoped James would come out on his side, like he always had. Otherwise, he truly had nothing.

He was sure someone was inside James's house, so when James himself pulled up in the driveway, Larry Lee was confused. Getting out of his car, James looked over in Larry Lee's direction and, with a sigh, headed across the street. Larry Lee scrambled out of his truck and was standing by the passenger door when James approached.

"Hey." Larry Lee said. James looked at him with a strange expression, detached and deflated.

"What do you want, Larry Lee?"

Larry Lee's emotions were all over the place, his fuse short. Riled by James's seeming indifference, Larry Lee shot back, "I want to know what you're doing hanging around Beth." James's face flushed, his eyes momentarily darting toward his house before he could stop himself. He clearly hadn't been expecting Larry Lee's question. "She's in there?" He growled, gesturing toward James's house.

"Why would Beth be here?" James hedged, but Larry Lee could see sweat beading on his forehead. "What business is it of yours anyway?"

"I saw you two at the Carriage House the other day." Larry Lee saw he was getting under James's skin, so he kept poking. "What's going on, James? I thought you were my friend."

James suddenly bristled. "Why, Larry Lee? Because I follow you around and pick up your messes? Because I'm here when you need a place to crash and I put up with your stupid tantrums? Face it. Being your friend hasn't gotten me anywhere. Actually, it costs me money. Fixing fences, cleaning up trash. I don't want to be here in Jasper forever. I've got to take care of me so I can get out of this hellhole."

Larry Lee thought about it for a moment, allowing for the truth of his cousin's words to sink in, and then said quietly, "You didn't answer my question."

James shuffled his feet. "Beth needed some help, that's all."

"Did she kill my mama?" Larry Lee asked, a tremor in his voice. He didn't expect the look of fear that momentarily swept across James's face, replaced too late by a stony glare. He did notice, however, the lack of surprise in James's reaction. With tremendous effort, Larry Lee kept himself calm. Losing it with James wouldn't bring his mother back. It wouldn't get him any closer to finding Beth.

"What'd she do, James? Finally gave you a piece? Surprised you still want her after everyone in town had a go." Larry Lee spoke slowly, angling every word to inflict as much damage as possible. He saw James cringe. Watched as his best friend's pride took a beating by his own hand.

"Get out. And don't come back." James turned and walked into his house, slamming the door behind him.

Larry Lee waited for a few minutes before getting back into his truck. Rage exploded in his chest and he beat his fists into the steering wheel until they hurt. He leaned his head against the wheel, gulping for breath, and waited for the storm inside his mind to clear.

35

Deputy Carver sat on the Simms's front porch, his head between his knees. Each breath took him one step forward to taming his stomach, which had been churning ever since setting foot inside the house. He'd never lost it at a crime scene before, but seeing Agnes Simms was a horror he'd never imagined.

Not that Pickens County hadn't seen its share of murder and mayhem. In nearly thirty years with the sheriff's department, Carver had seen death so often it had become second nature. People always thought living in a small town meant you were safe. Carver knew that wasn't always true, but the mangled remains of Agnes Simms's body was more than he'd bargained for.

"You all right?" Deputy Morrison said, taking a seat next to Carver. A wave of foul-smelling air wafted in Carver's direction, following Morrison out of the house, and Carver kept his head down a moment longer, determined not to vomit.

"I'm okay," Carver said. His voice shook a little bit.

"The boys from crime scene are here. Robert came up from Atlanta to help them out. It's going to be a while."

Carver was listening, but his tongue was tied. He'd known

Agnes Simms since they were kids, had shared drinks with her husband and busted both of her children. His history with the Simms family was fraught with drama and mixed emotions. Still, Carver could feel the fury, the pure hatred that had given rise to Agnes's death like a sick, terrifying heartbeat pulsing through the house.

"I can't go back in yet."

"No need, but I would like to hear your thoughts, when you're feeling up to it."

Carver looked up and saw the concern in Morrison's face. *I must look pretty bad.* At times like these, Carver relied on sarcasm, a snarky comeback, to keep his emotions at bay—to save face. Right now he didn't have it in him.

"This is the first time in all my years in law enforcement I'm not sure I want to do this anymore." Speaking the words aloud provided relief, Carver felt his body lift, the weight of the situation alleviated a little bit. Morrison sat quietly, for which Carver was thankful. It took a few more minutes before he was able to pull himself together.

"You know what I think, Morrison? You reap what you sow. Every bit of meanness, every cruel thing Agnes ever did to anyone just came back to her a hundred times over."

"I know what you mean. I remember making a stop here once on a domestic call. Agnes and Beth Ann had been walloping on one another, but when I got here, Beth was all apologies while Agnes threatened to whoop my ass. She was about as mean a woman as I've ever met. Ballsy too. Just laughed when I threatened to slap some cuffs on her."

Carver sighed. "I've known Agnes all my life and I believe she was born that way. Used to sit next to her husband every day at the bar and wonder how he lasted as long as he did. So, what do you think happened?"

"I think someone took a knife—probably serrated, there was a lot of tearing around the wounds—and stabbed Agnes maybe fifty, sixty times. Some of the stab wounds are clean punctures. Others look like the knife was raked across her skin. Maybe the assailant wasn't really paying attention to what they were doing. Probably they were out of their ever-loving minds at that point. Definitely a crime of passion. Whoever did this was full of hate, wanted to make her suffer."

Carver nodded.

"We haven't found her hands."

The image of the stumps where Agnes's hands had once been sent Carver's stomach lurching again.

"Local girl was murdered, more than seventy years ago, and her hands were cut off. I was reading a story about her a few years ago in the *Progress*. Seemed like the husband might have had a thing for hands, some kind of fetish." Carver tried to remember what he'd read about the story, but couldn't come up with anything specific. "This doesn't feel like that for me. Feels like something more angry."

"I agree," Morrison said, then quietly added. "Do you think Larry Lee did this? Agnes kicked him out. He was definitely angry. Course, he's generally angry about something. Do you think he could do this?"

Carver thought for a moment. "No. I don't think this was Larry Lee." His chest tightened as he considered all the possibilities. A vision of mutilated dogs in an abandoned shack hijacked his thoughts followed by a jolt of cold dread. "Oh God. The dogs." Carver felt the bile rising in his throat.

"The dogs?" Morrison asked.

"The dogs at the shack. She's been practicing."

"She?" Morrison parroted, but then his face lit up in understanding. "Beth." The word came out as a whisper.

"Morrison, we need to pick up Larry Lee and bring him in to the station. I don't think he's safe out there."

36

"Ma'am. Ma'am. Are you all right?" The voice sounded distant, muffled, like a dream. Alice felt groggy. She shifted the weight of her head, which felt heavy and slow, like she was under water.

"Can you open your eyes, ma'am?" The voice was closer now. Insistent. Alice couldn't see anything and she thought, *aren't my eyes open?* There was something unusual about the thought and Alice began to panic. Why can't I see anything? A rush of adrenaline surged through her and when she finally consciously made an effort to open her eyes, she was relieved to see images coming slowly into focus. A concerned face. A uniformed body. *Where was she?*

"Mrs. Bennett?" The face was talking to her.

"Do I know you?" she asked, and was surprised by the strain she felt in her chest. Her voice sounded far away, feeble.

The face held a grim expression, but offered a hasty smile at Alice's questions. As her vision came into focus, Alice realized the face belonged to a woman, familiar somehow. She tried to access her memories, but thought was difficult, hazy.

"We met last week, Mrs. Bennett," the woman said, either

clueing in on Alice's expression or reading her mind. Alice noticed her uniform: the staff and serpents on one patch, a red cross on the other. The paramedic who'd helped her after the attack on Joylyn. But why was she here?

"Am I hurt?" Alice grew frustrated. A memory drifted close to the surface but she couldn't quite catch it. Then it all came rushing back. The car slamming into them. Will's face, red and terrified. Hitting the ditch. The airbags deploying. "Will?" she asked, turning her head to face the passenger side. It was empty.

Looking back at the woman, confusion giving way to hysteria, she asked, "Where is Will?"

The confused look on the woman's face was enough to drive Alice over the edge. "Where's Will!" she screamed, frantically trying to get out of the car.

"Hold still, ma'am. Let me help you get the seat belt unfastened." She felt the other woman reach across her torso and gently unfasten the belt, carefully moving it away from Alice's body. "Please stay here until I can assess your injuries."

"I'm not injured!" Alice yelled, still struggling.

As if on cue, Alice felt pain. First in her chest, then her cheek. Soon the pain was everywhere, enveloping her body. "Oh God," she moaned, leaning back into her seat.

"Where does it hurt?" the medic asked, examining Alice's body. Alice moaned in response.

"Can you move your arms?" Alice complied. "How about your legs?" Again, Alice complied, but not without wincing as pain shot up her back and into her neck. "Please stay still. We're bringing a stretcher."

"Where's Will?" Alice asked again weakly, though she made no further attempts to move.

The medic looked at her again strangely. "Was Will in the car with you, ma'am?"

Frustrated, Alice snapped, "Of course he was!"

Unfazed by Alice's tone, the medic simply replied, "We haven't found anyone else, ma'am."

It took hours before the hospital was willing to discharge Alice with pain medication and orders to rest for at least a week. They'd ruled out concussion, broken bones and internal bleeding. There were bruises and abrasions all over Alice's body, including a long ugly stripe across her torso where the seat belt had held her tight. Morrison and a deputy she didn't recognize fired off questions as the hospital staff poked and prodded Alice, leaving her physically and mentally exhausted.

She'd reluctantly called Margaret, knowing she'd have to talk her out of rushing to Jasper. Morrison had explained if they didn't find Will soon, he'd have to talk to Mae as part of his investigation, but Alice was still holding out hope they'd find Will sooner rather than later—and that he was all right. She gathered her things and followed the deputy to his car for a ride into the police station to give a formal statement.

Someone had seen Alice's car in the ditch and called an ambulance, but by the time the cops arrived, Will was gone. There was a small smear of blood on the door handle, and it looked as though someone had been dragged, but all traces of Will vanished within feet of the car. Morrison delivered the news cautiously, as if gauging changes in Alice's mental state with each word.

Unfortunately, there weren't many clues to Will's disappearance. They could see the car that ran them off the road had pulled up beside them. No witnesses had come forward. Alice had been knocked out and had no memory of anything that happened after the crash. The sheriff's department urged her to return to Atlanta with promises to call if there was any news. Instead, she'd made them go over every detail with her again as she tried in vain to make sense of it all.

"He may have hit his head and wandered off," Deputy Morrison suggested, though without much conviction.

"I suppose," Alice replied. "Have you located Beth Simms yet?"

"Um, no," Deputy Morrison said, hesitantly. "But when we went out to the Simms house, we found Agnes Simms."

"Why wouldn't you? She lives there, doesn't she?" Alice asked, only half engaged in the conversation. She drummed her foot against the ground nervously.

"No," Morrison continued, and the sound of his voice gave her pause. "We found Agnes Simms's body. She was dead. Had been for days."

"What was wrong with her?" Alice asked, not registering the look on Deputy Morrison's face.

Again, Morrison paused before speaking. "She was murdered, Alice. Someone stabbed her to death."

Alice gasped. She'd begun to think along the lines of the feud, that someone was out to get the Bennetts. The murder of Agnes Simms cast a shadow on every assumption she'd made, every conclusion she'd drawn. "Who would do such a thing?" she asked, her voice shaking.

"We're going to pick up Larry Lee Simms."

"You think Larry Lee killed his mother?"

"I don't know what to think, Alice. We have to bring him in to question him. We're still looking for his sister, Beth." Alice noted the dark circles under Morrison's eyes, the way he shifted his gaze as he spoke. He was exhausted and searching desperately for answers that weren't there. She knew the feeling, and wasn't entirely surprised when he added, lamely, "Larry Lee used to carry around a hunting knife back in high school."

Alice sighed, disgusted. "Don't you think that's a little convenient?" she asked, thinking about Larry Lee's claim that he was being set up. His story rang true with her, felt familiar to her, maybe too familiar. She couldn't separate her feelings about Larry

Lee from her own experience with her father. To be accused of murdering your tormentor when you didn't do it was adding insult to injury.

Morrison looked Alice in the eye with something akin to disappointment. "It's possible, but right now he's the only lead I have to follow. I hope when we find Larry Lee that we'll find Will too. Safe," he added, seeing Alice's expression.

Alice shuddered. *If only.*

Larry Lee had been parked at the drive-in, sipping a soda and pondering his next move. When he finished his drink, he drove up to the library to use the computers. For the second time in recent days, he knew something was wrong the minute he walked in the door.

Charlene Walker looked up at Larry Lee like she was seeing a ghost. As he approached the circulation desk, she leaned forward and whispered urgently, "You need to get the hell out of here, Larry Lee."

"Finally have time to talk to me, eh?" Larry Lee said smugly, but he could feel the tension in the air and it was making him very uncomfortable.

Charlene frowned. "I'm serious, Larry Lee. Someone ran Will Bennett and his wife off the road out near the highway about an hour ago, and the sheriff's office has already been in here looking for you."

"For me?" Larry Lee felt idiotic the minute the words were out of his mouth. Of course they were looking for him. Anything goes wrong in Jasper and it must be Larry Lee Simms. No wonder someone was trying to frame him. He was a sitting duck. He looked all around him like a caged animal.

"There's no one here right now," Charlene said, but she was

still whispering. "You're in real trouble, Larry Lee. You need to get as far away from this town as you can."

"You don't know the half of it," Larry Lee muttered.

"That's where you're wrong." Charlene seemed about as uncomfortable as a person could be. She looked over her shoulder and leaned even further over the counter. "Listen, Larry Lee. I've had my heart set on you since the first time I saw you when we were kids. Right now though, I don't want to have anything to do with any of you, but I don't want to see you in trouble either, and if you stay here, that's exactly where you'll be." She was about to say something else when the doors opened behind Larry Lee. He tensed, imagining handcuffs being slapped on his wrists, but he saw Charlene relax. He glanced quickly behind him, relieved to see an older woman he only knew in passing walking towards the stacks.

"Get out of here, Larry Lee," Charlene hissed. Then she got up and walked back into the administration offices. Larry Lee scurried out to his truck. He still didn't have a plan, but his brain was finally wrapping around a seemingly unbelievable idea. It was possible that when his mother kicked him out, she might have been trying to save him.

37

Thump, thump, thump.

Alice woke with a start when she heard the thumping of footfalls across the ceiling above her bed. At first, she was disoriented. She scanned her surroundings and remembered she'd taken a room at the Woodbridge Inn—too nervous to stay at Mae's house alone. By the time the deputy had finished his report, it was getting dark in Jasper, and Alice was tired down to her bones. The doctor had warned her she'd wake up feeling sore, maybe enough to stay in bed, but Alice was determined to help search for Will. Deputy Morrison had reluctantly agreed to pick her up in the morning.

Dawn was breaking and only a faint light was visible through a split in the curtains. Alice sat up slowly, acutely aware of every muscle in her battered body. She kneaded her neck with aching fingers until she could almost turn her head from side to side without shooting pain. Fumbling for the prescription bottle next to her bed, Alice gulped some painkillers and lay back down to think while the medicine kicked in.

She pictured the look on Will's face when she met him at the restaurant yesterday—distracted, guilt oozing from every pore.

He'd sworn fervently he would never betray her, and yet he'd been with Beth Simms. What had they been doing? Alice chided herself. She knew what they'd been doing. Still, she couldn't entirely believe it. Will's sense of honor and loyalty were deeply engrained, one of the many things that had attracted Alice to him. Growing up in a household devoid of those qualities, Alice had clung to Will's chivalry, to his decency, like a moth to the flame. She realized now how accurate that analogy was. Even if Will hadn't slept with Beth, Alice wondered if she would ever trust him again.

Finally, Alice dragged her weary body out of bed and into a hot shower. Savoring the heat against her skin, she stayed in until the water became tepid. She stood in front of the mirror and examined the darkening bruises on her chest and hip. In a day or two, she'd look like the abused girl she'd been twenty years ago. She'd never used a car accident before to explain away her injuries. She smiled ruefully before putting on yesterday's clothes. The pain was breathtaking, but she was a pro at working through physical pain.

As she was sitting down to tie her shoes, there was a knock at the door.

"Who is it?" she asked, warily.

"It's Deputy Morrison. Are you ready to go?"

Alice opened the door and took in the deputy's face, puffy from exhaustion, stubble framing a usually clean-shaven chin. She wondered if he'd slept at all.

"Yes. Let me get my shoes on." When she'd finally finished, panting from the effort, she picked her purse up off the chair and swung it over her shoulder, only to yelp and pull it off.

"Are you all right?" Morrison asked, concerned.

"As all right as I can be, under the circumstances," she said hastily, immediately regretting the agitation plain in her voice. The deputy's expression remained constant. He was probably used to dealing with people's frustration. Despite the doctor's reassurances that she'd feel better in a few days, she doubted her body would ever feel whole again.

"We've been out all night in the field where we found your car. There's no sign of Will. Wherever he is, he didn't get there on his own."

Alice nodded. The news was as she'd expected, but the extinguishing of what little hope had remained still stung.

"So," she said, exhaustion holding tight to her lungs, making each word heavy and harsh, "where do we start?"

By noon, Alice was beginning to feel delirious. Any doubts she'd had about the doctor's orders to rest were gone. To make matters worse, they'd found no trace of Will or either of the Simms. Alice had ridden along to the Simms property, which was still a mass of police tape and investigators. It was a run-down old cabin—dilapidated, uncared-for—in the middle of the beautiful Georgia woods. Only half a mile from Mae's house. Alice had passed by every day on her walks with Rosy, never paying it much mind. Now, as she stared at the broken house, she tried to imagine living there, but her brain was too tired. All she could see was isolation, a breeding ground for abuse and neglect.

The Carriage House had become a refueling stop for the search teams. They'd exhausted the area surrounding the crash site and were chatting quietly over coffee. When Alice walked in with Deputy Morrison, a hush fell over the room. She walked to the back and took a seat away from the crowd, not caring whether every eye in the restaurant was on her—and they certainly were—needing to rest her weary body. Morrison ordered them both coffee and then joined her. They sat in silence. Alice was lost in thought when she felt someone standing beside her.

"How are you holding up, Alice?" Jim Davis's friendly voice caught her wandering attention. He was still wearing a jacket and looked tired. He'd been out all night with the searchers.

"Thanks for helping, Jim," she said, offering a feeble attempt at a smile. "I'm doing okay." She stretched her arms, wincing as her stiff muscles popped with pain. "I may have to lie down for a while. How's Judith?"

"I came from my house, checking up on her and all. She's having a good day today. I told her about the search and she wanted to come, dear thing." Jim's eyes crinkled with mirth. His apparent affection for his wife made Alice's heart ache a little less. "I convinced her to stay at home but promised I'd come in and do my best to help you."

"Would you sit with me for a few minutes?" she asked, feeling stronger in Jim's presence. She wondered with a pang of envy if Jim had any children. What would it have been like to have a father like Jim Davis?

Jim nodded at Morrison and took a seat next to her, offering comfort by proximity. Alice was really beginning to zone out when another sheriff's deputy approached the table. Morrison stood, had a whispered conversation, and then turned to Alice. "They think they've found the car that hit you. It's by the lake, behind some brush. Looks like it was Agnes Simms's car."

Alice took the news like a shot of electricity to the pit of her stomach. Feelings of anticipation at finding Will mingled with fear over finding him dead, causing her chest to constrict painfully. She stood unsteadily.

"Stay here." Deputy Morrison put a gentle hand on her shoulder. "I'll let you know what we find."

Alice's expression turned to steel. "After all this, if you think I'm waiting around here, you're out of your mind. You can either take me with you or I'll start walking." She pushed past Morrison and stomped out of the restaurant, feeling all eyes on her again as she went.

They drove past Mae's house in silence, taking a dirt road near the top of the hill toward the lake. Alice had passed by the road dozens of times on her walks, but never ventured past all the overgrown brush and brambles to see what was at the end. Now she saw the crushed front end of the car and trembled.

Having survived her father and her own self-destructive tendencies, Alice had always thought of herself as tough, but the reality of the last few weeks had finally taken their toll. She understood her father's outbursts, especially after alcohol took over her life. It was pretty simple really. He was a mean, abusive drunk. End of story. But this violence—this cold, calculated violence—was beyond her.

Alice followed Morrison out of the squad car, earning her a frustrated look and exaggerated hand motions to get back inside, but she couldn't obey. She wouldn't. Reluctantly, Morrison turned his attention to the abandoned car.

"Charlie, go slow," Morrison said to his fellow officer. Gesturing for Alice to stay back, they approached the car, guns drawn, every footstep measured. Alice held her breath, counting the seconds it took for them to reach the car, peer inside, and declare it empty. After that, things moved faster. Someone opened the door and began inspecting the front seat. Another jimmied open the trunk, examining the interior with a flashlight. "Nothing back here," he said.

"More blood," came a voice from inside the car. "Is crime scene on the way?"

Alice let out her breath in a rush. Morrison walked forward, looked inside, and then over to Alice. "Just a little bit," he said, reassuringly. Alice was not reassured. The deputies searched in and around the car, then headed out into the surrounding forest. Alice waited, watching, clenching and unclenching her fists while she continued to count.

A movement caught her eye across the water and Alice realized how close they were to Mae's house. She could see the dock jutting out in the water and the roof peeking above the lower trees. She studied the shoreline wondering what had made her turn her head.

"We'll need to call in a team to dredge the lake," Morrison said, appearing beside her and causing her to jump. Seeing the look of horror on her face, he added, "And a more thorough search of this area." He gestured toward the tree line.

Alice still stared at the Bennett dock, allowing a blanket of numbness to shield her from her mounting panic. Morrison followed her gaze and asked, "Did you see something?"

Alice shrugged. "I don't know. Maybe. Something moved."

Morrison looked at the dock and then his face twisted. "When was the last time you were at Mae's?"

"Four days ago?" Alice guessed, thinking back over the past few days. Then, suddenly, the realization hit her in the face. "They're in Mae's house." It wasn't a question.

Morrison called his team over and asked, "Who checked out the Bennett house?"

"I did," a short, balding man said from the periphery of the team. "I didn't see anything unusual."

"Did you go around the whole house?"

The older deputy hesitated. "Yes, but I didn't go inside. It was locked up tight." Both deputies looked in the direction of the dock.

"Okay. Let's assume Will Bennett was able to walk out of the car. Can you make it from here to the dock on foot?"

Another officer chimed in. "No. There's a rock wall all the way out to the water between two of the houses."

"That's, what, two houses away from Mae Bennett's'?"

"Yes." Then the officer paused. "The water level is low right now. You might be able to walk around the wall at the waterline. Might get a little muddy."

"Let's go," Morrison said, scrambling around the car to lead the charge. He glanced back at Alice, but she shot him a look that shut down any further attempts to keep her from following.

38

As the search for Will progressed, Larry Lee sat in his truck on a side street in Jasper near the hardware store. He'd been sitting there for hours, staying far enough away from his mother's house or the Bennett house so as not to arouse any more unwanted attention. By staying out of sight, hopefully he would stay out of trouble.

He'd almost convinced himself to get out of town before anything else could happen, when he spied Beth and Jeffrey Hatcher. It hadn't been two weeks since Larry Lee saw Hatcher, but those two weeks had aged Jeff. His shoulders sagged and seemed grayer. Larry Lee almost felt sorry for him.

On a whim, Larry Lee followed them. They were driving an unfamiliar car, and Larry Lee stayed as close as he could as they made their way up toward the lake, taking the back road that came down from the Salvation Army camp. There was only one place they could be heading: the Bennett house. But why? Everyone in town knew Mae Bennett was staying in Atlanta now. And he'd heard the cops were still swarming Agnes's house.

Larry Lee parked his truck along the road and walked through the woods toward the Bennett house. He spied the car Beth and

Jeff had been driving parked up the hill from the Bennett's property. It was empty. Making his way cautiously down the hill, Larry Lee's head and hands began to sweat, his heart racing.

With a sinking feeling, Larry Lee realized everything that had happened lately—to him, to Alice and Mae Bennett—was leading up to this point. Visions of Beth with her cold smile, her maniac laugh, her dead eyes forced their way into his mind. Whatever came next, he knew he needed to face her, to catch her at whatever she was doing and put a stop to it, the way he should have done so many years ago.

He'd reached the driveway to the Bennett house and leaned around the bushes to get a sense of what was going on. There was no movement and Larry Lee was beginning to doubt himself when he heard a scream—shrill and full of pain—come from inside the house. Firming his resolve, Larry Lee crept toward the front door.

39

As he neared the front door, Larry Lee heard his sister's piercing voice.

"You're not the one in control here, Will," she screeched, "Just shut up! Shut up!"

A mumbled response. A groan.

"Shut up!"

The *thunk* of something hard hitting flesh followed by more groaning: the word "Alice" laced with pain and sorrow.

"You won't be here to help her, Will, but don't worry, I'll take special care of her." Beth's voice had gone silky, almost seductive. She was toying with him, like a cat with a mouse. It made Larry Lee shiver.

Carefully, Larry Lee opened the door, praying it wouldn't squeak, thankful there was no screen to complicate matters. With all the commotion inside, Larry Lee was able to slip into the foyer undetected. There, he froze again and listened.

"You are a bastard, Will Bennett." Beth's voice had gone quiet and deadly, like a lion ready to pounce. "You're just like me. A cold, heartless bastard. That's why we were so good together. Then you killed my baby and you stole my chance at a different life." She cackled, her voice growing wild with rage and pain.

"I'm sorry," Will croaked weakly, his voice heavy with defeat.

"Sorry? You're sorry?" Beth's words were becoming manic again, her anger palpable. Larry Lee knew Will was in deep trouble. Beth continued, her voice rising back to a shrill scream. "You left me lying there, Will. You left me for dead. Went back to school. Went on with your life. Your job, your fat, ugly wife. Like none of this even happened. Like *I* never existed. Then you come around here now telling me to back off, to watch my back." Beth laughed. "You don't get it, Will. You never have. This is my show and I'm not done until every last one of you is dead."

Beth moved down the hall, then she yelled, "Take him in the bedroom."

Will groaned as someone dragged his body across the carpet in the hallway. Larry Lee felt as if his feet were glued to the floor. He had no love for the Bennetts, had nearly killed Mae Bennett himself, but the murderous tone of his sister's voice was sick and terrifying. He thought about Alice Bennett—the damaged wife—and the fate that awaited her if Beth was left unchecked. Larry Lee didn't care one lick about Will Bennett, but he wouldn't let Alice bear the burden of all this misery.

Sneaking quietly across the sitting room, Larry Lee made his way toward the sound of Will's groans. As he approached the first room, he saw Jeff Hatcher struggling to get Will's body across the threshold. Will probably outweighed the guy by at least fifty pounds, and at the moment, Will was deadweight. Larry Lee saw beads of sweat on Jeff's face as he tried to carry out Beth's orders. When dragging didn't work, Jeff moved into the doorframe to push Will's legs aside.

Larry Lee sprang, grabbing Jeff around the neck and squeezing with every ounce of his strength. Jeff's arms flailed wildly, knocking into the door and dresser beside it.

"What's going on, Jeff?" Beth's voice came down the hall, but sounded muffled by a door. When Jeff didn't answer, Larry Lee heard a toilet flush. He knew his time was running out. He let go of his stranglehold on Jeff and pummeled him hard and fast on the head and face, not giving the other man time to respond or even defend himself. He shoved Jeff across the room and grabbed Will Bennett's arms, dragging him back out into the sitting room, knowing the noise was sure to bring Beth flying down the hallway.

He'd made it most of the way into the room—the front door was in his sights—when he felt a stabbing pain in his shoulder. Dropping Will in a heap, he turned to face Beth. Her hand held a hunting knife, now slick with Larry Lee's blood. Her eyes were dark and remorseless.

"What are you doing here, Larry Lee?" she purred, eyeing Larry Lee hungrily. He could see the tension in her muscles. She was ready to spring at him, to stab him and kill him. Her eyes now sparkled with bloodlust. Larry Lee was terrified. "I'm not finished playing with Will yet."

"You don't have to do this, Beth," he said as gently as he could, looking down at Will's still body lying beside them. Fear gripped Larry Lee, causing his hands to shake. The pain where she'd stabbed him throbbed angrily down his back and into his arm.

A puzzled expression came over her face. "Why wouldn't I?" she asked. "What do you care? He's just a Bennett."

Larry Lee had uttered those words so many times in his life. Only now did he realize how hollow his hatred for the Bennetts was. He envied them, coveted what they had, but he had no real malice. Not the way Beth did. "What did Will Bennett ever do to you?"

"Oh, I remember. You weren't around that summer. Will knocked me up and then he beat me until the baby died." Larry Lee's jaw dropped in shock. Seeing the look on his face, she laughed. "Didn't know that, brother dear, did you?"

A momentary pang of sympathy turned quickly to anger. "You mean the summer I was in prison?"

Beth faltered. Her head seemed to clear for a moment. "Oh."

Larry Lee felt the anger grow, and he lashed out at Beth. "Yeah, oh. Tell me Beth. Did Will Bennett rape you like Oscar Clement did?"

A look of confusion appeared on Beth's face. "You don't understand, Larry Lee. He hurt me." Her voice was suddenly shaky, her eyes distant. Larry Lee saw how far gone Beth was in that look.

"Who? Oscar Clement? That boy was nearly dead when I got there. What did he do to deserve that, Beth?" She didn't answer.

Larry Lee took a step toward his sister and she backed away, giving him a surge of confidence. "Did Will Bennett really get you pregnant?"

Beth blushed, making her look nearly human again. "I don't know. Maybe. He could have." She looked at her brother, pleading. "I was gonna make him marry me. I could have gotten out of here."

"You think Will Bennett would have married you?" Larry Lee's tone was mocking.

A wide range of emotions flashed across Beth's face. Anger. Sadness. Desperation. It was like watching a roulette wheel, wondering where she would end up.

"He hit me, Larry Lee." She finally muttered, sounding like the scared little girl Larry Lee had rescued from his mother's angry fists time after time, but her eyes were still lifeless. "He hit me so hard, it killed my baby. I was in the hospital for a week. Don't you see, Larry Lee? He deserves to be punished."

Larry Lee paused. Up until a few weeks ago, he'd have agreed with her wholeheartedly. Before long, he'd probably find himself in jail for his attack on Mae Bennett. He thought of Alice Bennett's face again, her willingness to hear him out, right here in this room. He ventured a fleeting glance at Will Bennett's unmoving form, folded awkwardly on the floor where Larry Lee had dumped him.

Then, he pictured his sister, slumped over a headstone in the cemetery, body shaking with emotion.

For a moment, he was paralyzed, unsure what to do. He could walk away. He could turn around now, walk back to his truck, and go far away. Will might die, but Larry Lee wouldn't be around to see it. It wouldn't be his fault anyway. Will had always gotten away with everything. Maybe this was justice.

Almost absentmindedly, Beth murmured, ". . . and then I'll find that fat bitch he married." Her voice trailed off, but in the silence that followed, Larry Lee saw the path of disaster that would follow Beth wherever she went. He looked over at Will Bennett's still form and found himself staring into eyes wide with panic. Will's face was pressed mercilessly against the floor where he'd landed. "Help Alice," Will's lips formed the words, but no sound escaped his lips. Then his eyelids slid closed and Larry Lee wondered if he was dead already.

From the lower floor, someone shouted and Larry Lee heard the door being kicked in followed by footsteps moving toward the stairway behind him. His body flooded with relief. The cavalry had arrived.

At that moment Beth lunged, shrieking, the hunting knife flashing in her hand. The blade tore into Larry Lee's jacket. He could feel the burn as it ripped through his flesh, the serrated edge mauling his skin. Instinctively, he jumped back, lashing out wildly at Beth's arm. By some miracle, he managed to knock the knife out of her hand. It dropped with a clatter to the floor. Beth looked stunned, out of her mind. Larry Lee stepped forward and swept the knife up.

Beth was looking at him with a menacing smile that pierced his heart. Her eyes were wild with malice. He pictured his mama lying dead in her bed, her hands chopped off, and he realized that the blade in his hand had killed his mother. In that moment, he saw the truth. Beth would never stop killing until she'd settled the score. It would never be enough. An image of Alice Bennett, bloodied and broken, flashed through his mind.

He tightened his grip on the knife and plunged it into Beth's stomach. She dropped as her knees gave way beneath her, forcing the blade up before Larry Lee was able to pull it out. Blood gushed out of her abdomen. Larry Lee felt his hands shake, but looking down at his sister, he saw she was still smiling.

"Some brother you are," she whispered with her last breath, a trace of a grin still visible on her lips as she crumpled to the floor. Larry Lee screamed, a guttural, animal sound that pierced his soul, leaving him empty.

They made it to the stone wall with Alice right on the heels of the search team. She could see footprints on the shore from where she stood. Morrison gathered the team again. "It looks like they may be in Mae Bennett's house. I want you three to go around to the front. The rest of us will go around by the dock. Low and slow, folks." He glanced back at Alice, but seeing her expression, he sighed. "Just stay back, Alice."

With every step they took, Alice's apprehension grew. Her muscles ached from walking over uneven ground and her vision was a little bit blurry, but she persisted, needing to see this through to the end for the sake of her own sanity.

They reached the dock and climbed up the hill toward the house. They could hear shouting inside, shrill and panicked. They quickened their pace, though it still felt to Alice as if they were slogging their way through quicksand. Morrison and the other deputies drew their guns as they approached the back door. A series of loud thuds and a shriek rang out as Morrison yelled, "Sheriff's office. Open up now!"

Morrison counted to three and kicked at the door. It took only a moment before the old wood splintered and the door opened with a groan. Morrison walked in swiftly, followed by the other officers, with Alice bringing up the rear. It took precious minutes to clear the lower level, Alice's pulse racing as she waited. Finally, Morrison ascended the stairs. Alice was the last one up and when she reached the landing, she saw all three officers standing with their guns drawn. "Drop the knife," Morrison commanded, the muscles in his arm tight as he aimed.

Alice heard the clank of metal hitting wood, and she took a step around the door, readying herself for the carnage she was sure to find. Throwing her hands to her mouth, she forced back a scream.

Standing in the middle of the floor was Larry Lee Simms, blood spattered over the front of his shirt and pants. A knife lay bloody at his feet, right next to the twitching body of his sister.

40

"Alice?" Deputy Morrison's voice poked through her foggy mind like a stick and she realized she'd fainted again. Alice opened her eyes and saw Larry Lee, handcuffed, seated in Mae's armchair, talking quietly with one of the other deputies. She heard a groan to her left and saw Will lying on the couch. Alice was lying on the carpet near the front door, right where she'd fallen, with Deputy Morrison squatting beside her. She tried to sit up but Morrison held her back.

"Stay still, Alice. The ambulance is on its way."

Alice sighed, looking over her shoulder at her husband. His skin looked pale, and she could see bloodstains on the side of Mae's sofa.

"Will?" she asked, feeling her head begin to spin again.

"He'll be okay. He's been stabbed and beaten, but the bleeding is slowing and the blade seems to have missed anything major. Won't be sure until the medics get here, but I think he'll be all right."

"Larry Lee stabbed him?" Images flashed through her head. Larry Lee with the knife, blood dripping from its gleaming blade and coating his clothing. Beth Simms lying on the floor, blood pooling around her. So much blood.

"No, Alice," Morrison rested his hand on her shoulder, steadying her as she began to tremble. "It looks like Beth did, or possibly her accomplice."

"Accomplice?" Alice's inability to string two words together was starting to get on her nerves, but she was too tired to form more complicated sentences. Trying to stay awake was becoming difficult.

"Local boy. Worked at the drugstore until a few weeks ago. Haven't seen much of him since then. We found a bottle of Benzos in his car up the road and some bloodstains we'll have to identify. Probably Will's, but I'm guessing that was from the car accident."

"Where is he? The accomplice." The word rolled thickly off her tongue.

"Larry Lee must have gotten the jump on him. He's unconscious, beat up pretty badly. We'll have to sort everything out, but it looks like Larry Lee may have saved Will's life."

Alice looked over at Larry Lee as he raised his head. Their eyes met, and Alice's breath caught as she saw her own experience —her powerlessness and triumph, her hope and horror—reflected back at her.

Alice watched the steady beat of Will's heart on the monitor beside his bed, allowing her mind to wander. She'd been discharged from the hospital, but had simply moved herself down to Will's room, where she'd been dozing at his bedside all morning. The doctors had sutured him, cleaned up his wounds, then left the nurses to tend to him. Alice sat by his side. He'd been drifting in and out of sleep for the last twenty-four hours. Each time he'd opened his eyes, Alice had looked away, unable to connect with him yet. Her presence was the most she could give to him.

"Alice?" Will's hoarse voice poked at the edge of her consciousness, snapping her out of her quiet thoughts.

"I'm here," she said quietly, moving closer. He looked toward her, and this time, she looked back, searching for something in his eyes that would ease the pain in her heart. She was surprised to see tears sliding down his bruised and swollen cheeks.

"I'm sorry," he whispered. "I'm so sorry."

Alice could see the effort it took to speak, and the part of her that wanted to reach out and take his hand screamed at her. She felt herself begin to shake, but she couldn't allow herself to be taken in again by Will.

"Can I get you anything?" Alice asked, keeping her voice as steady as she could.

"No," Will replied. He kept his eyes on her as silence filled the gap between them. Something between them was broken. Alice could feel it, like someone had taken hold of her body and was attempting to tear it apart limb from limb. It was a familiar ache—grief, deep and unrelenting.

"I spoke with Margaret this morning. She's bringing Mae up today to see you." Each word cost her something. Breath. Energy she simply did not have. "I'm going to go to the hotel and get some rest. I'll be back tomorrow."

Tears continued to spill down Will's bruised face, but he remained quiet. Alice stood to leave, pulling her bag painfully over her shoulder.

"Goodbye," she said.

As she turned to the door, she heard Will's voice like a whisper on the breeze as he echoed her: "Goodbye."

41

It would be days before Mae's house was ready for her to move back in. Margaret moved Mae out of the resort and into her apartment in the interim. Larry Lee had given Beth's companion Jeff quite a beating, and it had taken a few days before he was able to tell a coherent story. Even then, the investigators realized Beth hadn't let him in on parts of her plan. Despite his part in all the horror, it was hard for Alice not to feel sorry for him.

Will spent three days in the hospital, bandaged and recovering from the trauma of their car accident and the assault. He'd been very quiet since fully regaining consciousness. Alice didn't mind. She didn't have much to say to her husband, and her visits to his hospital room were filled with a silence that made her feel weary. Margaret was also a frequent visitor, and Alice was heartened to see the siblings mending their broken relationship, though progress was slow.

Larry Lee Simms was in the county jail, waiting to see whether he'd be charged for his attack on Mae Bennett—a confession he'd made in the aftermath of his sister's death and that had unfortunately made its way back to the district attorney. Mae, for her part, refused to testify against Larry Lee. It was obvious that Beth had intended to kill Will, and Larry Lee's timely intervention was the only thing that had stopped her from doing so.

Had Beth been in her right mind, perhaps she would have murdered him before Larry Lee arrived, but with her vision clouded by fantasies of revenge, she'd opted for pain over a quick kill. This fact alone may have saved Will's life, but knowing it would haunt him.

After being discharged from the hospital, Will had come to stay with her at the Woodbridge Inn only after agreeing to her stipulation of separate beds. Pain had kept him from sleeping well. Alice had spent many hours listening to him thrash and moan. Her own pain had begun to subside, but emotional turmoil kept her awake. The next morning, Will was on the phone with work when she decided to take a walk, needing some time on her own. The close proximity was making it impossible for her to think clearly.

Alice settled back in her chair at the Carriage House. She savored each bite of homemade granola, every sip of coffee. Everything tasted better this morning. Alice was no stranger to reprieves and she realized she'd been granted another one. Life was short, and she was more determined than ever not to take it for granted.

"Good morning, Alice." She looked up into Jim's smiling face.

"Morning, Jim." Alice had been approached several times with well-wishes from people she'd seen every day in the diner. Many of those faces had been distant before, but now that the drama had ended, life in town had settled into the quiet, peaceful atmosphere in which she'd found it all those weeks ago.

"May I join you?" Jim asked. Alice nodded and Jim gestured over his shoulder. An older woman in a floral housedress walked up beside the table. "This is my wife, Judith."

Alice smiled, her first genuine smile in days. "I'm pleased to meet you, Judith." She took the woman's hand as she and Jim sat down and ordered coffee.

Judith's skin looked thin across her hands and Alice saw she was very frail. Her labored breathing and the tremble in her fingers showed Alice how big an effort this meeting was for her.

"I asked Jim if he would bring me into town this morning to meet you." Judith's voice was soft and melodious with a lilt that made Alice think of Georgia pines and peach preserves.

"I'm so glad you did. Jim has spoken so sweetly of you. I'm very pleased to make your acquaintance." Alice was touched to see the tenderness in Jim's eyes as he patted Judith's hand.

"She's my best girl," he said, fondly. "I'm sorry you couldn't meet her under happier circumstances."

Alice nodded, trying to think of something to say, but Judith spoke before she had a chance. "I'm sorry all this happened to you, Alice." She smiled, but there was something sad in her smile. "Jasper is a beautiful little town, but we're not immune to the uglier parts of life."

Alice's stomach knotted a bit. She wasn't sure how much more drama she could take, and desperately searched for a way to circumvent the direction the conversation seemed to want to go. "I don't suppose any town is perfect," Alice offered weakly. "Still, I'm glad I got to meet you. Jim has been such a good friend to me."

"You know, Alice, I haven't always been the best man. Judith can tell you, I've done my fair share of stupid, sometimes horrible things. I've been grateful to have this girl by my side through it all. I'm glad I could help you. This whole situation reminds me how lucky we are." He smiled and took Judith's hand. "How lucky I am to have so much love in my life."

Judith beamed, looking at her husband with such love and pride Alice couldn't help but warm a bit in the glow. "We both hope you'll come and see us the next time you're in town."

"Of course I will," Alice said, moved to tears by the older couple's affection for one another, though she wondered if she would ever come back to Jasper. Her future was so uncertain.

Jim stood and helped Judith to her feet. "I'm sorry to make this visit so short, but I'd better get Judith home to rest. I'll see you around, Alice." Alice bade them goodbye. As she watched them go, she thought about her own marriage and the dull ache that had become a constant companion squeezed at her heart.

Alice was finishing up her coffee when a new voice interrupted her thoughts. She looked up to see a sheriff's deputy, older than Deputy Morrison—rounder, balder—but with a kind face. He looked down at her solemnly when he asked, "Mrs. Bennett? Do you mind if I sit down?"

Alice nodded, and he took a seat beside her. The waitress swooped up behind him to deliver a steaming cup of coffee.

"Thank you kindly, Patsy," he said, winking at her, which caused the woman to blush.

Turning back to Alice, he said, "I'm Leland Carver. I think you're more familiar with Deputy Morrison."

"Yes," Alice said, curious about why Carver had suddenly appeared.

"How's your husband doing?" Carver asked, watching her closely. She suspected this was to gauge her reaction.

"He's doing much better, thank you. I don't mean to be rude, Deputy, but what can I do for you?"

Carver sighed. "I'm sorry, Mrs. Bennett. I can't imagine what you must be going through right now, and I'm sorry to disturb you, but I wanted to talk with you about something. About Larry Lee and Beth Simms, actually."

Alice frowned, but nodded at him as she readied herself for whatever the deputy might have to say.

"I've lived in this area my whole life. I spent my childhood in the mountains, very near the Simms, until my father got a job at the marble company and we moved into town. Mother wouldn't hear of moving into Tate. Both her sisters lived here in Jasper and since she didn't drive, she wanted to stay close.

"I knew Larry Lee and Beth's mother, Agnes. She was a hard woman, even when she was younger. Very cold. Very prone to fits of temper."

Alice interrupted, her voice stern. "She was physically abusive to her children, Deputy Carver. No need to sugarcoat it for me."

"Yes, she was. Especially with her daughter, Beth." He paused for a moment, a pained look on his face, before he continued to speak.

"Yes, Agnes was vicious and her husband was a drunk. Spent most of his time at the local bar. I'm ashamed to admit that I spent a lot of time right there beside him."

"I heard their father died."

"He did. Drank himself to death. Things were already bad for the Simms kids, but after their daddy died, everything got much worse. Larry Lee was nearly expelled from school. Beth was doing drugs, sleeping around. Larry Lee managed to get out, joined the Navy. After he left, Beth came unglued. Larry Lee came home from the Navy and a few years later, he was sent to prison for assaulting the boy Beth was dating, Oscar Clement."

"I know Joylyn Clement, Deputy Carver. She doesn't seem to think Larry Lee was the one who assaulted her son."

Carver nodded. "Neither do I, but he was found guilty anyway." Carver sighed, his shoulders drooping. "I should have done more for him."

Someone should have, Alice thought. "Why are you telling me all this?" she asked, frustrated and exhausted by what had become a very stressful morning.

"Because what happened with Beth Simms was horrible, but also tragic. Because I don't think Larry Lee will ever recover, and I feel like someone ought to know his story. Theirs—his and Beth's."

Alice scrutinized the deputy's face. It was etched with regret.

"Anyway, at some point, while Larry Lee was still in lockup, Beth got pregnant."

Alice's heart jumped. "How do you know?"

"My ex-wife was a nurse on the maternity ward at the hospital." Sadness crept across his features for the briefest of moments before he continued. "She'd come in to the hospital bloodied and bruised. Looked like someone had given her a real beating, but she wouldn't say who. She was bleeding. They almost lost her. They did lose the baby. After she left the hospital, she was never sober again. It wasn't long before she hooked up with a local boy and hightailed it out of town. Honestly, I thought we'd seen the last of Beth Simms."

"What about Larry Lee?"

"He came home from prison, tried to make it on his own, but before long he was back at home, taking care of Agnes. He drank a lot. Got into trouble a lot." Carver paused again, and then said, thoughtfully, "I went to see Larry Lee yesterday. In all the years I've known him, I've never seen him look so defeated. He always had that fight in him, that spark. Got him into trouble plenty of times, but I think it's how he survived all those years with Agnes." His words hung in the air, leaving Alice feeling like he wanted something from her.

"I still don't know why you're telling this," Alice said. "There's nothing I can do for Larry Lee and his sister is dead. I don't understand why he confessed to pushing Mae."

"Don't you?" Carver asked, his voice hushed. Alice blushed under the intense scrutiny of his gaze.

Carver looked at her long and hard before continuing. "I don't know you from Eve, Mrs. Bennett, but I get the feeling you might know a little something about having a hard life." She started to protest, but he held out his hands in surrender. "Please, hear me out. I think Larry Lee needs forgiveness. He's serving time right now for a crime he never would have been caught for, but he came clean, though I damned well wish he'd kept his mouth shut." No one had been happy with the judge's harsh sentence. "He's got no one in this world, and he needs something, atonement maybe. I think you may be the only one who can give him what he needs."

That afternoon, Alice went to the hospital to check in on Joylyn, still reeling from her conversation with Deputy Carver. Alice knocked softly on the hospital room door.

"Come in," a man's voice responded, one she didn't recognize.

Opening the door, Alice was relieved to see Joylyn Clement sitting up in bed, a handsome man sitting next to her. Upon closer inspection, Alice could see the thin white lines of old scars on his forehead and cheeks. He stood and reached out a hand.

"You must be Alice Bennett. My mother has been telling me all about you." His smile was warm and genuine. "I'm Oscar," he said, offering his hand.

"Hello, Oscar. I'm very glad to get to meet you. Your mother has spent hours talking to me about you." He smiled, blushing lightly, but she could see the worry in his eyes. He pulled an armchair closer to Joylyn's bed and gestured for Alice to sit.

"Hello, Joylyn." Alice took Joylyn's hand in hers, finding comfort in how warm and soft it was. The last time she'd seen Joylyn, the older woman had looked on the edge of death.

"Hello, Alice. Tell me, how's Will?"

Alice's face fell. "He's doing better. They released him from the hospital yesterday. He'll be in pain for a while, but he'll be all right." Alice couldn't help but look at Oscar when she said this, thinking of the beating he had taken, leaving scars that were still visible, and, she suspected, many that were not. For one fleeting moment, Alice wondered what kind of torment Will would endure, how long the memories would stay with him. But she couldn't allow compassion to crack her shaky outer shell today.

Oscar looked at her thoughtfully, then said, "It's okay, Alice. Mother told me what happened with Larry Lee and Beth." He winced when he said her name. "I don't have any love for Larry Lee Simms, but I'm glad he got to Will when he did."

Alice nodded, her voice caught in her throat. She thought of Larry Lee, alone in a world that had been worse than unkind in its indifference. Her heart ached for the child Larry Lee had once been, and for her own stunted childhood. Combined with Carver's words, the ache was turning to guilt. She turned back to Joylyn.

"Do you remember what happened to you, Joylyn?"

"Beth Simms." The old woman sighed. "Here I thought Larry Lee was the one to fear. I walked up to see Mae and Jeffrey Hatcher grabbed me. I kicked and fought like a wildcat but all it did was tire me out. He took me into the woods near Mae's house and there was Beth, looking strung out and crazy. She yelled at me about ruining her life. Of course, I argued that she'd ruined Oscar's life. Never did know when to keep my mouth shut," she chuckled. "Next thing I knew, she was on top of me. It wasn't long before I passed out and woke up here."

"How are you feeling?"

Joylyn grinned. "Oh, achy. Old. I guess it took a real beating to get this stubborn old girl to see reason." She smiled up at Oscar where he stood on the other side of the bed, and then she took his hand. "Oscar is taking me home with him. I should be discharged tomorrow."

"When will you leave town? I know Mae will be heartbroken if she doesn't get to say goodbye."

"I spoke with Margaret this morning and we'll be dropping in to see Mae in Atlanta on Friday."

Alice fought back tears. She'd grown very fond of Joylyn and was sad to see her go. She reminded Alice of her grandmother and had become an integral piece of her Georgia experience.

"Well, I hope you'll keep in touch. I'm going to miss those peach pies."

Joylyn patted her hand. "I'll leave you my recipe. Lord knows

Oscar isn't going to be taking up baking to satisfy my sweet tooth."

"Can't get Georgia peaches in New York, Mother," Oscar said, but he was grinning. "But I can't wait to introduce you to cannoli."

Alice said her goodbyes, giving Joylyn a gentle kiss on the cheek and exchanging phone numbers with Oscar. Then she made her way back to the hotel to work.

42

"Well, Alice. This isn't the piece I was expecting, but it's riveting," Nancy said. Her enthusiasm was palpable despite the distance, a trait Alice had always appreciated about her editor.

Alice sighed. "It's been very thought-provoking being here in Georgia. Things didn't go as planned, but I feel good about bringing Juanita Jones back into the public sphere of consciousness. I hope maybe it'll help someone."

"It's shocking what her husband did to her. I wonder what was wrong with him."

"We'll probably never know. You have to remember, mental health issues were taboo back then and since Juanita was a woman, not to mention his wife, they didn't look very closely at it. It's probably a miracle he was even convicted. I'm sure that was due largely to the heinous nature of the crime—and her popularity." Alice's heart went out to all the abused women who were overlooked because they didn't fit society's image of popular, or even normal.

"And the part about the feud. That was shocking. I didn't think things like that still went on in this country."

Alice smiled. In searching for Juanita Jones, Alice had found something much more profound than one woman's story. She'd learned a very real and nearly fatal lesson about keeping secrets. She'd reintroduced Juanita Jones to the world, but she'd also given voice to Beth Ann Simms, a woman who would probably be demonized by her community for years to come but who Alice couldn't help but feel some empathy for despite her anger.

She'd written about the Simms / Bennett feud as one of the underlying causes for Beth Simms's eventual undoing. She wondered if Beth had lived whether she could have been saved from herself and whether the rest of them would have survived her. If Larry Lee hadn't intervened, Beth's reign of terror would have extended beyond Joylyn, Will and, of course, Agnes. The story of Beth chopping off Agnes's hands had swept through town like wildfire. Her desire to get back at those who'd wronged her was a force unto itself, uncontrollable and beyond reason.

Jeffrey Hatcher had survived Larry Lee's attack with bruises, broken bones and a punctured lung, but otherwise no permanent damage. He would stand trial for his role in Agnes's death and Will's kidnapping, as well as the assault on Joylyn. He claimed he'd had nothing to do with Agnes's murder. Alice thought that might be true—Agnes's murder was much too personal—but with Beth dead, Jeff would endure the full force of the law and public condemnation. He'd already been removed from the prison's general population as a safety precaution.

"When are you heading back?" Nancy asked, interrupting Alice's train of thought.

"I'm not sure," Alice replied tentatively.

"Is Will well enough to travel?" Nancy had always been fond of Will. Most people were.

"Yes. He's flying home tomorrow." Alice paused, taking a deep breath to calm her nerves as she spoke the words she'd been rehearsing in her mind. "I'm not sure Georgia is done with me. I've learned so much being here." *More than I wanted to know, in some cases,* Alice thought, but then she chided herself. Avoiding the truth had never been a good coping technique for her.

"Is there more to the Juanita Jones story?"

"Maybe." Alice paused. "I need some time to get my head on straight."

"Is everything okay?" Nancy asked, and Alice could hear the concern in her voice. The clicking of Nancy's keyboard had stopped. "Are you feeling all right?"

"Yes," Alice answered simply. She'd run Nancy through the events she'd lived through like a journalist reporting dispassionately on a story, skipping over the more intimate details, the ones she wasn't ready to share or that cut too deeply. She was still processing her feelings about Will, the things she'd learned about him and what he'd done to Beth Simms. She knew better than to judge someone on the mistakes of their past. Lord knows she wanted people to forget about hers, but Alice couldn't think about Beth and Larry Lee Simms without thinking about her own story, all of which complicated her feelings toward her husband.

Then, there was the matter of Larry Lee Simms. The district attorney had grudgingly decided not to pursue charges against Larry Lee for killing his sister. In the hours following her death, however, Larry Lee had confessed to a stunned Deputy Carver about his attack on Mae Bennett. Despite Mae's refusal to testify against Larry Lee, the DA was steadfast in his desire to see Larry Lee behind bars.

Will had been furious with his mother. He was having nightmares that kept him from getting sleep, leaving him irritable and frustrated. His physical wounds were beginning to heal, but Alice knew there would be emotional fallout that would fester if Will didn't seek help.

In reality, Alice saw in Will the need for revenge. Having witnessed firsthand the destruction that kind of anger left in its wake, she felt disgusted by it. As it was, Larry Lee had been tried and convicted for the assault, which, now that she knew more about Larry Lee's history, seemed especially harsh punishment for a man who had ended up saving so many lives. Alice thought everyday about what Deputy Carver had said about Larry Lee, about whether she could face him, but she knew she wouldn't have the courage or the clarity of mind to even consider a visit to the prison until Will was back home.

She and Will had moved from the Woodbridge Inn into Mae's house. Mae was able to walk for longer stretches without her walker and needed less care. She'd decided to return home, over a barrage of protests from Will and Margaret, accepting regular visits from a home health nurse and respite providers in exchange for her continued independence. Alice had supported that decision, putting her at odds once again with her husband.

Will walked in the front door, having taken Rosy for a walk. "Listen, Nancy. I have to go, but I'll call you next week." Nancy started to protest, but Alice disconnected the line.

Will hung up the leash he'd insisted on buying for Rosy. The dog shook furiously at the harness she now donned day in and day out, still unused to the feel of being restrained, but Will wanted Mae to keep Rosy close by on walks and Alice had agreed.

"Hello," he said, taking a seat on the couch beside Alice. They'd been tiptoeing around one another for days, all of their interactions cordial, but formal. Will slept downstairs in the guest room, while Alice staked out the upstairs couch in anticipation of Mae's return—and to avoid any intimacy with her husband. They'd moved back into Mae's house to get everything ready for her return, which was scheduled for the following day. She'd come home and Will would leave. What Alice would do was still uncertain.

"I took the last load of garbage down to the dump this morning," Will said. "We should maybe go get groceries so Mother won't have to worry about food for the first few days. She'll be able to drive soon, but the home health aide will do some shopping and light cooking in the meantime. Have you gotten your plane tickets yet?"

Alice frowned. "No, Will. As I told you, I'm not sure when I'm coming home. I want to make sure your mother gets settled and I'd like to follow up on a couple of things that came up for my story."

"Mother will be fine, Alice. You can do your research from home." There was an insolent tone creeping into Will's words. Alice studied him closely, really taking in this man who was so used to getting his way. When they'd met, Alice had found this quality sexy and alluring. Will was self-assured. He knew what he wanted. Another time, Alice would have compromised or simply adhered to Will's plan, but she wasn't the same woman she'd been then. Will seemed so willing to go right back to the way things had been, unchanged, when all Alice wanted was to move forward. She didn't begrudge his need for normalcy, but she wasn't willing to follow him down that road.

Turning to face him, Alice mustered up her courage and said, "I need some time. When I came here, I wanted you to see how much I loved you, how much I was willing to do to be a part of your life. But everything that's happened, well, it's changed me. I still love you. Very much, but I feel like I don't know you."

Alice could see the hurt in Will's eyes, but she continued. "I realize I've been painting a picture of a perfect relationship. One where I'm not an alcoholic and you're the perfect Southern son." She took a deep breath. "I want the chance to think about who I am and what I want. When I do come home—if I come home—I'm going to want to take things slow. We need to get to know each other, for real this time. No holding back. No secrets or lies."

"I never lied to you," Will said gruffly, and Alice saw tears forming in his eyes.

"I saw you that day, Will. The day of the accident. I saw you with Beth Simms."

The color drained from Will's face. "You don't understand."

She cut him off. "You're right. I don't understand because

you've never told me. You don't talk to me about your past, about how you're feeling or what you want. You don't understand me either, not really. This whole trip has been like a nightmare that I'm just waking up from. And you're part of it. I need time to make heads or tails of it." She could see the way her words wounded him, but she kept her voice steady and calm.

"I thought I could control Beth," he said, his eyes pleading, hands shaking. "I thought I could make her leave you alone."

Alice cocked her head, a question forming. "How did you know it was her?"

"The pills. It occurred to me after I left that Beth was always high on something. If someone was going to use drugs to mess with my life, it would be Beth." Will's voice took on a frantic edge as he pieced the scenario together for Alice.

"Mess with *your* life?" Things were beginning to make sense, but Alice couldn't help but feel angry with Will's assumption that he could control everything around him. "This isn't all about you. That woman could have killed Mae. She ran us off the road. I could have died, too. All those weeks you knew she was here in town, you suspected she was up to something. I can't imagine the arrogance it takes to put your family members in harm's way just to protect your image."

Will hung his head, but Alice continued. "See, this is exactly it, Will." She sighed heavily. "There are times when I look at you and I see the man I fell in love with. Then, there are moments like this when I don't understand you at all. You're like a stranger to me."

"Are you leaving me?" Will's voice was soft, vulnerable, unlike any sound she'd ever heard from his mouth. For the second time in their marriage, he looked genuinely shocked.

"I'm asking you to give me the space I need without any guarantee things will work out the way you want them to. I know it's a lot to ask, but I think you owe me that." She braced herself for a retort, but it never came. Will's silence filled the room, pressing against her chest like a vise.

Alice sat at a small table in the prison, picking at a snag on one of her nails and wondering if she'd been crazy to come. The plastic chair she occupied was causing her back to ache. She'd been searched and scrutinized so thoroughly she'd almost lost her nerve. Pushing the memories of her own arrest aside, she soldiered on.

She looked up and saw Larry Lee Simms being escorted to her table. He wore a drab prison uniform, but he was clean-cut and looked remarkably well for having been locked up for a month. Alice had attended every day of Larry Lee's trial, spending most of the time deep in thought about the differences between them, not exactly sure what she had to gain by this exercise but unable to control it. Her life had been hard, and in many ways, Larry Lee's story wasn't much different from her own. Which made her wonder how she'd managed to rise above it all when Larry Lee couldn't. Of course, Alice had had her grandmother for a while—a stable force in her otherwise chaotic childhood.

"Hello, Alice," Larry Lee said as he sat down across from her, looking bewildered. "I'm surprised you came."

Alice studied his face. She expected to see hopelessness and defeat. Instead, she saw strength and resilience. "Hello, Larry Lee. You're looking well."

Larry Lee's trial had been an eye-opening experience for Alice. Given what she knew of Larry Lee and his family, she'd expected nothing: no mercy, no compassion, no attempt to untangle the web of abuse and deceptions that had brought Larry Lee to this place. Instead, she'd seen a town rally for one of its own. Deputy Carver testified on Larry Lee's behalf, painting a particularly compelling picture of a man who had done the right thing and deserved leniency. Beth Simms would never be tried for her crimes, but the criminal justice system ensured Larry Lee wouldn't be punished for them either.

In the end, it was his assault on Mae that had come back to bite

Larry Lee. He'd been behind bars a little over thirty days when Alice decided it was finally time to go see him. She was looking for closure, but being face-to-face with Larry Lee had the opposite effect—unanswered questions swirled violently in her mind. Larry Lee spoke before she had a chance to organize her thoughts.

"Why are you still here?" Larry Lee asked. "I mean, in Georgia. I thought you'd have been out of here as soon as you could. I know I would."

"To tell you the truth, I'm not entirely sure." Alice hesitated. She'd planned to thank Larry Lee for saving Will's life, to tell him how much she appreciated him, to make a difference in his life, but now that she was sitting across from him, the words wouldn't form. Instead, she asked, "How are you doing? I mean, are you okay in here?"

Larry Lee gave her an odd look and shrugged. "It's not as bad as the last time."

Alice imagined all the ways prison might provide a sense of comfort for a person like Larry Lee. During the trial, Alice had realized how little Larry Lee had to cling to in this life. His cousin James had disappeared. Suspecting Beth may have had a role in his disappearance, the sheriff's office had put together a search party. When questioned about James, Jeff Hatcher had been particularly tight-lipped, but they'd still managed to find his body dumped unceremoniously in the woods behind the Simms house—another broken person in Beth's wake.

"I'm sorry about your mother," Alice said softly, still lost in her thoughts. With his mother and sister gone, Larry Lee had no one left. Her heart ached for him.

Larry Lee nodded, though his expression remained fixed. "She was a mean old woman, but she didn't deserve to die like that."

"When my father was killed," Alice ventured, "I felt the same way. I'd thought about killing him myself a million times, but seeing him that way didn't seem right." She closed her eyes. In the silence that followed, she thought about her father, trying to come up with a single good memory, but falling short. What had made him the way he was? She really didn't know. When she opened her eyes, Larry Lee was staring at her, his blue eyes piercing her soul.

"I know what you're thinking," she said. "You think because I'm Will Bennett's wife, I can't imagine what you're going through."

Larry Lee shook his head. "No. I think you *do* understand. That's why I came to you at Mrs. Bennett's house that day." He paused, as if grasping for the right words. "The first time I saw you, well, the first time I really knew who you were, there was something about you that stood out to me. Something . . . damaged." His cheeks flushed and he cast his gaze downward, unable to keep the eye contact with his words floating between them. "Sorry," he muttered.

"There's no need to be sorry, Larry Lee. You're right. I'm damaged. I didn't realize how much until I came here. I thought I'd made a new start in my life, but I guess old habits are hard to break. That's one of the reasons I can't leave yet. I don't think I can leave until I figure out how to stand on my own two feet." This time it was Alice's turn to blush. In minutes, she'd shared more about her own state of mind than she'd ever shared with her husband.

As if he could read her thoughts, Larry Lee said, "I think you should know. The day Beth died, Will asked me to help you. To save you."

His words were like daggers to her heart. She'd accused Will of extreme selfishness, and maybe that was true, but in the end, he'd been thinking about her, trying to protect her. Did knowing that make a difference? She wasn't sure.

Alice nodded at Larry Lee, but couldn't think of anything to say. It didn't look like he'd expected her to respond. They sat in silence, but it wasn't uncomfortable. There were so many things Alice had wanted to say, yet it was a struggle. She realized her reasons for visiting Larry Lee had been self-serving. She thought she could say something to ease his mind, to give him peace. Instead, he'd let her open up, share some of her own experience, given her hope. Even now, Alice saw Larry Lee was working up the courage to say something himself. She gave him time.

"I keep thinking about Beth," he said, his voice shaky. She could see tears in his eyes. "About how life might have been different if I could've kept Mama from beating on her. I couldn't help her, though. I didn't know how."

"I used to wonder about things like that too, about my mother and my father. I used to wonder how the people around me could let the abuse happen, right in front of their noses, and never rescue me from it." Alice looked at Larry Lee and smiled timidly. "I think sometimes things happen the way they do, and we can't fix it. We can only move forward and try to live better."

Larry Lee's eyes fixed on her. His pained expression began to relax, making his features softer. Alice caught a glimpse of Larry Lee as he might be, and again, it gave her hope.

"I wondered . . . if you would tell Mae Bennett thank you for me."

"I will." Alice stood up as the guard approached to escort Larry Lee back to his cell. "I'm sorry about your sister, Larry Lee. I'm grateful for what you did, but I'm sorry about Beth."

Larry Lee nodded though his eyes looked sad again. "Me too," he said, and he followed the guard out of the room.

43

The sun shone brightly, turning the kudzu a brilliant green. Alice shivered every now and then, imagining ghostly apparitions among the vines when she allowed her imagination to roam. Mostly, she watched out for snakes. She inhaled the fresh mountain air, kicking up dust along the unpaved road as she made her way down to Mae's house.

In a few months the heat would force her out of the house earlier in the day, but for now, Alice enjoyed the sunny afternoons. As she approached Mae's, she saw a car she didn't recognize in the driveway. For a moment, she thought about turning around and heading back home, but she told Mae she'd be by and she hated to disappoint.

Coming around the bend, the porch came into view with its new permanent ramp and handrails. Mae was completely back on her feet, but the events of the past year had convinced her of the need to make improvements to the house—just in case. With Alice renting Joylyn's place, Mae was able to stay in her house alone with only minimal intervention from home health aides. Alice was a daily visitor, taking care of some of Mae's needs, but, more importantly, forging a strong, lasting relationship with her mother-in-law—hoping it would last regardless of the fate of her marriage with Will.

With Will on her mind, Alice was startled to see him sitting on the bench that now sat where bushes had been. He was watching her walk up the drive. Will had gone back home after the matter with Beth Simms was settled, and though he and Alice were still talking frequently, he hadn't been back to visit and she hadn't come home. Instead, she'd taken her savings and rented the cottage Joylyn had called home for so many years. It was cozy and she did her best to care for Joylyn's garden.

"Hi, Alice," Will said softly. He had dark circles under his eyes and a few day's hair growth on his chin.

Alice approached slowly. "Hello, Will. What are you doing here?" She hadn't meant the question to come out harshly, but it did and she didn't apologize. She'd come to understand her relationship with Will had been built on her compromising and apologizing. She was done with all that.

Their relationship was in a state of limbo. Neither had spoken the word divorce, but after almost nine months living in different states, separated by more than miles, reconciliation seemed like wishful thinking. Most days, as Alice went through her routines, she was able to put it out of her mind and take one day at a time, but seeing Will made her heart melt. Standing this close without reaching out to him took effort.

"I came to see you, actually," he said, worry lines appearing around his eyes. His fingers drummed against his knee; his fidgeting made the chair squeak.

"Oh?" Alice asked, not knowing what to say. She'd been expecting Will to end things one of these days. The uncertainty of their situation really wasn't his style. Will liked things orderly. He tied up loose ends. He was a finisher. She wondered if today was the day they were finished.

Will sighed. "I know you're still angry with me and you have every right to be." This was not what she'd been expecting. Alice felt her pulse quicken, as he continued timidly. "I want you to know how sorry I am that I hurt you."

Alice studied Will before responding. "I'm not angry with you." She paused, collecting her words carefully. "When I was drinking, I lied. All the time. When I stopped drinking, I made a promise to myself that I would be honest. That I would own my decisions. My actions. As soon as I met you, I started lying again, not overtly but by omission. I wanted you to see the best side of me. That's why I never told you about being an alcoholic, about being accused of murdering my father." Before Will had returned home, Alice had come clean with the rest of her story, no longer scared about how he would react. "I didn't want you to know those things about me, so I pretended to be something I wasn't."

Will nodded, staying silent so Alice could finish. Another shocker. Will usually finished her thoughts for her. The old Alice usually let him. She went on, "I came here to take care of your mother because I wanted to show you I was committed to you, to our marriage."

"But?" Will asked, his face wracked with tension.

"There's no but. While I was here, I realized we really didn't know each other, despite our years together. I learned a lot about you and your life. Not from you, but from this place. Things I didn't like. I wished you'd told me, but I understand why you didn't."

"I never wanted you to come here. I knew you'd see what a fraud I was. All the things I'd done, things I'm ashamed of. I guess I didn't want you to know this side of me either, but I didn't know it would get that bad. Then, I thought I could control it, fix it, but you were right, Alice. I couldn't control Beth, and I see now I shouldn't have tried to. I should have told you what was going on."

"Yes, you should have," she said, matter-of-factly. Her tone remained even, but it was important that she hold Will accountable. They would never be on even ground if she didn't.

"There are some things I want you to know." Alice braced

herself. She knew she wouldn't like what Will had to say, but he needed to say it and she needed to hear it from his mouth. "When I saw Beth the first time I visited, I did not sleep with her."

"Will, I . . ." she started, but he held up a hand to stop her.

"Please, Alice. I need to say this to you. I've done many things I'm not proud of. I was arrogant, like you said, and I treated you badly before you ever came to Jasper, and after, too. I made things so much worse through my actions and inaction, but I need you to know I did not sleep with Beth. I need you to know I would never do that to you."

Alice nodded. There was nothing for her to say.

"I also want you to know what I did to Beth back in college was unquestionably the worst thing I have ever done in my life. It changed me. I made an effort to never lose control of my emotions again. It also made me hard. What I did to Beth was inexcusable. I want you to know I know that."

Will's body relaxed where he sat. She could see he'd been nervous to tell her, scared even. She would need time to process this information. For the moment, she gazed steadily at her husband, trying to see him as the man he was. Not the man she'd married, the perfect, always-in-control man she'd allowed to take over her life, losing herself along the way. Instead, she studied the man in front of her—more flawed than she ever would have imagined, but also beautiful in his imperfection.

Will paused. "I'd like us to start over, Alice. I want to be where you are and I want to know everything about you."

The pressure in Alice's chest threatened to explode. She felt tears creeping into her eyes. She fought an internal battle between the part that wanted to embrace Will, to pull him back into her life, and the part that urged caution, the suspicious part. For a few minutes, she simply stood there unable to move one way or another. Finally she pulled herself together.

"I think I'd like that."

Alice moved forward and sat silently beside Will. She kept her hands folded neatly in her lap, but the warmth emanating from his body made her heart race. She didn't know what the future would bring for them, but this moment on the bench—a moment grounded firmly in the present—it was enough to hope.

ACKNOWLEDGMENTS

My undying gratitude to my editors Caitlin Berve and Laura Mahal for their dedication in helping me take this book to the next level. To Carl Graves for the beautiful cover design. And to Penny Sansevieri and the team at AME for their work on getting *All the Broken People* into the hands of readers.

Thank you to Larry Cavender and Barbara Cline who brought Juanita Jones into my life. Alice and I will never be the same and we hope this book will honor Juanita and help keep her memory alive.

A huge shout-out to my fellow writers. To Laura, Ronda, Sarah, Sheala, Joe and David for supporting me and helping me make my writing better. To Valerie and Kerri for your insights - I'll miss you Valerie. To Joe Konrath for giving me the kick in the pants I needed to get this book out the door.

To my family and friends, thank you for your love and enthusiasm. To Dave Schenwar for all your input and encouragement. To my mother-in-law Betty who was always so supportive and helpful and without whom I would never have discovered kudzu. I will miss hearing stories of Allen's childhood. To my children for thinking my writing career is cool. And to my husband for telling me to "keep writing" no matter what. Thanks for doing life with me.

ABOUT THE AUTHOR

Amy Rivers is the author of *Wallflower Blooming* and *Best Laid Plans & Other Disasters*. She has been published in *Flash! A Celebration of Short Fiction*, *Chicken Soup for the Soul: Inspiration for Nurses*, and *Splice Today*, as well as *Novelty Bride Magazine* and ESME.com where she is a regular contributor. She was raised in New Mexico, educated in Washington State and now lives in Colorado with her husband and children. *All the Broken People* is her first novel of psychological suspense. For more information, visit www.amyrivers.com.

CPSIA information can be obtained
at www.ICGtesting.com
Printed in the USA
LVHW032109051219
639556LV00005B/903/P